THE BIG FREE

The

BIG FREE

A Novel

MARTHA B. BOONE

NEW YORK

NASHVILLE • MELBOURNE • VANCOUVER

THE BIG FREE

Published in New York, New York, by Morgan James Publishing. Morgan James is a trademark of Morgan James, LLC. www.MorganJamesPublishing.com

The Morgan James Speakers Group can bring authors to your live event. For more information or to book an event visit The Morgan James Speakers Group at www.TheMorganJamesSpeakersGroup.com.

ISBN 9781683504122 paperback
ISBN 9781683504139 eBook
Library of Congress Control Number: 2017900721

Cover Design by:
Rachel Lopez
www.r2cdesign.com

Interior Design by:
Chris Treccani
www.3dogdesign.net

In an effort to support local communities, raise awareness and funds, Morgan James Publishing donates a percentage of all book sales for the life of each book to Habitat for Humanity Peninsula and Greater Williamsburg.

Get involved today! Visit
www.MorganJamesBuilds.com

"We shall not cease from exploration, and the end of all our exploring will be to arrive where we started and know the place for the first time."
T.S. Eliot

DEDICATION

To my loving husband, Jesse D. Boone

And

To all of my great teachers, mentors, and professors of Tulane Surgery and Tulane Urology.

Special thanks to Dr. Norman E. McSwain. While being a Tulane professor and director of trauma surgery, Dr. McSwain still found time to be a reader for my book until his death in 2015.

TABLE OF CONTENTS

CHAPTER 1
Charity Hospital, New Orleans

July 1, 1982

First Day

Dr. Elizabeth Roberts walked through the back door of the most notorious trauma center in America. It was her first day as a doctor. Her name tag was proudly displayed on her new, starched, white doctor's coat.

As she passed the noisy, crowded waiting room, she heard a patient shout, "When is it my damn turn? I been here all damn night!" Elizabeth noticed many of the angry and impatient people were speaking out loud to nobody in particular.

The aromas of fear, blood, sweat, alcohol, and dirty diapers filled Dr. Elizabeth Robert's nose.

As she walked through the last of the swinging doors and into the inner sanctum of the accident room, she spotted a woman standing in front of the nurse's desk. She was giving orders to other nurses. Elizabeth had been told to look for a tall woman with skin like caramel. She must be the charge nurse.

"Hi, I am Dr. Elizabeth Roberts, and I am the charge resident for Tulane Surgery this month," said Elizabeth in her friendliest Charleston accent.

"Well, I'll be damned! I heard they were sending me some kind of Southern belle, but I never expected a pink hair bow, pink plaid socks, and penny loafers, for God's sakes!" Head Nurse Lavinia Robichaud laughed loudly.

Elizabeth trembled. She had never liked for anyone to shout. She felt frozen with fear. The nurse did not introduce herself.

Elizabeth stared at the big, beautiful, Creole queen. "Well, I was to report to Nurse Robichaud. I assume that is you? What do you consider appropriate attire for my new position?"

"My God, who talks like that? Just saying 'appropriate attire' tells me all I need to know about you, honey. Just in case you did not happen to notice, this is the busiest accident and trauma emergency room in America! Accident means blood. Girl, people come through that door behind you, shot, stabbed, beaten, bleeding, and crazy on drugs and adrenaline. Many have to be restrained. All you gonna learn in that goofy outfit is how to get blood out of your clothes. Who told you to wear your fancy pearls to work in the ER?" said the nurse.

Elizabeth stood horrified in the middle of the chaotic hall lined with patients, busy nurses, and frightened new medical students. Nobody had spoken to her with such disrespect in her life. *Who was this crazy and mean-spirited woman?* Elizabeth began to understand why 50 percent of the first-year doctors, called interns, were fired or quit by the end of their first semester in Tulane Surgery.

The nurse continued her tirade as she leaned closer and looked up to read Elizabeth's name tag. "And another thing, *Dr. Elizabeth Grace Roberts,* do not under any circumstances come down here with your name tag on! Honey, this place is full of prisoners, drug dealers, and criminals. They do not need to know who you are. All those fancy manners that you learned in South Carolina do not apply here. Get that name tag off your white coat now!"

Gathering a hint of her courage, Elizabeth said, "Okay, clearly I have a lot to learn. What would you have me wear? What is the 'dress for success' clothing for dealing with murderers and drug dealers?"

Nurse Robichaud saw the fear in Elizabeth's eyes. But the smirk on her lips was obvious too.

"Get yourself some high-topped black leather tennis shoes. Get something that you can hose the blood off and that comes up high on your ankles to keep the blood from running into your shoes. Get dark socks, unless you want to spend your nights getting the blood out of those pink plaid argyles. Never wear that khaki skirt down here, and that pale pink Izod shirt has to stay in the on-call room for conferences at Tulane only," said the nurse.

The other nurses, an orderly, and two patients were staring in Elizabeth's direction. All action stopped to observe Elizabeth's instruction. Even the cleaning lady was leaning on her mop, riveted.

Nurse Robichaud had her hands on her hips as she barked out commands like a drill sergeant to a young recruit.

"Pull that mass of blonde hair back and up so they can't grab it. Get some cheap scrubs and bring lots of them because you will need to change frequently. Forget that white coat you are obviously so proud to wear. It will be ruined the first five minutes down here. Keep it in the call room for conferences with professors. And never, ever, tell anyone your name! You really do not want 'visitation' from any of our customers. That should do for starters," said Nurse Robichaud.

The nurses with whom Elizabeth had worked in South Carolina had been much sweeter and more deferential to the doctors. Nurse Robichaud did not fit her expectations for a charge nurse. She seemed to relish shaming the new intern. *At least*, Elizabeth thought, *she seems passionate about her work. Despite the nurse's aggressive behavior, I am still the doctor and I am still in charge…*

Nurse Robichaud ignored Elizabeth and returned to her chart work. Elizabeth was determined to do her duty. She stepped closer, squared her feet, and said, "Thank you for your advice, Nurse Robichaud. Can you tell me why that man we passed is tied down to that gurney? He is obviously bleeding. And why is he left in the hall with a surgical mask on his face? He must feel claustrophobic with that mask covering his nose and mouth. Why would we treat a patient so harshly?"

Nurse Robichaud, irritated by the interruption of her charting, looked up and said, "*Wow!* You really do not know anything, do you? That man is on crack cocaine. He has the physical power of two men. He is currently out-of-his-mind-crazy, and he is a spitter!"

"Why is he covered in blood?" said Elizabeth.

"He has all that blood all over him because he tried to head-butt one of New Orleans' finest during his arrest for beating his dealer. Head wounds bleed a lot, so it looks worse than it is. He cannot really be helped until he settles down from the crack. If you tried to stitch him up, he would spit his HIV-laden sputum in your beautiful little face, and you'd spend the next hour washing out your baby blues. As he is, *doctor*, he is closer to a rabid dog than a man. We have to triage in here, decide who might die soon, and be sure to take care of them first. Don't you worry about him, my little crème puff. He will get taken care of as soon as he is in a condition that he won't harm the staff or further harm himself," said the nurse.

"So who makes these life-and-death decisions of triage?" asked Elizabeth.

Losing patience with the new intern, Nurse Robichaud roared, "I do, until you have some damn sense."

"And exactly who determines when I have some sense?" said Elizabeth.

"Dr. Norman McSwain and I do. And if you give me any more attitude, you will take a long time to get any sense. Dr. McSwain is a world-famous trauma surgeon, a tough taskmaster, and a great teacher, if he thinks you are a hard worker. He does not waste time on fools. He and I have been at this together for over fifteen years. If you follow instructions, you will learn a lot. If you give me any trouble over anything, you will have to deal with him. Believe me, you do not want that for yourself," said the nurse, who turned to walk away.

Elizabeth persisted. She needed to know how to do her job.

"But, Nurse Robichaud, I was taught that the doctors are in charge and the nurses follow instructions from the doctors. That's why they are called 'doctor's orders,'" said Elizabeth.

Nurse Robichaud laughed so hard that her buxom chest shook. "You can try that, *doctor*. But you got your diploma in June. And it is just July. More people are killed in July in teaching institutions than any other month. Ain't nobody with any sense gonna do a damn thing you say until I okay it, in July! Unless they want to lose their jobs, that is. I heard that on paper you look like a smart little crème puff. But you need to remember real people die down here. Hell, girl, they die down here even when we do everything right. If you listen to me, fewer people will die, and that is our goal in July."

The nurses and orderlies and housekeepers nodded in unison. Elizabeth realized all of these people knew more than she. She felt like a toddler just learning to walk.

Giving Elizabeth her full attention, Nurse Robichaud said, "Please, do us both a favor and try to realize that your butt just fell off the turnip truck. All kidding aside, the best thing new doctors can do in July is realize that they don't know anything and latch onto the smartest, most experienced nurse they can find. Please realize that last month, while you were sitting with a book taking your Advanced Trauma Life Support quiz, I saw and cared for over one hundred real-life patients, many of whom had life-threatening injuries."

Elizabeth felt confused and disoriented. "But why did they tell me that I was the charge resident? At orientation, they made a very big deal about my having to know everything that goes on down here. They told me that I was responsible," said Elizabeth.

"Honey, you are the charge resident. Being the surgical charge resident in the accident room means that for one month, you carry the target. Everything that goes on down here has to be explained by you," said Nurse Robichaud. "It is part of your education. You will be grilled about every four to six hours by a doctor above you. You will have to explain anything that goes wrong on Friday afternoon at a big surgery conference in front of everyone in your department. If you don't wet your pants or cry in public, you will have to do it over and over again. But looking at you today, your time at Tulane Surgery could be short!" said Nurse Robichaud.

"And what happens to the doctors who don't do it your way?" asked Elizabeth. She refused to be intimidated by the nurse.

"Well, the really arrogant ones, I let them sleep through the good cases. You will be so chronically tired after a few days of having your sympathetic nervous system constantly staying on high alert that you could drop and sleep anywhere.

Hell, you could probably cuddle up next to that crack addict by the weekend," said the nurse.

Elizabeth shuddered at the thought.

"If you act like a fool, I will usually push you to the side and just do what needs to be done myself. If you really cause me grief, I will set you up with Stormin' Norman McSwain and tattle on you and work to get you fired. It usually works, too. The world does not need one more arrogant know-it-all doctor. I am here to see that does not happen. And in your case, we certainly don't need a frozen-with-fear but obstinate debutante. So what's it gonna be, Crème Puff?" asked Head Nurse Lavinia Robichaud.

After a very deep breath, Elizabeth said, "Well, ma'am, I don't like being bullied. But I am also not stupid. My goal is to leave here knowing as much trauma surgery as a new doctor can possibly know. I definitely want the benefit of your many years of experience. I will do exactly as you wish until such time as I feel it is not good for the patient. As long as you allow me to treat every person who comes in here with dignity, I will do whatever you tell me to do. Even though I did, as you said, just 'fall off the turnip truck,' you will find me to be a quick study and a hard worker. If taking really good care of these patients is the game plan, we will make a great team. I would, however, appreciate it if you could keep the bullying and demeaning to a minimum," said the doctor. Elizabeth had planted her feet firmly in position and was leaning slightly forward and making eye contact with the nurse. She stood erect and felt determined. She thought bullies required firm action.

"You just might make it, Crème Puff. You just might be okay," said the nurse, trying not to laugh.

A young male orderly stuck his head around the door and said, "Lavinia, there's a prostitute and her pimp fighting in Room Eleven, and the police are tied up in the waiting room. Can you send some of the fresh new meat in there to attend to them?"

"Sho, baby, I got just the person right here," said the nurse in her melodic New Orleans accent. "Dr. Roberts is just dying for something to do. Go to Room Eleven with Jorge and see what you can learn, Elizabeth."

As the nurse turned to walk away, she called over her shoulder to Elizabeth, "And just so you know, *you* ain't in charge of nothing down here! My job is to keep your lily-white butt from killing anybody in the month of July. Because, Crème Puff, you don't know nothing, and I need my job!"

Elizabeth was horrified that the nurse in charge would scream at her in front of patients and other staff members. She had known this month would be challenging, but she had thought the challenges would come from learning large volumes of scientific knowledge, learning better eye-hand coordination in surgery, and getting better at speaking before her esteemed colleagues. She had not realized that verbal abuse and blatant disrespect from some of the nursing staff would be a part of the challenge. She had been at the top of her medical school class, but had to admit to herself that the only person she had ever treated in a trauma scenario was a Low Country boy who fell off a deer blind and accidentally shot himself in the leg.

As she looked down the corridors of the trauma emergency area, she saw more pain and suffering and fear and bleeding than she had seen in four years as a medical student. To her right was a half-clothed drunken woman with abrasions on every limb. She had a large cut over her left eye, and blood was running down her chin. To her left was a sobbing man who was curled into a ball on a bloody gurney, speaking in Spanish, while intermittently asking for his mother in English.

This is what I wanted, Elizabeth reminded herself. If she was going to be one of the first women in urology, she'd have to survive the gauntlet of general surgery, and she was hoping to learn as much as was humanly possible. Since Elizabeth was a little girl, she had watched all of her relatives work hard and do their duty. Her family was full of quiet heroes who got up every day and took care of their jobs and their families. She thought that greatness was nothing more than doing what you were supposed to do every day, whether you felt like it or not. She had chosen medicine as her duty, and it was very important to her to do her duty well. She hoped to return to South Carolina and be a local surgeon.

She thought about the rules of etiquette that applied in South Carolina and wondered why they did not seem to apply here. Nurses at home had been respectful to doctors. She yearned for that respect. She knew that she could adjust to anything. She just had to learn the ropes.

Her thoughts were interrupted. "Come with me, Elizabeth."

Elizabeth turned and followed Nurse Robichaud to the nurses' station. The nurse tossed Elizabeth a pair of green paper scrubs. "Here, put these on. They will save your clothes for today. Just be careful because they are thin and tear easily. Lord only knows what you got on under that prom queen get-up," said the head nurse.

Elizabeth appreciated the scrubs and tucked them into her on-call bag to change into later.

"I'm ready to start," said Elizabeth.

"Okay, so you want to get right down to learning, do you?" said Head Nurse Robichaud. "Go to Room Eleven and take a policeman with you. There's a prostitute in there who apparently did not complete her work assignments for the night and has been stabbed multiple times by her pimp for her poor work ethic. Try to clean her up, and remember all those gals likely have that new virus that's mysteriously killing folks."

Mischief in the form of a nurse strutted away as she called over her shoulder, "Oh, and remember to protect your own self, girl. That one doesn't usually spit, but she has been known to bite. We don't know how the patients can give you that virus, but it is always best to act as if anyone can give you anything infectious and protect against it."

Before Elizabeth opened the door to Room Eleven in the trauma suite, she was hit with a smell that combined the metallic odor of blood, the sour sweat of poor hygiene, and the acrid essence of fear. Elizabeth knew that opening that first door was the beginning of a life of exploration that would continue for many years, if she managed to make it through this first month.

The examination room was small, old, and shabby; its walls were covered in peeling mint-green paint. The floors were sticky and yellow. Many years before, they might have been cream-colored tile. Now they were the color of tobacco-stained teeth. The aging monitors hung from the ceiling. Blood pressure cuff, paddles for resuscitation, and tubes for intubation were all within an arm's length. Everything necessary for running a code was attached to the walls with heavy metal bolts and locks. Surgical lights that no longer functioned were overhead. A small aluminum goose-neck floor lamp took their place. Three people were crowded into the cramped, dingy space.

A skinny black woman with both eyes violently blackened and nearly swollen shut lay in dirty, bloody, and torn garments. Long ago, when the clothes were new, they were meant to be seductive. She cowered under the glare of an arrogant, enraged, and hate-filled black man. He was in the exam room with the permission of the prostitute. He was there to guard his property.

"You took yo sweet time getting in here, doc. We been waiting over three hours fo you! This gal ain't worth all this, man. And this officer ain't doing nuttin' but harassing me. Charity sucks the big one, man," said the pimp.

Elizabeth watched as his angry eyes darted around the room. He seemed to be speaking to nobody in particular. His shouts of discontent were for general consumption. He made no eye contact with anyone. He attempted to pace in the small space. His agitation was palpable.

The police officer's badge identified him as Alois Thibodeaux. He stood on the balls of his feet with plenty of anger of his own, poised to spring if needed. One hand rested on the top of his Beretta 9mm pistol. "Hey, doc, you need me to calm them down, ma'am?" said the officer.

Elizabeth had no idea what the officer meant by "calm them down," but the burning fire in his bright blue eyes gave her the uncomfortable feeling that violence was usually met with violence here.

"No thanks, officer. I think that if you will just remain nearby, we will be okay," said Elizabeth as she studied the medical chart. "So, ma'am, I see that you have been involved in some kind of altercation. Is that correct?"

The patient laughed, and her pimp joined in.

"Yeah, I guess you could call it an 'altercation,' but it was more like a damn beating and stabbing, if you want to know the truth," said the woman. She looked at the angry pimp and giggled again.

"What is so funny?" asked Elizabeth. Nothing about a man beating a woman seemed funny to her.

"Well, I ain't never seen nothing quite like you. Yo little pink bow, yo little pink shirt, and yo little pink socks, you about the funniest-looking doctor I ever seen," said the prostitute as she continued to stare at Elizabeth and laugh.

Elizabeth realized that in her excitement, she had forgotten to put on the paper scrubs as Nurse Robichaud had instructed.

The pimp said, "Miss Lady Doctor, you look so damn weird, I thought Mardi Gras had come in July! No wonder that mean nurse call you Crème Puff. With all that pink, yo look like an ice cream flavor to me."

Officer Thibodeaux moved closer to the pair as he gained in height and body tension. "Shut up, you low-lifes! Keep it up and I'll wipe those stupid grins off your stupid faces," he said.

Elizabeth noticed that the patient covered her mouth to hide a broken front tooth while her pimp grinned and exposed two bright sparkling gold teeth with diamonds in the middle of a fleur-de-lis. Obviously, the prostitute was not the recipient of the money she made using her thin and abused body.

Even though this was her first patient as a licensed medical doctor, and Elizabeth was very nervous, and they were attempting to demean her, she felt great compassion for the woman, who was embarrassed enough to cover her mouth due to a dental issue. No woman at any level of society wanted to show a jagged front tooth, even this prostitute. In Charleston, a woman's appearance certainly mattered. No Charleston woman went out of her home until her hair was combed and her clothes were clean and her makeup was applied correctly.

"Well, since it ain't Mardi Gras, and it is July, and we at Charity, I guess they just got a new crop of don't-know-nothing doctors, and yo stupid butt was lucky enough to hit the jackpot and get the shiniest and newest one of them all. I just hope she ain't dumb," said the pimp.

The policeman moved at lightning speed and grabbed the pimp by the arm and slammed him against the wall. The pimp screamed, "Po-lice brutality! Po-lice brutality!"

Officer Thibodeaux snapped out his baton and waved it in the face of the angry man. He growled, "One more disrespectful comment to the doctor and you will get some of this and some of me. And trust me, you will remember both!"

"Come on, man, you gots to admit, the doc here does look kind of foolish in that outfit she got on. Who comes down here looking like some damn candy-assed cheerleader to work with the likes of us?"

"Shut your trap. Last chance," said the angry officer.

"Why can't you remove him to the waiting room, officer?" asked Elizabeth.

"Because *she* doesn't want him to go," said the officer, pointing to the patient.

Elizabeth had never been so close to physical violence. The meanness and aggression of the two men in this small space was frightening and felt uncontrolled. The men in her life in South Carolina, black or white, had been genteel. Men had always been her helpers. Whether it was Mr. Willie, the black man who worked side by side with her grandfather on the farm, or her four uncles, or her teachers or neighbors, Elizabeth had never feared men. She snapped out of her reverie and remembered she was supposed to be in charge. She tempered her shock at the threats of violence and said, "Officer, I think it might be to our best interests if you escort this gentleman to the waiting room and let me attend to the patient."

"Sorry, doc, the rules say that I have to stay with you, and I can't let him wander around. So he can either sit on the floor and shut up while you do your work, or I can handcuff him to the wall and he can stand—his choice," said the officer.

Elizabeth turned to the pimp. "Sir, please sit on the floor in the corner so that I can focus on the patient. I am sorry that there is no chair for you or the officer." Both men seemed surprised by her forced gentility. The pimp complied and sat in the corner.

"Okay, let's get started. I will give you a little pain medicine in your IV and we can start to remove those bandages and see what we have to stitch up," said Elizabeth. As she held a syringe and reached over the patient to get the IV tubing to inject pain medication, the patient lunged off the bed and tried to bite Elizabeth's arm. Elizabeth had many years of handling farm animals and was agile at avoiding bites. She had always been thin but strong. This was her first human biter, but the same principles applied. Shock and revulsion filled the young doctor.

Unfortunately, Elizabeth squealed and brought Nurse Robichaud running. "Crème Puff, I told you to cover up, to change clothes, and to remember that she was a biter! Things are busy out here, and I don't have time to clean you up from a human bite! Get that gown, those gloves, and restrain her, right now!" shouted the nurse.

She spun around to face Officer Thibodeaux. "And as for you, officer, why did you not restrain this woman? You have dealt with her before, and you know how she gets when you come near her with a needle."

Officer Thibodeaux looked embarrassed. He shrank a little and his shoulders drooped slightly. "Lavinia, I wanted to restrain her and him, but this doc here did not want me to. The doctor seems overly concerned about her feelings and the patient's dignity." Elizabeth saw the wily smile on his face and felt his disdain for her.

"Forget her dignity. This is about getting the job done and keeping the staff safe. Do it the way we always do it and do not try anything new, particularly in July! Damn, Thibodeaux, I thought you were one cop that I could count on!" said the nurse.

"I got it, Lavinia, I got it," said the officer as he roughly restrained the prostitute and her pimp.

With the patient in four-point restraints and every limb tied to a corner of the gurney, and the pimp handcuffed to the wall, Elizabeth could start her work.

As she pulled off the first dressing, the patient howled. The wound site was horrifying. Her skin was covered in old and new cigarette burns, and she had been stabbed superficially at least twenty times. Elizabeth turned, and for the first time as a doctor, vomited into the nearest trash can.

She wiped her mouth on a rough paper towel and continued working.

Instead of turning his head, the officer gawked. "Well, I guess this gal gets the prize of the week for the most stabbings. It looks like your brother was willing to lose himself a meal ticket to release his anger. Baby, you so ripped up, you look like confetti on a Mardi Gras float!" said the officer. He seemed amused.

Elizabeth could not believe the officer had just announced that the man with the patient was her brother. She shuddered to think that a brother could be so sadistic and barbaric to his own sister. Why would they accept this bondage as a way of life?

"I fail to see the humor in this!" said Elizabeth. Oddly, the prostitute, the pimp, and the officer were giggling in unison. Elizabeth had read about dark humor, but this was her first experience of it. Elizabeth wanted to feel more joy while caring for her patients. She wanted to like them, and she wanted them to respect her. This bizarre scenario was not what she anticipated her life as a doctor to entail.

The pimp napped on the floor while Elizabeth worked. His anger had disappeared while he slept. The officer remained at attention, watching Elizabeth's every move. The patient was sedated and cooperative.

After an hour of painstakingly cleaning, dressing, and exploring the wounds, everything was completed. As the last of the antibiotics ran in the IV, Nurse Robichaud stuck her head in the door and asked, "How's it going in here?" The pimp awoke.

Before Elizabeth could speak, the officer said, "Doc's a little slow, but I'd let her work on me. She is thorough and her stitching is very neat. This ol' gal is gonna look about as good as she can, given her chosen life."

Simultaneously, the patient was screaming at the nurse, "I'm gonna get you, you fat mulatto witch. You sent some new don't-know-nuttin' honkey in here to sew me up, and you ain't even check to see what she do. I will get you for this!"

The nurse looked at her rude patient with warm eyes and said, "This ain't the Windsor Court Hotel, baby. Complain to the State of Louisiana. They pay your bills with my hard-earned tax money! I'm sure they have a complaint department just waiting for your call."

Elizabeth was stunned. She did not expect praise for her hard work, but profane verbal abuse of the nurse was not expected either. And the nurse's disrespectful answer was even more shocking. Elizabeth wondered if there was a better way to get the education she craved. Did she really need to work in this den of iniquity to learn surgery?

No longer covering her mouth, the patient continued to berate the nurse and the doctor. Her anger seemed genuine and mostly directed at the nurse.

The officer and the nurse just laughed in unison, and Nurse Robichaud remarked, "Another satisfied customer."

As the officer was removing both of their restraints, the pimp gave the young doctor an appraising look from head to toe and said, "Hey, baby, yo is kind of hot in a skinny white girl way. Since you clearly ain't gonna make it at The Big Free, you might want to take my card and come do some real work after you fail here. I am sure that I could find some market fo yo. Those ol' boys from Metairie might pay big fo a white girl with all that blonde hair."

After a moment's surprise, Elizabeth realized the humor in the situation and reached out, took the card, and said in her best Charleston fake debutante drawl, "Why, thank you, sir, I will keep your employment opportunity in mind."

Nurse Robichaud and Officer Thibodeaux were bent at the waist howling as Elizabeth exited Room Eleven after treating her first patient as the surgical charge resident in the infamous accident room at Charity Hospital in New Orleans.

CHAPTER 2

The Elevator

Elizabeth finished her first meal from a vending machine. She hoped that honey buns and cola drinks would not be her typical meal. She never had food that was not fresh and freshly prepared. Between her family's farm and the fresh seafood easily available in the Low Country, she had never eaten food that came in packages. All the women in her family were good cooks. The sticky sweet bun was nasty and smelled like chemicals, but she was starving from her fourteen-hour shift and ate eagerly.

She tossed the food wrappers into a trash receptacle and ran quickly back to the emergency room, where she heard Nurse Robichaud call, "Elizabeth, run upstairs to the blood bank on the seventh floor and bring back every unit of O-positive blood that they have! Hurry up! This is a matter of life and death for two people!"

The nurse was obviously agitated, but Elizabeth felt compelled to argue. "But, Nurse Robichaud, I was told on the first day to never, ever leave the accident room during my twelve-hour shift. In fact," she continued, "I was told specifically that I would be fired if Dr. McSwain came by and I was not here and ready to do whatever needed to be done. I can't leave."

The nurse whirled around, moved closer to Elizabeth's face, and growled, "There is a woman who is eight months pregnant with a class three abruptio placentae! She is bleeding so hard from the placenta separating itself from her uterus that she could die! Every second that you stand here arguing with me is a second that she is closer to God, and her baby is losing brain cells due to hypoxia." It was obvious to Elizabeth that Nurse Robichaud was becoming exasperated and wasn't impressed by Elizabeth's protestations.

"I cannot leave this emergency room in July! Too many doctors and nurses do not know what they are doing to be left alone in July! You have to do it. This errand is more important than your job! It is about the life of a mother and her unborn baby," the nurse continued. "Now, unless you want to explain to Dr. McSwain how you killed them both by ignoring my wishes, I suggest you hightail it up to the seventh floor! I will call the Tulane chief resident down to cover for you, and I will explain to Norman, if need be. Now, go!"

Elizabeth was glad that last night she had gone to Kinney Shoes and found the black leather high-top tennis shoes Nurse Robichaud suggested as she ran to the lobby of Charity and rang for the elevator. While she waited the few minutes for the elevator to arrive, Elizabeth marveled at the beauty of the hospital lobby. Charity was constructed in the 1920s, and the lobby was Art Deco in design. Everything was symmetrical and modern, and the colors were vivid in comparison to the drab functionality of the remainder of the hospital. Inlaid into the center of the lobby floor was a beautiful round medallion of the seal of the State of Louisiana, the 1838 founding date, and the words, "Union, Justice and Confidence." Elizabeth had read about the history of Louisiana. The center of the seal depicts the "pelican in her piety," a brown pelican that has wounded her own breast to feed her young. Three drops of blood splatter from her breast. Elizabeth thought it quite fitting for a charity hospital to be adorned with that emblem. She felt proud to be part of a hospital with such great history.

Suddenly the doors to one of the four working elevators opened. Elizabeth jolted out of her reverie and back to the business at hand as a throng of tired doctors, nurses, students, and techs piled out of the elevator.

As Elizabeth entered the car, the elevator operator said, "Good morning, baby, where ya going?"

"Nurse Robichaud said for me to hightail it to the blood bank or lose my job. She said for me to get all the O-type blood they have and to make it fast," replied Elizabeth.

As the old doors creaked closed, Elizabeth read the name badge of the operator. Miss Albertha Simmons was a healthy-looking black woman who could have been thirty-five or sixty-five. She was all smiles and pleasantries and had incredibly kind eyes. Elizabeth noticed the other folks piling into the elevator. Two young adolescent black women, wearing visitors' badges, were dressed in short shorts and halter tops. They were drinking Cokes out of open cans, despite the sign that read "No food in elevator." In the other corner was an anxious-looking medical student with a Tulane badge pinned on his short white coat. In the wheelchair in front of the student was an overweight white male patient in a psychiatric straitjacket, mumbling the same phrases over and over.

"Well, if Nurse Robichaud said we'd better hurry, we'd better hurry! I will just set this old buggy so that it will not stop until the seventh floor. If I was you, baby, I'd take the stairs on the way back down with that blood. That nurse don't usually like to wait."

Obviously, Nurse Robichaud's preferences were widely known. As the elevator chugged along, Elizabeth wondered how a forty-story hospital had become a place where everyone seemed to know everything that was going on at any given time. In her short forty-eight hours since starting her new job, it seemed that the walls of Charity really did talk.

Abruptly, the elevator stopped. As metal squealed and the floor rocked, Elizabeth came to attention. The lights in the elevator dimmed, the adolescents began to scream, and the patient in the wheelchair muttered louder and faster.

"Don't anybody panic. We're just between floors. The elevator does that sometimes. It will be okay," said the operator.

The air in the elevator seemed to immediately become thick, warm, and musty. Elizabeth had never been stuck in an elevator before, but she remembered from her sixth-grade safety class that it was very important to stay calm. She said to nobody in particular, "Just take a few deep breaths and take your own pulse for a minute to calm yourself."

In response, the wheelchair patient insisted in a Mississippi drawl, "Come over here, baby, and give me a kiss. I need something to drink. Yeah, some loving and a cold drink would do me good."

Simultaneously, one of the adolescents announced, "I have claustrophobia, and y'all better get me out of here! I do not want to be in no old elevator when it starts to freefall like they do in the movies."

The medical student chimed in, "It is my day in the bullpen, and nobody is going to accept that I was stuck in an elevator as an excuse for being late! I am going to be crucified for not being there on time with this patient."

The anxiety and heat in the elevator rose quickly.

"Baby, do not worry," said Miss Albertha to the adolescent. "This elevator is held up by two-inch-thick metal cables. Freefalling elevators only happen in the movies. I been sitting in this same elevator for forty years, and I'm still here. The most that is going to happen here is we'll be stuck for a while."

Elizabeth continued to remember what she learned in the sixth grade. She reached over and hit the bright red CALL button. *That should alert someone to come rescue us in a timely fashion*, she reasoned.

Miss Albertha said, "Doc, that button don't work. It ain't been serviced in years."

"What do you mean?" asked Elizabeth. "I thought by law all elevators had to have regular service."

"Honey, this is Louisiana, and this is Charity Hospital," Miss Albertha explained. "As long as one of our four elevators can get the bleeding folks up to the twentieth-floor operating room that is good enough for the folks who give out the money in Baton Rouge." She shrugged. "In my forty years here, I can count the times any elevator saw a serviceman on one hand. Four out of four elevators has to be down for a serviceman to appear. That's the way it's done here. The Big Free does everything with nothing. The budget seems to only cover things that don't work at all."

Elizabeth looked at her in disbelief.

"You can hit that red button all day and ain't nobody coming. But if it makes you feel better, keep hitting the red button," said Miss Albertha. "I won't stop you."

"I can't breathe, I can't breathe, I feel faint!" said one of the adolescent girls. "Help! I need some help!"

The situation was deteriorating quickly, and Elizabeth recognized action was needed. "Okay," she told the girl. "Sit on the floor. The last thing we need is for you to faint. You can't fall and hurt yourself if you're sitting on the floor." Elizabeth took a pen from the front pocket of her white doctor's coat and pulled an empty sheet from the patient's chart hanging by a clip from the arm of the wheelchair. She handed both to the girl on the floor. "Do you know how to play Tic-Tac-Toe?" she asked.

"Are you nuts? I can't breathe, and you want to know if I can play Tic-Tac-Toe? What kind of doctor are you?" asked the adolescent.

"Well, she sho ain't no lung doctor, even I can tell you that," said her friend.

"Listen to me," Elizabeth said with as much authority as she could muster. "I want both of you to sit in the corner and play Tic-Tac-Toe until I tell you to stop." She addressed the girl who said she was feeling faint: "You are having a panic attack, and you need something to focus on besides your situation. Just keep playing Tic-Tac-Toe, and take a slow, deep breath each time you make a mark," said Elizabeth.

"Come on, baby, give me a kiss. Just a little kiss is all I need," said the patient in the wheelchair. Elizabeth looked at the patient and the panic-stricken medical student. She noticed that under his white straitjacket the patient had a full erection. She felt alarmed but recalled a very rare disease that explained his actions. "I need something to drink. I need food. I am hungry. And I sure need some loving," said the patient.

The pockets of Elizabeth's white lab coat were filled with food. She had already learned that the long ER shifts and constant work caused her to miss regular meals. She dug in her pocket and pulled out three peanut butter crackers wrapped up in cellophane. She handed them to the med student and said, "Slowly feed him the crackers to keep him occupied. His hands are tied to his chair and he cannot feed himself. Just feed him half a cracker at a time, and dole them out slowly." Elizabeth looked at the girls playing Tic-Tac-Toe in the corner and asked politely, "Could I please have the remainder of one of your Cokes? The two of you can share the other, and our patient will be much calmer with something to eat and drink."

She handed the Coke can to the med student and turned her attention to the elevator doors. She wondered if the doors could be jimmied open. Was there anything in the elevator that could be used as a tool? She remembered Nurse Robichaud's terse warning and started to feel a little panic of her own.

Then the elevator operator started to sing.

"One these mornings soon, I'm gonna lay down my cross and get me a crown," sang Miss Albertha. Elizabeth marveled at the beauty of her deep contralto voice. She immediately recognized the old gospel song and joined in. "Gonna lay down my heavy burdens, and you know all God's sons and daughters that mourning now will drink that old healing water soon," they sang. Elizabeth felt a jolt of pleasure in singing a familiar song. *Maybe New Orleans wasn't so different from the Low Country of South Carolina.*

As Elizabeth tried to recall more information she learned in sixth grade about elevator safety, the calming influence of the beautiful gospel song tamed her anxiety about being delayed.

Elizabeth's voice, an untrained alto, joined Miss Albertha's stunning church choir voice, which was full and melodic. "And we gonna live on forever, we gonna live on forever. Fly, Lord, and never falter cause I'm gonna move on up a little higher," sang the two. The spell was broken when Miss Albertha stopped singing and asked, "Girl, how do you know that song? I would have never guessed you to know that song."

"My Daddy's mother, my Granny, saw Miss Mahalia Jackson at Carnegie Hall in 1950. She bought 'I Will Move on up a Little Higher' on an old 78rpm vinyl record and played it regularly till she died. My Granny loved gospel."

"Well, I'll be," said Miss Albertha. "What else do you like?"

"I love all the old standards: 'You'll Never Walk Alone,' 'Amazing Grace,' 'How Great Thou Art.' You know, the songs most people know," said Elizabeth.

"I don't mean to break up old home week with you ladies," the medical student interrupted, "but my patient is getting down to his last cracker, it is getting hot and stuffy in here, and I have to get to bullpen. The surgery department staff is waiting on me, and they are not a particularly patient group, so if you don't mind breaking up your gospel fest, I'd like us to come up with a plan for getting out of here."

Elizabeth leaned over in the dim light to read the medical student's name tag. Right below Tulane it read "Larry Silverstein." She smiled at him and said, "Okay, Larry, what plan do you have? What do you know about getting out of an elevator without a call button?"

As Miss Albertha hummed "Amazing Grace" in the background, the girls continued Tic-Tac-Toe, and the patient slurped his confiscated Coke, Larry stammered, "Well, I don't actually have a plan at this moment."

"Okay, then. If you don't have any ideas, then your job is to be quiet and not add to the confusion," Elizabeth told him. "Pull the patient's wheelchair up against the far corner, and come over here and help me try to pull these doors open."

As the doctor and the student pulled on the elevator doors to no avail, they yelled for help. But the adolescent girls and the patient were disturbed by their yelling, and they started to bellow.

"I can't breathe," said the claustrophobic girl.

"Give me some sugah," implored the patient.

"I want my mama, and I want something to eat," said the other girl.

Again, Elizabeth tried to maintain a sense of order. "Okay, everybody calm down," she said. "Larry, feed the patient the last piece of cracker and the rest of the Coke. Girls, get back to Tic-Tac-Toe and deep breathing. Miss Albertha, start singing. I am going to try tapping out Morse code with my keys on the metal. Maybe that will carry up the elevator shaft," said Elizabeth. She thought back again to sixth grade. Three short, three long, three short was Morse code for SOS, the universal distress signal. Dit 3, dat 3, dit 3 was all she could remember.

Three dots, three dashes, three dots. She had no idea if anyone would hear her, but she felt like she needed to do something.

Elizabeth loved to spend her free time reading about strange, rare, and unusual diseases, and as she tapped the SOS code with her keys, the name of the elevator patient's esoteric disease came to mind. As she continued to tap on the metal door with her keys, she said, "Hey, Larry, I can help you with bullpen. Your patient has Klüver-Bucy disease. It is caused by bilateral temporal brain injury or disease. Most frequently, meningitis or trauma is the cause. Since your patient has obviously had a craniotomy, I'll bet his was traumatically induced. Patients with Klüver-Bucy get this strange desire to eat, drink, and constantly have sex. Fortunately, they are almost never violent or aggressive. So when you get to bullpen and he starts jabbering about having something to drink and wanting a kiss, you will happily be able to 'stump the chump' and tell the professor, in detail, about your patient's disease," said Elizabeth.

Larry said, "Are you sure? I have never heard of that disease. I don't want to look like a fool in front of Dr. McSwain." He seemed dubious. "I really do not know why we have to have this archaic bullpen experience. None of the other medical schools do this to their students and residents. Even though Dr. Ochsner, one of the proponents of the bullpen, has been dead for years, Tulane continues this psychologically taxing ordeal. Somebody in the surgery department still thinks it is a good idea to push students and residents to maximum stress as a training tool for thinking on their feet. I find it barbaric," he concluded.

"Larry, I think you are wrong," argued Elizabeth. "Being a surgeon requires that you really be able to work under duress. The surgery professors like to keep you on your toes so when a real-life stressful situation occurs, you are ready. Surgery, unlike internal medicine, is more like the military in that regard."

"Look, Larry," she went on, "when you spend hour upon hour reading esoteric things in medical books that you think you will never use, always remember today. Every single thing you ever learn will be used some time, some place, and to someone's benefit. No matter how tired you get poring over those books, remember today and your hyper-oral, hyper-sexual patient and his rare brain disease," said Elizabeth.

The elevator started to jerk and move. It dropped about two feet and stopped, and the doors opened. They had been trapped less than five minutes, but it seemed like a week to all involved.

As Elizabeth bolted out the door and ran to the blood bank, she called over her shoulder, "Good luck in bullpen, Larry!"

"Quick! Quick! Give me the blood that Nurse Robichaud called to reserve!" shouted Elizabeth through the window of the blood bank.

"I was just getting ready to take my break," said the technician behind the counter as Elizabeth lunged through the window and grabbed for the tall pile of pints of blood sitting on the counter.

"No time for the usual courtesies, sorry," said Elizabeth.

"Hey, you better come back here! That blood has to be signed out. You better get back here right now!" shouted the tech.

Elizabeth, grateful for her tennis shoes, hurled herself and the pints of blood down seven flights of stairs. She ran headfirst into Dr. Norman McSwain as she bolted through the swinging doors of the accident room. She tossed the blood to Nurse Robichaud and turned to face her boss.

"So where have you been? Your job is to be here at all times. What part of your job description did you miss, Dr. Roberts?" bellowed Dr. McSwain.

Elizabeth trembled with adrenaline and looked up into the face of a man oozing testosterone, intelligence, and intensity. Six feet of him loomed ominously over her. At five feet and ten inches tall, few people loomed over Elizabeth.

"I got stuck in an elevator on my way to the blood bank, sir. It is only my second day, and someone had to get the blood. The chief resident was covering so I could leave to get the blood. The patient really needed the blood."

"YOUR job is to never leave this accident room during your shift! If I or any other staff person comes down here at any time, it is your duty to know every single thing that is going on and be ready and able to report on it at a moment's notice! How exactly were you going to carry out those duties from the elevator?" yelled Dr. McSwain.

Elizabeth looked up and saw Nurse Robichaud looking over Dr. McSwain's right shoulder. With her eyes, Elizabeth implored the nurse to defend her, but the nurse's cold stare told her she wasn't going to help Elizabeth. Elizabeth felt betrayed and angry. The nurse had specifically said that she would cover for Elizabeth with Dr. McSwain. The nurse's betrayal stung.

After a deep breath, Elizabeth looked into the eyes of the toughest trauma surgeon at Tulane and said simply, "I am terribly sorry, sir. It was an error in judgment, and it will never happen again."

"See that it does not happen again, doctor," said McSwain.

At least Nurse Robichaud had the decency to look away sheepishly as she threw me to the wolf, thought Elizabeth as the young doctor stalked away.

Her next assailant was Dr. Peterson, the angry Tulane chief surgery resident. "How dare you call me down here like some lackey to cover for you while you run off to powder your nose!" he said. "I am not your chump. You are mine!"

Elizabeth realized she was defenseless again. She snapped to attention and said, "It will never happen again. I apologize."

A slight grin pulled at the corner of the chief's mouth, and Elizabeth realized that this commotion might be some type of initiation. But she also knew the patient's needs were urgent and real. Nurse Robichaud probably had her priorities straight, even though Elizabeth suffered in the eyes of her superiors.

Surely these people could not be this angry and this adamant all the time? But if the chief grinned after dressing her down, and Dr. McSwain had not fired her on the spot, maybe she was not failing completely.

Elizabeth looked to her left and saw that the patient with abruptio placentae had four units of blood infusing. While the doctors were talking, the nurses had pushed in the blood. The Obstetrics staff doctor examining her said, "It's time to head to the OR. She is stable enough to move now."

As the patient's gurney was wheeled away, Dr. McSwain said, "There are two questions to ask yourself every day, intern: What have you done for humanity today, and what have you learned today?"

Elizabeth was thinking that she had kept people calm in a stalled elevator and had learned not to trust Nurse Robichaud. But she imagined Dr. McSwain would not be pleased with the truth.

"There was a patient with Klüver-Bucy syndrome in the elevator, a textbook case. He constantly asked for romance, food, and beverage. He behaved exactly as I'd read in the textbooks. It was fascinating. I will never forget him," said Elizabeth.

Dr. McSwain chuckled. "I hate to break your heart about your great medical discovery, but what you found in that elevator was nothing more than an LSU student. All they are good for is sex, eating, and drinking. I think their school motto is 'Beer, Booty, and Bar-B-Que'!"

Elizabeth knew the rivalry between the two medical schools of Tulane and LSU was robust. But she was surprised to hear a tenured professor of surgery ridicule a student from another medical school. The emergency room seemed to bring out the jocularity in everyone.

As Dr. McSwain strolled away, still laughing, the chief resident bent down and whispered in Elizabeth's ear, "What Dr. McSwain neglected to tell you is that the Tulane Surgery motto is 'Surgery, Scotch, and Sex'! And events usually occur in that order."

CHAPTER 3
The On-Call Room

On her third day as a doctor, Elizabeth finished her second twenty-four-hour shift in the Charity trauma suite. She headed upstairs to find her on-call room. The on-call room was the place where medical students and interns could rest and clean up between shifts without leaving the hospital. She changed from her bloody scrubs into a skirt, blouse, and clean white coat for today's clinic assignment.

The hospital staffing in the trauma unit was organized so that Louisiana State University Medical School and its trauma team rotated coverage of the trauma unit for twenty-four hours with Tulane Medical School. So every day was either LSU day or Tulane day in the trauma suite. On LSU days, when they weren't on trauma duty, Elizabeth and all the other Tulane residents and students were expected to work in the various clinics that were run by Charity Hospital, the nearby Veteran's Administration Hospital, and the private Tulane Medical Center clinic across the street from Charity.

Elizabeth was weary and excited by the idea of a warm shower. The ER patients were often dirty, and she loved to be clean. Her muscles ached from the tense environment and the long hours of trauma duty. Twelve hours of farm work had never made her so tired.

She had been assigned to share a room on the hospital's twelfth floor. As she walked the mint-colored halls and strained to read the faded sixty-year-old numbers on the battered wooden doors, she finally found Room 1207. *Seven has always been my lucky number,* she thought as she threaded the giant brass key into the old lock.

As the heavy battered wooden door swung open, Elizabeth saw two fellow residents that she'd met during orientation. "Hi, guys," she greeted them. "I guess I will be bunking in here with you."

"What? Are you kidding me? They're putting the only girl in here with us?" shouted Dr. Michael LeBlanc, incredulous. "Man, they are starting to haze you early, Dr. Roberts, making you sleep in here with Dr. Parker. He snores like a freight train, and his farts are the most toxic around! You'll hear the covers levitate on his bed, and then toxic dark fumes fill the room. The worst part is that our window is jammed, and our fan is broken! We could die from rooming with him," laughed Michael. Dr. Anthony Parker laughed and accepted the complaints.

Elizabeth chuckled nervously. She remembered that the tall, handsome, blonde LeBlanc was a native of Lake Charles, Louisiana, and had been an LSU student before joining Tulane Surgery. Thus, he was considered a traitor by both sides. She was comforted to be rooming with someone who had been at Charity for four years and might help her to learn the system more effectively. Her thirty-two cousins had taught her the value of running with a strong pack.

"I hope that you guys don't mind my being assigned to this room," Elizabeth said. "I guess it is easier if we are all in one place, for communication purposes. I thought it odd also, that they would put men and women in the same space. But despite the fact that there are forty floors in this hospital, it appears that sleeping space for doctors is limited." She looked around the small room. Three metal cots resembling army rejects were arranged in a space that barely contained them. Barely one foot of space was between each cot. The three windows had yellowed roll-up shades that were frayed on the edges. Elizabeth felt as if she were in an army barracks.

"At least we do have a private bathroom, and we won't be in here at the same time very often. Would you mind if I take a drawer for my personal items?" asked Elizabeth.

"No, no, go right ahead and take whatever you need. You can have whichever bed you want also," said Dr. Anthony Parker. Elizabeth remembered him from orientation, too. He was from New York City, had attended one of the island medical schools in the Caribbean prior to coming to Tulane for internship and surgical residency, and had scored very high on the early testing. People called him Tony.

Michael interrupted, "I don't really care where you put your personal items. But I need the bed by the phone. Sometimes, late at night, I like to check in with my women friends."

"Yeah, while listening to me snore, you can also listen to lover boy call three or four women and tell each one how much he loves them and how she is the only one for him," said Tony in disgust.

"Come on, man, I protest! You are giving the cute young lady doctor the wrong idea. I am really a family man at heart," protested Michael.

"Come on, Michael. Your idea of a family is five rich wives, you as the only husband, and every woman fighting the other for your affection," snorted Tony.

Elizabeth looked around the room as the two continued their banter. She saw several aging pin-up posters. Farrah Fawcett in the red one-piece swimsuit was above her bed. Bo Derek with the beads and the tan swimsuit hung beside Raquel Welch's famous poster as a seductive cave woman. Farrah and Raquel were above Tony's bed, and Raquel appeared to have been there for a decade. Above Michael's bed was a newer grouping of *Penthouse* magazine cutouts of completely nude women. Elizabeth had never seen naked women displayed in such a manner. Someone with artistic flair had placed them carefully. She wondered who had done that.

Tony Parker followed her gaze, saw the display through her eyes, and suddenly looked horrified. He was one of the blackest men that Elizabeth had ever seen. He was built like a pit fighter from Roman times, with massive shoulders and arms. Despite his size, he radiated kindness. "We can take that crap down *today*. If we had known you were bunking here, we would have made that happen already. I am so sorry," he said.

Tony glared at Michael.

As he reached to pull down the first pin-up girl, Michael protested, "Tony, man, those posters are a Tulane Surgery institution. Some of them have been up there more than twenty years. I don't think that we should take them down just because we have a female in surgery now." He looked at Elizabeth. "Hell, she might not even make it till Christmas, and we would have broken a twenty-year-old tradition for nothing."

Above his protests, Elizabeth said, "There is no need to take them down. They do not bother me. I would, however, like to put a poster of my own liking over whichever bed will be mine."

She smiled and remembered her father had always taught her to concentrate on the battles that really mattered. Nudie pictures above the beds of grown men seemed silly to her, but were not terribly offensive. After all, she was a doctor and saw the naked human body every day.

"I'd also like to know the reason for this particular tradition. History always interests me," said Elizabeth.

As Tony hung his head in embarrassment, Michael explained, "Well, we need inspiration. This surgery stuff is pretty hard work. The hours are long. The patients are extremely sick. The staff can be brutal. And we are the low men on the totem pole. We need something to keep us going and cheer us up when the going gets tough. We need something to remind us that there is a world outside of Tulane Surgery."

"Okay, that makes total sense," agreed Elizabeth. "But I need some inspiration as well, so I will bring my posters next week and hang them in a spot that is not already occupied. There is no need to move anything of yours or to break any traditions," said Elizabeth.

"Well, I hope to God that we are not going to have to look at a pile of dangling peckers from *Playgirl* magazine. That would give me endless nightmares," said Michael.

Elizabeth winked at Tony Parker and said, "Well, Dr. LeBlanc, I guess you'll just have to wait a week to see what inspires me. After all, a girl needs inspiration, too." *Dealing with these boys is going to be easy.* Twenty-two of Elizabeth's thirty-two cousins were male, and growing up with them had taught her much that served her in good stead as she navigated the male- dominated bastion of general surgery. In growing up with her cousins, she had trained with the masters in hand-to-hand combat, food fights, pranks, and merciless teasing. She was unlikely to have to fight for the last biscuit with these two. And probably neither of them would dangle a garden snake over her while she napped. *Compared to my male cousins, these two will be a piece of cake.*

Tony looked away from Michael and toward his newest roommate. Switching away from the jovial banter, he asked, "What happened with that case last night? I heard a pregnant woman was bleeding out in the ER? Everyone said that Dr. McSwain and Nurse Robichaud were really worked up."

Elizabeth looked down at the brown concrete floor and was flooded with sadness.

"It was a real scary and rare case. The placenta disrupted from the uterus in the patient's last trimester. The mother made it after complete hysterectomy, but the baby did not make it. The little boy was stillborn. It was very sad. We got the mother resuscitated and got fourteen units of blood into her. But the baby had been without adequate oxygen for too long." She sighed. "I did three months on obstetrics in Charleston and never even heard of this condition."

"Elizabeth, you will find that things you have read in medical textbooks to be rare happen around here all the time," said Tony. "This place has pathology in volumes that you will never see in most training centers. Your challenge is to stay awake and not miss anything. An abruptio placentae carries a 95 percent chance of death to the mother and the baby. The fact that even one of them was saved is just wonderful!"

"Well, while you are celebrating the greatness of The Big Free, just remember that somebody's butt is going to hang out to dry over this one. Nobody is allowed to die during the watch of the Tulane Surgery team. If someone dies, the staff will crucify the doctor covering the case. Tulane Surgery takes any death personally. Somebody will have to explain everything about this case to the professors.

Make sure it is not you, Dr. Roberts. Always remember Nurse Robichaud is Dr. Norman McSwain's number one spy, and believe me, she tells him *all!*" said Michael.

"Oh, Michael, don't be so paranoid," said Tony. In his voice, Elizabeth noticed a combination of the staccato cadence that she associated with people from the northern United States and an island lilt. The northern staccato dominated his accent when he was agitated, like he was now.

"Nurse Robichaud has known Dr. McSwain for many years," Tony continued. "They are close colleagues. All employees tell Dr. McSwain everything. He is a cross between the hospital god and the hospital ghost, ever-present and all-knowing. The nurses in the trauma suite are only one part of his thick network," said Tony Parker.

"Don't kid yourself, dude—every nurse in this entire hospital is in love with Dr. Norman McSwain," opined Michael. "They cannot resist that whole testosterone-laden Marlboro man routine. He doesn't smoke, but he sure has the cowboy persona. The guy is smart as can be, an excellent surgeon, and every woman's idea of the bad boy she can rescue and turn into a family man."

"Why, Michael, you sound a little jealous," said Elizabeth. "Besides, Dr. McSwain is practically an old man. I'll bet he is every bit of forty-three years old!"

"You have not seen him over at Joe's bar after hours," Michael said. "He can drink any twenty-year-old under the table, and women flock to him like the alpha male he is known to be."

"Well, whatever he is or isn't in his personal life, he is one of our most respected professors. I think we should commit our time to learning from him instead of gossiping about him," said Elizabeth.

"Well, aren't you little miss goody-two-shoes!" laughed Michael. "I bet you are scared to death of him. When he gets next to you with all that testosterone, I'll bet your little Southern belle self can hardly breathe! Tell the truth, Elizabeth. Have you swooned at the feet of McSwain yet?" He glanced in Tony's direction. "Look how red she's getting, Tony! I'll bet she's under the spell of McSwain, just like all the nurses."

As Michael was speaking, Elizabeth had felt her face redden, the heat rising from her chest to her forehead. She assumed by now her ears were glowing pink. In point of fact, men who were overly masculine scared her. On the farm, men and women worked closely together and did many of the same jobs. But particularly handsome, powerful men were out of her realm of experience.

She felt it best to ignore Michael's taunts and change the subject. Still flushed and embarrassed, she turned to her overnight bag and began to unpack. "I am happy to organize myself around whatever system you gentlemen have in place. But I would like you to honor one request." She turned to them, a plastic container in her hand. "The tan soap in this aqua box that has the word *Clinique* on the outside is my personal face soap. I would appreciate it if you would refrain from using it. It is a girl thing and special to me. That is my only, one, little request," Elizabeth said demurely.

As she continued to unpack, she noticed Tony automatically gave her privacy by diverting his eyes from what she was removing from her bag. But Michael, on the other hand, looked as if he were ready to climb in the bag, like he was unable to wait to see what might come out next. He seemed riveted by her Clinique face soap box. She felt vexed by Michael's excessive interest in the contents of her overnight bag.

Elizabeth again gazed at the wall of scantily clad women and observed that they were all white women—blondes, brunettes, and redheads—but no posters of black women. Tony Parker was most certainly black. So maybe none of those posters were his idea. Maybe he would be a potential friend for Elizabeth. She sensed that he was a respectful man in general and had what her grandmother referred to as proper home training.

She decided to ask for his advice. "So, Tony, what do you think of Nurse Robichaud? Is she our friend, or is she not to be trusted?"

"Well, I think she is just like Dr. McSwain," Tony replied. "I think she cares about the patients, the quality of care given, and the education of the people who come through her area. You have to realize that yesterday when you were sent to the blood bank at Charity, she had dispensed other interns to run to the blood bank at Tulane Medical Center and the VA Medical Center—all of them getting blood for the same patient. Her connections are far-reaching, and she will do whatever is required to get the job done. Your assigned task was only a small part of what she orchestrated to try to save that woman and her baby. If not for Nurse Robichaud's actions and her network, the mother would have likely died, too.

"You see, Elizabeth, Nurse Robichaud is a bit like a general directing an army," he explained. "She admires intelligence, loyalty, and hard work. She is constantly aware that bad things can happen in July when everyone is new and unfamiliar with the trauma service. Her greatest fear is to disappoint Dr. McSwain," Tony concluded.

"Well, that is only part of the story, Tony," Michael chimed in. "You may be a second-year resident, and Elizabeth and I may only be interns, but I spent a senior rotation in that trauma room, and I can tell you Nurse Robichaud is completely loyal to those patients and Dr. McSwain *only*! She knows that half of us will not be here by Christmastime." He looked at Elizabeth. "In all honesty, this girl could be the first one to go. Nurse Robichaud is not going to get attached to anyone until she is damn sure they will make the cut and don't quit."

Elizabeth felt a spark of anger toward Michael and wondered why he thought that she would be more likely to get fired than him. She vowed silently to prove him wrong.

"You made it through step one of Nurse Robichaud's gauntlets, Elizabeth, by not crying, not lying, not fainting, and not blaming her when she threw you under the bus right in front of McSwain. She fed you to the lion and you didn't waver. That was a good move, doctor. Most interns that are told not to leave the emergency room for any reason would never leave, especially when a nurse was giving them the order," said Michael.

"You did what was required for the team, and Nurse Robichaud was disloyal and did not stand up for you. She would not take the blame for your leaving your post, even though she ordered you to do so. There was no way that she would admit giving an intern instruction that contradicted Dr. McSwain's orders," said Michael.

Elizabeth realized that the nurse was just trying to take care of the patient and was using anyone to get the job done.

"The way I heard it, Dr. McSwain was standing over you, snorting like a bull, and you stood your ground and apologized. I heard you did not make any excuses, and you did not cry. That is the Tulane Surgery way. There is no crying in surgery. You take your licks, and you keep working. One tear or one excuse and the new chick could have been out early," said Michael.

Elizabeth could not tell if he was complimenting her or threatening her. There seemed to be a bit of each in his diatribe.

Michael was ready to change the subject. He turned to the wall of posters and asked, "Hey, you never did tell me—which lovely lady you like the best?"

"Come on, man, leave it alone. Haven't you ever heard of sexual harassment?" Tony gave Elizabeth a disgusted but sympathetic look.

Elizabeth allowed her eyes to roam across the wall. She grinned. "I don't care much for the crotch shots as they remind me too much of STD clinic. But, hey, it is hard to beat Farrah Fawcett in that red bathing suit!"

Michael looked horrified. Now his wall of beauties would be associated in his mind with sexually transmitted diseases. At that moment, he hated Elizabeth.

Tony and Elizabeth shared a laugh.

"It's time for me to get going. I think I'm scheduled for the Angola prison clinic today," said Elizabeth.

She gathered her things and dressed in the small bathroom, grateful for the modicum of privacy that it gave. There was no time for a shower today and no time for breakfast, either. She left hurriedly for clinic.

As the door to the on-call room closed, Michael said to Tony, "I can't wait to place a big, black, curly pubic hair on that fancy face soap of hers and watch her scream and squeal. Now that will be real entertainment!"

"You are one sick dude," Tony told him. "I guess that is what happens when you grow up with no sisters. If you had sisters, you'd know that the consequence of sisterly retribution is never worth the satisfaction of the prank."

CHAPTER 4

Sister Marion

Elizabeth ran down the stairs from her on-call room on the twelfth floor to the third floor to start her first outpatient clinic at Charity.

Dr. Edward Peterson was the chief surgery resident, and it was his responsibility to assign interns to the various clinics Tulane was responsible for staffing. Today Elizabeth was scheduled to work the prison clinic with Sister Marion O'Heaney. Dr. Peterson met Elizabeth in the hall in front of the elevator, right before she entered the prison clinic. He came to make sure the new intern met her assignment. He chuckled under his breath as she approached and advised, "Dr. Roberts, be careful with those Angola prisoners. They would like nothing better than to create some serious mischief with a naïve lady doctor. A woman doctor in the Angola prison clinic is a completely new experience for everyone involved."

Elizabeth didn't need him to tell her this, but she didn't interrupt him.

Dr. Peterson continued, "You have never been around men like these before, Elizabeth. In all seriousness, keep your eyes on the prisoners at all times. Never let their prison guard get more than a foot away from you. These prisoners are constantly thinking of a way to get away. How he might escape comprises 90 percent of a prisoner's waking thoughts. You can imagine what the other 10 percent involves." There he was, smiling again. Elizabeth didn't take the bait.

Elizabeth had known Dr. Peterson only a short time and thought him to be lazy. He spent his days and nights in the operating room or entertaining himself with good food, Saints' football season tickets, and any available nurse. He did not seem willing to be involved in teaching medical students or interns, and he didn't appear interested in participating in the lower-level duties of patient care in the hospital and clinics.

Elizabeth thought he seemed to relish taunting her about working with the Angola prisoners.

She stood at attention as he droned on. "Elizabeth, they will not care about your well-being at all if you are caught between them and their freedom. If one attempts to get away, drop to the floor and make yourself as flat as possible. The guards are not afraid to shoot the prisoners right in the clinic, if needed. This is a rare occurrence, but just be ready to drop to the floor and roll your entire body under the nearest metal table. And if you have time, be sure to push that mean old nun in front of you."

"Thank you for the advice, Dr. Peterson," said Elizabeth calmly. She thought certainly Dr. Peterson was trying to frighten her for his own entertainment. If one nun could run the clinic, the security must be good.

Elizabeth had read about Angola Prison. She knew it to be a maximum-security prison for the worst criminals in Louisiana. The prison was named after the country in Africa from which the slaves of the former plantations originated. Louisiana's most violent prisoners called Angola home, including those awaiting execution on death row. Angola had housed many famous prisoners in its time. Elizabeth was determined to not allow Dr. Peterson to frighten her.

The chief continued, "Sister Marion O'Heaney is the last of the Ursuline nuns, the religious order that ran Charity Hospital from its beginning in 1736. The old bat probably came with the building and might be the only person in Louisiana meaner than the Angola prisoners. In fact, if a situation presents itself where you have to choose between the sister and the prisoners, go with the prisoners. They will likely just use you as a hostage. Sister, on the other hand, has been rumored to eat interns in her morning porridge," laughed Dr. Peterson.

Elizabeth's eyes were wide with shock. "How can you have such disdain for a woman who has given her life to God and to Charity?" she challenged him. "You seem to have equal disdain for our nurse, the nun, as you do for our patients, the prisoners. And where exactly will you be while I am seeing the forty prisoners coming to our clinic today? If you are so concerned about my well-being, why won't you be with me on my first day?"

"Honey," Peterson told her, "I am abandoning you. I am good and scared of Sister Marion. I will be at my apartment, nowhere near that woman! She keeps an up-to-date list of my many transgressions, and I am sure that when her mean butt gets to the pearly gates, she intends to read all of them to God. I do not plan to give her anything else to report to the big man on Dr. Edward Peterson."

Great, she thought. *This is just like the military. He's the sergeant, and I am the new recruit. I get the worst assignments, and he goes to lunch.* "I guess arguing is pointless, right?" asked Elizabeth.

Elizabeth knew that she was the new guy, and, as such, she was expected to do the work nobody else wanted to do. She was not expecting to do jobs above her level. But she was hoping Dr. Peterson had more of a team approach.

Elizabeth had watched the LSU doctors work together in the accident room and thought that their chief was a better leader and worked to teach his interns. In the very short amount of time that she had known him, she thought Dr. Peterson demanded much of her and taught her little. Elizabeth wondered why Tulane's chief was not more like LSU's.

On her family's farm in South Carolina, everyone worked. Orderly division of labor was the key to the farm's survival. The younger cousins were assigned to muck the mule's stall and do the backbreaking work of picking up rotten pecans from the ground in the family orchard. The older cousins had more responsibility and reported directly to her grandfather. Everyone was treated fairly and everyone worked hard. Nobody was allowed to slough off their duties on others. She wondered how Dr. Peterson had survived to be the chief.

"Yep, you best head down to the bowels of the basement of Charity and submit yourself for duty to the tutelage of the most infamous nun in the system and the worst prisoners Louisiana can cough up. And, yes, I am headed to lunch. Don't forget my sage advice. If guns come out, tuck and roll." He started to walk away, but then turned back to Elizabeth.

"You might like to know that the hospital gossip mill reports that the sister has never worked with a woman doctor before, and that the old bat is all aquiver!" reported the chief. Elizabeth wondered what he meant by that, but she decided not to ask. "*Good luck* to you," he said, and he was gone.

While Elizabeth waited for the elevator to the basement, she read a brass plaque about the history of Charity that was mounted between the elevator doors:

> FOUNDED IN 1736 FROM A GRANT GIVEN BY A FRENCH SHIPBUILDER. THE BUILDING THAT IS CURRENTLY USED WAS NOT THE ORIGINAL BUILDING. CHARITY HOSPITAL NEW ORLEANS IS THE SECOND OLDEST CONTINUALLY RUNNING HOSPITAL IN AMERICA. ITS ORIGINAL NAME WAS L'HOPITAL DES PAUVRES DE LA CHARITE, ROUGHLY TRANSLATED AS 'A HOSPITAL FOR THE POOR.'

The elevator was slow, as usual. Perhaps Miss Albertha was taking a critical patient up to the OR. Elizabeth took the stairs. She had learned that tardiness was not the Tulane Surgery way.

As Elizabeth exited the stairwell in the hospital's basement, she smelled mildew. The area that housed the clinic was below sea level, moldy, and ancient. The familiar mint-green color of the walls contrasted with crowds of men in bright orange prison wear and clanging metal chains and shackles. The prison guards carried 9mm semiautomatic guns and wore dark navy police uniforms labeled "Angola." Elizabeth thought her father's advice about carrying pepper spray in the big city would not be helpful here. These men were not the type to be deterred by pepper spray. They looked feral and hostile. The smell of fear—

that acrid, pungent, over-ripe odor—was everywhere. The men's implied menace made Elizabeth tremble. Nobody smiled. Everyone was tense and ready to spring into action.

As Elizabeth rounded the corner, she heard the voice of an older woman with a distinct Boston accent talking loudly in her direction. "Come along, *doctor!* You are three minutes late for *my* clinic," Sister Marion admonished her. "This is America, and even though these men are the worst murderers, serial rapists, gang leaders, drug dealers, and anyone's idea of the prisoners from hell, they have a legal right to quality medical care. Each one has insisted to the prison doctor that he has a medical condition that can't wait, so here we are! Today you will examine forty of the most feared prisoners in America. So, obviously, we have lots of work to do and you are late! Hop to, intern!" Elizabeth remembered that no resident at orientation had anything nice to say about Sister Marion.

Elizabeth was surprised to find that Sister stood only four feet, eleven inches tall. Her bones were tiny and her posture impeccable and she had the power of the pope in her countenance. The nun was dressed all in white, topped off with a white cornette wimple that towered nine inches above her tiny head. The wings of the heavily starched cap protruded six inches on either side of the nun's head. It was hard not to chuckle. *That hat has a life of its own,* thought Elizabeth. She was reminded of the nuns in the 1960s TV series *The Flying Nun.*

As Elizabeth stepped closer to Sister Marion, she said, "I am sorry that I'm late. It is my first time here, and I did not know exactly where the clinic was located. I will not be late again."

"Harrumph," mumbled Sister Marion. As she got closer, Elizabeth noticed the nun's sparse hair was mostly white. It had a pinkish hue that indicated it was probably red when the nun was younger. Now it formed a tight white bun with curls escaping the sides. Her brilliant and fierce blue eyes were surrounded by thin, pale, saggy skin.

Sister Marion carried her meanness around her mouth. Her lips were thin and pale and formed a straight, severe line across her lower face. Her jaw was tight and her teeth were clenched in a perpetual scowl. Elizabeth remembered one of the many unkind nicknames that she had heard applied to the nun. "Old chicken lips" was a popular descriptor used by many of the more senior male residents. "She doesn't smile. She has never smiled. Nobody at Tulane has ever seen her smile," was how another resident described her.

Sister Marion said, "I want to be completely clear with you, Dr. Elizabeth Roberts. I do not tolerate tardiness in my clinic. We do not want to have patients waiting around starting trouble while we are drinking coffee. We start on time, we work hard, and we finish on time. Do you understand me, young lady?"

"Yes, ma'am," said Elizabeth to the miniature monster in thick white support hose.

"I want you to remember, at all times, that many of these men have committed heinous crimes against women and children," Sister Marion continued. "They need know nothing about you that could lead them to be able to contact you from Angola. Most certainly, you do not want a very unwelcome visit once they are released. Do you understand me?"

Sister stood very erect and pointed her wrinkled blue-tipped finger at Elizabeth. Her white cornette bobbled slightly as she swung her finger in the doctor's face. Up close she looked much older than her sprightly gait suggested.

"They have little to contemplate during their incarcerations, and you do not want to give them any reason for you to be on their minds. I never wanted a woman in this clinic. You were forced on me. The chairman of surgery at Tulane insisted that 'all residents and interns in Tulane Surgery are treated equally and that nobody is given special consideration for any reason.' So just know that two women in the basement of this God-forsaken hospital with forty dangerous men was not my idea."

Elizabeth felt afraid. The nun was more convincing than Dr. Peterson.

"There is only one armed guard for every five prisoners," she explained. "They are shackled from their necks to their hands and to their feet. But the guard will have to take some of those chains off for you to examine them. Be aware of your surroundings at all times. That little worm of a chief resident should be down here with you, but he's probably more afraid of the prisoners than you," said Sister.

No, he's really afraid of you, thought Elizabeth to herself, remembering Peterson's words. "This is how it works. The prisoners are locked in the wire cage that we use as a waiting room. They are shackled to each other and to the floor, and some are shackled to the guards. One prisoner at a time, accompanied by one guard, will be removed from the cage and put behind an exam curtain. You examine the prisoner behind that curtain. We do not have examination rooms here. You will simply pull the curtain to provide privacy when it's time for the exam," said Sister.

"Go behind that last curtain in the back," Sister Marion told her, "and I will bring the first chart and your first patient. The guards are to stay with you at all times. Remember the danger. I see that you had the good sense to remove your name tag. Do not engage any of them in idle conversation. We are not here to socialize, doctor. The clinic is a charity endeavor for the prisoners of Angola, and you are providing medical care, not making new friends. Are we clear?"

"Yes, ma'am," said Elizabeth.

Elizabeth moved to the area behind the curtain. The nun barked like a drill sergeant, "First patient!" Elizabeth shuddered, and her hand shook slightly as she reached for the chart.

She quickly scanned the prisoner's chart. This patient had been admitted to Charity Hospital every six weeks for the past eighteen months because he had been chronically urinating blood. The medical term was "gross hematuria." His Angola prison sentence came after he had killed his young wife during a drunken blackout. Apparently, the unfortunate woman had been having relations with the prisoner's younger brother in the prisoner's marital bed. Elizabeth could understand crimes of passion, even though violence was not a part of her family's life.

"What are you doing, doctor?" Sister Marion interrupted. "I gave you explicit instructions to avoid anything to do with them personally. Reading his prison history has nothing to do with why he is here! Medical service is what we give here. All you need to read is his medical chart."

Elizabeth felt anger rising as her belly tightened and her shoulders tensed. "Please do not rob me of seeing the tiny thread of humanity that might still lie in some of these men, Sister Marion," she said tersely. "I am not ready to be an automaton. I am a physician, and I intend to be one, no matter the patient before me."

As the curtain was pulled back and the first prisoner arrived, Sister said, "Well, then, do it quickly! We have forty pieces of precious humanity for you to examine today, doctor!" Elizabeth thought the nun was ridiculing her; she seemed slightly amused. *Could her meanness be partly bravado to cover the nun's own fear?*" wondered Elizabeth.

Elizabeth heard the prisoner shuffling toward her before she saw his emaciated face. He was a very pale man with deep, dark purple smudges beneath crystalline aqua eyes. His filthy blond hair was plastered to the sides of his face. His chart said that he was twenty years old. Elizabeth waited for him to speak. "Speak up, son. We don't have all day," said Sister. Elizabeth noticed that she was not as harsh as a moment ago when she was speaking to her. She sounded almost kind.

"Miss Doctor Lady, I am sorry to say that I have blood dripping from the end of my penis," said the prisoner. If Elizabeth were in different surroundings, she would have smiled at his accent, which was pure Plaquemines Parish, Louisiana. Elizabeth had heard the dialect in the ER earlier this week. It was quite distinctive. The prisoner reminded her of Jim Morrison, a handsome rock star whose life had been taken by drug addiction. His enormously muscled black guard interrupted, "Get over there to the doctor girl. We ain't got all day for your foolishness."

Elizabeth studied his chart, incredulous. "I see that you have had this same problem on every single admission. That seems odd to me, sir," she said.

The guard laughed under his breath.

Despite her fear and Sister's warnings, Elizabeth said to the guard, "You will have to unshackle him, at least in the front, so that I can examine him, please."

"Sure, doc, this one ain't going to give you no trouble at all. He is everybody's best girlfriend, and he ain't going anywhere. We started you out with him 'cause he won't hurt a fly," said the guard.

Elizabeth sat on a rolling stool as the guard unlocked the front shackles and the patient's baggy orange prison pants fell to the floor. "I am very sorry, ma'am. I know it is a mess down there, and I am sorry that you have to see it." The prisoner's apology seemed sincere to Elizabeth.

From the other side of the curtain, Sister Marion said, "Get on with it, doctor."

"There certainly is blood dripping from your penis," Elizabeth observed. "I have not seen this before. And you have a lot of scar tissue down here," she said as she looked up into the face of the prisoner. He was red from his chest up. He looked like an embarrassed boy, not a hardened criminal.

As the prisoner blushed, the guard growled, "Don't be giving him too much pity, doc. He done this to himself. He works all month in the commissary to sneak a couple of staples out of the middles of magazines so he can jam them in his manhood, make himself bleed, and get a few days in The Big Free. It is his sick little way of getting a holiday from Angola. Every time he makes bright red blood come out his pecker, we have to bring him in. It's the law."

Elizabeth fought to hide her disgust. "Could you please bend over the table so that I can complete the remainder of your exam? I need to examine your prostate and rectum to be sure that the blood is not coming from there."

The embarrassed prisoner squeaked, "Do I have to bend over? They usually just admit me when they see the blood."

The guard looked on with disdain and instructed Elizabeth, "Look, doc, here's what's going on here. This little blond filly stays alive inside Angola by being the girlfriend of the biggest buck on the yard. He gets to keep his life, but he gets sold around for favors like cigarettes, candy, phone time, and God knows what else. You might say that our little friend here is a little used up."

Fighting back a wave of nausea at hearing the guard's words, Elizabeth said to the patient, "Yes, sir, I do have to examine you. An entire exam is required if I am to properly diagnose you." The prisoner obediently bent over the exam table.

Elizabeth gasped as she stared at the prisoner's scarred, red, swollen, and partially everted anus. "I am so sorry that this has happened to you," she said. "You must have been through hell to be in this condition, sir." As bile rose from her stomach, she fought her desire to beg for his release. Everything in her being cried out with compassion for the patient. How could one human being do this to another human being? It hadn't occurred to her that such horror existed.

From the other side of the curtain Sister said, "Doctor, just culture him up and get him admitted. He will have to stay for a week just to get the antibiotics and for you to get him on the operating schedule to get that staple out of his private parts."

The prisoner said, "Thank you, Sister."

The nun leaned in toward the patient and whispered, "You only have six more months to go, son. Seventy months down and six to go, son. Godspeed to you."

To Elizabeth, she admonished, "Chop! Chop! Dr. Roberts! We've got many men to go!"

The prisoner pulled up his pants. His shackles refastened, he shuffled out with the guard holding his arm. As he passed the cage where the other prisoners were held, the catcalls began. "Have a good rest, baby. We will sure be missing your sweet self, and we will be looking forward to your return!" the other prisoners taunted him.

Sister Marion shouted, "Move it! Faster, guard! Faster!"

Elizabeth felt her composure slipping. "I wish I was big and strong and could crawl in that cage and beat the hell out of those monsters! How dare they treat another human being like that!" exclaimed Elizabeth, trembling with rage. She threw the chart on the counter, breathed heavily, and scowled at Sister Marion. "Why exactly can't we do something about this? When children are abused, we report it to the state. What exactly could we do to stop this? *This is insane!*"

The nun lunged at Elizabeth and hissed in her face, "Look here, girl. You are not the judge, the jury, or God. You are simply the doctor. Your job is to treat all the prisoners the same. That man will be back in here every six weeks until they let him go. All you can do, besides attend to his medical care, is pray for him, and pray for the monsters that are doing this to him. You are no judge. You are the doctor. Each one gets the same care. Whether victim or perpetrator, we treat them the same. So shake it off! Here's the next chart." Sister firmly placed the chart in Elizabeth's trembling hands and spun around.

"Yes, ma'am, I am ready." As Elizabeth's fury settled into a deep ache, the nun moved efficiently toward the cage and retrieved the next patient.

Two enormous black men, muscled from head to toe—a guard and a prisoner—came around the curtain. Both had several blue-ink tattoos. Both were over six-and-a-half feet tall. Except that the guard had a gun and a blue uniform and the prisoner wore shackles and orange, it would have been impossible to discern which was which, prisoner or guard. Anger and meanness emanated from both.

The prisoner sneered, "My, my, my. Ain't you the prettiest, sweetest, little white thang?"

The guard whipped out his baton and tapped the shackled man on the side of his head. "Look, buddy," he said, "one more word out of that big mouth of yours and you are going back in the truck and the party is over!"

"Hey, dude, I am just trying to help her out here. Ever had a big black man, baby? You know the saying, 'Once you go black, you never go back'!" chuckled the prisoner.

The guard whacked him harder and shouted, "That's it, slime ball. You are going back in the truck." As the prisoner was hauled away with no exam, Elizabeth marveled that the patient's thick neck muscles could withstand such a beating. An ordinary person would have been knocked unconscious by those blows to the head. The prisoner showed little reaction. It was as if he had been thumped with a finger.

As he was dragged past the other prisoners in the holding cage, Elizabeth heard him shout, "Hey, guys, she is super skinny, but super fine for a white chick. There is a lot for us to dream about tonight, dudes." Elizabeth heard the sound of one last crack to the prisoner's head. It was the loudest, and the talking stopped. After the third blow, the prisoner staggered and required the support of two guards.

Elizabeth felt a wave of shame as she realized that she felt pleasure in his beating. *He was rude, and he deserved it,* she thought, though she felt uncomfortable to be judgmental about a patient. Sister was right. She should not judge. But she could not resist a quick reading of his chart.

The prisoner had been a linchpin dealer of crack cocaine. Elizabeth remembered reading about the effect that the introduction of crack cocaine had had in inner cities. When the crack folks came to New Orleans and took over much of the Mafia's turf, it was not good for the city. That was because prostitution and graft had been effectively controlled by the Mafia, so average citizens were rarely affected by criminal goings-on. The crack crowd was different. The average citizen felt the lawlessness and brutality of the drug wars between the gangs vying for power. The number of violent deaths tripled. The young black men in the projects participated in a new form of slavery, becoming slaves to the highly addictive drug and the crack lords. Prostitutes, especially young women, also became crack addicts and were caught up in the turf wars that followed. There were no longer any safe neighborhoods in New Orleans.

This particular man was notorious for beating the fourteen-year-old boys who worked as his drug runners when they were caught skimming off the profits of his crack trade. To teach a lesson, the dealer prisoner had the boys' ears delivered in bags to their grandmothers' front doors. He was awaiting death in Angola for committing multiple murders.

Elizabeth's attention was brought back to the present moment by the nun's shouts as she marched in front of the remaining caged prisoners. "Okay, you bunch of buzzards, listen up! Just one more disrespectful comment to *Doctor* and I will close this clinic down for the day, and all of you will go back to prison without being seen! Do I make myself clear? *One more comment and we are done here!*"

Is she a nun or a Boston cop? Elizabeth wondered. No matter, there was quiet from the cage.

Elizabeth stood tall, fought her emotions, and forced a neutral countenance onto her own face as Sister pulled back the curtain to reveal the next patient. She realized the prison clinic was physically challenging. One doctor seeing forty patients in one day was more than most could manage. But she was unprepared for the emotional burden. She realized for the first time how sheltered she had been in South Carolina. Hers had been a very sweet life. Her heart felt heavy and her hands felt tremulous. She did not want to know the depth of man's depravity. She wanted to heal people and not be traumatized herself. She fought the strong urge to run from the clinic and never look back. After seeing only a few patients, she felt emotionally drained.

"Chop! Chop! Doctor!" said Sister.

The menacing man—six feet, five inches tall—had two guards with him. Their name tags revealed that Captain Aucoin and Sergeant Dubois were his handlers today. The prisoner was greasy with sweat. His strong, foul odor suggested his bathing was sporadic at best. Two sets of chains hung from every appendage. Elizabeth felt the resentment and hostility that exuded from his every pore.

She glanced at his chart and quickly read: serial rapist, serial murderer, highly recidivistic, high escape risk.

Oh, joy, she mumbled to herself. She was starting to feel exhausted to the bone. She had taken two naps in forty-eight hours of hard work and hadn't had an actual meal in more than two days. Instead, she'd enjoyed whatever food could be gotten from the vending machines in the entrance to the stairwells between the hospital floors. Her fatigue, hunger, fear, and disgust were mounting, and she fought off the desire to sit in the corner and cry herself to sleep. But she knew there was no crying in Tulane Surgery.

The prisoner said, "Doc, no joke. I got some kind of knot on my left ball. It came up about five days ago. It don't hurt. I just want to make sure it ain't no cancer."

Elizabeth sat on her rolling stool, pulling her skirt as far down over her legs as possible. The last thing on earth that she wanted to do at that moment was examine this man. She thought, *I am an intelligent, educated woman from a good family in South Carolina. My father would have a stroke if he saw this. What am I doing in a dark, dirty clinic with a mean nun asking the guards of a serial rapist to unshackle him and pull down his pants?* Suddenly, happy vignettes from her days at her family's farm danced through her memory. The mooing cows, the sweet smell of the apple orchard, the taste of a hot tomato freshly picked from a vine, the refreshing feeling of cool well water on a hot summer day, and the sight of horses running in the grass calmed her.

With a heavy exhalation, she said to Captain Aucoin, the largest of the guards, "Please loosen his chains enough to pull his pants down. I can't examine him unless I can get to his groin."

"Doc, do you know who you are dealing with here?" said Captain Aucoin. "He's probably just caught something again and needs some penicillin. Taking anything off him is too dangerous, ma'am."

"Yeah, and I shore don't want to be in here when he exposes hisself," said Sergeant Dubois.

"The other doctors just have Sister give him the shot in his arm. They don't ever actually touch him, ma'am," said Captain Aucoin.

"Well, sir, I appreciate your advice. But if your diagnosis is correct and he has gonorrhea repetitively, then it is likely a resistant strain of the bacteria, and we will need a culture to cure it. But if he really does have a lump on his testicle, it is my duty to be sure that it is not cancer. So either way, his pants must come down," said Elizabeth. She was struggling to sound authoritative, though she was feeling scared to death.

"Cancer is too good for him," said Sergeant Dubois.

The prisoner turned desperate. "Please, please, ma'am. I beg you to not put that metal swab up my privates. When you docs do that, it feels like somebody is running a razor blade up in there. I'd rather get stabbed with a shank in the liver than have that swab in my manhood. Please, ma'am, don't do it."

Elizabeth wondered if his victims had begged as he was now begging.

"Really, miss, I do not want that culture. I am telling you that I do not have the clap. I got a knot on my ball. Please, no culture," reiterated the prisoner.

"Look, doc, he is doing this to himself," interjected the captain. "He keeps going back to the same place and getting the same thing. That skinny little white dude you treated first thing today is his main girlfriend. They keep passing diseases back and forth. My man here just can't resist!"

Elizabeth was energized by a wave of blind fury. Loathing momentarily consumed her. As her heart hammered she fought her instincts to take the easy route and ignore her sworn responsibility as a physician. "Look, gentlemen, I am the doctor," she told the two guards. "Do not try to tell me my duty! We are either going to do this right, or we are doing nothing."

She looked at the prisoner. "If you want to be examined, get your pants down now. If I see any discharge coming from your penis, you will be cultured. I will be as gentle as possible, but those are your *only* options, sir." As Elizabeth spoke, hatred for the patient and his crimes and her sworn duty as a physician battled for her conscience.

Elizabeth could hear Sister rustling outside the curtain, letting Elizabeth know she was very near, but she didn't speak.

"This is a bad idea, ma'am, but you asked for it," said Captain Aucoin as he reluctantly began removing the first set of shackles.

"I am out of here," said Sergeant Dubois. "Angola does not pay me enough to have to look at all that. I will stand behind the curtain with Sister, but I am not going to be in here for this."

Elizabeth felt perspiration accumulating in her hairline as the orange pants and shackles fell to the floor. She forced herself to scoot the rolling stool closer to the prisoner's groin. The prisoner saw the metal swab lying on the counter and whispered, "Please don't hurt me, doc."

Elizabeth hated him for what she imagined him to have done to the prisoner they had admitted. But under that hatred lay her compassion. *No matter how twisted the man is*, she reminded herself, *he is a human being.*

As the remaining guard stepped to the side, the prisoner lunged forward, his body falling on top of Elizabeth's like a giant, heavy, black wall. Elizabeth felt the rolling stool fly from under her bottom and shoot out behind her. She hit the nasty floor with a jolt, and the prisoner's full weight crashed on top of her. Her skirt flew up to her waist as it caught on his chest shackles, and her lower spine was pressed into the floor as his genitals met her pubic bone. A half second later, his heavy chest pounded her chin, and she lay on her back on the floor—dazed, disoriented, and repulsed.

Hysterically, she tried to squirm out from under the prisoner, screaming, "*Rape, rape, rape!*" She had never known such fear.

She looked around the prisoner's neck and above her saw Sister Marion O'Heaney with a baseball bat positioned above the prisoner. On either side of the nun stood Captain Aucoin and Sergeant Dubois, their semiautomatic weapons drawn with the safety released. A third guard, who seemed to materialize from thin air, pressed a gun against the base of the prisoner's skull, three inches from Elizabeth's face.

"Get up, you nasty piece of trash, before I blow your brains out! I have been waiting three years to blow you away! Get up this second or my dream will come true!" The bellowing guard pushed the barrel of his gun deeper into the base of the prisoner's skull.

Simultaneously, everyone realized that the prisoner was not moving. His 240-pound body was dead weight on top of Elizabeth. The pelvic grinding she feared was not happening. She attempted to crawl backward, like a crab, but she made no progress. The prisoner was too heavy.

"Put that gun up before you shoot the doctor," commanded Sister Marion. "Pull this man off her immediately," she demanded as she lowered her bat.

As one guard held his gun on the prisoner, the other two grabbed the prisoner's chest chains and prison shirt and hoisted him off Elizabeth.

Elizabeth quickly jerked her skirt down and looked into the prisoner's face as he was being hoisted up. Elizabeth felt great relief in no longer being in physical contact with him. She noticed the prisoner's eyes were unfocused. He was breathing shallowly, and a large gash in his forehead was bleeding briskly.

"Oh, my God," said Sister. "That man was not trying to rape you, doctor. He fainted when he saw that metal-handled swab, and now we are going to have to send him to the ER to get his head stitched up!"

The guards pulled the limp prisoner onto the examining table. Sister said, "Quick, doctor, get that culture while he is still out."

The guards laughed, Sister fumed, and Elizabeth cultured the prisoner. Sister put a large ice pack on the prisoner's head and gave him two shots of penicillin, one in each arm, before he was fully awake.

As he was coming to, he chastised Elizabeth. "Miss Lady Doctor," he said to her, "I told you that swab was a bad idea."

CHAPTER 5

The Louisiana Rain

The remainder of the day's Angola prison clinic was less eventful. The guards and other prisoners were tired of waiting and wanted to make sure that everyone was seen before time to return to the prison. The fainting prisoner had stolen an hour from the schedule.

"Come on, men, get yourselves together and stop the foolishness," said Sergeant Dubois as he banged his baton on the bars to get their attention. "You know the prison warden will be mad as hell if all of you are not seen by the doctor today. He does not like us bringing you back to Charity two days in a row. There will be half rations of food for the whole group if we don't get everyone seen."

Captain Aucoin said, "You have two choices. Either you stay quiet and get seen by the doctor, or you keep up the chaos and drama and get carted back to Angola unseen. You'll be very hungry by the morning if the warden gets angry."

"Yeah, and don't think we won't tell the warden exactly who caused the problems. He will get a full report on anyone foolish enough to keep us from accomplishing our job," said Sergeant Dubois.

Elizabeth thought, *The guards sound as if they are threatening these violent men with their father's wrath. Would that really work?*

The remaining prisoners seemed calmer. Maybe it was fatigue, or hunger, or earlier seeing three big guns pointed at one prisoner's head that calmed them. Elizabeth really did not care. She just wanted to finish the clinic and get out of there.

To Elizabeth, the shock of having the worst thing that she could possibly imagine happen early in the clinic calmed her. *If the worst has happened and I'm still here working, how bad could it be?* she thought.

Sister worked like a robot. She had run the clinic hundreds of times, and she called each prisoner into the exam room, guided Elizabeth through the choices for treatment, and moved to the next man.

"Doctor, pick up the pace. We have five left, and I want to clean them all out today," said Sister Marion.

"Yes, ma'am. I am moving as fast as I can," said Elizabeth.

The guards seemed amused by the woman doctor. As the clinic progressed, they became more and more helpful. After the fainting prisoner was taken to the emergency room, Elizabeth had overheard the guards laughing among themselves. She knew that she and the prisoner were the brunt of the jokes, but she really did not care. Her relief at not being attacked made the jokes tolerable.

Captain Aucoin said, "Hey, doc, that was the last one. You have completed your first Angola prison clinic and lived to tell about it. I want you to know, me and the other guards are impressed with you for sticking with it today. Not many women would have gone through what you did and kept working. If you ever want to be the Angola prison doctor, we'd be happy to put in a good word for you with the warden."

Elizabeth saw the glint in his eye and knew he was teasing her. The abject violence of two hours ago was gone. Standing before her was a man who could have been one of her male cousins, picking at her for falling off the family mule.

She said, "I will keep that career choice in mind. One of my many long-term goals was always to either help my patients or shoot them. Angola could certainly fulfill both criteria."

She signed the paperwork containing the names of the prisoners she had seen and handed a copy to the guard and to Sister Marion. She felt an enormous sense of relief as the last prisoner shuffled in his orange prison suit and shackles out the clinic door.

While Elizabeth and Sister Marion completed the last of the clinic's paperwork, Elizabeth said, "How have you done this for forty years? I am so tired and drained that I can hardly complete this paperwork. You are three times my age, and I can't keep up with you."

Sister laughed and said, "You'll get used to it." Elizabeth could not imagine how that statement would ever be true.

The boredom of the paperwork could not keep Elizabeth's attention. Her mind wandered to the comfort of her apartment and her bed. She was deep into thought about the comfort, quiet, and safety awaiting her at her little efficiency apartment when an orderly she recognized from the emergency room came through the clinic door.

The nun looked up and gave him a grimace that was likely Sister's version of a smile. "How are you today, Jorge?"

Since he appeared just as the clinic ended, it was obvious he knew Sister Marion's routine and that they were friendly.

"Hey, Sister Marion," he said, "I am very sorry to report the rain is really coming down out there, and it doesn't look like it is going to let up anytime soon. I hate to be the bearer of bad news, but I know you are down here in the basement level with no windows and that you have no idea what the weather brings."

The nun slumped in frustration and instantly looked ten years older. "Thanks for letting me know, Jorge. You know I hate riding my bike in the rain."

"Where do you live?" Elizabeth asked.

The tired nun mumbled, "About a mile up Poydras Street. There is a dormitory home for the nuns there."

"Why don't you let me drop you off? My car is in the lot behind Tulane. The parking lot is in a covered garage just across the street, and we won't get wet if we go through the underground tunnel between Charity and Tulane," Elizabeth offered.

Sister Marion looked confused. "I can't leave my bike here overnight. Someone will steal it in a minute. I'd rather get soaking wet than leave my bike."

Elizabeth explained, "Your bike will fit perfectly into the back of my car. It is no trouble to load it up and drop off both of you at the door of your dorm. I certainly would not want your cornette hat to get wet. It looks like it is a lot of work to starch and iron."

Astonished by Elizabeth's kindness, the nun's eyes grew wide and she was momentarily without speech.

Then Sister said, "Nobody has ever offered to give me a ride home."

The heaviness of that statement washed over Elizabeth. "Well, I will be here on and off for the next few months, and anytime I am here I can certainly give you a ride when it rains."

The nun would not release a full smile from her lips, but a momentary sparkle came from her bright blue Irish eyes. She retreated to the back of the clinic and returned with an ancient Schwinn bicycle. She handed the bike to Elizabeth and grabbed a large brown box.

Sister Marion and Elizabeth did not speak as they left the basement clinic and made their way through the underground tunnel. The underground portion of Charity and the underground portion of Tulane Medical School were attached by a tunnel. The doctor walked Sister's bicycle through the tunnel as the diminutive nun struggled with the weight of her box. The two exited the tunnel and waited in front of an elevator in the basement of the medical school.

The women waited quietly. Suddenly the elevator doors opened and a group of male doctors hurried off the elevator. When they recognized Elizabeth, their chanting began, "*Rape, rape, rape!*" They hustled down the hall in a pack, taunting Elizabeth over their shoulders.

The women could hear the doctors' raucous laughter even after the elevator doors closed behind them.

Elizabeth was mortified. Sister was angry. "Don't let it get to you, doctor. The Charity Hospital grapevine is quick and brutal," she said kindly. "Anything humiliating that happens to anybody makes the rounds in about fifteen minutes, and the story will get bigger and more dramatic as it is passed around. It's not personal. They do it to everyone. Honestly, they could close down the phone system in the entire hospital and the community gossip mill could suffice."

Elizabeth was almost too tired to care. *How could so much happen in eight hours? Surely only soldiers and policemen knew this kind of weariness. Medical school had not prepared her for this.*

The nun clung to her box covered in brown paper as Elizabeth rolled the bicycle toward her car. She had offered to carry the box, as Sister appeared to sway under its weight. But the little old nun clutched the box like her only child was contained within.

Elizabeth was glad to see her old, gray Volkswagen Rabbit was still where she had left it the day before. Elizabeth thought, *One advantage of having a rusty old tin can of a car is that nobody wants to steal it, even for the parts.*

Together they lifted the bike and loaded it into the rear compartment, secured with bungee cords left over from Elizabeth's sailing days. Sister Marion and Elizabeth got in the front seats, and they started off.

"Sister, would you like me to put that box in the back seat so you don't have to endure its weight in your lap?" Elizabeth asked.

"No, thanks," said Sister as she clutched the box tighter. Elizabeth was too tired to argue.

They silently made their way down Poydras Street in the pouring rain. There was sunshine through the clouds but no sign of the rain abating. Elizabeth thought about the beautiful afternoon showers she had known in Charleston. They were cool and refreshing, but nothing could match the relief of the afternoon Louisiana rain. The days in New Orleans were the muggiest she had ever experienced. By three in the afternoon, Elizabeth felt as if she were trying to breathe through a heavy wet sponge. Afternoon showers in New Orleans were divine.

Elizabeth pulled under the porte cochere to allow the nun to disembark in a dry spot. Elizabeth lifted the old bike with chipped paint from the back of her car and stabilized it while the nun secured her box on the bike's back storage rack.

As the nun walked away, pushing her bike, Elizabeth clearly saw the words *Bud Light* on a side of the box where the brown paper had come undone.

Sister called back over her shoulder, "Thanks, Dr. Roberts."

"Goodnight, and thank you, ma'am," replied Elizabeth.

Elizabeth chuckled as she drove away and thought a case of Bud Light was a reasonable way to cope with the horrors of the Angola prison clinic. She vowed to make sure that she had a case of beer for Sister most Fridays and that the brown paper was better secured to keep the nun's secret safe.

After Elizabeth dropped Sister Marion at the nuns' dormitory, she drove out Airline Highway to her efficiency apartment. The highway had been appropriately named by Governor Huey P. Long in 1933. It ran from New Orleans, past the New Orleans airport, to Baton Rouge, and past its airport. As driving over potholes in the pavement jolted Elizabeth's aging car, she wondered if the potholes also were a relic from Governor Long's time.

The highways were not usually crowded during the hours Elizabeth drove. Few people traveled to work at four o'clock in the morning and came home at nine or ten at night as Elizabeth usually did. She had been at Charity for over thirty-six hours, and now, more exhausted than she could ever remember being, she prayed she would stay awake in the six o'clock rush-hour traffic. This evening, Louisiana rain, the traffic on Interstate I-10, bumpy Airline Highway, and splashing mud stood between the young doctor and her bed.

Elizabeth's Volkswagen Rabbit had cost only $900. It had served her well through eight years of college and medical school, but the salty air of Charleston had rusted the car severely. The floor on the driver's side was rusted through, and in some spots Elizabeth could see the road beneath her. When it rained heavily, like it was tonight, mud splattered through the holes in the floor of the car and stung her ankles. She was careful to avoid placing her feet near the larger holes in the floor since she never knew when a rusty area might give way, making her feet a little too intimate with the pavement.

Elizabeth knew her reflexes were slower than usual after a day and a half on duty. She struggled to keep her feet away from the holes in the floorboards and to navigate the innumerable Airline Highway potholes with care. The crowded highway, the pouring rain, and the obviously frustrated drivers made the trip home intolerable. As traffic came to a halt, Elizabeth started to cry. Previously, crying had been a rare activity for her, and she surprised herself when her crying turned into sobs and her shoulders shook with grief. As mucus from her nose ran down her face and tears soaked her blouse, she croaked out angry screams. *Why? Why do the prisoners have to be so hateful to one another? Don't they have a tough enough life just being confined? Why? Why is there such abject poverty right next to obvious wealth in New Orleans? Why would a brother pimp out his sister? Why? Why does Nurse Robichaud have to be so stern? Why can't she show a little compassion? Why all that meanness? Why all that horror? Why would people treat one another in such a hideous manner? Why did I choose Charity Hospital? Why did great surgical training have to be so difficult?* She wanted to be a healer, not the brunt of hospital jokes. She beat her steering wheel with her palms until her hands ached as much as her heart. Could she do this? As the traffic started to move again, she wiped her eyes with the back of her hand and wondered if she even wanted to continue to try. Maybe she should quit before they fired her.

An eighteen-wheel semi-tractor-trailer truck pulled dangerously close to her left front bumper and loudly blew his air horn in frustration. The doctor was not moving fast enough, in the pouring rain, to suit the trucker. *Why was New Orleans so uncivilized?* she wondered. *Why did I choose such a difficult route to my goals?* It was all too much.

As suddenly as they began, Elizabeth's tears and screams turned to laughter. If she was going to make it to her bed, she would have to pull herself together and focus on the road. She was not interested in having a "white light" experience she remembered hearing patients describe during her senior year in medical school.

One of Elizabeth's last rotations before coming to New Orleans had been a cancer ward. Many times a patient would code, and if the patient had not specifically asked to be allowed to die, the medical team would have to perform cardiopulmonary resuscitation. Since near-death oncology patients didn't usually live long under the best of circumstances, the senior staff would frequently allow greater participation by the more junior doctors if a patient coded. When life was nearly over and the medical battle was ending, the patient's comfort and the family's comfort were the only concerns.

Elizabeth remembered the amazing resilience of some of the cancer patients. Often a patient who had gotten chest compression to restart his or her heart the night before would be sitting up in bed and eating scrambled eggs the next morning as though nothing out of the ordinary had occurred. The very elderly seemed to be particularly hardy. Elizabeth believed anyone making it to eighty years old had to be tough. She did not completely understand how any of that birth and death stuff worked, but it fascinated her.

She always came in early to check on the people who had coded and made it back. When a patient coded, Elizabeth thought she could feel the person's essence—the soul, perhaps—still lingering in the hospital room for a time. One minute the body appeared to be uninhabited and the next minute it again was fully animated. To the young doctor, death felt like the opposite of birth. In birth, one minute there were two people in the delivery room, and then suddenly there were three. In death, one person went away. It almost seemed like magic.

Elizabeth often had a premonition about when a patient was going to exit his or her body. Usually, it felt to Elizabeth as if the patient who died had actually made a conscious decision to leave their body for good. Those patients did not survive even extreme measures on the part of the medical staff. Over and over she watched patients become much more lucid and communicative shortly before they left their bodies. She loved to listen to their white light stories, and she felt honored to be present at a patient's transition.

The patients loved to share those stories with Elizabeth, and their stories were surprisingly similar. "Honey, it was not bad," one woman told her. "I did not see some big white guy on a cloud with a white beard. I did not see anyone who appeared to be Abraham or Jesus. But there was white light, and there was calm, and there was peace. It was not scary at all." Hers was a typical tale of a near-death experience. Some patients talked about their near-death experiences as if they were a new adventure, even as they continued to eat their rubbery scrambled eggs. The casualness with which her patients spoke of the experience of being near death captivated Elizabeth.

But tonight Elizabeth did not want to wake up in Room Four of the Charity ER with Dr. McSwain standing over her and interrogating her about her poor driving. She also did not want to explain to Nurse Robichaud why she was late for her shift. So she put her focus back on getting to her apartment safely.

As the rain finally slowed, Elizabeth pulled into the cracked asphalt driveway of her apartment complex. She had not put much time or effort into choosing her new home. Because she knew that she would be there rarely, she opted for cheap and easy. Her stipend from Tulane was eighteen thousand per year, a salary that provided little in the way of creature comforts. Since she expected to work more than eighty hours a week, what did she really need? *Most nights,* she had reasoned, *I'll be sleeping in the on-call room at Charity.*

As she got out of the car and stumbled toward her apartment, she saw her new neighbor standing in her doorway. Mrs. Eloise Kaczka, a Polish lady from Milwaukee, reminded Elizabeth of the famous comedian Phyllis Diller. Her voice was gravelly, and her usual tone was a cackle. Mrs. Kaczka held a Chihuahua named Buster, and her hair was always teased at least six inches high. She loved to combine hot pink and orange in her fashion choices and home décor, and tonight she was dressed in very tight, hot pink pants. In her hand, she held a gold cigarette holder with rhinestones encircling the base. Elizabeth had never known anyone like Mrs. Kaczka. But she was sweet and unfailingly friendly. She spent her days at home alone with Buster, while her husband, whose name was Larry, worked the oil rigs.

"Hey, docta, ya look a little worn around the edges tonight," said Mrs. Kaczka in greeting. "At least ya home at a decent hour. How do they ever expect ya to get a man when all ya do is work, work, and work?"

"Mrs. Kaczka, the last thing I need is a man," laughed Elizabeth. She smiled and reached to pet Buster. He nipped at her fingers and began to squirm and whine.

"Stop it, Buster! Act like you have some manners!" scolded the neighbor. Buster hated everyone but Mrs. Kaczka. "What is all that mud around your legs?"

"My car has some rust in the floorboards and when it rains heavily, a little mud shoots up into the car," said Elizabeth.

"Jesus H. Christ!" exclaimed Mrs. Kaczka. "I thought ya doctas was rich. What's the matter with that hospital? They pay ya nothing and keep ya there to all hours. Have the people down here, in the South, not realized that whole slavery thing is over with?" She looked at Elizabeth and shook her head. "As cute as you are, you could get a handsome, rich man and forget all this foolishness. I can see an ugly girl having to work this hard, but not someone as cute as you. I advise you to find a rich and handsome doctor, get yourself knocked up, and retire, honey. That's how they do it on the soaps."

"Oh, Mrs. Kaczka," said Elizabeth, "you sound a lot like my mother."

"Well, speaking of mothers, when is the last time you ate something? Do they feed ya there? Oh, who cares, even if you did eat, you can eat again—you're skinny!" she exclaimed with a laugh. "Come on in here. Larry is out for his big bowling night, and I just made a stew with pork, kielbasa, and sauerkraut. You need to eat a big bowl. Since ya ain't got no man yet, ya don't have to be worrying about the gas!"

"Well, maybe just a little bowl," Elizabeth replied, realizing she was indeed ravenously hungry. "Then I am headed straight to bed." A home-cooked meal sounded heavenly. "Thanks, Mrs. Kaczka," said Elizabeth sincerely. It felt good to be mothered by her neighbor, especially since her neighbor was such a good cook.

CHAPTER 6

The Bet

Elizabeth slept deeply and fitfully and awoke feeling lifeless and sore. She had set three alarm clocks to be sure she would wake up on time, and now all three flashed 4:00 a.m. as she sat up in her hideaway bed. When her feet hit the floor, she thought, *Is this what being a doctor feels like? Maybe I'm really not a doctor.* Surely being a physician was more of a cerebral pursuit. Being a Charity Hospital doctor felt more like a physical challenge than a mental one at four in the morning. Her first two days at The Big Free had left her sore from head to toe. Her body felt like she had been fighting in the roller derby. She had a tender lump on the back of her head from when she hit the floor after the Angola prisoner fainted on top of her. She noticed bruises on her arms and legs and torso that could not be explained. She bolted off the bed after three minutes of reverie. Dr. McSwain and Nurse Robichaud would be greeting her soon, and detailed preparation, she felt, was her only chance for success. Gone were the mornings of sipping coffee and reading poetry before school. Her five-minute shower and the banana-and-yogurt breakfast she ate while driving would put her in downtown New Orleans at 4:20 a.m.

Her trauma shift did not begin until seven, but Elizabeth had learned at orientation that in Tulane parlance, a trauma room shift that started at 7:00 a.m. meant that she was to know everything that had happened in the past twenty-four hours and be ready to explain it all while on trauma rounds with Dr. McSwain, Nurse Robichaud, and Chief Surgical Resident Dr. Edward Peterson. Her hope was to get every pertinent piece of information for every patient on an index card before Dr. McSwain and Dr. Peterson appeared.

Perfect organization, she believed, would save her from her ignorance. Elizabeth was rushing constantly to try and get everything done. Her mind raced and she found focus difficult. Her stomach felt queasy thinking of the large number of patients awaiting her. At her medical school in South Carolina, students cared for no more than four patients at one time. She had heard that the accident room at Charity could be treating as many as thirty people concurrently, and she knew that when she was on duty all the patients in the accident room would be her responsibility. She had signed up for the most rigorous, elite surgical training. She thought she was prepared and capable, but that did not mean she wasn't frightened.

She drove in the dark, and she parked in the dark, in one of the worst neighborhoods in America, jogging quickly to the back door of Charity Hospital. On the ramp leading up to the large sliding-glass doors at the emergency room entrance stood the leftover people from last night's emergency room activity. A cross-section of the entirety of the hospital was represented in the smoking area— prostitutes, pimps, desperately sick patients, exhausted policemen, ambulance drivers, off-duty nurses, and doctors. As she passed them, Elizabeth smiled and said, "Good morning." A few of the men smiled back, but most looked on in surprise.

Elizabeth had changed her wardrobe as Nurse Robichaud had suggested, leaving the pink hair bow, the pink argyle socks, and her penny loafers at home. But she refused to relinquish her grandmother's pearls, and she wore them proudly with her scrubs. In front of this seasoned crowd, Elizabeth felt scared, naïve, and inadequate, but despite her fear, she vibrated with excitement. She longed to be a valued member of the team.

The Charity Hospital calendar was divided into twenty-four-hour intervals, from seven o'clock in the morning one day until seven in the morning of the next. The long days rotated between staff members of the medical schools of LSU and Tulane. Every medical student, intern (first-year doctor), junior and senior resident (two to six years after medical school), fellow (the post-residency elite doctors getting special training), and medical school faculty followed the time-honored rotation. Every patient coming through the doors of the emergency room during Tulane's twenty-four-hour period was the responsibility of the Tulane team of doctors. At seven o'clock on the next day of the month, anyone who came into the emergency department was an LSU patient. The days of rotation between the two medical schools continued through the calendar.

Over the decades, the calendar rotation caused great conflict between the doctors of the two schools. According to the division of hours, every patient entering Charity Emergency Department was either a Tulane patient or an LSU patient. If a critically sick patient checked into the emergency department five minutes before the seven o'clock shift change, the patient was the responsibility of the medical team on duty, and that doctor, who had been working twenty-four hours at that point, could not go home until that patient had been admitted to the hospital and handed off to go to the operating room or to the team of admitting doctors.

This admission policy, and its potentially unintended consequences, could mean the difference between a twenty-four-hour shift and a thirty-six-hour shift for an intern or resident. Even though the charge resident may have already been on duty for longer than twenty-four hours, he or she was required to remain on duty until the last admitted patient's plan of care was determined. Typically, patients were discharged from the emergency room after receiving care or being sent to the operating room for surgery or admitted to a hospital ward. The process didn't always go quickly or smoothly.

A large part of the charge resident's job in the emergency room was to make certain that the charge resident's team, whether LSU or Tulane, did not get any dumps. Dumps were particularly complex cases that entered the trauma room in the last minutes of a twenty-four-hour rotation and were "dumped" on the roster of an exhausted surgical team. Dr. Peterson had explained the system to Elizabeth in detail. He made it clear that Elizabeth was to be a wall to prevent any manipulation of the schedule to favor LSU, and he warned her that any excess work for him would not be looked upon favorably.

The jockeying by charge residents to prevent the last-minute admissions was legendary. Handsome residents from Tulane and LSU had been known to make romantic overtures to the triage nurses to persuade them to change a patient's admissions time. Marriage proposals at the triage desk in the waiting room were not unusual. Abject begging and the promise of a romantic dinner at Commander's Palace were routine—never mind that no resident could afford that restaurant. With triage nurses, it was the thought that counted, and they seemed entertained by the constant attempts to court their favor, even with lies.

Being female, Elizabeth did not have the option of romancing the triage nurses, so she knew she had to get to the ER very early. Her opportunity to protect her team from late hits depended upon surveying the landscape and being familiar with the players. Manipulation was not her strong suit, so she thought keen observation of her surroundings and diligence would have to suffice. She could compliment, bat her eyes, make sweet jokes, and charm with the best of them. She knew how to apply the wiles of a Southern belle, if absolutely necessary. But she doubted beguiling behavior would work in this environment.

Elizabeth approached the triage nurse station, located just inside the ER entrance, and introduced herself to the nurse on duty. "Hi," she said, smiling. "I am Dr. Elizabeth Roberts. How are you?"

The nurse, with no name tag, looked up from her long list of waiting patients. "I am too busy for chitchat. Livvy already warned me about you." Elizabeth's heart sank at the mention of Lavinia Robichaud's name. Elizabeth was not looking forward to seeing her, as she was still smarting from the rebuke Nurse Robichaud had given her in front of Dr. McSwain, but she was anxious to learn from her. She hoped that they could get on fresh footing and that her education would be a bigger priority than her hazing. Nurse Robichaud's shift didn't start until seven, but she usually arrived around six-thirty.

"Here's what you need to know," the triage nurse continued. "There are about thirty-five patients you need to know for rounds with McSwain, unless, of course, some of them die in the next hour." The nurse's faded and brassy red hair exposed an inch of light-brown roots. Her nails were painted orange, and the polish was chipped. Good grooming obviously was not mandatory for triage nurses. Elizabeth thought this nurse resembled a bone-tired leprechaun. *Maybe,* she mused to herself, *she had misplaced the pot of gold at the end of her rainbow.*

"Thanks very much," said Elizabeth, still smiling. "Where do you suggest I start?"

"Storming Norman McSwain arrives right at seven, and he likes to start with the most critical patients and move on to those who are malingering. If he finishes his coffee before you have presented the patients needing surgery, he won't be happy. So I suggest you go right to the LSU charge resident and start following him around to see who is the sickest," said the nurse.

"Thanks. What time does the chief resident get in?" asked Elizabeth.

"It depends," said the nurse.

"On what?"

Chuckling under her breath, the nurse looked up. Her green eyes were cold and resentful as she replied, "It depends on the quality of the piece of butt under him in that call room of his!"

"Oh…okay," said Elizabeth.

"It's just best to assume that you are on your own. Try to watch your back. You can be sure he is watching his," offered the nurse.

The nurse looked down at her large stack of charts and appeared to dismiss Elizabeth. Suddenly, she looked back up and said, "Listen, doc, you seem like a nice enough girl. I will give you another little tip. There is a thoracic patient back there, and that means you will get an early visitation from *the* Dr. Harrison Lloyd White III. He is so tough that he makes Norman McSwain seem like a sweet baby panda. Any patient that comes in with a chest wound involves Dr. White. He demands to be notified of anything that happens between the neck and the diaphragm of every patient. That is his kingdom, and he is the king! Even Nurse Robichaud gets a little nervous around him."

"Thanks for the advance warning. But what's the big deal about him? He is not even staff, is he? At orientation, I saw his name on the Tulane list of fellows, and he was listed as a seventh-year resident in cardiothoracic surgery. The roster clearly listed him as a fellow, not full-fledged professor," said Elizabeth.

"Honey child, he is a Tulane Surgery legend! He is brilliant. He has a photographic memory. He comes from an old New Orleans blue-blood family that has had doctors in it for five generations. He went to Tulane undergrad, Tulane medical, Tulane Surgery, and now Tulane cardiac surgery. Though their blood is blue, the way his family loves Tulane, it may be tinged a little green!" She smiled. "Honestly, he is a brutal perfectionist toward himself and everyone that comes near him. Rumor has it that he mostly lives in the hospital, and has for many years. He has not seen the light of day in a decade and is the whitest person you will ever meet. He is so white that he makes Dracula look tanned. The story around here, if anyone is foolish enough to joke about him, is that he was the Louisiana leader of the Hitler youth!" said the nurse.

Elizabeth thought it surprising that the nurse was joking and laughing about Hitler. Her uncles had fought in World War II, and Hitler was no joking matter on the farm.

Elizabeth said, "You mean he is a racist?"

"Nah, I mean nothing like that. He just takes it all so damn seriously. He is a little too tightly wound, if you know what I mean." She shrugged. "The population here is too mixed for racism. If you are a real racist, you get out of New Orleans early. There is nothing but mixed blood in this city. A real racist would run for the hills," said the nurse.

"And," she continued, "don't be surprised if Dr. White thinks it's not a good idea for women to be in surgery. None of the women in his bloodline work. They are part of the 'lunch-at-Galatoire's' crowd. They spend their days raising money for art shows and the Catholic Church. But that's New Orleans."

Elizabeth thought the nurse was trying to frighten her; she was getting tired of being afraid, and it wasn't five o'clock yet. "So what do I need to do to be ready for Dr. Perfect?" asked Elizabeth.

"Well, if you will bring me a cup of coffee when you get back to the nurses' station, I will tell all," said the nurse.

"If you save the skin on my hide, I will bring you coffee every morning that I am here. But if I am going to be your morning servant, I need to know what to call you. Queen? Madam? Your Highness?" said Elizabeth.

"Queen of the Universe will do for now. I am not telling you my name until I am sure that you won't use it to blame me for anything! But as for the coffee deal, I am in!" said the nurse. "Always remember Dr. White is the king of surprise. He likes nothing better than to sneak up on unsuspecting first-year doctors and grill them on tiny details that nobody can remember. Interns are fodder for Dr. White."

Elizabeth's eyes grew wide and her posture rigid. She had never experienced a teacher who purposefully tried to upset his student.

"Why would he use that teaching method?" asked Elizabeth.

"He can't help it. His intensity just boils over. He'll focus his piercing blue eyes on you and make you feel like a gnat nailed to a mat. If he senses that you are the least bit off-guard, he'll ask probing questions in rapid succession." She glanced at her watch. "I have watched him sear experienced residents, and it's not pretty. Here's my advice: Run and get my café au lait, and then get in there and learn every tiny detail about that thoracic patient, and quite possibly, you will be fine," said the nurse.

Elizabeth marveled at everything she was learning via the hospital grapevine. Surely the nurses were too busy to be bored. It did seem the doctors provided the nurses endless entertainment. Eager to get to work, Elizabeth turned to leave.

"Oh, by the way," the nurse told her, "Livvy and I have a little bet going that Dr. White won't be as hard on you as he is on the boys. You resemble his younger sister, you see, and he has been raised to be super nice to women. I think his knight-in-shining-armor routine will override his Tulane devotion. Livvy thinks he's going to incinerate you just like he does all interns. My bet is that he will take one look at your loveliness, remember his debutante parties, and not have the nerve to skewer your butt." The nurse laughed and shook her head. "But we'll see. I have not won a bet with the head nurse in a long time."

"What is at stake with the bet?" asked Elizabeth.

"The usual bet between Livvy and me is a beer at Joe's on Friday night. But this is a high-stakes bet. We are betting a steak dinner at Charlie's in uptown," said the nurse.

Elizabeth had heard enough. "I'd better get hopping," she said. "I only have two hours to learn everything about everyone before the gods of Tulane Surgery appear."

"Hey, don't forget my coffee, intern!" said the nurse.

"Yes, Queen of the Universe," called Elizabeth as she moved through the swinging doors and into the trauma suite.

Elizabeth looked into the face of a young LSU intern who looked harried and nearly devastated. The badge he wore identified him as Dr. Adrien Lambert, but he did not introduce himself. "How's it going?" she asked him. "I thought I'd come a little early and get the lay of the land." She smiled and hoped he'd be comforted.

"How's it going? How's it going?" Lambert repeated. "It's hell on earth. That's how it's going! I have had four 'Room Fours' in the last three hours and two had to have their chest opened down here in the trauma suite."

He stood in the hall of the emergency department with a clipboard in hand, stethoscope around his neck, and spots of blood on the lower legs of his scrubs. Nurses, X-ray technicians, orderlies, and housekeepers buzzed around him. Elizabeth saw the open doors to a large trauma- equipped suite with "Room Four" above the door. Several people were rapidly cleaning and restocking the room. In orientation, she had been told Room Four was the room where the emergency medical technicians brought the most critically injured patients. If someone was on the verge of death from trauma, they were brought here.

"It's July. The medical students don't know anything yet and are worthless. My chief resident is in the OR and has had no time to help me out. Nine people need stitches before I can turn them over to the Tulane charge resident. And the prostitute with stab wounds in the bed in Room Nine has probably got that new virus, so nobody wants to go in there. So who the hell are you, and why are you asking me stupid questions?" said Dr. Lambert, the LSU doctor in charge.

Elizabeth stepped back a foot and continued to force a friendly smile.

"I am Dr. Elizabeth Roberts," she told him, "and I am the Tulane Surgery charge resident. I will take over in two hours. If you help me get the lay of the land on all the most critical people, I will help you clean up the stragglers so you can get out on time."

He looked her up and down and laughed.

Incredulous, he said, "Am I hallucinating? Are you my fairy godmother? Is this some kind of sick joke? Did my chief send you down here to mess with me?"

Elizabeth was surprised that he did not immediately take her up on her generous offer.

Dr. Lambert said, "I was told at orientation to never, ever trust a Tulane resident at turnover time. I was told that Tulane knows every dirty trick imaginable to try to get LSU to admit the really sick patients to their service."

"This isn't a trick," Elizabeth assured him. "I'm pretty quick with simple lacerations for an intern. I can knock out those nine patients in an hour."

"You don't even look like a doctor," Lambert protested. "Why should I trust you? You're wearing pearls in the accident room, for God's sake. This must be a new trick." His suspicion was palpable.

Elizabeth ignored his tirade. "What's your name?" she asked, though she'd already read his badge.

"Look, I don't have a lot of time. My name is Adrien Lambert. I am from Opelousas."

"I have never heard of Opelousas. Is that where the horses are from?" asked Elizabeth.

"No, you are thinking of Appaloosa, which is a type of spotted horse. Opelousas is the town where the Tony Cachere spices are made. Louisiana is all about the food. Everyone explains where they live as it relates to cuisine. Mr. Cachere made a spice concoction that is famous in Creole and Cajun cooking. He's a hometown celebrity. You don't sound like a local," said Dr. Lambert as he turned to walk away.

Elizabeth felt foolish. She knew a good bit about mules and workhorses from her days on the family farm, but she was ignorant about horse breeds. And as for spices, she knew salt and pepper. She felt ignorant, as usual, in general.

She followed him, uninvited. "Dr. Lambert, where do we start?" she asked.

"I don't mean to be rude, Dr. Roberts, but I really do not think that this whole 'we' thing is a good idea," Lambert told her. "I was specifically told to watch out for Tulane tricks, and this feels like a trap to me. I can't see any good reason for you to be here this early when your shift does not start for two hours!"

Elizabeth was insistent. "I think that it makes all the sense in the world to have a smooth transition, Dr. Lambert. Besides, I am inexperienced and could use your knowledge. I have not had any trauma experience, and you have been at LSU for four years as a medical student and have been in trauma cases many times." She could tell he was still dubious. "I will help you with the more mundane parts of cleaning up the night," she offered, "if you will teach me about some of the more complex parts that I have not seen. Do we have a deal?"

"Okay, Dr. Roberts. You drive a hard bargain, and I don't have the time or energy to spend arguing with you. Come on," said Lambert.

"Please call me Elizabeth."

"All right," he said. "I am Adrien."

He pushed open the nearest exam room door. Elizabeth saw a very tall black man with dreadlocks and a clear tube that looked like a garden hose coming out of his chest. He was too tall for the gurney, and his head and feet nearly hung off the ends. Her interest was piqued with the realization that he must be the chest patient the nurse had told her about, the one Dr. White would want to see. Elizabeth took out her index cards and quickly scribbled notes, giving this patient's case her entire attention. She did not want Dr. White to be disappointed in her performance today. She felt exhilarated, thinking about how she would impress him.

"This guy, Mr. Green, was stabbed about one o'clock this morning," said Adrien. "He arrived by ambulance with a tension pneumothorax. He was drunk and combative, but we finally got a chest tube in, drained the blood, and got him breathing normally again," said Adrien.

"In my Advanced Trauma Life Support course, I learned that a tension pneumothorax can kill someone very quickly. His chest cavity would have been filled with blood and air that could not escape and would have collapsed his lung on the other side, right? So how did he make it here?" asked Elizabeth.

"One thing you'll learn about New Orleans is that the trauma staff at Charity has invested a lot of time and resources to train everyone to respond to emergencies. Dr. McSwain is on a first-name basis with the ambulance people and the police. The emergency medical technicians in this town are well-trained and unequaled anywhere, except for military MASH units. Dr. McSwain has seen to their training personally," Adrien told her.

"In this case," he continued, "the EMT in the field recognized the patient's trachea was deviated to the side. Despite the fact that Mr. Green was drunk and belligerent, the EMT managed to put a needle in Mr. Green's chest and got out the excess air as a temporizing measure. That made the difference. Mr. Green will never realize it was that EMT who really saved his life," said Adrien.

Mr. Green appeared to still be drunk. He snored loudly, and alcohol-laden fumes came out with each exhalation.

"So what does he need now?" asked Elizabeth.

"He should be good to go upstairs to the surgery ward. The chest tube will allow him to heal the wound. The stab wound will close on its own, and it's unlikely he will need major surgery," said Adrien.

"Great, who is next?" asked Elizabeth as she completed her index card on the chest patient. Satisfaction filled her as she realized good preparation could save her from public humiliation. Hard work had always smoothed her way. Maybe Charity and Tulane Surgery wouldn't be all that different than challenges she had faced in college and medical school. She had always succeeded by thorough preparation and attention to detail.

"The patient with appendicitis is in the examination room next door to Mr. Green, and she is heading up to the OR. The gunshot wound to the leg in the last room on the end is stable and headed upstairs for an angiogram. He never really dropped his blood pressure at the scene or here, and so I doubt he has any major arterial injury in that leg, but we'll get the angiogram study to be sure," explained Adrien.

"I read about something called 'compartment syndrome' that can develop later from the swelling due to the trauma of the bullet going through the tissue. I read that it can compress the important structures and cause the patient to lose his leg later, just due to excess swelling. How do we make sure that does not happen to him?" said Elizabeth.

"Look, you are making this more complicated than it needs to be," Adrien told her. "The job down here is to get them somewhere else and out of the trauma area. Whether they go to the morgue, the operating room, the orthopedic floor, out the swinging doors to home, jail, or get admitted, I do not really care!" said Adrien.

Elizabeth saw Adrien's lack of sensitivity as due to his fatigue. She hoped that she never got so tired that she did not care.

"I understand the general principles of the job of the charge resident in the accident room," replied Elizabeth, "but what about the principles of good patient care? If this man's leg swells and the swelling cuts off the circulation, he could lose his leg. That is important to his care also, don't you think?"

"Okay, consult orthopedics. They will hate you, but if you must, consult orthopedics. This guy is a drug dealer, and he has been in here every three months for years. This is the life he chose," said Adrien.

Elizabeth was surprised to hear him speaking disparagingly in front of a patient. The doctors were standing right in front of him, at his bedside. If commentary were necessary, surely it could occur outside of the examination room, in the hall.

"Dr. Lambert, he is our patient. Whatever else he might be is none of our business. I'll put the call in to orthopedics. They can yell at me," said Elizabeth.

"I knew you'd be a pain in my rear!" barked Adrien as he turned to stalk off.

"No, I won't be," Elizabeth said, following him into the hallway. "I am headed to stitch up your HIV patient that nobody wants to touch. I will keep up the teamwork until you accept that we can be friends and help each other, Adrien. You'll see," said Elizabeth, as she hurried behind him and spoke to the back of his head.

"*Remember*, she could be contagious with that virus the CDC has yet to identify, Miss South Carolina," said Adrien, calling over his shoulder as he scurried into another examination room.

Elizabeth went two exam doors down the hall and opened the door to be confronted with the backside of an emaciated black woman. Her hair was in disheveled braids and her backbone protruded beneath the cheap cotton hospital gown. Her feet were calloused and exposed from the bottom of the gurney. A thick pad with blood seeping through covered the back of her upper left arm.

Elizabeth softly said, "I am Dr. Roberts, and I am here to help you. What is your name?"

"My Moman used to call me Helaina, but I answer to 'Girl' mostly," said the woman. She grimaced as she turned to face the doctor.

Elizabeth saw protruding eyes with yellow where the white should have been. Not only did Helaina have a bleeding wound, but she appeared to have hepatitis too.

"Be careful, doc, I have contagion," said the patient.

"I know, ma'am. Don't worry about me. I will take precautions," said Elizabeth.

"Tell me, Helaina, what happened to you?" asked Elizabeth as she donned sterile gloves, a surgical mask, and a plastic gown to protect herself.

"I used to be a nurse's aide right here in The Big Free," she began. "I loved my job. But my brother got me on drugs and he got in big debt with the wrong people. He started selling me out to men to pay our bills, and he forced me to do things that any woman would be ashamed to do."

Elizabeth stopped getting dressed and looked into the shame-filled face of Helaina.

"Our Daddy died on an oil rig, and our Moman died of breast cancer, so it was just him and me. I got sick pretty quickly, with the weight falling off me, and have been sick much of the last year. When I'm sick I can't work. Sometimes my brother gets real mad when he can't rent me out for a quick buck. Last night, he stabbed me in the back of my arm when I was trying to run away from him." She shook her head. "He used to be such a sweet boy, till he got on drugs," said Helaina.

Elizabeth looked at the jagged cut on the back of her arm. It was superficial, but Helaina had almost no body fat, and her brother's serrated knife had cut through muscle. As Elizabeth methodically cleaned the wound and carefully stitched the muscle and skin, she found herself quietly praying for Helaina.

"I tried to get on hospice, but they are full right now," Helaina told Elizabeth. "It seems like crack is really taking over the city." She paused. "I appreciate you trying to help me. You seem like a nice lady. I ain't got money for antibiotics. Miss Nurse Livvy usually gives them to me."

As Elizabeth finished her last stitches and lightly bandaged the wound, the door opened. Adrien Lambert hesitantly stuck his head in.

"Where do they keep the antibiotics that they send home with the patients?" said Elizabeth.

"There is no such thing," Adrien told her. "The patients at Charity have to get their prescriptions filled at a pharmacy just like anybody else."

"But this patient said that she gets antibiotics from Nurse Robichaud," protested Elizabeth.

Adrien shook his head. "I can't believe that woman takes her own money from her own paycheck to buy antibiotics for the scum of New Orleans. She gets Dr. McSwain to call in large bottles of antibiotics to various pharmacies, and she pays for them and gives them out like candy to anyone who has a sad story. She is a bleeding heart like no other," he said in disbelief.

"I don't want to be any bother," Helaina said when she heard the exchange between the doctors. "I had no idea Nurse Livvy was buying them. I thought it was some kind of Charity program." She averted her eyes with shame. "I would never want to make Nurse Livvy pay for anything for me."

"Girl," said Adrien Lambert, "the state government of Louisiana can't even afford Tylenol for the patients we have in the hospital now. The doctors run across the street and steal it from the private hospitals." He touched Elizabeth on the elbow and said, "Hey, thanks for your help. You are okay for a Tulane doctor. Everything seems pretty quiet right now. See you tomorrow."

"Thanks for your help, Dr. Lambert. Get some rest," said Elizabeth.

After the door closed, Elizabeth said to Helaina, "I think that he is wrong. I think we can get some antibiotics for you. Just wait here a moment. Tulane has antibiotic programs about which LSU is not aware." *God forgives little lies,* thought Elizabeth.

THE BET | 77

Elizabeth ran to the front of the hospital and grabbed the long-forgotten coffee from the vending machine near the stairwell. She knew the triage nurse would likely know about the antibiotic stash.

She carried the coffee in front of her like a peace offering to the triage nurses' station. "I thought you forgot me!" said the nurse.

"I am sorry this took so long," Elizabeth apologized. "There is just so much to do. Where can I get antibiotics for a patient to take home with her? She has no money."

"Oh, my God, don't tell me we got another Nurse Lavinia Robichaud on our hands!" the triage nurse threw up her hands and exclaimed. She stood up and leaned close to Elizabeth's face. "You can't help all these people! You will starve trying! What you see happening in the Charity Emergency Department is mostly self-inflicted misery. Most of the people coming in here made life choices that led them into places where they were shot, stabbed, or beaten." The nurse pointed to the large front doors of the emergency room. "Do you really think innocents come through those doors?"

Elizabeth squirmed as nearby patients stared. "I don't know about everybody. I just know that this one lady really needs her antibiotics, and she can't afford them."

"You cannot run around spending your hard-earned money on them. The one you do something for today will be the one who mugs you tomorrow. Give them two dollars and you'll get your window broken and your radio stolen for your kindness. Do not do this to yourself," said the nurse.

Elizabeth thought, *I hope I never get that jaded.* She stood firm and said, "Please, where does she keep the antibiotics?"

The triage nurse sat back on her chair, crossed her arms before her chest, and appeared defeated.

"They are under the damn counter in the nurses' station. A group of us fools contribute whenever the stash gets low and try to make sure there is always something there when it's needed. You are a big sucker. We really don't need another bleeding heart around here," said the nurse.

"Thanks!" called Elizabeth over her shoulder as she trotted back to the trauma suite.

Under the nurses' desk was the biggest bottle of prescription sulfa antibiotics Elizabeth had ever seen. She counted out enough for seven days, wrapped them in a clean specimen cup, and headed back to Helaina's examination room.

Helaina was sitting up, ready to leave. "I told you that he was wrong," Elizabeth said as she handed Helaina the plastic cup full of large white pills. "Here you go. Take one every twelve hours until they are all gone, and report to the LSU clinic in a week to get the stitches removed. Take care."

"You a nice lady, miss. Thank you," said Helaina. She shuffled out the door, down the hall, through the sliding-glass doors, and out into the early morning.

As Elizabeth turned to walk up the bustling hall, she spotted Nurse Lavinia Robichaud. It was still early—only six o'clock—and Elizabeth knew the nurse's shift started at seven.

"Well, well, look who is here all bright and early—Miss Crème Puff!" Nurse Robichaud greeted her. "You got some little dark circles under those baby blues. How were your first two days?"

"Very educational, thanks for asking. Why are you here so early?" asked Elizabeth.

"It is still July, and I want to make sure that none of you freshly minted doctors kill anybody on my shift. I have to be here early and stay late to keep an eye on the fresh meat that just got out of medical school three days ago and thinks they know it all," said Nurse Robichaud. With her hands on her hips and head moving from side to side, she dared a challenge.

Elizabeth had no time to argue with the nurse or to absorb her verbal thrashing. She felt the pressure of the start of her shift and knew that she needed information. "Do you have any suggestions for my first rounds with Dr. McSwain, Dr. Peterson, and Dr. White?" asked Elizabeth.

"You need to know what you are doing, and you need to be prepared. So since there is no chance that you can possibly know what you are doing at this point, you had better be super prepared. If I were you, I'd get here two hours early and go from exam room to exam room and try to know everything about every patient and keep doing that until the doctors arrive for rounds. Things can change quickly down here, and you do not want to be caught with your pants down, so to speak," said the nurse.

"That has been my plan all along. I was hoping you might have more detailed advice that might help with each doctor's expectations of me," said Elizabeth.

Suddenly, Nurse Robichaud looked startled as she glanced over Elizabeth's left shoulder and down the hall of the emergency department. The nurse appeared to force a smile onto her own face. "Good morning, Dr. White, it is great to see you so bright and early," said Nurse Robichaud.

Elizabeth turned to introduce herself and looked into a pair of intense blue eyes. Dr. White was of average height, average build, and average coloring, except for the paleness of his skin. But the raw energy vibrating from him was anything but average. His intense stare was scalding.

He only looked at Elizabeth for a second and then directed all his attention to Nurse Robichaud.

"Good morning, Nurse Robichaud," he said politely. "It is very nice to see you, too. I hear there is a chest patient down here. I'd like to make rounds early, as I have a heart valve to replace at seven at Tulane this morning. I guess the Tulane crowd has not made it in yet, so maybe you could take a moment to direct me?"

Elizabeth thought him every inch the genteel New Orleans aristocrat the triage nurse had described. She understood the meaning of the phrase "old money." She had met many of his ilk while in school in Charleston.

The nurse stepped back, grabbed Elizabeth by the elbow, and thrust her forward toward Dr. White.

"Well, as a matter of fact, Dr. White, this woman is your new charge resident for July. This is Dr. Elizabeth Roberts, and she is apparently an early riser, too. She will be quite happy to show you around." Nurse Robichaud scurried away, leaving Elizabeth with the chief cardiothoracic fellow.

Dr. White tried to hide his surprise. The two stood facing each other uncomfortably. He shuffled his shiny shoes on the yellow-tiled floor, and she looked down at the floor to steady herself.

Elizabeth automatically extended her hand, and with her best Charleston manners said, "Hi, I am Elizabeth, and I am pleased to meet you, Dr. White."

His hand was hot. His fingers were long and soft. The men in Elizabeth's life all had calloused hands; this man was different. If her eyes had been closed, she might have thought that she was shaking hands with a pianist. He smelled clean, like warm limes. Elizabeth was excited and scared and anxious. She thought, *I have never met a man quite like this guy before. I really want him to think me smart and teach me all he knows.*

She quickly withdrew her hand before he could sense her tremble. After momentary eye contact he said, "I want you to take excellent care of anyone who comes to the trauma center with chest trauma. I usually let the second-year residents do the surgical cases, but I take full responsibility for anything that goes on with any chest case in the entire Tulane system. So whether you are working in the Charity Emergency Department, or the Veteran's Administration, or the Tulane Hospital, ultimately you always answer to me," said Dr. White. He pulled his beeper out of his coat pocket.

"Here is my pager number," he said, showing Elizabeth the label on the device. "Memorize it, and call any time. Do not make any decisions on your own. We follow a strict chain of command at Tulane Surgery. You evaluate the patient. You call the chief of General Surgery, and he will evaluate your evaluation. If he needs me, he will call me. If he is in surgery or can't be reached, you call me. That's why I want you to have my beeper number. I am the one who calls the professors. Do you understand?" said Dr. White.

"Yes, sir, I understand," said Elizabeth. She savored the sound of his soft, drawling, New Orleans patois.

"Let's get down to it. I have a long surgery schedule today," said Dr. White. His posture was ramrod straight, and his clothes were starched and immaculate. He was the first truly clean doctor that Elizabeth had seen in the trauma department. He walked briskly.

Elizabeth talked as she struggled to keep up with Dr. White's pace. She wondered, *How does he know where to go?*

"The patient, Mr. Green, is a twenty-eight-year-old black male, stabbed in the left costovertebral space in the anterior axillary line, around one o'clock this morning. He was initially unresponsive at the scene. Apparently, an EMT put a needle in his chest wall and released a tension pneumothorax. The LSU charge resident inserted a chest tube upon arrival, and he has been stable ever since. He has a high blood alcohol level of 0.12. But he was alert and talking the last time I saw him."

"Good," said Dr. White.

Elizabeth glanced up at the clock. It was only six-thirty in the morning, and she was organized and had all her patients memorized. Deep inside, she hoped that Dr. White was impressed. She felt a twinge of pride as she walked into the exam room.

As they passed through the door, she was immediately horrified to see the tube had come out of the man's chest and was lying on the gurney beside him.

"Mr. Green! Mr. Green!" shouted Elizabeth. The patient was not responding to verbal commands.

"It appears that your assessment was completely erroneous!" bellowed Dr. White. "This man could die any second, you idiot!" He shouted through the doorway, "Nurse Robichaud, bring a fresh chest tube setup immediately."

As he turned back to the patient, he saw Elizabeth's hands were shaking as she worked. As she examined the patient she reported aloud, "His pulse is strong; his trachea is deviated to the right. His breath sounds are absent on the left side. His jugular vein is distended in his right neck. He is breathing very fast at twenty-six times a minute."

"Move out of my way, intern!" Dr. White commanded. "While you are assessing this man, he is dying." He deftly drew on a pair of sterile gloves and stuck his fingers into the site of the stab wound through the patient's chest wall. When Dr. White pulled open the ribs between his fingers, an audible release of trapped air shot out between the doctor's fingers. Elizabeth watched the trachea move to the center of the patient's throat. Simultaneously, the monitor showed the man's heart rate decrease, and the patient's inner lips immediately looked less blue.

Still holding the man's chest wall open, Dr. White grilled Elizabeth. "So, *intern*, what just happened here? Tell me the entire likely sequence of events and the mechanism of this patient's near-demise on your watch. *Now!*" said Dr. White.

Elizabeth was awestruck by his quick action and terrified by his aggressive questions. She was fighting not to tremble visibly. "It appears Mr. Green's chest tube was inadequately secured and had come out since I last saw him, causing a reversion to his original problem with the sucking chest wound. Every time he tried to take a breath, he sucked more air into the cavity between the lung and the chest wall. That air compressed his lung and created tension that kept him from inflating his left lung. As the tension became greater, his respiratory condition became more labored. We found him a few minutes before it might have been too late," said Elizabeth.

"So, *doctor*, this man was brought into this department stable and was found dying while under your care, due to stupidity! Is that what you are telling me? This patient is in one of the best trauma centers in the world and he almost died because the charge resident did not check his chest tube to be sure it was properly secured? Is that your assessment?" said Dr. White.

Elizabeth was angry and embarrassed. She looked at Nurse Robichaud, who had just appeared with the requested supplies. The nurse wore a smirk on her face. Both Nurse Robichaud and Dr. White knew that it was not yet Elizabeth's shift, so technically she was not in charge. They knew it was the LSU resident who had not properly secured the failed chest tube. They knew what had happened was not Elizabeth's fault.

Elizabeth knew this, too, but her earlier sense of pride had turned to shame. She felt a sense of intense failure and fear at the magnitude of her responsibility. She remembered Tulane Surgery was organized like the military, and she was a grunt. Nobody cared that the LSU charge resident was truly at fault.

"Yes, sir," she said contritely to Dr. White. "Your description is accurate."

Dr. White glared at her as he held his long, white-gloved fingers in the man's open chest wound.

"What would you have done if I had not been here, intern?" said Dr. White.

"Sir, I have never seen anything like this before," Elizabeth told him truthfully. "I would not have known to put my fingers in the man's wound. So I would have done what worked in the field for the EMT. I would have put a large needle in his chest on the left side to let the air out while calling the nurses for a new chest tube setup. But now that I have seen your demonstration, I would try to do what you just did."

"Have you ever put in a chest tube?" asked Dr. White.

"No, I have not," said Elizabeth.

"Have you ever seen anyone put in a chest tube?" said Dr. White.

"I saw one placed in the operating room when I was in medical school. But I was standing behind three people and could not see very well," said Elizabeth.

"I am short on time this morning. So we will forego the usual Tulane tradition of 'See one. Do one. Teach one.' And go straight to 'Do one.' Nurse Robichaud, please set up the chest tube procedure. Dr. Roberts will put it in now," said Dr. White.

"Got it right here, doctor," said the nurse. She had anticipated his need. A trembling new nursing student rolled the sterile surgical tray toward the patient's gurney. "Dr. White, it is, until seven o'clock, still an LSU day. Should their resident be doing this?" asked Elizabeth. She wondered where Adrien had gone.

"Since they nearly killed the man, I do not think their services will be needed, intern," Dr. White replied. "Deciding who does what is not your job. Never question me again," he said sternly. "Your job is to follow my orders."

Mr. Green looked oddly normal to Elizabeth, considering he had a hole in his chest and a doctor standing beside him, casually holding that hole open with his fingers. The patient did not look scared or worried or in distress. He seemed to sense that Dr. White was helping him. *Of course,* she thought, *the alcohol in his blood might be helping him achieve this level of serenity.*

Dr. White turned all his attention to the patient. "Sir," he told him, "we are going to numb the area between your ribs. Then Dr. Roberts is going to make an incision just above the rib under your armpit and put in another tube. I am very sorry that the last one came out. Dr. Roberts will make sure that this one does not come out." He turned to Elizabeth. "Won't you, Dr. Roberts?" asked Dr. White.

"Absolutely," said Elizabeth, wondering exactly how that would occur.

The patient snorted and drifted into alcohol-induced sleep. The smell from his mouth made Elizabeth momentarily turn her head away.

Dr. White spoke calmly to Elizabeth, as if he were speaking to a spooked horse. As he spoke, Elizabeth felt as if she were watching a great conductor conduct his simplest symphony. Dr. White's anger and aggression had evaporated, and he was focused on the job at hand. The man who had been named "teacher of the year" for the last three years stood before her, giving her directions.

"Clean him off with betadine, Dr. Roberts. Nurse, give the patient two milligrams of valium IV now," said Dr. White.

As Dr. White continued to hold the snoring patient's chest wall open with his gloved fingers, Elizabeth sterilely wiped the entire chest wall with the brown antiseptic. She was very careful not to drip any of the strong antiseptic into the patient's chest cavity.

Elizabeth felt much calmer as she filled the syringe with lidocaine, numbed the patient's chest wall, and took the scalpel in hand. Dr. White calmly talked her through every step.

Holding the surgical scalpel had never frightened Elizabeth. The instrument felt like a natural extension of her hand. She opened the patient's chest a few more inches and drained the accumulated blood into a basin.

"Good so far," said Dr. White.

Elizabeth picked up the new sterile chest tube that looked and felt like a clear, stiff garden hose and started toward the open chest cavity.

Dr. White said, "Place the tube in the most dependent portion of the chest cavity to drain out any remaining blood."

As Elizabeth followed his instruction, the tube passed into the back of the chest and a large amount of bright red blood flowed into the clear tube. None of the blood was clotted.

Elizabeth knew that for the amount of time that the patient had been in the ER, he should have definitely clotted his blood, unless it was fresh bleeding.

Dr. White calmly addressed the patient as the bright red blood continued to flow, "Sir, who is with you today at Charity?"

"Nobody, doc," said the man.

"Sir, we are going to take you to the operating room and explore your chest to see why you are bleeding so much. You will likely lose a piece of your lung. You have high blood-alcohol content and cannot legally give us consent. Is there someone that we can call to get consent?" said the doctor.

"No, I have nobody," said Mr. Green.

"If we don't do the surgery, you will likely bleed to death," Dr. White told him. "Do you consent to the surgery, Mr. Green?"

"I can see all that blood running out of my body, faster than you can pump it in. I might be drunk, but even a drunk can see something has to be done. You look like you know what you're doing, so go ahead with it," said Mr. Green.

Dr. White leaned into the face of the patient and whispered, "I will take good care of you, sir." Then he turned and began barking orders.

"Nurse Robichaud, call the Charity operating room and tell them that we need to bring this man up now! It appears that his lung laceration is still bleeding. Then call the Tulane operating room and tell them that I will be a little late starting that heart valve replacement."

His gaze fell on Elizabeth. "Dr. Roberts, type and match your patient for four units of blood and run in two bags of intravenous fluid. I prefer lactated ringer's solution. Now! He needs immediate surgery. His lung is lacerated and bleeding. Intern, remember this lesson. Healthy people and children can lose a lot of blood before they look really sick. Their hearts are strong and you won't necessarily be able to tell how badly they are bleeding until it is too late. Always remember to keep a close eye on anyone who has been stabbed. One minute they are talking coherently, and the next minute they are dead," said Dr. White.

"Hey, doc! Am I going to die?" asked Mr. Green.

"Not in my hands! But you might consider getting a better class of friends when you get out of the hospital," said the doctor.

The patient laughed and grabbed his side, realizing the garden hose, called a chest tube, was still there. The gallows humor surprised Elizabeth. Talking about death and laughing seemed strange to her.

"Should I call Dr. McSwain?" asked Nurse Robichaud.

"I will call him. He has two hernia repairs at Tulane this morning, and he helped with a car wreck last night. He's likely getting his requisite four hours of sleep as we speak. We will not need him for this surgery," said Dr. White.

As Dr. White walked out, Nurse Robichaud stood beside Elizabeth and offered, "Let me show you how to suture and tape that chest tube so a Mack truck could not pull it out." Elizabeth stepped aside to give her room to work. "You have to tape it in several places," she said as she placed pieces of tape, "so no matter how hard it is pulled on, it will never come out by accident. If it falls out again," she warned, "Dr. White will kill you, and even though it's only been three days, and I am not the least bit attached to you, I do not want to start all over again with a new doctor."

Elizabeth was shocked to see that the blood kept running out of the chest tube and into the bag set up by Nurse Robichaud. As Elizabeth continued to tape the tube to the patient's chest, the redheaded triage nurse entered the room and hung two units of blood on the IV pole.

"So how'd it go with Prince Charming?" she asked Lavinia.

Nurse Robichaud said, "You lost again, Aoife! I can almost taste my free steak dinner!"

Elizabeth made a mental note of the triage nurse's name.

"Dr. White did not seem to notice that Dr. Roberts is female. Her beauty had *no* effect on him. He gave her a royal hazing, just like he does all the rest," she said with a satisfied chuckle. "If she had not known everything a book could teach her about tension pneumothorax, he would have eaten her for lunch. He was poised and ready to rip her up! But even though she was stammering and shaking, Crème Puff could answer all his questions, so he let her put in her first chest tube."

The two nurses talked as if Elizabeth were not standing between them working on the patient's wound dressing.

Nurse Robichaud continued, "I was holding my breath, wondering if Crème Puff was going to have a seizure, faint, cry, or get the tube in. At one point, she looked worse than the patient. She really could have gone either way." Both nurses were laughing. Elizabeth felt indignant, and the patient snored.

Nurse Robichaud said, "But you still owe me that steak dinner. I told you, Aoife, to Dr. Harrison Lloyd White III and Tulane Surgery, a good patient outcome is all that matters. No pretty little intern is going to turn that one's head. Charlie's Steak House, here we come!"

CHAPTER 7

Buster

Elizabeth was lucky today. She was going to be able to go home to her apartment. The days and weeks were running together. She had been at Charity for several days. Finally, she would get to sleep in her own bed in privacy. Her clinic assignment at the VA was short. Nurse Mikey had a cold and he rescheduled all the routine veteran visits. Tulane had sent over an extra resident to help out, and Elizabeth was driving home in the daylight. She planned a long, luxurious night of sleeping.

She cooked a package of ramen noodles for her dinner and ate them while she sat on her rented couch and enjoyed being alone. She felt safe and relaxed and happy. All she desired in the world was ten hours of suspended consciousness. Her nervous system was overstimulated and desperately yearned for inactivity.

Elizabeth fought sleep as she boiled her noodles on the stove, threw in the flavor packet, and pulled one of her two bowls out of the cabinet. She sighed with satisfaction as she slurped the last of her salty, chicken-flavored noodles.

Eating food while seated had become a luxury. Eating slowly wasn't usually an option, either. Elizabeth chuckled, thinking of the looks of horror on the faces of the women in her family if they could see her standing in front of a vending machine, gobbling her dinner, a Little Debbie roll, dressed in dirty scrubs. Leisurely dinners while seated at a dining table with an ironed tablecloth and polished silver—the way meals were served at her father's mother's home— seemed a distant dream. Meals were less formal at the farm, but good manners and slow eating while conversing were the norm.

Elizabeth had wanted rigorous surgical training when she chose Charity. But the endless volume of people who had been shot, burned, stabbed, overdosed, beaten, and killed was overwhelming. She knew that she had already learned more as an intern in a few months at Charity than she learned as a medical student during her entire two years of clinical study in Charleston. Her education was coming at such a fast pace that she felt overwhelmed. Surgical training had, thus far, stripped Elizabeth of simple pleasures that she regularly took for granted, such as being able to do things at her own pace. She had never rushed before becoming a surgery intern, but now she rushed all the time. But tonight she was not going to rush. Tonight she took her time as she showered, brushed her teeth, and dried her hair. Grooming herself leisurely felt decadent and comforting.

She crawled into her bed before the sun was down and slept deeply for an hour.

Then, the frantic knocking began. "Please, please, please, doctor, open up!" Elizabeth woke with a start and recognized the voice of her neighbor, Mrs. Kaczka. "It's Buster— something has happened to Buster!" Mrs. Kaczka said.

Her banging was loud and incessant. In her somnolence, Elizabeth thought Mrs. Kaczka said something was wrong with her husband.

Now wide awake, Elizabeth bolted to the door and found Mrs. Kaczka, her hair in rollers and dressed in her orange fuzzy bathrobe, carrying her unconscious Chihuahua, Buster.

"Doctor, you gotta do something! Buster was playing on the floor with his toys, and suddenly I heard him coughing and then he fell over!" said Mrs. Kaczka.

"Mrs. Kaczka, I am not a veterinarian. I do not know anything about Chihuahuas," said Elizabeth. While she felt pity for the frantic woman, she also despised the yappy little dog that always tried to bite her. *How was this happening?* She longed for her quiet, cool bed.

Mrs. Kaczka ignored Elizabeth's protests and thrust the dog into her hands.

Buster's body was warm but limp, so whatever had happened to him was recent. Mrs. Kaczka was crying and begging. Elizabeth realized the quickest route back to bed might well be trying to help the dog. She remembered her trauma training algorithms. The steps to resuscitation were simple, and either they worked or they did not. Every surgeon knew the steps by heart. *Could a mean little dog be much different from a crack addict? Maybe the same rules of resuscitation apply,* she thought. *I'll try anything to get back to bed.*

She grabbed the dog by his hind legs, held him upside down, and gave him a good shake.

Mrs. Kaczka looked on and chewed her fist, but did not interfere.

Nothing happened. Buster was still unconscious. Mrs. Kaczka started wailing and flapping her arms. The front of her orange fuzzy bathrobe opened up to reveal a see-through black negligee and more loose skin than Elizabeth wanted to see. *What a freak show…and all I wanted is sleep.*

Elizabeth was wide awake now.

"Be careful, doctor, Buster is old," cried Mrs. Kaczka, wringing her hands as she danced around Elizabeth in a circle, praying and shrieking. "Please, doctor, help my dog."

"I told you that I am not a veterinarian," said Elizabeth, who was cross and tired. It was clear that the neighbor was not going to the veterinarian. Elizabeth was short on ideas and feeling resentful. Home was not a place where she wanted to feel incompetent—there was plenty of that feeling to be had at work. Right now, all she wanted was sleep.

"Please, doctor, please!" said Mrs. Kaczka.

"I am trying everything that I know to try," said Elizabeth, as kindly as she could.

Next, she rubbed the dog's sternum to try and assess its level of consciousness. When she pressed her knuckles deeply into Buster's chest the dog did not move. Not responding to a deep sternal rub was a bad sign. The tiny monster was really out of it. Elizabeth felt sorry for her neighbor, but not all that bad about the dog.

Having lived on a farm, she knew animal death was commonplace. She found it hard to understand the near-worship of some pet owners.

"Oh, my God, oh, my God, I love Buster more than Larry," Mrs. Kaczka told her. "You gotta save him, doctor! That dog means more to me than my husband ever has!" *Wow,* thought Elizabeth. *Did Mrs. Kaczka just say that she loves the dog more than she loves Mr. Kaczka?*

She turned her full focus back to the unconscious animal. Elizabeth recalled that the opening of the airway was the most important thing in helping an unconscious patient. She could not imagine herself giving mouth-to-mouth to a dog she had seen licking its private parts, a dog that had tried to bite her at least ten times. Not to mention the hideousness of his nasty old dog breath. Giving Buster the "kiss of life" was unimaginable. The eerie keening sound coming from her neighbor impelled the young doctor forward in search of a remedy.

She remembered using the Heimlich maneuver and laid the Chihuahua's chest against her left palm, slanted his head toward the floor, and pounded his back with her right palm. Immediately, a shiny purple bead shot out of the dog's mouth, and Buster proceeded to vomit on Elizabeth's gown and feet. The dog immediately started to rally. Buster coughed a few times and then snarled at Elizabeth.

"It's a miracle, doctor!" exclaimed Mrs. Kaczka. "You saved Buster! Thank you so much!"

Mrs. Kaczka beamed with happiness and relief. Despite herself, Elizabeth felt proud and relieved that the evil little creature lived on to snap again.

"I can't believe my baby choked on a stupid Mardi Gras bead," Mrs. Kaczka said, almost to herself.

Elizabeth stared at the growling, bug-eyed rat-dog and thought of how much she did not like some of the patients she treated at Charity. A drunken convention-goer was not much different than Buster, but at least at Charity someone else cleaned up the vomit.

Mrs. Kaczka apologized for Buster's lack of gratitude for Elizabeth's lifesaving ministrations. "He does not mean to growl and snip at you. He is just old and does not like strangers," she explained. She didn't offer to help Elizabeth clean up.

"It's not a problem, Mrs. K.," Elizabeth assured her. "It is just that I am so tired. I hate to be rude, but I have to clean up this mess and get back to bed."

"I know, honey, you look exhausted," said Mrs. Kaczka sympathetically. "Remember my advice—get a nice husband, stay home, and relax. If you got a good man who likes to work, you could stay home all day, just like me," she told Elizabeth on her way out the door.

Elizabeth threw her gown in the garbage, washed her lower body in the shower, mopped up Buster's vomit from the floor, and tossed the purple bead on top of her ruined gown. *What to do now?* She had such an adrenaline rush from the dog drama that she knew sleep would be impossible. She looked at her watch and it was eight o'clock. She knew that her family would be finishing dinner and the dishes would be done. South Carolina was an hour earlier than New Orleans.

As she put on a clean nightgown and looked at her clean, soft bed, she realized that she longed for some connection with her family. She felt lonely. She had been so busy at work that she had forgotten that she knew nobody in the entire state of Louisiana. There wasn't one person who knew anything about her or really cared about her. She particularly missed her father, who disliked little dogs as much as she did. He would find this story funny. She did not have long-distance service on her phone, due to the cost. But she felt it might be acceptable to call home collect and send a check to reimburse her parents when she got paid at the end of the month. She was careful with money, didn't go out much, and mostly ate at the hospital cafeteria. Her expenses were low.

She dialed the long-distance operator from her wall phone in the efficiency apartment's kitchen area. "I'd like to make a collect call to Mr. Zeke Roberts at 838-397-7717," said Elizabeth. "My name is Elizabeth Roberts. Of course, I'll speak to anyone who answers."

"Hold on for confirmation," said the operator.

"Hello," said Elizabeth's mother.

"Will you accept a collect call from Elizabeth Roberts?" said the operator.

"Well…I guess so," said her mother.

"Your party is on the line and accepts the charges," said the operator.

"Hi, Mom, it's me, Elizabeth," she said unnecessarily, not knowing what else to say.

"Hi, honey. How much is this going to cost?" asked her mother.

"Don't worry, Mom, when the bill comes just tell me how much I owe you, and I will send you a check," Elizabeth promised. "How are you and Daddy?"

"We are fine," her mother assured her. "When are you coming home? The family reunion is next weekend, you know, and everyone is expecting to see you, Elizabeth."

Elizabeth thought, *Mom doesn't remember anything that I told her about my schedule. She wants the same thing that she has always wanted...me home and participating in the family.*

"Remember, Mom, I do not get any vacation for a year, so I have to miss the reunion. I cannot be there this year," Elizabeth reminded her. "Remember, I sent you and Daddy a letter with my schedule for the internship year. But next year, I will be sure to request vacation time for the family reunion."

"I really wish you had stayed here," her mother told her. "I just can't understand why you put yourself through all of this. No respectable Southern girl should be living alone in *New Orleans*, of all places!"

Elizabeth wanted to cry. She craved comfort and understanding. She wanted to have a few laughs about all the crazy things that had happened to her.

Elizabeth sighed. She knew this familiar diatribe. Her mom had never been to New Orleans but was insistent that it was a bad place. Her mom did not want her to be a doctor. Her mom wanted her to be a teacher and marry a South Carolina farmer. Her mom had a high school education and her family were all farmers. She did not want Elizabeth to get outside of her comfort zone in life. No matter how hard Elizabeth tried, she could not get her mother to understand why she wanted to do what she wanted to do. Many, many times, she'd tried to explain her decisions to her mother. Each step of the way, whether leaving for college, or going to do research, or going to medical school, or leaving for surgical residency, Elizabeth had tried to explain to her mother her choices. Elizabeth's mom didn't agree, wouldn't listen, and she didn't understand. Arguing was useless. Elizabeth had resolved to be pleasant and accept that she and her mother might never see eye to eye. She would love her mother and accept that they were very different.

"Mom, it is really nice to hear your voice. But is Dad home?" Elizabeth was nearly frantic to speak to her father. She didn't want to rehash old territory with her mother. She wanted to tell her father about all the events of her first few weeks at Charity. She wanted to be consoled, not lectured.

"No, sweetie," her mother said. "He had to go out to the farm. A few of the cows broke their fence and got in the highway. Your grandfather and uncles needed help getting the cows back in and the fence repaired, so they called and asked Dad to come out and assist them. And of course, he was glad to help." *I'm not so sure about that,* Elizabeth thought, but she didn't disagree. "He will be so sorry that he missed your call," her mother continued. "But we should probably get off the long-distance line. There is no telling how much this is costing you."

"Okay, Mom," Elizabeth agreed. "I love you. Tell Daddy and everybody that I love them. Goodbye, Mom."

Elizabeth sat heavily on the floor with her back to the wall, feeling waves of disappointment and loneliness. She loved her mother, of course, but they had never been able to fully connect. Their conversations were always superficial. They did best when they stuck to news of the thirty-two cousins, the weather, and Mom's church news. Elizabeth always felt her mother never approved of her on some level. Elizabeth knew she was not the daughter her mother wished she had.

Her father, on the other hand, was Elizabeth's best friend and her most enthusiastic fan. He came from a family of strong women, and he understood her need to excel and understood her personality. He was proud that she worked hard, got good grades, and excelled at school. He cried with joy when she received a full academic scholarship. She longed to tell him of the conditions of her work and of her fears of failure. He would understand, and he would encourage her and give her helpful advice.

She laughed at the thought of him chasing the wandering cows. Zeke Roberts was a town guy, and he really did not like farm life. He had gone to Clemson for two years and worked in an office at Georgia Pacific doing forestry surveying for most of Elizabeth's life. The "family farm" belonged to Mom's family, not his. As a dutiful husband and family man, he participated in farm activities when it was necessary or required. But he did not love the farm the way her mother's family loved it. Chasing down cows after dark was his idea of some kind of hell. Elizabeth giggled, momentarily cheered at the thought. But then the loneliness returned, and she cried and tried to remember the sound of her father's voice and his words of motivation.

For as long as Elizabeth could remember, whenever she was upset her father would say, "Take it one day at a time, little girl. Today wasn't everything you wanted. Go to bed with a clean conscience and hope for better luck tomorrow." Tonight she recalled her father's advice, and she did exactly that. She'd saved Buster. She'd been a good neighbor. She hoped she'd be able to talk soon with her father.

As she drifted off to sleep, Elizabeth decided if she was not fired when the cut came in December in the surgery department, she would find a new apartment in New Orleans, a place to live that was closer to the hospital and away from Buster and Mrs. Kaczka, who was just too much like Mom. Elizabeth was happy that she had only taken a six-month lease. Already, she was weary of being told she should quit medical training and find a nice husband. *Being an intern is stressful enough,* she thought, *without someone constantly reminding me that there's an easy way out.*

CHAPTER 8

A Manual Should Come with This

Elizabeth arrived very early to the emergency room. She had stopped at Café du Monde and gotten giant go-cups of hot chicory coffee for herself and the triage nurse. They seemed to usually have the same shift in the ER, and the nurse was the only person who regularly smiled and seemed to want to help Elizabeth. A daily cup of coffee was a small price to pay for a potential new friend in the triage area.

Elizabeth ordered the same things every morning at Café du Monde and arrived at the same time. Most mornings, one of the Asian waitresses ran out of the restaurant when she saw Elizabeth pull up to the curb and would hand her a bag of steaming cups of coffee through the car window. The waitress smiled and bowed, and Elizabeth gave her cash and sped away.

Frequently, they included *lagniappe*, the southern Louisiana French term for "a little something extra." Sometimes it was an extra beignet; other times it was a larger size of coffee than she had ordered. Elizabeth was grateful, as she knew that curbside service was not typical of Café du Monde. Most customers stood in line on the sidewalk and waited to be seated. With the help of the waitress, Elizabeth's morning breakfast pick-up routine took three minutes. The ritual gave Elizabeth an excuse to drive the edges of the French Quarter in the wee hours of the morning and have a sweet exchange before beginning the rigors of her work at Charity.

She parked in the Tulane garage and sped across the street. As she jogged through the back door of the Charity emergency room balancing the bag of goodies, she saw the triage nurse's fiery red hair sprawled on her desk. She appeared to be asleep. A line of waiting patients milled around her. No one was willing to wake her up.

Elizabeth stood in front of the nurse's desk and softly said, "Good morning, nurse." Even though she had been bringing the woman coffee for a while, Elizabeth realized that she had never been told the nurse's name. She had heard Nurse Robichaud call her a name that Elizabeth assumed to be a nickname. But Elizabeth had never been told the triage nurse's real name.

The nurse slowly raised her head and looked momentarily dazed. She focused on Elizabeth and said, "Is that you, Crème Puff? I sure do need my coffee. Last night was a killer, but I got it real nice and quiet for you now." The nurse's eyes were bloodshot, and Elizabeth thought that she looked worse than some of the patients. The emergency room was amazingly quiet for five in the morning, and Elizabeth felt grateful.

"I am embarrassed to admit this, but I do not know your name. We get so busy around here that common courtesy is sometimes forgotten," said Elizabeth.

"You won't know it after I tell you, either, Crème Puff. Both of my parents are Irish. They love to drink and decided to name me the weirdest Irish name they could find and make my life hell. My name is Aoife...pronounced EE+FA. Ain't that a hoot?" she asked, clutching the hot coffee.

"I think your name is beautiful. It sounds as if it would be the name of a fairy princess," Elizabeth told her sincerely.

Aoife snorted when she laughed. "Don't make me blow coffee through my nose with your silliness! Back in the sixties, my parents were doing a lot of drugs.

In between drug fests, they were celebrating their Celtic-ness. My full name is Aoife Dearg Patrick, after a female character in Celtic mythology, also a redhead, who was considered a great warrior. They were into the whole feminist thing, too." She shrugged. "As a kid, it was just awful. Having parents who did drugs and having a weird name was quite the burden. But now I don't care. New Orleans is full of odd folks, and nobody notices down here."

She looked up at Elizabeth. "Thanks a lot for the coffee. You really do not have to bring me coffee. I will help you anyway. Livvy does not like us to be too nice to the interns. But I like you, and a bribe is not necessary," said Aoife. She reclined in her chair and sipped the coffee while the patients formed a line beside her. Elizabeth noticed that everyone in the line was content to wait.

"Bringing you coffee started as a mild form of bribery," Elizabeth replied, "but now I like the look on your face when you see me with the cup. I like to start out my day knowing I made at least one person happy."

"In that case, I am pleased to help you. This coffee is much better than anything available at The Fistula," said Aoife.

"What's The Fistula?" asked Elizabeth.

The nurse laughed and said, "In medical terms, as you probably learned in school, a fistula is an abnormal connection between two organs, usually caused by inflammation or infection. One example is a fistula between the bowels and the bladder. A fistula is usually pretty nasty—nothing anyone would ever want." She shuddered, then continued, "But at The Big Free it's also the name we give to the little café in front of Charity Hospital New Orleans. The café is located between Tulane Avenue and the hospital's front door, and we affectionately call it The Fistula." Aoife smiled. "The food is nasty as can be. In fact, it is the only place in New Orleans where you can get bad food."

Elizabeth wondered if there was anything about Charity that wasn't in contradistinction to the rest of New Orleans. Some of the best restaurants in the world were in New Orleans, and New Orleans was a city known for good food. Elizabeth knew these facts, even though her work gave her no time to think about the food scene and no money to experience it. *Why would Charity have The Fistula?* she wondered. She pulled herself back to the present moment and focused on her work.

"Thanks for the tip. As interns, Tulane pays for three meal tickets at the Charity cafeteria every day when we are on the ER schedule to work. So far, I am eating from my Charity meal tickets, out of the vending machines, and from my neighbor. I will avoid The Fistula, if possible," said Elizabeth.

"Here's another tip," Aoife said. "If you are counting on eating in the basement cafeteria with your meal tickets, get down there before the orthopedic residents do. They descend upon the place like an elephant herd and eat everything in sight. Both Tulane and LSU hired oversized hunks this year. I think the whole lot of them played football! They are handsome, sweet-talking giants who charm the cafeteria ladies into giving them more than their fair share. I have been in line behind them—they get eight pieces of bacon to my one!" She smiled. "I actually saw one of those brazen manipulators bring the bacon server a bouquet of flowers! I guess if you are a seventy-year-old black lady with crack-addicted grandsons, a nice young man bringing you flowers will turn your head every time. I advise you to get there early, because orthopedics is shameless and I don't want you to starve."

Once again, Elizabeth was reminded of how Charity was like life on the farm. Her larger male cousins did try to take more than their share of the food. The girls learned early to eat with one hand and guard their plates with a knife in the other. Elizabeth credited her ambidextrousness to defensive eating tactics she learned at the farm. She learned sometimes she had to guard to her left, and sometimes she had to guard to her right. *Defensive eating also made for very good peripheral vision,* Elizabeth mused. Defending her plate from her older cousins had made her a much better surgeon.

"I'd better get to the accident room. The LSU charge has started to count on me for minor suturing, and I'm happy to report my stitching is getting better every week. Have a good morning, Aoife," said Elizabeth.

As she passed through the doors to the trauma area, an unusually pungent odor caught her attention. Dr. Lambert stood in the middle of the hall writing on a chart. He was standing up straight, for a change. He usually leaned on whatever was closest to him, Elizabeth had observed, as if the furniture were all that was holding him erect. This morning he looked relatively clean, and less exhausted.

"Good morning, Adrien. It looks pretty quiet down here," said Elizabeth.

"Shush!" he said, putting a finger to his lips. "Let's keep it that way. It was wild in the early evening, but all we have now is a half-dozen superficial stab wounds, a voodoo treatment gone awry, a botched suicide, and a psychotic guy who is pretty banged up from a fall. It's about as quiet as it gets here."

"What is that smell?" said Elizabeth. The whole place reeked with the stench of rotten meat dipped in an acrid broth.

"Have you not come across a voodoo concoction yet?" said Adrien.

"No, I know nothing of voodoo," said Elizabeth.

"Well, you will get your fill of it down here. New Orleans is full of folks who go to the local voodooiene for a cure before coming here. Even though they do not pay a cent to come to Charity, many locals trust the voodoo priestess more than they trust us. But when things get bad, they show up here," said Adrien.

"That is ridiculous! Who does that? Why would anyone go to a crackpot instead of getting state-of-the-art medical care?" Elizabeth was incredulous.

"Louisiana has a long history steeped in the cultures of the islands. West African slaves brought the voodoo traditions with them, spread the traditions among the population, and today voodoo practices are ubiquitous in the black and white communities. Have you heard of Congo Square?" said Adrien.

"No, I love history, but the last eight years of my life have been full of science. It's been ages since I read a novel, and I haven't watched television in three years," Elizabeth admitted.

"We don't have time for a history lesson this morning, but ask Nurse Robichaud sometime. She knows a lot about voodoo and can tell you some great stories about voodoo in this ER," said Adrien.

"Okay, down to work. Who needs the seamstress this morning?" asked Elizabeth.

"Begin in Room Eleven. He will be an interesting start to your day," said Adrien.

Elizabeth smiled and greeted people as she walked down the hall to Room Eleven. She made a habit of speaking to all the orderlies, nurses, and cleaning people because she understood that they were all part of the team that made medicine work, and she knew that nobody could take good care of patients without them. Charity was perpetually short-staffed and underfunded, and everyone had to be willing to do everything. Doctors mopped up messes. Maids and janitors ran blood to the lab for the nurses during emergencies. Strict job descriptions had no place in a hospital like Charity, so Elizabeth tried to ensure that everyone on staff was aware she appreciated them.

She walked through the swinging, wooden double doors of Room Eleven. Like everything in the ER, they creaked when they moved. Humidity and stifling heat ruined equipment, furnishings, and people quickly. Charity supposedly had air conditioning, but it was only noticeable in the surgical operating rooms. Everywhere else, fans churned warm air.

The patient on the gurney in Room Eleven was naked, and his arms and legs and chest had been tied to the gurney with sheets, with a particularly tight sheet across his chest and pelvis. He was staring at the ceiling, talking to someone only he could see. He was covered in lacerations. Elizabeth immediately thought of a phrase that her grandmother used when one of the kids went through a barbed-wire fence. The patient was "cut to ribbons."

As he continued talking, Elizabeth grabbed a surgical gown from a nearby cabinet and donned two pairs of surgical gloves. The room was small and sweltering, and the patient was sweating as much as he was bleeding.

She felt curious and concerned. She approached slowly so as not to startle the patient.

Elizabeth quietly inspected him. His chart said he was forty-two, and he had short and stylish dreadlocks. The bone structure of his face was delicate, and his skin was mocha. His limbs were long and thin but much muscled. He seemed not to notice Elizabeth was beside him.

Suddenly a young doctor came through the door and said, "Hi, I am Louis Trahan, the third-year LSU student rotating on psychiatry this month, and this is my patient, Mr. Biniam Adisa. He has schizophrenia. Despite our best efforts, we have not been able to get him out of his current state. He talks to someone day and night. We have seen no family, and he never speaks to any of us."

"So what happened to Mr. Adisa?" asked Elizabeth. "How did he get so cut up?"

"Even though he does not seem aware of his surroundings, he had shown no signs of being aggressive or dangerous to himself or to others, so he was placed in the general population in the day room on the psychiatric ward. For many days, he sat peacefully talking to his imaginary friend, not bothering a soul. When prompted to eat and drink, he would do so," said the student.

"Our team on psychiatry was finishing our rounds of the ward," he went on. "We ended with the patients in the day room. Mr. Adisa was our last patient. We have been baffled and frustrated that none of the usual antipsychotic drugs have helped him, and we were trying to figure out what to try next. It is hard to do much with no family to give consent, and he certainly cannot give consent for himself."

"Don't antipsychotic drugs take a long time to take effect? How long has he been at Charity?" asked Elizabeth.

"He has been my patient for a month, but I think he has been on the psychiatry ward for several months. Yes, it can take four to six weeks for drugs to take full effect, but we should have seen some improvement after a week," said the student.

"Okay, so you guys are making rounds and trying to figure out what to do next. That does not explain his plethora of cuts," said Elizabeth.

Mr. Adisa, the patient, continued to talk in a language that Elizabeth had never heard. He bled from his many cuts and still seemed not to notice his condition or the doctors in the examination room.

"The chairman of psychiatry had been talking about using electroconvulsive therapy as a last resort before we implant a deep brain stimulator. We typically try two to three antipsychotic drugs, then a series of three to four shock treatments, and if that does not work, we move on to surgery and implantation of the brain stimulator."

"What is a deep brain stimulator?" asked Elizabeth, pulling out an index card to take notes.

"It's a device that's implanted in the base of the brain," said the student. "A psychiatry professor has been working with a neurosurgery professor to help people who have failed to improve on drugs and have not benefited from multiple treatments of electroconvulsive therapy."

"How does it work?" asked Elizabeth.

"Nobody really knows," said Louis. "It is a bit of mad science, if you ask me! I have seen a few patients improve, but many end up with a big cut in their skull and no improvement in their condition. The neurosurgeon takes a three-centimeter plug of bone from the base of the skull and places a metal device where the bone used to be. The device makes for an impressive X-ray," laughed the student.

"What do you mean?" said Elizabeth.

"On a plain skull X-ray, it looks like the patient has a beeper in the back of his head. The crazy thing is three centimeters wide and made of surgical steel. On X-ray, it looks like the patient has a metal box in the back of his head," said Louis.

"You still haven't told me how he got so cut up," Elizabeth interjected.

Louis said, "This is where the story gets interesting. We always talked right in front of Mr. Adisa, like we're doing now, as he never seemed to know what we were saying or to show any reaction. And we never strap him to his chair because he is always docile. As the chairman started outlining the details of implanting the deep brain stimulator, the patient became agitated. He was not looking at us or directing any energy toward us, but his conversation with his imaginary friend got much more animated," said the student.

"Suddenly, he bolted from his chair, streaked across the floor, picked up the TV in the day room with amazing strength, and threw it through the window. Then he jumped out through the hole in the window made by the TV. Thank God psychiatry is on the second floor," said the student.

Elizabeth's mouth fell open, and she turned to look at the student. "Is this a joke?"

"I kid you not. The TV fell on the concrete, smashed to pieces, and made quite a racket. Mr. Adisa fell into the oleander bushes in front of the hospital. The bushes broke his fall, and the fall knocked him out long enough for us to roll a gurney out the front door of the hospital and retrieve him. He did not fight us. He was cut up and bloody from the window glass, as you see. But when he woke up, he resumed his usual rant in his foreign language."

Elizabeth stood still for a full minute, marveling that the man was even alive. She made a mental note to check carefully for orthopedic, spine, and skull injuries from the fall. She chuckled to herself, realizing that suturing a trauma patient who had been already admitted to the hospital was a true piece of irony.

The LSU student kept nervously talking in the direction of the wall. "He looked like a rag doll flying out the window and just lay there in a pile on the bushes in front of The Big Free, bleeding away. I never imagined there could be blood and gore in psychiatry!"

The patient continued to look up at the ceiling and speak in the foreign language and ignore the two doctors.

Elizabeth approached him with gloved hands, holding pieces of white gauze soaked in antiseptic. She needed to clean his cuts to determine which ones needed stitches. She decided to start with his lower legs and feet. "This is a pretty big job—would you mind helping me?" asked Elizabeth.

The medical student looked horrified. He stepped back two feet in the tiny room and moved behind Elizabeth.

"Sorry, but I am going into psychiatry. I don't do blood," said the student.

"But you are a doctor, and this man is your patient," insisted Elizabeth.

"Yes, you are correct. And I will do all in my power to try to figure out why he is talking to people who aren't there and use every drug that I can find to help his mind. But I would faint if I touched that blood," said the student.

Elizabeth was shocked. She had heard surgery interns joke about doctors who did not want to get dirty or touch patients, but she did not imagine such people really existed. Who would go into medicine never intending to touch anyone? Yet here was an example of that type of doctor. She was irritated and felt little compassion for the student.

"Okay, just stand out of the way and hand instruments to me from the sterile tray," she told him. "Put on gloves and stay behind me so you don't see the blood and faint. I do not have time to sew you up, too," said Elizabeth. She thought of one of her father's mother's favorite sayings, used when someone had been irritating: "To each his own."

The medical student had turned his back to Elizabeth and the patient and stood holding his gloved hands high in the air, like a TV doctor. He looked quite silly as he talked to the wall and refused to look at the patient. He handed gauze sponges soaked in antiseptic over his shoulder to Elizabeth. She noticed he was dripping betadine on his white coat, but she was too irritated to warn him that betadine stains would never come out. She decided buying a new white coat would be his penance for being a doctor who hated the sight of blood.

"What language is he speaking?" asked Elizabeth.

"One of the psychiatry orderlies is Ethiopian, and he told us it is a dialect closely related to Amharic. Our orderly told us that there are eighty-eight different dialects spoken in that region. He cannot fully understand what the patient is saying," said the student.

"Did you try having the orderly speak to him in his language?" asked Elizabeth.

"Sure we did. Many times we tried. The patient does not seem to realize that the orderly is there, either. Mr. Adisa is truly in his own world. The orderly picks up bits and pieces of what Mr. Adisa says. Much of it is about God and religion. The orderly thinks Mr. Adisa is a Coptic Christian. He said that he frequently mentions something called the Ethiopian Orthodox Tewahedo Christian Church in Addis Ababa," said the student.

"Have social workers tried to find anyone in the Ethiopian community in New Orleans who might know his family? Surely that community can help find his family," said Elizabeth.

"The budget for the social workers was cut deeply in the governor's last budget, and they now mostly work with children. Adults with social problems are mostly on their own," said the student.

Elizabeth thought about how important social workers were at the county hospital in Charleston. They were the ones who made sure certain patients had what they needed to carry out their doctors' orders after they were discharged. She wondered how Charity could function without a good social worker team.

Mr. Adisa did not move at all while Elizabeth cleaned his wounds. She knew that the antiseptic had to sting some. She injected lidocaine, and again Mr. Adisa acted as if she did not exist.

"Maybe the orderly could ask Ethiopians if anyone knows someone from Mr. Adisa's hometown or from that church. Is the town called Adidas?" asked Elizabeth.

"No, silly woman," the student said to her. "Adidas is a running shoe. His hometown might be Addis Ababa, the capital of Ethiopia."

She began suturing the patient's wounds.

Elizabeth was not knowledgeable about geography. She knew Ethiopia was in Africa, but wasn't sure she could find it on a map. She'd never known anyone who spoke Amharic. She did not want to say so, but this was the first time she had ever heard of the language or the city. Nobody in her family had ever been outside of the United States, except to go to war.

Elizabeth had finished the leg cuts and was moving up the body. The patient continued to talk and seemed nonplussed by her care. She wondered if he thought he was getting a particularly rigorous bath.

"What time is it?" asked Elizabeth.

"Six-fifteen," said the student.

She decided to let Dr. Lambert and the LSU team finish the backside of the psychiatric patient. She wanted to move swiftly through the remainder of the patients in the ER and be ready for Nurse Robichaud and Dr. McSwain. "Go and get the LSU charge resident. His name is Adrien Lambert. If you stand in the hall and call his name, he will come to you," said Elizabeth.

All of the wounds that she could clean, suture, and dress sterilely had been done on Mr. Adisa's front side. Turning him over would require taking off the restraints, and she would need help for that.

"Yes, Elizabeth, what's up?" asked Dr. Lambert.

"It is still an LSU day, and this guy is more complex than a mere suturing job. He dove from a second-story window and needs complete evaluation for injuries to his bones and skull. You'd better save some time in the X-ray suite for him and call orthopedics or neurosurgery if you find anything," said Elizabeth.

"Wow, after only a few months you are getting quite bossy," laughed Dr. Lambert.

Elizabeth knew that he liked her and appreciated her team spirit, but she also knew when she demonstrated the take-charge behavior valued in her male counterparts that she was considered aggressive and bossy. Teasing and nagging had always worked with her male cousins, and since she had no female mentors in surgery, she'd been trying those same tactics at Tulane, with mixed results.

"Yep, you'd better get hopping, Dr. Lambert," Elizabeth told him. "I love you, but I am not taking a dump from LSU for my team. Love only goes so far in the accident room," she teased.

"Threat received, Miss South Carolina!" said Dr. Lambert as he walked off toward the radiology section of the trauma suite.

Elizabeth knew she needed to find out about the rest of her patients, including the one whose stench permeated the hallway. Though she hated bad smells, she knew they were part of the life of a surgeon. She noticed the smell became more pungent as she approached the exam room. It smelled like something was rotting.

She pushed one side of the old swinging doors open and peeked inside the exam room. The smell was nauseating. A man with a huge, stinking dark rag tied with string to his left hand sat on a metal folding chair with the hand propped on the white sheet of the gurney. He smiled, revealing an open space from a missing front tooth, and said, "Bonjour, cher."

Elizabeth had never seen a dark-skinned person speaking what sounded like French. She had read about Cajuns, but had only seen a few in the ER so far. "How are you?" asked Elizabeth.

"J'ai gros couer," said the patient with a very sad face.

"I am sorry, but I do not understand you. I will try to find someone who speaks your language. Do you understand English?" asked Elizabeth.

"Ax for Livvy, cher," said the man. His body sagged, and he put his head on the gurney close to his smelly hand. He looked exhausted.

Elizabeth left the examination room thinking, *Does anyone in this crazy state speak English?* Even though it was just six-thirty, Nurse Robichaud was already at her desk.

"What's up, Crème Puff? Saving lives on the LSU dime again?" asked the nurse.

Elizabeth ignored the nurse's jab.

"I could use some help," she said. "The gentleman in Room Three has a nasty rag on his hand and is speaking what I think is Cajun French. I can't communicate with him, and he specifically asked for you."

"Not him again!" exclaimed Nurse Robichaud. "That is Etienne Comeaux. He was abandoned by his family and some Cajuns from Bayou Lafourche took him in, and he has forgotten how to speak regular English. He understands English, but he stubbornly sticks to that Cajun French."

"He has the nastiest rag on his hand that I have ever smelled," said Elizabeth.

"Yes, he is one messed-up dude. Cajuns don't usually do voodoo. But Etienne visits a voodooiene and has her treat his ailments. If results don't come quickly enough to suit him, he shows up in here. He never follows our instructions. He just smells up the place and wastes everyone's time," said Nurse Robichaud.

"Do you have time to translate?" asked Elizabeth.

The nurse put her cup of coffee on the desk and moved silently toward the exam room, obviously irritated but resigned.

Elizabeth followed, wondering what was on that rag.

The nurse burst through the exam room door and startled the patient. "Etienne Comeaux, what are you doing here again?" she scolded him. "I told you to let Dr. McSwain sew that finger back on you and give you some antibiotics! My nurses spent an hour teaching you how to change your dressing sterilely, and here you are back in here wasting my time with your nasty poultice," said the nurse. She shook her finger in the face of the patient and spoke loudly.

The man sat erect, pointing to his stinky hand. An animated conversation waged between the two in fragmented French. Elizabeth noticed Nurse Robichaud could hold her own in the odd language. The discussion heightened in tone and timbre, and eventually the patient slumped as the nurse donned sterile gloves and started pulling off the poultice. Whatever was said, it looked to Elizabeth like Nurse Robichaud had won, at least temporarily.

As she cut off the poultice, the nurse turned to Elizabeth and said, "This man nearly cut his finger off with a saw about three weeks ago. Dr. McSwain wanted to take him to surgery to reattach it as best he could. This fool is afraid of doctors and particularly afraid of anesthesia because some of his voodoo buddies told him anesthesia will steal your soul. So he went back to the voodooiene and got a poultice."

The smell got stronger as the layers were removed. The patient sat stock still and turned his head away from the wound and the nurse.

"Do poultices ever work?" asked Elizabeth.

"Unfortunately," admitted Nurse Robichaud, "sometimes they do work. The body has amazing healing abilities. I don't know if the voodoo poultice works, or if the patient's faith heals the wound, or if God truly does watch out for fools. Maybe the body can heal more on its own than we realize. But to answer your question, poultices work frequently enough that folks keep going back to get them."

Elizabeth was riveted. She loved science. She loved the study of medicine. She was fascinated by everything about the body. But she recognized medical knowledge was limited and that the wonders of the body weren't well understood.

"What is in that poultice that's so stinky?" said Elizabeth. She stared at the soft, moist, disgusting looking mass perched over the patient's thumb.

"Different foolishness is used for different ailments. This one is pretty standard. It has a copper penny, some kind of animal fat, ground cockroaches, ground coffee, the dried hind foot of a rabbit supposedly found in a graveyard, and a wad of gum moss—all tied together with kitchen string. The stink is from the animal fat and the cockroaches," said the nurse.

"Wow, you'd think the concoction would cause infection and rot off his entire hand," said Elizabeth.

"Yep, seems like it," replied Nurse Robichaud. "I'll bet he has a buckeye chestnut in his left pocket for luck. Many folks around here believe carrying a buckeye chestnut in their pockets prevents death. You will hear them say 'no man ever dies with a buckeye in his pocket.'"

The patient reached into his pocket with his other hand and produced the buckeye. He smiled. Apparently, he did understand what the nurse was saying, but he chose not to speak English.

When the last of the poultice was in the trash can and the nurse had cleaned the entire wound with antiseptic, Elizabeth was surprised to see Etienne's hand looked pretty good. His skin was pink all the way to the tip of the finger, and the edges of the wound were growing together. He could not bend the swollen finger, but it did not look infected.

"Well, I'll be damned. Wait until Norman—I mean Dr. McSwain—sees this. He will be shocked and amazed," said the nurse.

Elizabeth stood mutely behind the nurse, peering over her shoulder at the patient's hand. It was amazing to see healthy tissue under that nasty poultice.

"Not bad, huh, cher?" said Etienne Comeaux. He grinned, childlike, at the nurse.

"Oh, now you can speak English? You are getting a tetanus shot today, or I will tell the guard to shoot you if you show back up at the front door of Charity. I am done with your foolishness. You got off easy this time, and your finger is healing well. But either you get the tetanus shot or the guards will shoot you the next time you stink up my ER! Understand?" said the nurse.

The laughing patient lapsed back into Cajun French, apparently agreeing to Nurse Robichaud's conditions.

"Crème Puff," Nurse Robichaud said to Elizabeth, "do not dress his wound. I want Dr. McSwain to see this before we cover it up. Things are a little slow right now so he can stay in this room while you run around and finish your rounds before the Tulane doctors get here. There is a botched suicide down the hall. You might want to check on her."

Elizabeth recorded everything that she could remember about the poultice patient, quickly and meticulously, on one of the index cards she kept in the left front pocket of her white doctor's coat. She wanted to be perfect, and she wanted Dr. McSwain to be impressed so she could make the cut and keep her job.

It was now six forty-five, and she knew the Tulane team would be here any minute. As she moved down the hall and into the exam room to see the patient who had attempted suicide, Elizabeth was focused on ordering her index cards properly.

Lying in four-point restraints was what looked to be a beautiful woman. A broad-shouldered male doctor was standing over her, wiping her face with moist sterile gauze as she moaned and thrashed about. The woman's arms and legs were long and tanned. She was naked except for a beautiful matching black lace bra and panty set. Her fingernails and toenails were painted, and the polish was not chipped. Elizabeth recognized the color. It was her mother's favorite Revlon red, Cherries in the Snow, which had a matching lipstick. Elizabeth never polished her fingernails; she did too much work with her hands. The polish on this woman's hands and feet was perfect.

Elizabeth could not see her face, but she could hear a gurgling sound coming from the woman's throat. As Dr. Cabellero, the neurosurgeon, turned his head to speak to Elizabeth, she caught a glimpse of the woman's face. The right side of her face was beautiful. A mass of chocolate wavy hair tumbled over the white sheets covering the gurney. Her right eye was bright, staring at the ceiling, and the iris was nearly black. Her brow was perfectly shaped, and her skin was smooth and olive-toned. But the left side of her face was gone. In its place was a bloody pulp of oozing tissue charred with gunpowder and flecked with pieces of bone and tooth enamel.

The handsome doctor leaning over the once-beautiful woman formed a surreal picture. Elizabeth felt dizzy and reached for the wall with her right hand for balance. Her knees seemed to want to melt underneath her. She had never seen or imagined anything like this.

The neurosurgeon noticed Elizabeth's horror-stricken face.

"You do not need to stay here for this," he told her kindly. "There is really not much we can do for her at this point. The LSU neurosurgery team is tied up doing a brain aneurysm. They called me to come in early to assess her."

The patient attempted to talk, but pink froth came from what had been her nose and her mouth. The teeth on the right side of her mouth were perfect and straight and bright white. There were no teeth and no cheekbone on her left side.

Elizabeth felt deep sadness. "What happened to her?"

"The usual. I spoke with her sister, who is in the waiting room. She said our patient was engaged to a wealthy New York lawyer, and she found out he was cheating on her. So she decided that she could not live without him, stole her father's handgun, and really made her life a mess. Honestly, Elizabeth, suicide should come with a manual. I get really exhausted trying to put people back together after the botched attempts at killing themselves. If they are serious, they shouldn't do it while drunk. All they have to do is hold the gun steady while pointing it straight back in their throat and pulling the trigger slowly. A manual would keep them from blowing off part of their head, and leaving *me* to clean up their mess. My poor patients with terminal brain tumors would give anything to exchange places with this silly and vapid woman," said the neurosurgeon.

Elizabeth was disturbed by his cold analysis, but she had never seen anything like this patient before her. She could understand the neurosurgeon's disgust. But the patient's choice, Elizabeth could never understand. *Suicide over a man? Unimaginable!* Suicide for any reason was unimaginable. Life was precious to her. Elizabeth placed her focus on helping the patient and away from the horror of the scene. Her equilibrium returned. "What can we actually do for her?"

"The most important thing at this stage is her airway. We must make sure that she does not strangle on her own blood, mucus, and saliva. Her tongue does not work well, and I have heavily sedated her. She does not really realize what is going on," said Dr. Cabellero.

"Is there anything that I can do to help you?" said Elizabeth.

"Yes," he said. "Please open another box of sterile sponges, and hang those antibiotics and hook them into her intravenous line. If you are not going to faint, please hold pressure on her nose, as one of the arteries there is trying to bleed briskly," said the doctor as he turned to take off his gloves. He went to the phone on the wall and called the operating room. Elizabeth heard him tell the LSU team, "She's stable, sedated, and has an adequate airway but should get a tracheostomy today." He further informed them that he was cleaning the wounds and dressing them as best he could in the emergency department.

Elizabeth put on sterile gloves and held pressure on the woman's nose. She wondered how the patient's wounds could ever be fixed. As she looked closer, she saw the woman's left eye was missing. The socket had been packed with sterile gauze. As Elizabeth felt the deep sorrow of human foolishness, the door swung open and Dr. Peterson walked through.

"Hey, Cabellero," Peterson greeted his colleague. "Another botched suicide. Damn, man, you seem to get one of these every week. Think these women are trying to kill themselves just to get a date with a rich Cuban dude?" He laughed and approached the gurney, standing behind Elizabeth.

"Wow, she really messed herself up bad!" Peterson continued. "Botched suicides generate lots of business for the plastic surgeons who try to fill the holes.

They'll have a year's worth of work on her, for sure." Elizabeth saw his gaze travel down the full length of the patient's body. "Nice underwear, though," Peterson commented. "What a shame, it looks like she used to be hot." He turned to Dr. Cabellero, who was still on the phone. "These gals get all jacked up about some guy doing them wrong, and then they don't even know how to kill themselves correctly. You know, Cabellero, you should write an instruction manual for them so they kill themselves properly. It could be part of the high school curriculum. If they are going to do it, they should do it right, I always say," joked the chief resident.

Dr. Cabellero hung up the phone and turned to face Dr. Peterson in the hot, small room. "*Get out! Get out, now!*" he said loudly. "I do not need your kind of help, and this patient certainly does not need your disrespect. Leave now before I do something that I later will be sorry for doing."

Dr. Peterson threw his hands in the air and backed out of the examination room. As he cleared the doorway he whispered, "Sorry, dude, I did not mean to bring up your being Cuban. I know that pushes all your buttons. No harm, no foul, Cabellero."

Dr. Cabellero continued working, muttering a few phrases to himself in lilting Spanish. Elizabeth did not know much Spanish, but she did hear the word *cerdo* several times and thought she remembered it meant "pig."

The patient's wounds were clean, and dressings were in place. The bleeding had subsided. Elizabeth and Dr. Cabellero moved to the hallway to complete their notes. He said, "Dr. Roberts, the really hard part starts now. She will have to remain sitting up to maintain her airway and to minimize swelling. As soon as the LSU team finishes the aneurysm case, they will clean the room and come for her and inspect the wounds better and put in a permanent endotracheal tube for her breathing. Her sister is devastated, as you might imagine. I am going to speak to her and ask her to call the remainder of the patient's family. I think it best that no one else sees her like this. They can see her after surgery," said Dr. Cabellero.

"Why is she not covered up?" asked Elizabeth.

"I have covered her repeatedly, but despite the restraints, she manages to kick the covers off. I think that even sedated and in this hideous condition, she senses how hot and muggy it is in the emergency room. She seems to not want any cover so I quit fighting her. The nurses will get a hospital gown on her as soon as they get a free moment," said the doctor.

Elizabeth was relieved that he had at least attempted to preserve the woman's dignity. She scribbled on an index card, fighting back her own tears. How did a woman go from engaged to having half a face? She really didn't understand. Elizabeth herself was not particularly romantic. She'd had a few boyfriends, but none serious enough that the thought of losing the relationship would make her want to harm herself. *Besides,* she thought, *I'm probably more the homicide type than the suicide type.*

"You are sure having a fast and furious education in the accident room," Dr. Cabellero observed. "It has been quite busy since you got here. How about I take you to Commander's Palace for dinner one night? You look like you could use a quiet, nice dinner away from this lunatic asylum."

Elizabeth leaned backwards and reached for the wall again. *Had this man just asked her for a date? After what they had just been doing?* She was stunned. Her upbringing kicked in and she heard herself saying politely, "That sounds lovely. Just page me and I will check my schedule."

Dr. Cabellero continued down the hall and out of the emergency room. Elizabeth was anxious and surprised by her own excitement at his invitation. He was obviously smart, refined, darkly handsome, and different from the men at home. Her father had cautioned her strongly against dating in the workplace, but she never had the opportunity to go anywhere else to meet people. Her surgical internship was all-consuming. It was either the men at the hospital or no man. Dr. Harrison Lloyd White flashed across her mind. She laughed at herself, thinking she might discuss men with Nurse Aoife.

She was brought back from her reverie by Dr. McSwain's voice. As he strode through the swinging doors with four students in tow, she heard him say, "Nurse Robichaud, what have *you* done for humanity today?" Elizabeth knew this question was his signature. He always focused the team on their primary purpose, their patients. He was loud, he was manly, and he was in charge.

This morning, Dr. McSwain wore a big smile on his face, and the smile was infectious. His long white doctor's coat with the kelly green Tulane emblem had his name embroidered over the pocket. Norman McSwain, Jr., M.D., Chief

Trauma Surgeon. He looked like a chief. He wore a bright-red cotton turtleneck, and a large medallion hung around his neck. Elizabeth did not know what the medallion represented, and she was too shy to ask. It looked like some type of animal part on a heavy chain. He wore tight blue jeans and a huge belt with the insignia of the New Orleans Police Department emblazoned in gold tones at his waist. It reminded Elizabeth of belts she had seen on rodeo riders. He looked intense and mischievous.

He walked right up to her with his group, waving his hand in the air in a circle, and said, "Shall we round, intern?" Elizabeth knew it was more of a command than a question. Thank God, she had everything on every patient on her index cards. She was prepared, and for the first time, a little relaxed about rounding with him. She was unaware of any potential disaster brewing in the ER.

"Yes, sir," she replied. "There is nobody terribly acute at this moment. Shall we start at one end of the hall and move from room to room?"

"Absolutely not!" McSwain said. "We do it the same way, every time. We start with the sickest patient and move to the most stable. That's the Tulane way, intern. We are always thinking triage. Every time I walk up to you in this ER, pretend that you are in a military triage area, and start with the patient in the most urgent need of care. Take me to that person first."

Elizabeth said, "Yes, sir."

He explained, "Part of your learning experience in the ER is to quickly assess the sickest patients and prioritize who needs care the most urgently. Don't take me to someone with a splinter on his finger while someone in the next room has his arm hanging off," said McSwain. Two of the Tulane students started to laugh nervously. Elizabeth realized they did not know that they could be the next recipients of criticism. She had heard Dr. McSwain chew on the students, too.

"I want to see you make progress every day in knowing what needs the highest priority. That is the basis of surgery. We are action people. We assess, we act, and we save lives. You and I are not going on a walk through the emergency department. We are assessing who needs to go to the operating room first. When I show up down here and wave my finger around in a circle, that means 'Take me to the sickest first,'" said McSwain. "Got it?"

"Yes, sir!" said Elizabeth.

She quickly surveyed her index cards while Dr. McSwain looked on in disdain. Focused on her cards, she did not see his growing agitation. When she looked up, his smile was gone, and a dark cloud of disappointment covered his face. Elizabeth wondered what he was thinking as she considered her patient choices. The guy with the voodoo treatment was interesting. Nurse Robichaud had said so. The psychotic guy who had jumped through the window had an impressive number of superficial wounds, but he was not critical. She would start with the patient who had attempted suicide. Her airway could get compromised, so Elizabeth deemed her the first priority.

She turned and headed for the examination room containing the poor woman who had unsuccessfully tried to kill herself. This time, as Elizabeth entered the room, the patient was in a hospital gown and covered with a sheet. Her bed had her sitting with her head straight up and she was leaning slightly forward to maintain her airway. She seemed more coherent and was moaning loudly. The nurses were changing the sheet; blood and mucus had collected on her chest from under her dressings. The students were visibly horrified.

Elizabeth started to speak, and Dr. McSwain interrupted, "Let's discuss her in the hall, intern."

When they were back in the hall, he turned to the medical students and said, "Every week, we have people come in the ER who try to kill themselves. It is one of the worst scenarios with which we deal. People think they have a problem that they can't live with, and then they give themselves a real problem. As a surgeon, it is something that I never understand. But, students, always remember that even though the job of a surgeon is to save them and treat whatever hideous wounds they have inflicted on themselves, *always* get psychiatry involved early. You don't want to spend hours and hours of trying to get them whole again only to have them kill themselves in earnest. When this woman realizes what she has done to herself, she will really want to die. So always remember to get psychiatry involved early."

Elizabeth caught a glimpse of why Dr. McSwain always got the teaching award that was voted by the Tulane students every spring. She was proud to be mentored by him and hoped she would be here next year to learn more from him.

He turned back to her and said, "Please continue, Dr. Roberts."

She picked out the index card with this patient's detailed information and started to recite in the time-honored fashion of the medical world. "She is a twenty-six-year-old Latin woman who sustained a gunshot wound to her left lower face around five o'clock this morning…"

With lightning speed Dr. McSwain snatched the stack of index cards from her hands and threw them on the floor at her feet. Elizabeth gazed into his angry, penetrating stare, having no idea what she had done to displease him.

"You are a surgeon, Dr. Roberts, not a stenographer," he told her. "At Tulane, we *know* our patients. We do not jot down little notes and read them to one another. Do not ever present a patient to me that you do not know! I never want to see those stupid little index cards again!" said McSwain vehemently. He turned to look for Nurse Robichaud.

Elizabeth was bright red and humiliated. Could she do nothing right with this man?

"Nurse Robichaud, take me on rounds this morning, and let Dr. Roberts follow us. I want someone who knows their patients to round with me. Let's go, team. Nurse, lead the way," said McSwain.

One of the students gave Elizabeth a sympathetic smile, but it was obvious many nurses and students were entertained by the show. Elizabeth's meticulous cards lay in a pile on the emergency room floor. She had an overwhelming desire to bend down and retrieve the long hours of work those cards represented. She knew that she dare not pick them up.

She wanted to quit right then and right there. But if she did, she knew that she would never forgive herself. *This is just one moment in time,* she told herself. *I'll survive this hazing and learn to do it the Tulane way.* She wondered if he was being particularly hard on her because she was a girl. She knew that working the accident room was one of Tulane Surgery's tools for weeding out weak ones. She vowed not to be weeded out as she followed along behind the group.

An hour later, rounds were finished and Dr. McSwain was off to Tulane for his scheduled surgery. Elizabeth sighed with relief knowing that she had a few hours to clean up the ER before he would be back. Nurse Robichaud had given him a cursory explanation of each patient. He never demanded much detail from her, Elizabeth noted. Theirs was a language of long acquaintance, and she didn't have to say many words to have him understand her message.

Elizabeth walked out to the waiting room to look for people who might be sicker than they appeared. Dr. Peterson did little to teach Elizabeth, but he did warn her that she was responsible for all patients in the emergency department, even if they had not been brought back yet.

So she walked from aisle to aisle, observing the patients. One boy had a red rash all over his body. His breathing was harsh and shallow. His mother said that he had been stung by a bee and that he was an asthmatic. Elizabeth approached Aoife, the triage nurse, and asked that the boy be taken back immediately to the medical side of the emergency room. Aoife called the charge nurse on the medical side, and the boy was taken to an exam room.

"Thanks, Elizabeth," Aoife said. "I did not appreciate his degree of airway obstruction. Good call, intern."

If felt good to get a compliment for a change. Elizabeth paused at the triage desk and enjoyed her tiny accomplishment and the comfort of a friendly presence.

"I heard Dr. Cabellero asked you to dinner," said Aoife.

"How do you already know that? It was less than two hours ago," said Elizabeth.

"Well, honey, he did it right out in the hall for God and everyone to hear," laughed Aoife. "Of course, that is hot news around here. We are always anxious to see which new doctors will hook up first. The Big Free is nothing if not a giant soap opera."

"Well, if that is the case, I am most definitely not going to dinner with him. I don't like to mix business and pleasure," said Elizabeth.

"Oh, don't get your panties in a wad," Aoife replied. "He is going to marry some girl from Miami that his family has picked out for him. He is harmless. He likes to get dressed up and take nice young ladies out to dinner to show them his genteel manners. He has lots of dough and takes out one girl per week. It is not a big deal. It will be a great meal with no pressure. And wait until you see his car!"

"Why does he do that? I thought people dated to try and establish a relationship," said Elizabeth.

"Not Dr. Cabellero," Aoife said. "He knows his destiny. He is just lonely, maybe even bored. New Orleans is not really his cup of tea. He is used to a cultured world full of well-mannered rich people. He is a gentleman, and you will be glad you went. So go get a good meal and enjoy yourself."

"What is Commander's Palace?" asked Elizabeth.

"Only the best damn restaurant in the world!" Aoife told her. "It is uptown where the rich people live, and the restaurant is run by an old New Orleans family. Everything is first class. I won't spoil it for you. Just go and experience it for yourself," said the nurse.

Luckily, Elizabeth's Granny was strict about table manners, so she knew where all the forks went and how to use them. But finding something to wear to a fancy restaurant would be a challenge. Elizabeth realized she did not own appropriate clothes. "I don't have anything to wear to a place like that," she said.

"Don't worry," Aoife assured her. "My roommate is tall and skinny like you, and I will borrow something from her. Why don't we keep it simple and stick with a black dress?"

"Won't I look as if I'm going to a funeral?" asked Elizabeth.

"No, honey, all black is high fashion among the moneyed crowd," said Aoife.

Elizabeth wondered if she should be taking fashion advice from a woman with chipped nails and hair color that had never occurred in nature, but she felt grateful that Aoife cared enough to try and help her.

"Sure, that would be great. If your roommate doesn't want to loan a stranger a dress, I completely understand. But if she is comfortable with the idea, I will take excellent care of it," promised Elizabeth. "But right now, I'd better get back to work. This ER is never quiet for long."

CHAPTER 9
The Male GU exam

lizabeth had finished the early morning rounds in the trauma ER and sutured all the patients, while teaching the medical students. She was still stinging from Dr. McSwain's rebuke, but happily anticipating a nice meal in her near future with Dr. Caballero.

Nurse Robichaud approached. She was rushing, as always.

"Dr. Roberts, please hurry and finish with the suturing in Room Ten. The resident, the one who was to have taught the male genital physical exam to the new medical students, is stranded on the highway. He had a flat tire on his way back from Alexandria today, and he's not going to get here on time. Dr. McSwain asked me to put you on it. You will teach six to eight female medical students. These women have not learned about or performed physical examinations on men before.

"The tutorial occurs across the street at the Veterans Administration urology clinic," Nurse Robichaud continued. "The head nurse over there is a man named

Mikey Sherman. He is a bit eccentric," she said, smiling, "but he will show you the ropes. I talked to Mikey a few minutes ago. He told me they have around ninety-four veterans waiting already. Get going!"

Elizabeth was heading toward the door when she heard Nurse Robichaud's voice again. "One more thing," the nurse said. "Please do not pronounce his name 'Mickey.' It is pronounced 'Mike-ee.' He is from Arkansas, he lisps, and has the worst Southern accent you have ever heard; but he is sensitive about that name. So remember to call him Mike-ee," advised Nurse Robichaud.

Going to another clinic today held no appeal for Elizabeth. She had worked the entire twenty-four hours before and was once again on the twenty-sixth hour of a twenty-four-hour shift. She had pronounced one man dead from a gunshot wound, helped to revive three people whose hearts had stopped from drugs and alcohol, sutured a dozen stab wounds, and reviewed the X-rays of a dozen patients who had been beaten or injured in car wrecks. She was hungry, tired, and emotionally weary. She longed for a shower and breakfast and a bed.

It wasn't that Elizabeth minded hard work. Her summers on the family farm had been all hard work, but it had a steady rhythm with periods of labor and periods of enjoying food and rest. The family laughed a lot at the farm. In college and medical school, she had held one to two jobs while attending on full academic scholarships. She had pressure to keep her grades high to keep the scholarships, but she had never been in a situation with such emotional turmoil. In college and medical school there were very intense periods of study and work with days and weeks of relaxation. The accident room of Charity's giant emergency room was all hard work, all the time. So far, there was not a lot of laughter, and much of the laughter that had occurred was at her expense. After taking a few deep breaths, she mentally accepted her new assignment, adjusting her attitude and her posture. *Going to the VA clinic might be fun.* Elizabeth loved treating veterans. While a student in South Carolina, she had worked at the Veterans Administration Hospital in Charleston. Both of her mother's brothers were veterans, and the veteran patients had always been respectful and appreciative. After days of working with the cursing, bleeding, drunk, and crack-crazed crowd at Charity, Elizabeth though the VA might be relaxing.

As she exited Charity Hospital, Elizabeth observed that after a long shift in the accident room, there wasn't much difference in appearance between the hospital patients and the staff. Everyone looked exhausted, disappointed, hungry, and generally spent. At least, she hoped, the VA clinic staff worked nine-to-five shifts, and the patients were likely to have slept in their own beds the night before. The veteran patients would be a welcome relief. Having to hide her name and always being leery of attack by her patients was wearing on her nervous system.

She walked from the back door of Charity Hospital, across a street full of potholes, and into the back door of the New Orleans Veterans Administration Hospital and Clinics. The emergency ramps leading to the two hospitals were fifty yards apart, but they were worlds apart when one considered the size of their budgets and the type of patient served. Charity was poor and state-run. The VA was federally funded and steeped in bureaucracy. Charity was the soul of the poor community of New Orleans—the place where most of the uninsured were born and came to die. It was also home to one of the best trauma centers in the country. If the president of the United States was shot in New Orleans, he would be taken to Charity. It was rumored that Dr. McSwain stayed at the hospital when important dignitaries visited the city. In contradistinction, the VA was staffed by career bureaucrats. Many were absolutely devoted to the care of the veterans. Some were just there to get a paycheck and wanted to move as slowly as possible and do as little as possible. Nothing changed quickly at any VA in which Elizabeth had worked. But they were all similar, and there was comfort to the young doctor in knowing what to expect.

Upon entering the VA Medical Center, Elizabeth smelled the industrial scent of alcohol associated with most hospitals. It smelled clean. The difference between a federal budget and the budget of the State of Louisiana was readily evident in the physical surroundings.

As she walked down the main hall, everything was clearly marked with large signs above her head. She easily found the waiting room of the urology clinic. She passed hundreds of men waiting in plastic chairs. Most were chatting amiably. Some were sipping coffee. A few were asleep, but sitting upright.

Elizabeth found it easy to differentiate the veterans of the two latest wars. Guys who had served in Vietnam dressed in what she called *rebel wear*. They wore biker T-shirts, leather pants or jeans, and lots of heavy chains. Some had long hair, and most seemed angry. Veterans of the Korean conflict and World War II were older and more conservative. Their laughter came easier, and they seemed less cynical. The older vets remembered the Great Depression, and Hitler, and Mussolini. They came home to celebrating Americans who honored their service. Vietnam vets were young during the 1960s, and came home to angry protests against the war they fought.

The psychological effects of their different homecomings were evident. Both groups had witnessed horrors average humans never saw. Elizabeth observed that the two groups didn't mingle. Nurse Sherman's running humorous monologue was their thin thread of connection. Elizabeth felt great gratitude to all veterans. She knew that without their service, her country might not exist. She felt honored to serve these brave men.

She could hear a Southern twang above the chatter. "Now, you fellas need to settle down. We have our first female doctor coming from Tulane today. She is going to teach the male genital exam to a bunch of the female medical students. So since all the gals are new, things could run a little slow this morning. I expect everyone's best behavior and cooperation. These are the young doctors of the future, and we need to help them learn as much as possible," said Nurse Sherman.

"Hey, Sherman, I already served my country," yelled a man in a wheelchair who wore a United States flag tied like a bandana around his forehead. "Why do I have to have some ignorant kid probing my privates?"

"Calm down! Nobody is going to make anybody get probed for anything," drawled Nurse Mikey Sherman. "If you want to help make these young women better doctors, raise your hand and I will pick a few of you. The rest of you can sit there like a lump of coal until Nurse Mikey gets to you."

Elizabeth couldn't help but notice the distinctive Arkansas twang Nurse Robichaud had mentioned. It was the accent familiar in Hollywood movies when the objective was to make fun of Southerners. Nurse Sherman's accent was particularly pronounced.

"I am tired of being treated like a guinea pig. I want to see a real doctor, not some clueless kid," yelled another veteran.

"Honey pie, when this old VA turns into the Ritz Carlton, you will know, because I will be wearing a top hat! And the very moment you see me in a top hat, you can have anything your little heart desires," said the nurse. "Until then, we are just doing the best that we can, and I'd appreciate a little patience and respect."

Mikey hadn't yet noticed Elizabeth, giving her the opportunity to observe him. He was tall and thin, with a Semper Fi tattoo on his left forearm. The eagle, globe, and anchor were obvious from twenty feet away. His eyes were sage green, and his mustache was brown and gray, but his hair was wiry and orange—a failed attempt at an auburn curly afro. Elizabeth wondered if Mikey and Aoife used the same shade of boxed hair color. None of the women in Elizabeth's family colored their hair, and nobody had a tattoo.

As Mikey turned to walk back into the clinic, Elizabeth watched his hips and arms move with an exaggerated sashay. She followed him into the clinic hall. Every veteran in the waiting room stared, mouths open, as she passed. Apparently the nurse wasn't kidding when he said she was the first woman doctor to come to this clinic.

"Nurse Sherman, I am Dr. Elizabeth Roberts. I am here to help teach the male urologic exam today," said Elizabeth.

Nurse Sherman pivoted and stopped short, looking Elizabeth over from top to bottom.

As Elizabeth got closer to him, she thought she smelled the fragrant odor of Elizabeth Taylor's Passion perfume. She also detected the smell of alcohol.

"Well, I'll be!" said the nurse, encircling her with an unexpected hug. "It looks like the world is modernizing a little. You are the prettiest thing around, and Nurse Livvy from The Big Free tells me that you are smart, too." He smiled.

I definitely smell alcohol, Elizabeth thought as he stepped back. She also marveled that the gossip ring ran from hospital to hospital.

"Thank you," she told him. "I am ready to get to work." She didn't want to waste time. As soon as this teaching session was over, she hoped, she could get some food.

"Good girl. Your new troops are waiting for you in the last exam room. This group is particularly green. They seem afraid of these sweet old vets, and for God's sake, one of them called me *sir*!"

Elizabeth noticed Nurse Sherman's lisp became more pronounced when he got excited.

"Every one of your gals is just gorgeous," he told her. "I suspect we'll be beating down erections all morning. It might be best if I pick the older guys to get started. If a ninety-year-old World War II veteran can cause your girls to blush with his manhood, well, you girls are on your own!" said Nurse Sherman.

Elizabeth was shocked to hear the nurse being so fresh within earshot of patients. But Nurse Sherman seemed sweet. Who was she to judge? At least he wasn't mean like Nurse Robichaud.

Nurse Mikey was off to the waiting room to secure the first volunteer. Elizabeth could see through the door that nearly every hand was raised to volunteer. True to his word, Mikey appeared to be picking older veterans for this tour of duty.

This clinic looked like every clinic everywhere. There was a long broad hall with examination rooms coming off either side at ten yards apart. The floor was cheap tile and the walls were another shade of mint green. The VA was cleaner and more recently painted than Charity. The clinic was warm, and except for a few complainers, everyone seemed calm and accepting. While Nurse Sherman chose the male volunteers, Dr. Roberts entered the last office in the clinic where the female Tulane medical students waited. Most looked anxious and fearful. When they realized their teacher was female, a few of them visibly relaxed. Elizabeth smiled when she saw they were gathered around an anatomy textbook titled *The Art of the Physical Examination*. Elizabeth remembered studying that text a mere three years before. She warmed to the task she had been assigned. She liked to teach and felt comfortable in that role. She had taught the night biology lab at her college and had helped teach anatomy dissection at her medical school.

"Good morning, everyone," Elizabeth greeted them. "Today we are going to learn the male genitourinary examination. Tulane usually hires a graduate student named Fred to be our patient. Apparently one of the young ladies from last week's group was a little overzealous with Fred's private parts, and he decided not to participate this week. Either that, or his rent was not yet due," said Elizabeth.

The young women laughed nervously at Elizabeth's attempt to joke. Elizabeth surveyed the students. These women looked like she used to look. They were fresh-faced and innocent. They were clean and smelled of bath soap and variously floral perfumes. Their clothes were freshly pressed and wrinkle-free. Their enthusiasm, like that of puppies, was infectious. Even though she had been on duty many hours, Elizabeth felt energized by them.

She smiled and walked toward them. She felt a stab of sadness at the thought of her own lost innocence.

Unfortunately, with time, Elizabeth thought, *they will learn that most disease is self-induced. They will counsel the diabetic who won't stop eating cupcakes. They will feel the frustration of the man with lung cancer who can't quit smoking. They will see the abused wife lie, for the third time in six months, that the bruises on her face, neck, and arms are caused by her clumsiness.* But today, these young doctors-to-be believed it was them against disease, and they were there to learn the physical examination part of the fight. They were the new troops. She shook the hand of each young woman, taking a moment to try to remember each name. She smiled, trying to put them at ease, and then said, "Please feel free to ask any and all questions. There is never any such thing as a stupid question. It is your duty as doctors to know all that you can possibly know, but please ask your questions before and after the patients have left the room, not while they are present."

She looked at their faces. "Remember these patients are not paid volunteers. These men fought for our country and gave much of themselves and their lives for our very way of life. Each and every one of them deserves to be treated with dignity. They volunteered or were drafted to make the ultimate sacrifice for our safety, and today they are volunteering to expose their most intimate body parts for your education. Please remember to ask before you touch them. Remember to thank them after you have finished your exam. Never say anything that could scare them or hurt their feelings. If you notice something that you think is abnormal, do not unnecessarily alarm them. Simply tell me after they have left the room."

Marianne, a tall young woman with gray-green eyes and strawberry-red hair, asked, "Will you tell us exactly what to expect with each man so we don't have any surprises?" Elizabeth felt she was looking at a beautiful, excited child.

"*Never!*" exclaimed Elizabeth. "All diseases can manifest differently in different patients. For the rest of your lives, you will be detectives. You will open an exam room door and enter with no idea what awaits you. Medicine is a field of investigation, mystery, and art—a cross between an ongoing Easter egg hunt and a whodunit mystery." She let that sink in. "Always remember that your patient is an individual, first and foremost. He will give you a few hints of his problem when you take his history. You will gain a few insights with your physical exam. Blood work and X-rays will further elucidate the matter. But an open mind, a willingness to truly listen, and careful contemplation will be your greatest tools."

"It all seems so scary and intimidating," whispered the student, Marianne.

"It is scary and it can be intimidating, but it is mostly magical," Elizabeth replied. "The healing powers of the human body will amaze you every day! You will never be bored. You will never know what is going to happen on any given day, and you will never know what awaits you on the other side of the examination room door. There is no other job on earth where people put themselves in such a vulnerable situation and ask for your help." She paused to emphasize her statement.

"Working in medicine is an honor and a privilege few people get. Remember that in your years of training you have other, more experienced doctors guiding you. Medical education is taught in a team, and there are always people around who know more than you and often people who know less. So always seek to listen to the doctors and nurses with experience, and always make sure that you teach the doctors and nurses who know less than you. Always ask for help if you need it. Keep the Hippocratic Oath in mind every day—particularly the part that says, 'First do no harm,' and you will be fine," said Elizabeth. She felt excited for the new students. She remembered her first clinical work, the part of medical school she most enjoyed. Her exhaustion was temporarily at bay.

"So, any questions before we start?" asked Elizabeth.

"Is it true that we have to stick our fingers up the anuses of these men?" a young Indian woman who had introduced herself as Jalpa Patel asked shyly.

"Yes, that is part of what we do. Cancers can form there, and a good doctor will probe every orifice looking for cancer. Once you get used to the idea of examining orifices and have done a few thorough physical examinations, you will find the mouth, the vagina, and the anus are similar. It is the idea of probing them that is a little shocking. Trust me, the patient is on the worse end of the deal," said Elizabeth. The students giggled nervously.

Jalpa did not smile. "I have never seen or touched a man of any type," she admitted quietly.

"That is okay," Elizabeth assured her. "You are a doctor now. This is your duty. It has nothing to do with being a man or a woman. There is nothing sexual about this examination. You are a doctor, and the person is your patient. That is all. Put everything else completely out of your mind."

Jalpa bobbed her head from side to side and spoke with a more pronounced accent, "Yes, madam, I will try."

"Now, ladies, we begin. The male GU system consists of the penis, the testicles and their structures, the skin covering the area, the groin on both sides, the anus, and the prostate," said Elizabeth as she pointed out each structure on a large, worn-looking laminated board on the back of the door.

"We examine the male patient standing up for the genitourinary exam," said Elizabeth.

"That seems awfully awkward," protested Jalpa.

"Again, we are not thinking of our comfort. We are thinking of how to best demonstrate pathology. We want gravity to assist us. Why might we need gravity?" asked Elizabeth.

Sally Smith, a cute black woman with a short afro and a winning smile, said, "We can't examine the testicles if we can't get to them. They are surrounded by a muscle called the cremaster that will pull them up into the groin when anything approaches, or if they get cold." The students giggled.

"Exactly!" said Elizabeth. "Good job, Sally. Also, when looking for a hernia, we want the patient standing so that the hernia will descend into the groin or the scrotum so we can see and feel it better."

The students seemed fully engaged in the lesson. Elizabeth felt gratified. *Things are going well.*

She continued, "So, ladies, you will sit on a rolling stool while your patient stands. Your eyes will be at about the level of the patient's pubic bone, and you will examine each structure carefully in the front. Then you will ask him to turn around and bend over the examination table. Then you will examine his anus and prostate. Be sure that you are wearing a pair of clean gloves, that you have inspected the gloves for holes, and that you use plenty of lubricant. You want to inform the patient that you are going to touch him, and make sure that he takes slow, deep, relaxing breaths. While he is relaxing himself, you can do the same by deep breathing with him. After he takes a few deep breaths, you are ready to enter his anus." Again, the girls giggled softly.

"Any questions?" asked Elizabeth.

Marianne said, "This is just plain disgusting." She screwed up her face to emphasize her disgust.

Elizabeth thought, *That one is destined for dermatology. Immaculate skin, hoity-toity attitude, and drop-dead gorgeous. Yep, dermatology, here she comes!* "Absolutely nothing about any patient is disgusting," Elizabeth rebuked her. "You are a doctor. The human condition, in all its variations, is before you to study, assist, and learn from. If you think examining a person to try to help him is disgusting, then you are in the wrong place, ma'am." She decided to lighten the message, adding, "Even if you work at the Clinique makeup counter, you have to touch people."

The student looked down and whispered, "I did not mean it like that. I just don't like the smell of feces."

Jalpa said, "I don't think anybody actually likes that smell, do they?"

Elizabeth said, "No, not really. But like everything about the body, you get used to it. But if you are really not a feces girl, you have just ruled out gastroenterology and general surgery as professions. A very productive morning for you, I'd say. Maybe eyeballs will be your thing. There's no smell there," she added gently.

Sally and Jalpa laughed. Marianne scowled.

"I think we are ready to begin. I will examine the first patient so you can see how it is done. I will not tell you of the findings until the patient has left the room. One to three of you will examine each man. I will decide how many exams each man gets, based on how I perceive him to be tolerating the process. Please decide among yourselves who is going first while I go get the first patient," instructed Elizabeth. She headed for the hall door.

Mikey was standing in the hall with several charts, talking to three veterans.

"Nurse Sherman, do we have a volunteer?" asked Elizabeth.

"Honey, we have a hundred volunteers," said Mikey. "One look at y'all sweet young things and every man out there was begging to be *the one*." He shrugged. "I picked a few of the older, genteel men to serve their country again," said Mikey. Elizabeth thought Nurse Sherman really enjoyed his job.

As the patient came into the examination room, Elizabeth gazed up from her seated position at a handsome octogenarian. His thin, pale white skin was in sharp contrast to his bright blue eyes. His crop of snow white hair protruded from under a once-expensive straw hat. His suit was pale pink seersucker. His tie was red, and he wore white bucks. He looked dapper and sweet, and he reminded her of men from Charleston. Despite his eighty-plus years and his time in war, his posture was upright, and he looked strong and happy.

"Good morning, young lady. Owen Richards at your service this fine morning," said the old gentleman in a Savannah drawl, as he extended a cool, soft hand and tipped his hat.

"Thank you for agreeing to help us, sir," said Elizabeth.

"I know you students have to learn on somebody. I have already donated my body to Tulane, so I figured you might as well get some use out of it while it is still moving around as well. I am from the Tulane class of 1915, and my blood is as green as the Tulane Green Wave mascot," laughed the old guy.

Mikey helped Mr. Richards to the end of the exam table. He winked at the young doctors and said, "Girls, this is one of my studs. Try to control yourselves." Nurse Sherman swished away as many of the students blushed.

"That nurse is an odd one and not particularly professional. The VA should be ashamed to employ someone like him," said the blonde student, Marianne.

Mr. Richards jerked his head around and looked indignantly into her eyes. "Even though Nurse Sherman is an unrepentant homosexual, he deserves your utmost respect, young lady. That man is a decorated Marine helicopter pilot. He flew his chopper in the most dangerous areas of Vietnam, saved hundreds of men, and was awarded a bronze star for extreme bravery in the Tet Offensive of 1968. While you were trying to learn how to ride a bicycle, he was watching his friends get blown up in Vietnam. That prissy nurse is a big war hero, and he is well respected around here. Please show him respect, girl. This clinic is lucky to have him," concluded Owen Richards.

Elizabeth was uncomfortable with the discord in the room and wished that she could come to the student's aid, but knew the old guy was right.

"Yes, sir," Marianne said. "I am very sorry, sir." She went to stand behind the other students.

Elizabeth tried to maintain decorum. She realized she was nearing her twenty-seventh hour at work, and fatigue was setting in.

"Okay, let's get started," said Elizabeth.

"Mr. Richards will face me while I sit on the rolling stool to examine him. Please pull your pants down and hold up your shirt, sir," Elizabeth requested.

"Yes, ma'am," said the patient. He slowly removed his straw hat, his seersucker coat, and his white leather belt. He handed each article of his clothing to a different student as if he were bestowing gifts.

Elizabeth remembered the first time she sat with her face ten inches from the genitals of a male stranger. She had been a virgin, and the sum total of her experience with male genitalia had been helping her uncle castrate hogs on the family farm in the summer. The only naked male bodies she'd ever seen were glimpses of her brother, her cousins, and her father on occasions when she had accidentally opened the bathroom door without knocking. As a new medical student, her first male exam was mortifying. Her goal today was to keep her instruction clinical and professional.

"Okay, Mr. Richards," Elizabeth told him. "You will feel me touch your genitals now." Her tone changed as she addressed the students. "First, students, we inspect the skin. Always look at everything. You can diagnose skin cancer, fungal infections, and genital warts just by looking. Any skin that is exposed on any patient should be carefully examined for disease. Skin can tell you a great deal about a person's health."

She continued, "Next, we will palpate the testicles, scrotum, and groin." Elizabeth reached out and tugged very gently on the patient's right testicle. "You have to feel all the structures of the testicle. On the back side is a structure called the epididymis. It wraps around the back of the testicle. Carefully feel all the structures of the spermatic cord. The spermatic cord comes out of the abdomen, runs along the inguinal area, and supplies the arteries, veins, vas deferens, and nerve supply to the testicle. Next, you lightly pass your index finger up into the groin from the back of the scrotum and ask the patient to turn his head to the side and cough. This is the best way to check for a hernia," said Elizabeth.

"Be sure that you have short nails on that finger, ladies!" advised Mr. Richards.

The students grinned. One tried to suppress a laugh.

"Yes, thank you for that tip, Mr. Richards," said Elizabeth. "It is very important for doctors to have short, clean nails." She went back to her narration. "Next, have the patient bear down as if he were having a bowel movement while you keep your finger high in the groin. This maneuver checks for hernia from the abdominal wall. These physical examinations are conducted on both sides."

"Then we move to the penis," she continued. "You will notice Mr. Richards is uncircumcised. Be very careful to inspect the skin that covers the penis and to gently pull the skin back to expose the head of the penis and to look inside the urethra. Putting a gentle stretch on the penis will assure that you see all the skin from the pubic hair to the end," she instructed.

The genteel old man stood straight and tall, his genitals exposed to the group. He smiled with pride. The students' eyes were wide, and their expressions were intense.

"You are doing an excellent job, Mr. Richards. Could you please turn around and bend over the exam table so that I can examine your anus, rectum, and prostate, sir?" asked Elizabeth.

"Sure, ma'am," he replied. "That is the *raison d'etre* of every old man, the yearly probing of the anus. I got my first finger-wave at age eighteen when I joined the army. God only knows what they could have been looking for back then." He giggled as he flipped up the back of his shirt and ceremoniously bent over to expose his white, flaccid backside.

"Again, students," Elizabeth directed, "we are observing the skin. Many men have hair around their anus. You want to be very careful not to pull that hair when you go inside the anus to examine the prostate. Make sure that you have plenty of lubrication on your glove, instruct the patient to take slow, deep breaths, and go in slowly. Be aware that a particularly anxious man will hyperventilate and cause himself to faint. So, while you are paying close attention to what you are palpating with your finger, help the patient to relax by reminding him to take deep breaths. Move slowly to ensure that you do not startle the patient," said Elizabeth.

Mr. Richards turned around and grinned. "When Mikey is doing the exam, all us guys know to make sure that both his hands are not on our shoulders when we feel something enter our rectum!"

The students' eyes popped open in unison. Every mouth made an O formation. Fortunately, no one uttered a word. Two of the students were beet red and glowing. Jalpa Patel had perspiration above her lip and seemed not to understand the patient's joke.

Elizabeth was shocked, but chose to ignore the comment. As a student, she had learned that when patients were frightened or uneasy, they frequently made inappropriate comments. Also, it seemed acceptable for veterans to poke fun at their own. *Unlike the gallows humor of Charity,* she observed, *humor is more ironic at the VA.* New Orleans seemed to bring out the playfulness in everyone. She never realized there was so much comedy in medicine.

"Mr. Richards, please take several slow, deep breaths, and try to relax your bottom. I will now enter your rectum, sir," said Elizabeth.

"Oh, joy!" cackled the old veteran.

"Students, it is important that you remember to always feel for cancers of the anus and the prostate," Elizabeth continued. "You will need to push a little to get to the end of the prostate. Many older men have very large prostates, but Mr. Richards' is a little on the small side."

Upon hearing that remark, Mr. Richards spun around. His face had turned red and his features were contorted. As he shook with anger, his penis bobbled in Elizabeth's face. "Young woman, I am an elderly man," he told her. "For your information, I am one of the best-endowed men in the Veteran's Home. Nobody, other than a couple of younger black veterans, has more than I do in the manhood department!"

Elizabeth was flabbergasted. As she quickly pushed back her rolling stool, she ran over the foot of Marianne, the future dermatologist. The student yelped loudly.

Still sitting on the rolling stool, Elizabeth leaned against the wall with the dirty glove that had just been in the patient's rectum, waving in front of her face.

"Sir, please forgive me," she implored. "I was not speaking of the size of your penis; I was talking about your prostate gland. It is a sign of youth for your prostate to be small. A smaller prostate is very desirable, Mr. Richards. Young men usually have small prostates, sir," said Elizabeth. She felt panic and embarrassment. *I'm the teacher. How could I be so insensitive?*

"Young lady, I faced down the Japs in 1941. I never expected to be demeaned in my own damn country," said the elderly veteran as he jerked his seersucker jacket, with an American flag lapel pin, from the hands of the student who held it.

"Mr. Richards, *please* accept my apology," Elizabeth said. "I did not intend to upset you. You are completely normal. I am sorry if I miscommunicated. This is my first time teaching this course!" she said, by way of explanation. Her eyes pleaded with Mr. Richards.

Mr. Richards was not placated by her penitence. He rushed out of the exam room, gathering his clothing as he went. Elizabeth slumped, dejected. As he moved down the hall, she heard him say, "Mikey Sherman, that one needs some lessons in manners. She told those girls that I was *small*, for God's sake! Everybody knows that's a damn lie!"

As Elizabeth shed the dirty glove and tried to recover her confidence and equilibrium, she heard Nurse Sherman say, "That's okay, baby, I will go in there and give it to her! I will make that girl sorry she ever messed with Owen Richards. I will beat her to a pulp."

Elizabeth hung her head and waited for Nurse Sherman. *If these students weren't here and I weren't responsible for setting a professional example, I'd be laughing hysterically,* she thought.

When Nurse Sherman entered the exam room, Elizabeth stood in front of the students and braced herself for humiliation. Instead, Nurse Sherman said kindly, "Honey, don't worry about him. He gets all dressed up so that he can get lots of compliments on how handsome he looks. The VA clinic, bingo, and his church are his only outings every week. All his friends have died. He gets bored waiting on Jesus to come for him. I was listening at the door," he told her. "You did nothing wrong. Mr. Richards is a little touchy because he used to be quite the hunk. He can't accept that he is old and dried up now. Short of asking him to marry you, you could not have given him enough attention. Please proceed, ladies. We have lots of men to see today," he reminded them.

Mr. Richards' tirade left Elizabeth feeling deflated and discouraged. *What else can go wrong?* She was tired of feeling inadequate. In fact, she was just plain tired. The enthusiasm and energy of the students had been keeping her alert, but now the fatigue of the last few weeks was starting to catch up with her. And so was her hunger.

Her goals changed. Teaching was secondary to basic animal needs for sleep and nourishment. She needed to finish the clinic and get some food. "We are behind schedule," she reminded the students. "Let's divide into groups. Each of you will examine one man and tell me of the findings in private. I will examine him after you finish. Lastly, we will have a group discussion." She smiled ruefully. "As you have seen, I have demonstrated perfectly what *not* to say. So remember to be extremely careful in your verbiage. Your patient is vulnerable. Who would like to go first?"

Sally, who was the only black student, raised her hand. "My mom is a nurse, and we went over this last night after dinner. I think I am ready." Elizabeth admired her spunk. Women were rare in medicine, but black women were the rarest.

"Nurse Sherman, please put one man in each of these last three exam rooms. We will try to pick up the pace a bit," Elizabeth told him.

"Great, I have three wonderful candidates," he said. "Each has known urologic pathology. Each man is over seventy years old and should be perfect for the job."

Jalpa looked terrified but determined. Elizabeth knew anticipating a new experience was always worse than having it, so she chose Jalpa to lead the first group. "Jalpa Patel, please go in Room One with the students standing beside you and examine the patient. After all three of you have examined him, return to the hall, and I will evaluate you," said Elizabeth. She said a silent prayer that Jalpa would not faint.

The rest of the students were divided into three groups. Elizabeth stayed with the third group in the room where Mr. Richards had been examined. Nurse Sherman ushered in the next patient. He was over six-and-a-half feet tall, and he smelled like an ashtray. His hair and nails were long and unkempt. His clothes did not match, and his teeth were sparse.

"Morning, y'all. I am Frank Brown. All I want is a plastic pecker. Mine don't work so good after the war. Mikey has it on order, and I have to wait my turn. He says my pecker don't work 'cause I smoke too much, but I know it was the stress of the war. My pecker worked just fine till I went to Korea," said the patient.

Meili Chen, an Asian student that smelled of jasmine, sat on the rolling exam stool and copied Elizabeth's exam technique. Her shiny, thick black hair hung down over her arms. Meili instructed the patient clearly, and he complied. The contrast between his poor grooming and the student's crisp cleanliness was stark.

Because the man was tall and the student was short, his genitals were at the level of her forehead, and she struggled to reach up to examine him. Elizabeth noticed white lace peeking from the sleeves of the student's white coat. The lace was about an inch away from the man's anus.

Elizabeth made a mental note to coach the students on proper attire for clinic. She remembered how her clothes had been ruined repetitively until she accepted the earthiness of the doctor's job and changed her wardrobe. *That's another big difference between the doctors on TV and real doctors.*

As Meili finished her examination of Mr. Brown with surprising efficiency and skill, Elizabeth was startled by a loud knocking on the exam door.

"Excuse me," said Elizabeth, opening the door a crack.

Standing on the other side, visible through the crack, was Jalpa, looking hysterical. "It is not wrinkled!" she exclaimed.

"What are you saying?" asked Elizabeth. "What is not wrinkled?"

Jalpa's head bobbed from right to left like a frantic metronome. "Dr. Roberts, *it is no longer wrinkled*. What do I do when it is no longer wrinkled?"

"I don't understand," said Elizabeth.

Jalpa exclaimed in a very heavy Indian accent, "Madame, it is not wrinkled! *It* is not wrinkled!" As her level of panic rose, she switched to her native language and spoke louder.

Elizabeth had no idea what the girl was saying or what language she was speaking. *Hindi, maybe?* "Please excuse me. And thank you, sir," she said to the patient. As she took off her examination gloves and squeezed through the partly open door, she said, "Students, meet me in the hall."

Jalpa was apoplectic. Her head was still bobbing. She looked angrily at Elizabeth and said, "You did not tell me what to do when it was no longer wrinkled!"

Mikey walked up behind her and asked, "Did that old fart get an erection? I really did not think he was capable."

Elizabeth saw the wink and the grin and knew that Mikey had been hoping for this moment.

Sally spoke up. "Jalpa went first. As soon as she touched him, that thing came up right in her face like a cobra waiting to spit. Jalpa has short arms and could not get anywhere near his groin without putting her face right next to his erection," Sally explained. "The patient had the good sense to look embarrassed, and I do not think that he did it on purpose." She grinned. "But the thing just hung in midair, and it would not go down, Dr. Roberts! It danced a jig right there in front of poor Jalpa's face."

Jalpa looked angry and betrayed.

Chalking it up to her extreme fatigue, Elizabeth realized she had forgotten to talk to the students about the proper way to handle an inadvertent erection. She also realized she had taken it for granted that Mikey would have chosen impotent men for the demonstration. But maybe Mikey needed a little fun in his day, too.

All of the students had gathered in the hall around Elizabeth, waiting for further instruction.

Like her favorite teacher from medical school always said, "Anything that happens creates a teaching moment." So teach she would.

"Let's go to the back of the clinic and talk about what happened," said Elizabeth.

Elizabeth entered the last exam room on the hall, and when everyone was crowded in, she closed the door. Nurse Mikey had rushed into the room at the last minute, determined not to miss the show.

Immediately, Jalpa began talking. "One minute it was hanging there all wrinkled and the next it was sticking straight up and bobbing before my face. I could not get anywhere near what I needed to examine. It seemed to follow my every move. Is that what they all do?"

Elizabeth fought back a belly laugh. Mikey did not attempt to control himself. As he slapped his thighs and roared with laughter, his orange mop of hair shook and his sage-green eyes glistened with tears.

Jalpa did not find it funny. Elizabeth bit her lower lip to gain control as she attempted to reestablish propriety.

"Jalpa, this is a natural response," Elizabeth said with all the dignity she could muster. "Some men get erections when they don't really want to get them. Sometimes a man's penis will get erect when you are trying to examine him. It happens almost all the time in children and younger men. What should we do when it happens?" said Elizabeth, addressing the group.

Sally said, "Thump it! A quick hard thump is required." She explained, "You have to thump it real hard to make it go down as soon as possible. The harder it gets the less likely it is to go down." Sally looked proud, and Elizabeth wondered where she had learned that piece of advice.

Elizabeth was frustrated. "No, Sally, that is absolutely *not* what you should do. What you are describing is akin to assault. You do not assault your patient," said Elizabeth.

The students stood at full attention, their eyes on Elizabeth. "The best thing to do when a patient gets an erection is to ignore it," Elizabeth told them. "Just act like it is not happening. As long as the man is not making lewd or inappropriate comments, he is probably as mortified as you are. An erection is a natural phenomenon. It happens more when you first start to examine men. They can tell that you are not yet proficient in your examination. You are probably touching them very softly, and you do not appear professional. So as time goes by, and you do more exams, it will happen less and less. But if it does happen, just ignore it and continue. Usually when they turn around for the rectal part, it will start to go down. If you feel really embarrassed when a male gets an erection, do the rectal exam first, change gloves, and then examine the front of the man," said Elizabeth.

Jalpa's face was red and her ears were glowing pink. "How am I to move it out of the way to get to the groin area? It was sticking up in my face, and I felt dizzy at the sight." Mikey made no attempt at restraint. He was laughing openly as tears continued to run into his scraggly mustache.

Elizabeth struggled to maintain her composure. "You have to move your face and your body slightly to the side, and position yourself at an angle so that the penis is pointing over your shoulder and not right in your face," said Elizabeth.

"I have never seen one before," said Jalpa, "and I don't really care to see another one, at this point." Looking to her fellow students, she asked, "Was that one larger than most?"

Nurse Sherman continued to bend over, slap his thighs, and laugh audibly. Tears were flowing freely down his cheeks.

"Honey," he gasped, "an erect penis can be anywhere from four inches to fourteen inches. His was about average at six inches. But don't you worry; many Indian men tend to run a little on the small side." He was still giggling as he left the exam room.

Now the entire group was laughing, including Jalpa. Elizabeth knew she and Nurse Sherman were supposed to be in charge. But he had left and Elizabeth couldn't quit laughing. Sally and Marianne had tears running down their faces from laughing so hard. Meili was wiping her face with tissue and still laughing.

Finally, Elizabeth fought to regain control.

"Students, we have learned a great deal today," she told them. "Let's review. Remember to never make any comment of any type in front of the patient regarding his or her anatomy. As you saw today, your words can easily be taken out of context." She paused, and then continued. "Remember to wear appropriate clothing. Wear clothes that can be washed. Keep jewelry to a minimum, particularly anything that dangles. Keep your sleeves shorter than your white coat sleeves. Examining patients can be an earthy job. Remember to treat everyone with dignity and kindness, and always ask before touching. Remember to expect the unexpected."

"Any questions?" said Elizabeth.

"I did not get to examine anyone," said Sally.

Elizabeth could only think of food and sleep.

"It is really important to me that I get to do the examination," said Sally.

Feeling the draw of doing her duty, Elizabeth said, "Okay, anyone who did not get to examine a patient, come by the ER during my shift and I will give you a private lesson. Bring your anatomy book and we will go over it all again."

"Cool, a private lesson works great," said Sally. Elizabeth thought, *They really do look like excited puppies.*

As they filed out of the exam room and into the hall, Elizabeth said, "And, ladies, if you remember nothing else from today, remember this: *no thumping*!"

When the last student had left the clinic, Elizabeth slumped against the wall, feeling she might fall sleep standing up. Mikey appeared with a cup of coffee and said, "You did great today. I think Miss Patel has successfully ruled out urology as her chosen specialty." He smiled. "Seriously, I am sorry about Mr. Richards' reaction; that old geezer surprised me. And sorry about that erection—he surprised us all! Jalpa's patient has been begging for a new plastic penile implant. I just struck his name off the list." Mikey shook his head.

"All these guys want the latest thing," he explained. "They are like a bunch of kids competing for a prize. They do not want another vet to get something they don't get. The government lets us implant ten penile prostheses per month at $6,000 each. My waiting list is eleven months long. Those implantable penile prostheses take up half my damn budget. Thanks for helping me reduce my list by one!

As the pair leaned against the clinic wall and sipped their institutional coffee, Nurse Mikey said, "I know you are dog-tired, baby. But Nurse Sherman considers this a successful clinic!"

CHAPTER 10
Gunshot Wound to the Chest

Elizabeth left the back door of the Veterans Administration Hospital and crossed the street to the back door of Charity Hospital New Orleans. When she accepted her internship in Surgery, she knew that meant she would have grueling twenty-four-hour shifts in the trauma emergency room, but she did not know that she would be working at clinics at Charity and the VA Medical Center and at private clinics at Tulane Medical Center on the mornings after her trauma shifts. She knew surgical training was harder than medical training, but she failed to take into account the staffing issues involved. If doctors who were scheduled to work the clinics were in the operating room doing emergency surgeries, then the doctors who were supposed to be sleeping had to fill in at the clinics.

Now it was five in the evening. She had worked twenty-four hours in the ER and eight hours at the VA urology clinic. She was exhausted, and she moved like a sleepwalker. The world around her was hazy and indistinct. Her stomach growled unremittingly, and she coveted her bed.

She hadn't realized thirty-two-hour days would frequently be expected of her. She intended to retrieve her overnight bag and go home to sleep for a few hours before her next shift in the major trauma area at Charity.

As Elizabeth walked through the door, Aoife, the nurse at the triage desk, called out, "Hey, doc, did you teach those girl doctors to *thump it?*"

Elizabeth came out of her fog and laughed, again amazed by the gossip mill that was the hospital system. Before she could walk from one building to the other, word of her latest adventures was spreading. The escapades of new doctors and medical students were wildly entertaining to the permanent hospital staff.

As she approached the elevators, bone-crushing fatigue settled in. She had never been so weary. Miss Albertha was running the elevator today. "Hey, baby," she greeted Elizabeth. "You look like The Big Free done took a bite out of you! You okay, girl? You are skinnier than you were just four days ago. What you been eating, honey?"

"I am fine, Miss Albertha. Let's sing some gospel while you take me to the on-call room. I think I need a nap before I try to drive home," said Elizabeth.

The old elevator doors clanged shut, and the car lurched upward. Elizabeth held the railing. Being with Miss Albertha gave Elizabeth a sense of peace and grounding in something sweet and pure and untainted. Elizabeth breathed deeply, smelled Miss Albertha's lemon-and-sunshine smell, and relaxed.

"Amazing grace, how sweet the sound," sang Miss Albertha as the elevator doors closed. She and Elizabeth belted out the words together, singing "that saved a wretch like me, I once was lost, but now I'm found, was blind but now I see." Being alone in the elevator with Miss Albertha was as comfortable as sitting on the front porch at the farm with Grandmother.

Elizabeth felt revived by singing and the soothing sound of Miss Albertha's powerful voice. As she inserted her key in the on-call room door's lock, she remembered a surprise she had brought for her roommates.

The on-call room was empty. Elizabeth chuckled as she eyed the pin-up girls on the walls. She had left her overnight bag in the on-call room, as always. She opened her bag and removed two black-and-white photos of the lowland gorilla she had studied when she was researching endangered species as an undergraduate. She loved this gorilla and reveled in removing a few of the pictures of naked women over her bed to hang photos of the gorilla in their place. Dr. Michael LeBlanc claimed the pin-ups were their inspiration. Elizabeth had decided to add her inspiration, a body she admired—a giant silverback male lowland gorilla. *Gorilla gorilla* was now pinned up right next to Miss June 1975.

As she taped the second gorilla photo above her bed, Elizabeth tumbled face first, still in her clothes, on the bed with the roll of tape clutched in her hand, under her torso at the level of her waist. She was completely asleep before her face hit the bed. She awoke nine hours later when she heard Michael LeBlanc exclaim, "What the hell!"

She turned over onto her back, felt a nasty cramp in her neck from sleeping in a distorted position, tasted yesterday's vending machine food in her mouth, saw the sun peeking through the window, peeled the roll of tape off her abdomen, and became panic-stricken, all in the same five seconds. She did not remember falling into bed, and realized it was the first time in her life that she had not brushed her teeth and washed her face before going to sleep.

"Oh, my God, I am going to be late!" cried Elizabeth as she leaped from the bed and ran to the bathroom. She was happy to find her Clinique face soap as she had left it, unused by the men.

She heard Michael say, "You have defamed our wall of inspiration by putting monkey pictures next to the most beautiful women alive! How could you? I knew they should have never let women in this program. What sacrilege!" Elizabeth laughed as she brushed her teeth.

She stuck her head around the bathroom door, holding the toothbrush like a baton, and said through a mouthful of toothpaste, "Well, Michael, different things inspire different people. For me, it is gorillas. Please do not call them monkeys. They are among God's most amazing creatures. Someday I'll tell you all about them."

In a hurry as usual, she made her way to the door of the on-call room. "Have a good day," she said to Michael. "I am headed back to the trauma suite." She wondered how often she'd never make it home.

"You'd better get to it. I heard from the LSU guy that there was a gunshot wound to the heart coming in, and *you know who* will be there and on your case, pronto!" said Michael as he threw himself on his bed.

Elizabeth decided not to wait for the elevator and ran down the stairs to the trauma suite. She had learned how to hold onto the railing and skip four to five steps at a time, throwing herself down ten steps while only touching two. It felt a bit like flying, she imagined. Forty flights later, she passed breathless through the swinging doors of the trauma emergency room and ran right into Nurse Robichaud.

The nurse's hand was on her haughty hip, and her eyes drilled into Elizabeth.

"How nice of you to join us, Crème Puff. Were you tanning at the local spa? God knows you need it," she sneered.

Elizabeth looked up at the clock. It was only six-thirty. She had thirty minutes until she was officially late, but she knew that she would have to hustle to catch up. *Will I ever be able to make the mark in this job? Nothing I do ever seems good enough!* thought Elizabeth.

"Where is Dr. Lambert, the LSU charge?" asked Elizabeth, still breathless from the stairs.

"Well, right this minute he is pinned down by none other than Dr. Harrison Lloyd White III. Dr. White heard there might be a gunshot wound to the chest coming in around turnover time, and he magically appeared," said Nurse Robichaud.

"Which room?" asked Elizabeth.

"You have been here a while and you still don't know where the major trauma goes?" Nurse Robichaud replied. "You people get dumber every year, I swear! Room *Four*. All major traumas go to Room *Four*." She looked exasperated. "They are reviewing the Advanced Trauma Life Support algorithm, which all Tulane personnel learn in orientation. I hope to God you remember it, because if you don't, Dr. White will be on you like white on rice this morning," she warned. Nurse Robichaud handed her a cup of thick black chicory coffee as she walked away.

As Elizabeth headed for Room Four, Nurse Robichaud added, "You should have been here two hours ago."

There was no job like Tulane Surgery. A seven o'clock shift meant different things on different days. Elizabeth needed to be in the ER early enough to know everything that was going on before anyone from the Tulane faculty arrived. Since she was sleeping when the ER was filling up, she had no way of knowing what awaited her and she certainly had no way to know when the professors would arrive. It often seemed that Dr. McSwain and Dr. White never went home. Unless she stayed awake twenty-four hours a day, there was no way to *be on time…* Elizabeth hated being late and didn't remember ever having been considered late until she came to Tulane. Now it seemed she was always late, always behind. There was just too much work to do, and not enough time to rest. The sheer volume of work was overwhelming. Nobody could do it all in one shift. *Everybody has to sleep sometime.* If only she could figure out how to learn everything she needed to know and not die of starvation in the process. *When was the last time I ate?*

Elizabeth was wrinkled and her head felt foggy. She had not changed into scrubs after yesterday's VA clinic, and she was wearing the clothes from the day before, the ones she'd slept in. She trotted into Room Four to find Dr. Adrien Lambert, Dr. Harrison White, and Dr. Norman McSwain standing in front of a chalkboard.

Dr. McSwain was explaining a new algorithm for treating gunshot wounds to the chest. Dr. McSwain was an innovator in trauma care, and he routinely worked with police departments, emergency medical personnel, and the military worldwide to determine the best methods for handling major trauma.

McSwain said, "Everyone knows major trauma deaths occur in the first few minutes due to blood loss. But among the patients who make it to the hospital, there are protocols that need to be followed to ensure that the largest number of people survives."

Adrien was the only LSU doctor in the room. His eyes cast rapidly back and forth to the door of Room Four. Elizabeth sensed he was looking for support in this sea of Tulane doctors.

Everyone ignored Elizabeth. Dr. McSwain addressed Dr. White. "So, Harrison, if the patient's blood pressure drops below 60 systolic, even if the pulse is strong and the patient is awake and talking, we are going to open the chest.

We know he has been shot near the heart, and we know that the lungs and major vessels are contiguous. So our new protocol is to open him up right here, put a big clamp across the largest artery in the chest, and try to keep his heart from stopping until we can get him to the operating room."

Dr. White's arms were crossed over his chest as he listened. He focused intently on the chalkboard and Dr. McSwain.

"This is going to be technically very difficult, Dr. McSwain," White said. "Cross-clamping the aorta in the emergency room would be extremely tough. Even when the patient is under general anesthesia it is not the easiest thing to do. When the patient is conscious, it could be much more difficult. Trying to open the chest, expose the major blood vessels to the heart, and clamp the aorta, down here with new recruits who can't even get to work on time, is a recipe for disaster," said Dr. White.

Elizabeth felt a cold chill run down her spine as the cardiothoracic fellow glanced her way. She felt piercing daggers shooting from his startling blue eyes.

Dr. McSwain said, "Well, that is why we are doing a quick run-through before they bring him in. We want all hands on deck and everyone to know what their job will be. We do not make progress in trauma surgery by being faint of heart. Saving lives is always dramatic. I've done this in the field, and it works well."

Dr. White looked down at the floor and accepted the advice of his professor. He did not look happy with the plan. But he looked resigned.

Adrien squirmed and shuffled behind Elizabeth as he addressed Dr. McSwain: "It is 7:10 a.m., sir, and I have to leave for the LSU cancer clinic." Elizabeth noticed he did not look at all sorry to be leaving Room Four after his long shift.

"Okay, son, head out. But you are going to miss all the action," said Dr. McSwain. To Elizabeth, Dr. McSwain looked like a kid at Christmas waiting to unwrap his red toy truck.

"Yes, sir," said Dr. Lambert. "I really hate to leave, but I am the designated clinic dog today."

As Adrien sped out the door, he whispered to Elizabeth, "Good luck, you're going to need it." From the emergency room hall, Elizabeth heard Nurse Robichaud yell, "Room Four, everyone! Get to your positions." As the trauma charge resident, Elizabeth bolted to her place at the head of the examination table. All surgery interns had to pass Advanced Trauma Life Support modules. They had practiced on dummies and acted the steps to the support of a patient in any trauma scenario.

Ten medical personnel amped with adrenaline flooded through the doors of Room Four, taking preassigned positions. Each patient was always a little different, but everyone had practiced their roles during teaching sessions with Dr. McSwain.

The swinging doors burst open and four emergency medical technicians wheeled a smiling black man in the door. The patient was strapped on a bright orange board with hand holes that made it easy to carry. Five thick black straps secured the patient at his ankles, thighs, waist, chest, and head. His upper body was naked, and an entrance wound from a bullet was visible just below his right nipple. His lower body, from ankles to waist, was covered in a pneumatic compression device. It looked like a giant black girdle.

Elizabeth knew Dr. McSwain had pioneered the use of the pneumatic compression device, which forced the blood from the lower body to the vital organs of the heart and brain in a patient who had experienced serious trauma and significant blood loss. Emergency medical personnel in the field and in triage areas of military medical facilities had little to offer a patient with serious injury prior to the development of this lifesaving compression device.

Treatment for trauma started in the field. Before arriving at the trauma emergency room, the well-trained EMTs would have started large intravenous lines in multiple locations, stopped bleeding where possible, poured in large amounts of fluid to sustain the circulatory system, supported respiration, and diverted blood from nonessential organs to the heart and brain.

As the patient was placed gently on the table in the center of the room, a swarm of nurses, doctors, and medical students surrounded him from every direction. A New Orleans police officer stood wedged in a corner. Elizabeth recognized Alois Thibodeaux from her first day at The Big Free. He nodded in her direction. Thibodeaux had dark, saggy bags under his eyes, and he slumped with his fatigue. He had aged visibly in the few months since Elizabeth's first day. Elizabeth wondered why.

An excited EMT, whose name tag identified him as Rob, gave Dr. McSwain a report about the events prior to coming to the hospital. Nurse Aoife called out, "His blood pressure is 100 over 70, and his pulse is steady at 94, doctors!"

"Dr. Roberts, get over here and put the Foley catheter in the patient's bladder," shouted Dr. McSwain. Elizabeth knew she was being given the job of the medical student as public punishment for her tardiness. Nobody liked inserting a catheter in the penis of a conscious patient.

Suddenly the patient looked up into the face of Dr. White and said, "Hey, Doc White, how you doing, man? I ain't seen you in a while."

The surprised doctor looked closer and said, "Mac Jenkins, what in the world are you doing back in here? I took a bullet out of your heart two years ago! I thought we'd turned you into an honest man!"

Dr. McSwain said, "Harrison, are you kidding me? Has this guy had a gunshot wound to the heart before?"

"Yes, sir, he sure has," Dr. White replied. "The last time we had to put him on cardiopulmonary bypass and open his heart to get the bullet out. He almost did not make it."

The patient's head was still strapped to the board. He looked up at the ceiling, grinned, and laughed.

"Yep, Dr. White is one stubborn dude. Every time I opened my eyes in that ICU, there he was staring at me with those big baby blues, willing me to make it. You would have thought I was his first-born child," laughed Mac Jenkins.

As Dr. White talked to the patient and Dr. McSwain, the X-ray team took a chest X-ray, the interns placed larger IV lines in case fluids and blood had to be given quickly, and Elizabeth inserted the catheter to monitor the patient's urine output. When the catheter tube passed his prostate, Mr. Jenkins pulled against his restraints and yelled, "Is that tube absolutely necessary? I am shot in the heart! Ain't nothing wrong with my manhood! Doc White, tell that lady to let go of my bird!"

Everyone ignored him and continued to work.

"I've been at this a long time," said Dr. McSwain, "and I cannot recall anyone shot in the heart twice who did not die."

Dr. White again leaned over the patient and asked, "What happened, Mr. Jenkins?"

"Well, doc, my wife is mean. She thought I was doing it with the neighbor, and she shot me! She's sitting outside in the waiting room, crying her eyes out because she loves me, but she is a passionate woman and jealous as can be. Of course, I ain't pressing no charges on her with the police. She's the one in pink foam curlers and the fluffy pink house shoes. She did not even take time to get dressed." He grimaced. "My chest hurts like hell, doc. It feels just like last time. That bullet is rattling around in my heart, doc," he said.

"Blood pressure 80 over 40 and pulse 120," shouted the assistant nurse. "His blood gas oxygen measurement is low, too."

"This cannot be happening twice," said Dr. White, shaking his head. "Get that chest X-ray to me immediately! Dr. Roberts, get your gown and gloves on and get that chest saw set up, *stat*! Nurse Robichaud, make sure everything is on the emergency cart. Once we start, there will be no sending out for anything. This maneuver will quickly go well, or *not*!"

Mr. Jenkins had stopped talking. His eyes were focused on a spot on the ceiling. His grin was gone, and his body had stopped pulling against the restraints.

Elizabeth was opening the sterile instruments, the students and nurses were pushing fluids in the patient, and all the junior members of the team were holding their breath in anticipation.

Dr. White looked at Dr. McSwain and said, "His heart is going to be stuck to the back of his sternum with scar tissue. It will be extremely hard to release his heart from the sternum without sawing through the heart in the process. Are you sure that you want to do it here?"

"Well, son," McSwain replied, "I'd say forget the protocol and let's go upstairs, but the operating rooms are full. The LSU boys have been running every room in this place for the last three hours." He addressed Nurse Robichaud. "Livvy, call upstairs and see if anybody is close to finishing their case."

As Dr. White slapped the chest X-ray on the viewing box, he whistled. "Dr. McSwain, the bullet is in the right atrium. Every time the heart beats, it moves with the motion of the heart. On each X-ray, it is in a different location, which means the bullet is bouncing around in his heart. It is a matter of time before he bleeds to death or this bullet gets lodged somewhere and obstructs the pumping of his blood. This is not going anywhere good."

Elizabeth thought, *Mr. Jenkins diagnosed himself.*

"I can't get his blood pressure, doctors! I repeat, I cannot get a blood pressure reading!" shouted the assistant nurse.

"Nobody is near finishing, Dr. McSwain," reported Nurse Robichaud. "All the operating rooms are full. We have no place to take this patient," she said as she hung up the phone.

Dr. McSwain said, "Okay, Dr. White. It is up to you, man. If anybody can get this guy's aorta cross-clamped in time to keep him from dying or being a vegetable, it is you. Go for it now!"

Dr. White glared at Elizabeth and said, "Intern, step to the other side of the table and do *exactly* as I tell you, and do it fast!"

"Yes, sir," said Elizabeth. Her heart raced. *This is why I wanted to come to Charity Hospital!*

"Intubate him immediately!" shouted McSwain to Elizabeth. She had practiced intubation many times and the tube went in easily.

"Pour betadine all over his chest!" Dr. White commanded Elizabeth. She complied.

"Hand me that scalpel," Dr. White instructed. "And be ready to cover the wound with gauze sponges as soon as I make the cut. Apply pressure to the bleeders, Dr. Roberts."

Elizabeth had never felt so alive.

She watched the cardiothoracic fellow move with unbelievable precision and speed. No movement was wasted. Every instruction was evenly orchestrated. Dr. White made a deep cut— one quick, deep, and graceful slash with the scalpel— from the notch at the top of the patient's breastbone to the end of his breastbone, just above the abdomen, completely exposing the patient's sternum. Mr. Jenkins screamed and lost consciousness. His blood flowed over Elizabeth's and Dr. White's gloved hands.

Elizabeth's stomach churned, and she suddenly felt dizzy. The patient's scream echoed in her head.

"Hand me the saw, intern," said Dr. White. She picked up the sterile chest saw. It looked like a heavy metal handgun with a right-angled hook at the end. Elizabeth thought, *This thing looks too indelicate to be anywhere near the heart,* as she handed the instrument to Dr. White.

Room Four was humming with energy. The members of the medical team knew their jobs and quickly performed them. Aoife breathed for the patient by hand with the Ambu bag. Dr. McSwain stood ready with the open-heart cardiac paddles to shock the heart directly if needed. The nurses constantly monitored the vital signs. Even the novices knew the next moments would determine whether the patient's heart would be sawed apart and inoperable, or whether he might have a chance to live.

Without Dr. White's heroic efforts, Mr. Jenkins' chance of living was zero. Opening his chest increased his odds of survival to 5 percent. Quiet tension prevailed in the room.

Elizabeth pressed sterile gauze against the skin edges and watched as Dr. White pushed his gloved left index finger behind Mr. Jenkins' breastbone, pushing his heart and the scar tissue from his prior surgery away from the underside of the breastbone as he sawed the bone to open the chest cavity with his right hand. Elizabeth felt goose bumps creep up her arms as she watched the handsome man work his magic. She had never seen such focus and determination.

"Intern, wake up!" Dr. White instructed, interrupting her reverie. "Keep pressure on those small, oozing blood vessels. This patient cannot tolerate losing any more blood."

His elbow was pressed into Elizabeth's arm as he forcefully guided the chest saw through the sternum to expose the heart. She leaned under his armpit to apply additional pressure on the skin edges. Elizabeth realized Dr. White had apparently abandoned earlier his starched white coat to a hook in the corner, and she saw his arms were thin for a man and very pale. In this moment, Dr. White was the only thing between Mr. Jenkins and death. Dr. McSwain and Nurse Robichaud were squeezing bags of blood into both of the patient's arms, while a medical student squeezed a bag of IV fluid. The race against exsanguination—bleeding to death—was on. *Could the team get blood into the patient faster than he was bleeding it out?*

The EMTs stood silently by, watching in awe. None of them had ever seen a chest opened in the emergency room. Their actions in the field had allowed Mr. Jenkins to survive to this point, and they weren't leaving until they witnessed the outcome. "Dr. McSwain, the heart is free from the sternum, and so far I have not cut into it," Dr. White said. "Dr. Roberts, hand me those long forceps." Elizabeth complied. "Now pull open the chest with that small metal retractor. Crank it open slowly, to avoid breaking his ribs," said Dr. White.

Elizabeth grabbed from the sterile tray an instrument that resembled a medieval torture tool. She placed the end of it through the opening in the chest cavity and cranked it open to slowly reveal the man's heart. She placed gauze sponges all along the edges of the cavity, under the retractor, to try to stem the bleeding with pressure from the retractor.

The sight of an open chest with the heart not beating, an inch from her fingers, overwhelmed Elizabeth. The beauty and awe-inspiring complexity of the human body never failed to amaze her. *How could anyone not believe there is a great, organizing power behind all of life? It is just too wondrous to be random.*

Elizabeth was holding pressure on every small oozing artery and vein that the edges of the retractor did not cover. Her hands were becoming numb, but nothing could make her let go.

Dr. White injected a large dose of epinephrine through a large needle, directly into the patient's exposed heart, and called for more epinephrine to be given intravenously. Dr. White put the intrathoracic resuscitation paddles directly on Mr. Jenkins' exposed heart and yelled "Everyone stand back!" as he attempted cardiac resuscitation.

"It's a no-go, Dr. McSwain," called Dr. White. "His heart is still not pumping, sir." But White wasn't giving up. "We're going again," called Dr. White, as he shocked the patient again. "Hand me that large clamp, Dr. Roberts! I am going to try to cross-clamp his aorta and see if we can get enough blood to stay in his heart to prime the pump to start pumping again."

Elizabeth stabilized the retractor with one hand and handed Dr. White a fourteen-inch-long clamp with the other. He reached deep into the man's chest cavity and clamped the aorta. Mr. Jenkins' heart began to quiver. Elizabeth could tell that Dr. White could not see the big blood vessel—he was able to do the maneuver by his memory of anatomy and by feel. His prowess amazed her.

"Hold that clamp and keep it steady," Dr. White told her. "No matter what else might happen in here, intern, your primary job is that clamp. Hold it steady for me! Hold that clamp like your life depends on it."

Elizabeth's mouth was dry and she was speechless. She continued to blot oozing blood with one hand and hold the clamp across Mr. Jenkins' aorta with the other. Her focus was at its peak.

She noticed that the squirting from the arteries was becoming more intense, and the blood was a brighter red. Oxygen was getting to the vessels around the heart. Rather than quivering as it had been, the heart started pumping.

Dr. White placed a long pair of the giant tweezers called forceps through the hole made by the bullet into the right top part of the patient's heart and pulled out a .22-caliber bullet. The surgeon released a laugh as he dropped the bullet into a metal bowl on the table. The bullet made a loud clanging noise as it hit the stainless-steel bowl.

"Well, I'll be damned," laughed Dr. McSwain. "I thought for sure that I had seen it all! Good job, son. Good job."

The hole in the patient's heart started bleeding profusely. Dr. White used a miniature needle holder and suture so thin that it was nearly invisible to the naked eye to sew the hole closed. The rhythmic pumping of the patient's heart grew stronger.

"Keep that clamp steady, Dr. Roberts. I do not want to see that thing move a millimeter," said Dr. White.

"His blood pressure is at 90 over 60 and his pulse is 98, doctors!" said Aoife.

"Great! We are moving in the right direction," said Dr. White. "Everybody, stay focused. Nurse Robichaud, call the OR and tell them we are coming up. They will have to open the room that is reserved for the president. Ronald Reagan is not in New Orleans today, and I want that operating room for this man. I will not take *no* for an answer. I know it's available and ready. Make it happen."

Nurse Robichaud looked to Dr. McSwain for confirmation.

"Lavinia, you heard the man," said Dr. McSwain.

"Yes, sir, Dr. White," Nurse Robichaud said. "I already called them when it looked like this cat had ten lives," she admitted with a laugh.

"Stay focused, team. Dr. Roberts, do you think you can hang onto that clamp for a while in the OR?" asked Dr. White. "My team is working at Tulane, and I will need some assistance."

"Sir, I am assigned down here, and Dr. McSwain said I was never to leave my post," replied Elizabeth.

"That's right, intern," said Dr. McSwain. "You are assigned down here for the month. I will call the chief resident to help Dr. White, but you can hang onto that clamp until he gets here."

Trying to hide her disappointment at not being allowed to go to the OR, Elizabeth said, "Yes, sir."

For the first time in her life, Elizabeth felt hero worship. Her father had taught her that most people have positive and negative qualities, and that nobody is truly better than anybody else. But to Elizabeth that day, Dr. Harrison Lloyd White III was in a category all by himself. She had never witnessed such a cool head, steady hands, and complete command of a tough situation. Every fiber of her being wanted to be just like him. She vowed to never give him any reason to doubt her, and swore to herself that one day she would emulate him.

Dr. Edward Peterson appeared at the door and said, "What's going on in here, guys? Looks like you've got the intern in the right position, covered in blood and hanging off a clamp."

Nobody laughed. Once again Dr. Peterson, the chief surgical resident, was somewhere else when important work was happening.

"Unfortunately, you are going to have to take over that chest clamp," Dr. McSwain told Dr. Peterson. "Dr. Roberts has not had a chance to make rounds since the LSU guys went to clinic, and she needs to do that. God knows what could be going on down here."

Elizabeth's hands were numb, and she was covered in blood, as Dr. Peterson had correctly observed. She reluctantly transferred the bloody clamp and the patient on the other end of it to the care of Dr. Peterson, though she did not relish relinquishing that duty to someone she did not fully trust. She was totally invested in the outcome of this patient, and she detested handing over the clamp to her chief.

Dr. McSwain said, "Make sure you write this patient's case up, Edward. Even if the guy does not make it out of surgery, this needs to go in the journal. This lucky or unlucky guy, depending on how you look at it, has been shot in the right atrium of his heart twice. Both times the same doctor removed the bullet and saved his bacon! Just amazing! This is why I love Charity Hospital."

Elizabeth headed to the nurses' station to retrieve an extra set of clean scrubs that she kept under the desk. Alarming other patients with her bloody clothes was not acceptable.

As Elizabeth headed for the doors, flexing her fingers, she moved past Dr. White. He mumbled, "Good job, intern. Next time you crack the chest." Despite her resentment of having to stay in the ER, Elizabeth felt an exhilaration she had never known. Though her part in removing the bullet had been small, she felt ten feet tall as she floated out of the Room Four trauma suite to start her ER rounds.

CHAPTER 11
Dinner at Commander's Palace

Elizabeth was elated. It was like being high—or at least what she thought being high would feel like. She remembered hearing men in her medical school class talk about the runner's high, but she had never experienced that euphoric feeling until she saw Dr. White pull the bullet out of Mac Jenkins' heart. As she finished her shift and headed for the back doors of the emergency department, the triage nurse, Aoife, walked toward her, carrying a brown Schwegmann's grocery bag and sporting a grin on her face.

"Hi, Elizabeth," she greeted her. "I have a date-night outfit for you. My roommate is a sweetie and was willing to contribute to the cause of getting you a life outside the hospital."

She opened the bag to show Elizabeth a pretty black silk dress. It was simple but luxurious. Aoife removed the dress from the grocery bag to reveal a pair of strappy black sandals with two-inch heels. The heels were a little worn, but the sandals were quite usable. The dress was Elizabeth's size, a six, and the shoes were only a half-size too big at size nine.

"Thank you so much, Aoife. You have more faith in me than I do that I will actually have a date someday," said Elizabeth.

"Of course you'll have dates, silly," said Aoife.

"I am touched that your roommate, a perfect stranger, would loan me her expensive and beautiful dress. I am also touched that you would take time out of your busy schedule to bring me the outfit. Thank you so much," said Elizabeth.

"No problem. This is the good part of New Orleans. We care about each other here. You really do look like you could use a night off and a good meal. The Big Free will eat your soul if you let it. We all need to be reminded that life is more than drama, trauma, and death. A rich hunk taking you out for a good meal will be a nice diversion," said Aoife.

Little does she know sleep and food are my great daily lusts, thought Elizabeth.

"How does your roommate come to own such a nice dress?" asked Elizabeth.

"Vicky is a nursing student who works part-time at Mrs. Yvonne LaFleur's dress shop in uptown. Mrs. LaFleur is the most fashionable woman in New Orleans, and working in her shop is a dream come true for Vicky. I am not sure how much money she makes there. I think mostly Vicky puts dresses on layaway and works at the shop to pay them off. But she seems happy with the deal, and her third of the rent gets paid. That is what I care about," said Aoife.

"I will take excellent care of the dress and shoes. They will look great with my grandmother's pearls. Even if Dr. Cabellero never asks me out, at least I will have a good dress when the opportunity does arise," said Elizabeth.

"Oh, he is going to ask you out," Aoife assured her. "He is a dependable man. I think your problem will be too many invitations. Half the men at Tulane are already in love with you, Elizabeth. You are so blind to it." She smiled. "Livvy and I laugh all the time about how you never notice when a man is staring holes in you with desire. You are so focused on working and not getting fired that these poor lugs don't have a chance. You could marry a doctor in fifteen minutes if you tried even a little bit."

Here we go again, thought Elizabeth. Another woman was trying to get her to marry what she was trying so hard to be. She decided to focus on the sweet gesture of the loaned dress and ignore the marital advice. Elizabeth smiled warmly at Aoife.

"I think that I'll take this dress upstairs and store it in the on-call room, just in case an invitation comes on a day when I don't get to go home after my shift," said Elizabeth.

"Good idea," agreed Aoife. "But you need to go home more. Living, sleeping, and eating Charity Hospital is not a life. I will see you tomorrow," said the nurse as she walked back to the triage desk.

Four patients were lined up, waiting impatiently. Elizabeth turned from the doors and headed back down the hall to the elevators. She took a service elevator up to the on-call room. As she rode up, she noticed the worn, dark, used look of the elevator. Everything at Charity needed a coat of paint and a good cleaning. She felt dirty after her ER shift and decided to take a shower before going home.

She entered the on-call room and was happy to find it empty. Usually either Michael or Tony was there reading, napping, or—in Michael's case—calling girls. A few moments alone were welcome.

The warm water of the shower washed over her tense muscles and relaxed them. The sweet almond smell of her shampoo erased the antiseptic smell of the ER. Even though it was morning, she felt sleepy and relaxed. Her adrenaline rush from the bullet-to-the-heart patient had worn off. She walked toward her bed in her clean scrubs and freshly washed hair and fell in. She was deeply asleep in thirty seconds.

Six hours later, she awoke to her squawking beeper. It was the Tulane operator. "Please call Dr. Cabellero at extension 5445 at Tulane Medical Center. I repeat, please call Dr. Cabellero at extension 5445 at Tulane Medical Center."

Elizabeth always awoke feeling disoriented when she slept in the on-call room during the day. She never slept well away from home, and the rotating sleep cycles did not agree with her circadian rhythms. As she stood up and crossed the floor to reach for the big black phone that sat on a metal table between Tony's and Michael's beds, her fog started to clear.

While she dialed, she realized that this call was likely not about a patient. She was not rotating on neurosurgery, and the chief neurosurgery resident was unlikely to need an intern's advice. This was a social call. The thought filled her with equal parts dread and excitement. Elizabeth liked men and thought Dr. Cabellero attractive, but she did not enjoy dating. She always kept those feelings to herself, as it did not seem entirely normal not to enjoy dating, and most women her age seemed to live for it. If Elizabeth were completely honest with herself, she'd admit she preferred a hot bath and a book to a night on the town. *But I will have to marry one day, won't I?* thought Elizabeth. So date she would.

"Hello, Cabellero here," said the neurosurgeon.

"Hi, Dr. Cabellero, it's Elizabeth Roberts."

"Hello. I apologize for calling at the last minute, but I checked the emergency trauma room schedule and saw that you are off tonight. You do not seem to have an open night for three more weeks, and I was wondering if you would like to join me for dinner tonight. At six-thirty?" he asked.

Elizabeth looked at her Timex. It was five-thirty now. She had the dress. She never wore much makeup. Her hair was clean and she had clips in her bag to put it up. She frequently wore her hair up for church, so she knew styling it wouldn't take long. And she was ravenous.

"That sounds lovely. When and where shall I meet you?" said Elizabeth.

"I know this is unorthodox, and I apologize in advance, but could we meet at the side door of Charity at six-fifteen?" asked Dr. Cabellero. "I have to finish rounds and pick up my car from the private lot at Maison Blanche. I usually pick my dates up at their homes and not on the street," he added, "but we are pushed for time. Commander's is full tonight, and the only table that I could secure in the garden room was for six-thirty. I want you to see that room. It is beautiful."

"There is no need to apologize. I realize that these are unorthodox conditions," Elizabeth assured him. "I don't usually go out with men that I have only seen a few times. But if you are good enough for Tulane, I am sure that you are an upstanding person. I will see you on the street by the side door of Charity at six-fifteen, Dr. Cabellero. What car shall I expect?"

"I will be in a small black sports car. And please, call me Ernesto when we are away from the hospital," said Dr. Cabellero.

Elizabeth heard the implication that they would be away from the hospital more than this one time. Her stomach lurched. She knew girls from college who routinely went out with men they did not like, just for a free meal. Elizabeth had no patience for spending time with anyone whose company she did not enjoy. Hungry as she was, she hoped she would like Dr. Cabellero's company.

"Great! I will see you then," said Elizabeth. She had forty-five minutes to dress, more time than she ever took to dress for anything. Luckily, Aoife's roommate's black silky dress fit perfectly. A loose French twist was easy for her, and her hair looked acceptable tousled on top of her head and secured with bobby pins and clips. She found a pink lip gloss in the bottom of her overnight bag. She observed herself in the cracked mirror of the dark and dingy bathroom. *Skinnier than usual, but not half bad...*

She took the service elevator again, feeling embarrassed to be out of her white coat in the hospital. Dressed for a date at six o'clock seemed odd, too. But then, her entire intern life was odd. Time in the outside world had started to blur, and the rhythm of her hospital shift was her only clock. She waited in the humid evening, feeling very conspicuous in the black cocktail dress, for only a couple of minutes.

She heard his car before she saw it. The loud, aggressive rumble was unlike any sound she had ever heard coming from any vehicle. *It sounds more like a train than a car.* Elizabeth learned to drive on the farm, first a combine, then a tractor. Nobody in her family owned any vehicle like the car she was about to enter. On the side of the black shiny car was the word *CARRERA*. There were two seats in the tiny rocket, and the wheels were wide and low to the ground.

Dr. Cabellero swerved to the curb, jumped out of the car, and ran around to open the door on Elizabeth's side. He paused for a moment to appraise his date's appearance.

"Elizabeth, you look beautiful. Thank you for joining me for dinner."

Elizabeth felt a little pride at his compliment, but mostly she felt embarrassed. She wasn't used to praise for her appearance. Hard work impressed her family, not looks. A person's looks were of little import.

Ernesto Cabellero held the door of the sports car for her, and Elizabeth folded her long, lean frame into the low seat. She inhaled the smell of the beautifully worn leather interior.

Dr. Cabellero returned to the driver's seat and engaged the gears. The Porsche rocketed forward. Elizabeth was pressed back into her seat from the force of the acceleration. *Not like my car,* she thought. Her car puttered along hesitatingly as if it could not decide whether to move forward or not. Her car sounded more like a lawn mower than a train.

This car roared aggressively forward with no hesitation. When they took the first right turn, she nearly banged her head on the side window, as she had not anticipated the speed with which the car could negotiate a corner. Going fast was exciting and new.

Both doctors were quiet in the small space of the car. Elizabeth enjoyed the roar of the engine and the feeling of riding a tiger to dinner.

Opera played softly on the car radio. Elizabeth smelled the musky lime scent of Dr. Cabellero's cologne. She glanced at him and noticed his fresh haircut and clean-shaven face. She appreciated his attention to detail. His nails were square and clean, and his dark suit and white-cuffed shirt were immaculate. Elizabeth wondered how he managed to keep such nice clothes in his on-call room at Charity. She wondered if the on-call room accommodations improved as a young doctor moved up the chain of command. She guessed that going to dinner all dressed up on a weeknight was something he did regularly. In Elizabeth's world, dressing up and going to a nice restaurant was for special occasions. The men in her family usually only wore suits on Sunday.

The car turned onto St. Charles Avenue and headed into the uptown area of New Orleans. Elizabeth had not yet ventured into this part of town. Her driving, for the several months she'd been at Tulane, was limited to the route on Airline Highway to Charity Hospital, and she had little time, money, or energy for exploring the remainder of New Orleans. Her world was the hospital.

From the vantage point of the small sports car, she looked up into the canopy of giant old oak trees that hung over the boulevard. The late fall sun glowed an orange-pink color through the moss-covered limbs. She noticed a few brightly colored plastic beads hanging scattered in the moss that dangled from the grand old oaks.

St. Charles Avenue in New Orleans was magnificent and grand. On her left was the rumbling streetcar, and to her right were stately mansions. St. Charles Avenue was passing too quickly; Elizabeth longed to walk the street and look in every garden. She knew from spending time in Charleston that the most beautiful parts of old homes were frequently in the back. Hidden gardens were her favorite part of the old homes near the Battery in Charleston. Breaking the silence, Dr. Cabellero said, "You will like the food here. It is typical of New Orleans, and everything is prepared to perfection. What are your favorite New Orleans eateries?"

Elizabeth could not help but giggle at his formality. She knew that she was out of her league with this cultured, experienced man. She felt no inclination to pretend that she was more than herself.

"My experience of the *eateries* of New Orleans has been limited to hospital vending machines, the Charity Hospital cafeteria, The Fistula café in front of Charity, and the all-night Popeye's on Airline Highway between my apartment and the hospital," said Elizabeth.

Dr. Cabellero looked horrified. They resumed their silence.

A few minutes later, he said, "All of that is about to change. This town is a food town. People here celebrate with every meal. I am happy to be the one to introduce you to the wonders of New Orleans cooking. Equivalent food can only be found in New York, London, and Paris."

To the tired intern, New York, London, and Paris might as well have been the moon. She had no experience with either and certainly could not compare cuisines. But she was starving. Any food would be good food to her.

Her date swerved to the curb in front of a bright aqua-colored Victorian home with an aqua-and-cream striped awning. At first glance, Elizabeth thought the restaurant exterior garish. An attendant opened her door after the car had barely come to a full stop. He was wearing a tuxedo and offered a white-gloved hand to assist her. Getting out of the low-lying car in heels and a silky dress was challenging. She was glad to have a chance to practice the maneuver with a stranger instead of Dr. Cabellero.

She heard another man in a tuxedo say, "Welcome back, Dr. Cabellero, it is great to see you. We have your usual table ready for you, and your favorite waiter is preparing your favorite wines."

They seem to know him. Elizabeth was impressed. She took his arm, and they walked into a dark-paneled, dimly lit entrance area. A third man in a tuxedo looked up from a line of guests waiting to be seated, smiled, and escorted the couple past the line and into the adjacent dining room. White linen tablecloths, ornate crystal chandeliers, gleaming silver, and sparkling glassware adorned every table. Even though it was early, every table was occupied, and the patrons were animated. Several people greeted Dr. Cabellero as they made their way up the stairs and into the garden room.

A tall Asian man stood smiling beside a table large enough for four diners. In front of the table, the entire wall was clear glass. On the other side of the glass was a huge, majestic old oak tree adorned with a few tiny white lights. The glow of the setting sun shone through the leaves. Elizabeth felt she was in a giant treehouse. The floor of the dining room was barely four feet from the magnificent tree. It took her breath away.

Beside her, the waiter said, "Hello, madam, I am Eric. I am Dr. Caballero's waiter. Welcome to Commander's Palace. I hope you enjoy the view, and of course, our food." He pulled out her chair, helped her get seated, and quickly disappeared.

Elizabeth felt her mouth hanging open and tried to regain her poise.

"This is so beautiful. Thank you for sharing it with me," said Elizabeth.

"The pleasure is all mine. Since you have not been here before, shall I order for both of us?" he asked. "Is there anything that you do not eat?"

"No, I like everything," said Elizabeth. She was embarrassed to hear her stomach grumbling in anticipation of what was to come. She had worked as a hostess at the Mills Hyatt House in Charleston during college and had learned much about good food from serving it to others. The chef frequently let the college kids taste the food at the end of the night, if any was left over.

"Okay, great! Then I will ask Eric to feed us. You will not be sorry," said Dr. Cabellero.

The waiter returned with a small army of assistants who poured water and arranged napkins and stood at attention quietly beside the table.

"What is your pleasure tonight, doctor?" asked Eric.

"Eric, this lovely woman is having her first dinner at Commander's, so why don't you feed us your best? Bring a little of everything. Our job will be to enjoy," said the doctor.

"Wonderful! Would you like me to choose wines also?" said the waiter.

"Actually, I am on call for the emergency room tonight, so I will just taste a few selections to entice my palate. I will not want whole bottles of wine tonight," said Dr. Cabellero.

Elizabeth had little experience with alcohol, as all the family members on Mom's side were teetotalers. She was already sleepy and did not wish to embarrass herself by becoming silly with wine. She decided she would sip what came to be polite.

As the waiter walked away, Dr. Caballero's beeper rang out. "Dr. Cabellero, please call the emergency room at Tulane Medical Center. I repeat, please call the emergency room at Tulane Medical Center," said the voice of the Tulane operator. The neurosurgeon looked disappointed but resigned.

"Excuse me, Elizabeth. I will go to the hall to use the phone so I don't disturb the other diners. When Eric brings the first course and the first wine, please do not wait on me to start," said Dr. Cabellero.

Elizabeth felt like a princess being served by an entourage. Everyone smiled and seemed happy she was there. She felt sorry for Dr. Cabellero, but she was relieved to not have to make conversation. She felt the hum of fatigue, and the need for sleep was starting its familiar buzzing in her head. The quiet beauty of Commander's Palace and having time alone suited her just fine. She gazed from the beautiful tree to the other diners. The people looked elegant and spoke softly. The clang of the silverware hitting porcelain plates and the tinkling of the crystal glasses touching each other provided a pleasant cacophony that droned in her head. She was deeply relaxed and grateful for the experience.

Dr. Cabellero rushed back to the table just as the first wine was poured and the appetizer appeared. A wonderful smell of garlic and fresh seafood wafted up from the table.

"This, madam, is Grilled Breaux Bridge Crawfish. It is paired with Dr. Cabellero's favorite Sauvignon Blanc. Enjoy!" said Eric.

"Thank you, Eric. This is a great choice," said Dr. Cabellero.

Elizabeth waited impatiently for her host to take his first bite. He picked up his wine glass and she followed suit. He lifted his glass into the air and proposed a toast. "To the prettiest woman at Tulane," he said.

Elizabeth was shocked. She wanted to be regarded as competent, not pretty. Pretty was okay, but smart was her goal. She squirmed in her chair, took a quick sip of the wine, and tried to relax. "Thank you," she said. "But since I am the only woman, the competition is not terribly stiff."

Dr. Cabellero laughed and began to eat his crawfish. After taking her first bite, Elizabeth wanted nothing more than to put her head down and devour the entire plate. It was the best dish that she had ever eaten. Hungry though she was, she tried to eat slowly and not inhale her food. She could hear her father's mother, her Granny, instructing her. Elizabeth knew Granny's dining mantra by heart. "Sit up straight in your chair. Take one slow bite at a time. Put your fork down between bites. When invited to dinner, your job is to enjoy the food and participate in the conversation. Your duty as anyone's guest is to be pleasant and engaging." Elizabeth vowed to follow Granny's rules as her stomach audibly gurgled.

Ernesto's beeper sounded again. He apologized and headed off to the telephone in the hall by the restrooms. Eric quietly had pointed out both to her in case she might need either. The other patrons did not seem annoyed. Elizabeth imagined that they had seen the doctor's routine before.

She finished her crawfish, sat silently, and sipped the wine. She fought the urge to reach over and eat Dr. Cabellero's crawfish, too. Her hunger was growing, not subsiding. The strong garlic smell was intoxicating.

The phone call was taking an inordinate amount of time. Elizabeth ate the tangy, crusty sourdough bread with herb butter. She wanted to dump the entire basket in her purse to eat later, but her Granny's voice still played in her head.

Dr. Cabellero returned, visibly upset. His brow was furrowed, and his jaw was clenched.

"I am very sorry, but I have to return to the hospital. Someone fell in the French Quarter at Pat O'Brien's and fractured his skull. I have to run to the Tulane ER and evaluate him to be sure he does not need surgery. Please stay. Eric will feed you. I may only be an hour. Eat slowly," he said with a smile, "and I should be back in time for coffee and dessert." He looked contrite, though he must have known she would understand. "I am very sorry, Elizabeth." He moved quickly away. She had no time to protest or offer assistance. She felt disloyal staying to dine while he went to work, but he did not give her a choice.

As she thought she heard the Porsche roar angrily away, she quickly switched Dr. Cabellero's crawfish appetizer dish for her empty one. Eric stood a respectful distance away from the table and allowed Elizabeth to devour Ernesto's appetizer. She thought about her grandfather's horses and how they always ran for the barn and the feed trough at the end of the day. She laughed to herself thinking, *I am just like those horses racing to the food...*

When she had finished Dr. Cabellero's crawfish dish, Eric approached the table. "Would you like some more wine?"

"I don't drink much, so a half glass should be more than enough for me," said Elizabeth. She knew that the queen of England—that other Elizabeth— could not possibly feel better served than she felt at this moment. The sun was setting, she felt immensely relaxed, and the hum of the conversation from the other patrons created a dreamy experience.

Eric came back with a soup that smelled of seafood and garlic with a hint of lemon and sherry. From her days when she worked at the Mills Hyatt House in Charleston, she thought that there was no food on earth better than a good soup.

"This is our famous turtle soup," said Eric. She could smell the strong alcohol he poured over the top. "The sherry is the *coup de gras.* Enjoy!"

The salty, dark, musky flavor of the turtle soup was divine. Elizabeth was quickly reaching satiety. She had not eaten a large volume of food at one time for many months. She wondered if she would be able to ingest all that the waiter would bring. As she finished the soup, she again felt the humming sound in her head that she had begun to associate with extreme fatigue. She decided to go to the restroom and splash some cold water on her face to revive herself.

As she started to stand, the waiter immediately appeared behind her and helped with her chair. Elizabeth felt a little dizzy, and the room seemed to spin for a second. As she stepped forward in the unfamiliar sandals that were slightly too big, she turned her ankle and stumbled. Eric caught her full weight and righted her in the middle of the dining room. Elizabeth flushed with shame, glad her date was not there to see her nearly fall. She tried to stand up taller as she walked through the dining room to the restroom. Her fatigue, full stomach, wine buzz, and loose sandals made for slow navigation. She was sure all eyes in the dining room were on her. It seemed to take forever to finally traverse the one hundred feet to the restroom. She threw cold water on her face and vowed to forego further wine. Her image in the mirror was slightly wavy. She had imbibed less than a full glass of wine, but she felt mildly drunk. After straightening her hair and dress, she proceeded back to the table.

Eric looked worried. "Are you okay, madam?"

"Yes, sir," said Elizabeth. "I am not used to drinking, and I am a little sleep deprived. I will drink water from this point on."

"No problem. Dr. Cabellero frequently doesn't drink at all, depending on his duties at the hospital. The chef used to be insulted, but we are used to the abstinent doctor now. Some nights the poor man spends more time on the phone in the hall than he does at his table. I admire his persistence in the face of frequent interruptions. Good food and the civilities of life are important to Dr. Cabellero," said Eric.

The cold water revived Elizabeth for a few minutes. Then the humming got louder and louder in her head, drowning out the conversations of the other diners. She fought to remain upright and awake. A waiter ceremoniously placed a beautiful crab salad with remoulade sauce in front of her. That was the last thing Elizabeth remembered.

She snorted and awoke confused. She smelled the intense odor of crabmeat very close to her face. She realized her lower body sat on a padded chair, and her face was resting on a table.

She felt completely disoriented and thought for a few seconds that she was in the emergency room. The crab smell reminded her of the po-boy sandwich one of the ER orderlies usually had for lunch.

As she came into full consciousness, Elizabeth remembered she was in the dining room at Commander's Palace, and she realized the entire right side of her face lay in the middle of her remoulade-soaked crab salad. Her hair, which had come loose on the right side, was marinating in the remoulade. Three concerned waiters stood at attention, blocking her from the eyes of other diners, guarding her while she slept in her salad. Elizabeth was mortified and hoped at that moment for a quick death. Granny's rules did not cover falling asleep in a signature dish at one of the best restaurants in America!

As she sat up, Eric handed her two napkins and offered to help her to the restroom.

Everyone around her stared as orange sauce ran down Elizabeth's cheek and onto the black dress. Once the other diners saw the beautiful young woman in the black dress was alive and seemingly well, the tension in the room melted into laughter. Sympathetic smiles emanated from most of the women, but many men were laughing openly. *At least Dr. Caballero isn't here to see this.* She realized she couldn't quite bring herself to call him Ernesto.

Just then Dr. Caballero returned to the room in a rush, just in time to survey the debacle. Elizabeth felt his hot hand on her upper back as he leaned over solicitously. She heard him ask her if she was all right.

Elizabeth was speechless with mortification.

"She fell asleep at the table. She was sleeping so soundly that none of us had the heart to wake her," explained Eric.

"That is completely understandable," said Dr. Caballero kindly. "She is working eighty to one hundred hours per week, and that makes it very hard to stay awake."

Dr. Cabellero's kindness and his pretending that what happened was normal made Elizabeth want to shriek with embarrassment. They were being so sweet, but nothing could take away how foolish she felt for falling asleep with her face in her salad.

Somehow, she knew, she had to take that long walk back to the restroom, clean herself up, and get out of the restaurant without crying. Elizabeth figured that the less fuss, the better. She stood up, less wobbly this time, and sauntered across the dining room with orange remoulade dripping down her borrowed dress and pieces of crabmeat bouncing to the floor with each step. The other patrons were riveted.

After the longest walk of her entire life, she collapsed in tears and surveyed the damage to the dress. She certainly did not have the money to pay for it, and she absolutely did not want to upset Aoife or Aoife's roommate. She removed the dress in the restroom and worked on it. Cold water did wonders to remove the spicy sauce. But nothing but a trip to a dry cleaner would get out that crab smell.

After crying and washing the dress for ten minutes, she started to laugh. Great globs of mucus ran down her naked torso as she hung her head over into the cold water of the sink. She had never had great luck with dating, and tonight seemed a continuation of that losing streak. She washed the sauce from her hair, out of her right ear, off her grandmother's pearls, and from her neck. She styled her wet hair as best she could and dried herself with the beautiful linen hand towels. She put the moist, black silky dress back on and exited the restroom.

When she arrived back at the table, Dr. Cabellero was contentedly eating his dinner. He looked up and smiled. The waiters were doing their best to act normally until a patron in the corner started to applaud. Within a minute, all the diners in the garden room at Commander's Palace were on their feet, clapping and hooting for Elizabeth's return to the table.

She was flushed from head to toe, but remained gracious as the waiter pulled out her chair and replaced her napkin across her lap. Elizabeth thought, *This is a crazy town. People here are very kind, but quite zany.* At home in South Carolina, people tended to ignore the foibles of others. In New Orleans, they celebrated foibles.

Dr. Cabellero looked tired as he calmly ate. He looked up and asked, "Would you like dessert and some coffee?"

"No, thank you," Elizabeth replied. "I am ready to leave whenever you have finished eating. I am really sorry to have ruined our evening," she apologized.

"You did not ruin anything," he told her. "I know the same kind of bone-weary numbing fatigue that you are experiencing. The work never gets better. The exhaustion is always there under the surface. I still feel it myself." He paused. "But what does come with time, I am happy to tell you, is the loss of fear. You will become so good at what you do that you are no longer afraid. Being afraid is what saps your energy and really wears you out."

Elizabeth was encouraged to hear him say one day she would no longer be afraid all the time.

She realized that she was mostly afraid of failure. She was not afraid of the work, or the hours, or the intensity.

"One part of my job that is very stressful to me is the fact that many people working in the hospital seem so mean," Elizabeth confided. "A little kindness and support would improve the workplace atmosphere of the hospital and the emergency room, too."

"Be patient, and the kindness and teamwork will come to you," Ernesto replied. "Try to remember you are not the only one who is afraid. Right now, everyone is afraid of the new interns. Everyone has to be more diligent and on guard to make sure the new doctors don't hurt anyone. Because of the nature of learning to be a surgeon, our errors are tragic and sometimes disastrous. No longtime employees at Charity or Tulane want to get attached to any intern. They know that half of them will not make the cut. So, from July first until the mid-December cut, they try to watch out for the patients, and they wait to see who will be chosen." He let that sink in. "They also help in the weeding-out process. I promise you, Norman McSwain will never hire anyone that Lavinia Robichaud thinks a bad doctor. One of her many jobs is to break in the new interns," said Dr. Cabellero.

Elizabeth noticed the crab odor was getting stronger in her hair from the heat of her head. She was ready to get home, shower, and make sure the borrowed dress was cleaned properly. Dr. Cabellero signaled Eric, and he brought the check.

As Eric pulled back her chair, he smiled and said, "It was so nice to meet you. We hope to see you at Commander's Palace again."

Trying to hold onto what little was left of her dignity, Elizabeth responded with what she hoped would be considered humor. "Yes, thank you. This is a lovely bed and breakfast. You must do a little work on your beds, though. I found my bed a little uncomfortable."

Everyone within earshot was laughing as the couple proceeded down the stairs and out to the street.

The little black Carrera sports car was idling noisily at the curb. Another man in a tuxedo stood guard by the open door to assist Elizabeth.

As she relaxed back into the soft leather seat, all she desired in life was her bed. Even though she missed half the meal, she was full from the rich, delicious food.

When they approached Charity, Dr. Cabellero said, "Are you sure you don't want me to take you home? You really need to get away from that on-call room more often."

"No, I have to be in the trauma emergency room at five in the morning, and that is only seven hours away. I might as well just crash here tonight. But thanks, anyway," said Elizabeth. She hoped his car would not smell like crabmeat tomorrow.

He ran around the car, opened her door, and stood at attention beside the car until she was safely in the side door of the hospital. He had not tried to kiss her goodnight. She was not surprised. She could see him smiling as he got back into his car. His roaring sports car moved away from the curb as Elizabeth entered the side door of Charity, grateful to be moving closer to her bed.

CHAPTER 12
Death in the ER

Elizabeth slept well and arrived in the trauma ER ahead of schedule. The embarrassment from her date had faded into the background of her psyche. It had been hours ago, and she chuckled at the memory of everyone clapping after she returned from the bathroom.

She felt light and airy and unencumbered. She thought, *I wonder what I will learn today.* She smiled as she walked through the swinging doors of the trauma emergency room.

Nurse Robichaud was the first to greet her and said, "Big excitement down here for you this week, huh, Crème Puff? It doesn't get much more exciting than Dr. White opening someone's chest and operating on his heart in the emergency room." Nurse Robichaud laughed as she sipped her coffee.

Elizabeth felt a thrill remembering Dr. White's prowess. His level of skill would forever be her goal.

"Do you think I could ever be as good a surgeon as Dr. White, Nurse Robichaud?" said Elizabeth, holding her breath as she waited for the answer.

"Honey, right now, I just wonder if you'll still be here in December!" Nurse Robichaud demurred. "I do appreciate you not fainting when Dr. White sliced that man open while he screamed like a banshee. That new trauma protocol was shocking, even to me. Getting that bullet out likely saved his life. If it had lodged in one of his heart valves, he'd have been a dead man. But cutting open a man's chest who was talking one moment before was a bold move, even for Dr. White."

Elizabeth nodded in agreement. "The protocol seemed barbaric at first thought. But I know it saved Mr. Jenkins."

"Dr. McSwain is forever trying to improve survival rates, and we have to be flexible, as he often changes our protocol for trauma," said the nurse. "You look like you have been on a pink cloud for days now over that case. But try to bring your little self down off that happy pink cloud and remember there are twenty-two new sick folks down here, and you are responsible for them all. The gods go to the operating room, and the peons stay down here with Nurse Robichaud."

Being back in the trauma ER and hearing Nurse Robichaud talk about Dr. White stimulated Elizabeth's memory, and she found herself daydreaming and reliving an earlier ER shift. Elizabeth had very much wanted to go to surgery with Dr. White, even if she would only have been hanging on a clamp in the intern position. She wanted to be near the action and near him. He was everything that she aspired to be.

Elizabeth longed for greatness. It really did not matter much to her whether people liked her or not, but she coveted her colleagues' respect. She wanted to be the one who was called when the patients were in dire need. She wanted Dr. McSwain to stand aside, trust her implicitly, and admire her the way he admired Dr. White. She yearned to do her duty and to do it well.

Elizabeth knew that she had a long way to go—at least six to eight more years of intense study. She felt she could likely endure anything if she knew that one day her skills would equal those of Dr. White.

"Come on, intern! Snap out of your fantasy world. We have lots of patients to see, and standing here yammering won't get the work done. Let's round," said the nurse.

Elizabeth followed Nurse Robichaud toward examination Room Six, still dreaming of her future greatness. She purposefully stopped herself from daydreaming further as she heard her grandmother's words of caution in her head: *Pride goeth before a fall.* Her grandmother started the day at the farm with a Bible reading, and Proverbs was a favorite. As they walked, Elizabeth noticed that the trauma department was more crowded than usual. Every examination room was occupied. Hospital gurneys filled with bloody patients lined every hallway. As she walked by each bed, Elizabeth tried to quickly assess each patient to make sure none was critically injured. They saw two well-dressed men tied to gurneys. Both were drunk and bloody, with cuts on their heads, and they were covered in their own vomit and blood. Nurse Robichaud checked their airways and made sure they were breathing, and she and Elizabeth moved on.

New Orleans was a party town. People came from all over the world to drink alcohol, listen to music, and walk the French Quarter. At orientation, Elizabeth recalled Dr. McSwain saying, "The police are excellent and keep the Quarter safe for most tourists. But a few imbibe too much, wind up on a dark side street, and wake up in the ER."

A floodtide of bleeding humanity constantly flowed into the emergency room. The volume seemed endless. "I have not seen the trauma ER this busy before," Elizabeth admitted. "It is a bit overwhelming, and I truly do not know where to start."

When she worked with Dr. White on the gunshot wound to the chest, time seemed irrelevant. The adrenaline rush, the excitement, and the need for total focus on their task had been the best part of her internship thus far. That kind of experience was why she had come to Charity. Today, the thrill had subsided, and she was left slogging through the more routine cases—the small mountain of people with minor trauma who filled the ER.

"It is chaotic down here," Nurse Robichaud concurred. "I think we should start at the end of one hall and work our way down to the end of the other side. My nurses have been making the rounds and keeping an eye on things. But many of them are nearly as green as you."

The trauma area was shaped like a giant letter H—two long halls with nine exam rooms on each hall. The center area contained the nurses' station, the emergency radiology suite, and the Room Four major trauma suite. The entire ER was quite shabby. The budget was tight and pretty was not a priority at The Big Free. Dr. McSwain was much more interested in having the best equipment than in having an attractive physical space.

As Elizabeth daydreamed of her future success and the admiration that would come from the cardiac fellow, she heard one of the drunken patients on a gurney they just passed vomit on the floor. She turned around to see him clutching his chest.

The man wore a nice, expensive-looking suit. He had a good haircut and was recently shaved. His eyes were extremely bloodshot, and they could not focus. *Another amateur drinker convention-goer.* Elizabeth and Nurse Robichaud turned around and headed toward him.

"Can you talk?" asked Elizabeth. The patient's eyes were wide, and he looked panic-stricken. He was shaking his head and pointing to his chest.

Nurse Robichaud said, "If he can't speak that means his airway is obstructed. Quickly turn him on his side and hit him on the back!"

Two nurses and a medical student helped Elizabeth turn the patient on his side and pound his back. After her experience with Buster the Chihuahua, Elizabeth half expected a Mardi Gras bead to pop out of his mouth.

"Be careful not to slide down in that pile of vomit, Elizabeth," cautioned Nurse Robichaud.

Suddenly the patient became quite limp, and when Elizabeth looked into his face, his lips were blue.

"It looks like he's aspirated, Nurse Robichaud," said Elizabeth, feeling her heart race.

"Okay, team, wheel him into Room Four. Elizabeth, grab the Ambu bag. Put the mask over his face and start trying to get some air into him as we move him. Nurses, be sure the setup for intubation is ready. We need to move him, *stat*! We cannot intubate him out here in the hall," said Nurse Robichaud.

As they arrived in Room Four, the student nurse said, "*I do not have a pulse! I repeat, I do not have a pulse!*"

Elizabeth felt his carotid artery, and the student was right—there was no pulse. She nodded to Nurse Robichaud to indicate the student was right.

"Code blue, stat! Full code blue!" shouted Nurse Robichaud.

Aoife appeared, running through the door, and said, "What the hell? One minute drunk and the next coded? What happened, Livvy?"

"He aspirated while we were standing six feet away, evaluating someone else. I had just walked by the guy, and he looked okay," said Nurse Robichaud.

Elizabeth was struggling to intubate him. "Can someone place pressure on his trachea? The tube does not want to go down."

A medical student stepped closer and pressed on the patient's trachea.

"No good, it's not going in. Call Dr. Peterson now!" ordered Elizabeth. Her hands shook and her heart raced.

"Nurse Robichaud, I am trying to bag him, and no amount of pressure will raise his chest. His airway seems completely obstructed," said Elizabeth.

"Turn him on his side again and sweep your fingers across the back of his throat and see if you can remove some of his vomit," advised Nurse Robichaud.

The student nurse said, "I cannot feel a pulse, and there is no blood pressure!"

"Want the paddles to shock the heart?" the medical student asked Elizabeth.

"It won't do any good if he does not have an airway. He must have an airway to circulate oxygen to his heart!" said Elizabeth as she raked her gloved finger through the back of the patient's throat. Her fingers encountered no obstruction. She knew that meant the patient's airway was obstructed further down his trachea.

"Dr. Peterson is not answering his page," said Aoife as she replaced the phone on the wall.

"Big surprise there!" intoned Nurse Robichaud. "Page Dr. McSwain, *stat!*" she ordered.

Elizabeth kept trying to intubate the patient, but because she could not get the tube in, she went back to trying to use the Ambu bag, squeezing it hard in an effort to force air to enter the patient's lungs. It seemed like an eternity, but they had only been working less than two minutes.

Elizabeth felt completely impotent. She tried to remember the various ways to get an adequate airway. All that was left was emergency tracheostomy. She had never seen one and certainly never done one. *Where was Dr. Peterson?*

"Bring the tracheostomy setup over here now," said Elizabeth.

She poured betadine over the patient's throat, and the thick dark-brown liquid splattered everywhere. Her hand was poised over his throat with the scalpel shining in the bright lights above when Dr. Norman McSwain entered. Her other hand was feeling for the soft cartilage of the throat.

"What's going on?" he asked.

"The patient came in drunk and vomited and aspirated in the hall while we were rounding, and I have not been able to intubate him," said Elizabeth.

"All proper protocols have been followed, Norman," said Nurse Robichaud.

Dr. McSwain pushed Elizabeth aside and grabbed the intubation equipment from the table. He snapped the patient's head back, jammed the metal laryngoscope through the patient's mouth, and pulled the man's entire head off the gurney as he stared down the patient's throat.

"Damn, he is totally blocked. Trying to pass a tube blindly will only make his airway more obstructed," said McSwain. He turned to Elizabeth.

"Intern, have you ever done an emergency cricothyrotomy?" asked McSwain.

"No, sir. I have never even seen one," said Elizabeth.

"Norman, he has been without an airway for five minutes," said Nurse Robichaud.

In one blast of movement, with no sterile gloves and no concern for his clothes and his white coat, Dr. Norman McSwain grabbed the scalpel from Elizabeth. He palpated the patient's neck with one hand and sliced it open with the other. Blood shot all over him and Elizabeth and across the patient's chest and upper face. Dr. McSwain threw the scalpel on the floor, grabbed the intubation tube, and jammed it through the hole he'd cut in the front of the patient's neck.

"Attach that Ambu bag and squeeze the hell out of it," ordered Dr. McSwain.

Blood continued spurting from around the tube, but the patient's chest rose and fell with each squeeze of the bag. He was breathing again.

"That, young lady, is an emergency cricothyrotomy!" said Dr. McSwain. Elizabeth was shocked, but thrilled.

The student nurse said, "Doctors, his pulse is thready and his blood pressure is 70."

"Run the code, intern. You know the sequence," ordered Dr. McSwain.

Elizabeth started calling out the sequence of drugs and maneuvers known to every doctor in every emergency situation. There were only so many things that could be done to support a patient who was attempting to die. Nurse Robichaud knew the sequence better than Elizabeth, and she anticipated the young doctor's every need. Epinephrine, lidocaine, magnesium, and oxygen flowed from the nurse to the doctor like a well-planned dance sequence.

The patient looked less blue. His pulse quickened, and his blood pressure rose slightly.

Every doctor and nurse knew that somewhere between six and ten minutes of no oxygenated blood circulating was the point of no return for the human body. After that period of time, cell death began.

Elizabeth had one hand on the man's bloody neck holding the endotracheal tube in place. Her other hand pumped the Ambu bag as if her life depended on it. The team looked on as Elizabeth enthusiastically pumped the Ambu bag with 100 percent oxygen. With intravenous fluids running to alkalinize his blood and drugs circulating to improve his blood pressure and heart rate, there was nothing else to do but wait.

Dr. McSwain stood shoulder to shoulder with her. Time was suspended in Room Four.

The student nurse constantly took the patient's vital signs. She reported, "Blood pressure is 90 and pulse is 88."

Dr. McSwain said, "Going in the right direction here. I wonder how many brain cells he killed?"

The staff always searched every unconscious patient's wallet for health information and for contact information for next of kin. The medical student was in the corner rifling through the patient's wallet. "It says here, Dr. McSwain, that he is a gynecologist from McComb, Mississippi. He has a picture with three daughters and a wife in the front of the wallet. There is no medical information in the wallet, sir."

"Damn, a drunken doctor at a convention ends up in Room Four. Poor bastard. I sure hope he's not a Tulane grad. Where is the chief?" said McSwain.

Nurse Robichaud said, "He hasn't been here this morning yet."

"Page him again, and tell him that I am looking for him in Room Four!" shouted Dr. McSwain, his impatience obvious. "Just because his daddy donated a wing to Tulane Hospital does not give him a free pass."

As Elizabeth looked down at the patient, she could see he was starting to become pinker and less blue. She thought, *Finally, Dr. Peterson's behavior makes sense. He can be a slacker because he is a rich boy whose father paves the way for him with money.* She resented those people.

Dr. McSwain turned to the student nurse and said, "Go out to the phone at the nurses' station and call the ENT team, and tell them to get down here. It looks like this guy is going to make it. They will need to convert this temporary tracheostomy to a semi-permanent one in the OR." She scurried off as if the hounds of hell were chasing her.

"Is there a best way to secure this tube, Dr. McSwain?" asked Elizabeth as she secured the tube to the patient's throat and dressed the wound.

"First, you secure the patient's hands. A tube in the trachea is extremely irritating, and his first response will be to try and pull it out. So secure his hands tightly while securing the tube," said Dr. McSwain as he tied the patient's hands to the gurney.

Nurse Robichaud was at the phone, again trying to reach the chief resident.

The patient's eyes popped open. He realized he could not speak and that there was something in his throat. His eyes were wide, and he started thrashing about in confusion. Elizabeth leaned over him and said, "You are in the emergency room at Charity Hospital. You aspirated and had to have an emergency procedure to get your airway opened. There is a tube in your throat so you can breathe. You are fine, and we are taking good care of you. Please lie back and try to relax. If you keep fighting, we will have to sedate you. Your hands are restrained to keep you from pulling out the tube."

The ENT team—the ear, nose, and throat specialists, or "booger doctors," as they were called behind their backs—arrived. "We'll take it from here, Dr. McSwain," said their chief resident as the other team members started to better secure the patient to the gurney for transport to the operating room.

"Thanks, guys," said Elizabeth as she watched them wheel the man away.

Nurse Robichaud was off the phone now, and Dr. McSwain had left. Elizabeth asked, "Is Dr. Peterson coming down?"

"Who knows? I get sick of babysitting him. I hope Dr. McSwain chews him a new one today. It's not fair to any of us that he just hides, especially in *July!*"

Elizabeth said, "Forget about him. Let's make rounds and see what needs our attention."

She and Nurse Robichaud went from room to room, giving orders and making plans with the nurses, medical students, and nursing students. They had finished the work in three examination rooms, and the routine suturing was assigned. Elizabeth knew she would likely do most of the work eventually because she was fast at suturing, and the students were slow. But they could get the work started by giving tetanus shots, cleaning the wounds, and numbing the areas to be sutured with lidocaine.

Nurse Robichaud opened the door to examination Room Eleven. "Oh, my God!" she exclaimed.

Elizabeth looked over the nurse's shoulder to see a man crumpled on the floor. His IV was wrapped around his leg, and blood was dripping on the floor from where the IV needle, which must have pulled out when he fell, had been in his arm. He was alone and unconscious.

"Dr. Roberts, get the Room Four team!" said the nurse.

As the same group of people who had just been assembled in Room Four gathered in the cramped exam room, Nurse Robichaud assessed the patient.

"He is breathing, just barely. His blood pressure is slightly elevated. His pulse is slow at 68. Who saw him last?" shouted Nurse Robichaud.

A frightened nurse said, "I did, Livvy. He is the guy who had been the line coach in a Little League baseball game. The bat flew out of a kid's hand and hit him in the side of the head. He complained of a headache, but was conscious at the scene, drove to the hospital himself with his family in the car, and walked in here with his wife and three kids. His name is Jeremiah Pierce. His wife called him Jerry. The last time I came by, he had a little nausea and asked the family to eat their hamburgers in the waiting room while he waited to see the doctor."

Elizabeth squeezed into the gap between the gurney, the wall, and the patient. She palpated Mr. Pierce's head and felt a big bump over the temporal bone on the side of his head above his ear. She felt a weak, slow pulse and yelled for the team to bring the emergency stretcher to move him into Room Four.

"Nurse Robichaud, please call neurosurgery immediately! His pupils are very sluggish, and he has a little blood dripping from his ear on the side of his head, near the injury," said a frantic Elizabeth. She looked down at the patient. He could have been any kid's dad. He had sandy brown hair that was due a trip to the barber, and he wore a faded plaid short-sleeved shirt and khaki shorts. His wedding ring was scratched gold, and he was deeply tanned, probably from coaching kids' baseball. She felt a big knot in her throat as she helped roll him over onto the orange board that had just been cleaned of the last patient's blood.

For the first time as a doctor, Elizabeth examined a patient to assess his level of coma. She had never seen a person in a coma in the emergency room.

She remembered from her textbooks that there were specific signs she should attempt to elicit. She took her knuckles and pressed deeply into the center of his sternum to try to determine his level of response to pain. She pressed harder and with more determination, but the patient gave no response. As she realized that Mr. Pierce had walked into the emergency room and was now unresponsive to deep painful stimulus, Elizabeth panicked, overwhelmed with the knowledge that she was insufficiently prepared for the job in front of her.

"Dr. Ernesto Caballero is the neurosurgeon on call now, and I have him on the phone, Dr. Roberts," said Nurse Robichaud.

Elizabeth ran to the phone, praying for instruction. She could hear music from the opera, *Madame Butterfly*, softly playing in the background.

"This is Dr. Caballero, I cannot come down. I have a brain tumor patient with her head completely open, and I am at the most delicate part of the procedure. You are going to have to tell me over the phone what happened and what you see now, and I will instruct you," said the neurosurgeon.

Elizabeth's panic was momentarily calmed by the beautiful cadence of Dr. Caballero's Spanish accent and the haunting music of Puccini. Surely, this calm, cultured man could solve her problem. He had been so gentle and kind when he returned to Commander's and found her asleep in her salad. Elizabeth thought, *Surely he can solve this problem, too.*

In the medical language known to every doctor and nurse, Elizabeth described her patient. "Sir, he is a thirty-two-year-old white male named Jeremiah Pierce. He walked into the emergency room complaining of a headache. He said that he had been standing on the line between the batter and the first baseman at a Little League baseball game when the bat flew out of the batter's hand and hit him over the left ear. He was never unconscious. He drove himself to the hospital. His family came with him. I was in another room and did not see him before the last five minutes. But according to the nurse's notes, his vital signs were normal and he was chatting with his wife and kids normally. We were working on a patient who had aspirated and required an emergency cricothyrotomy, and this patient ended up waiting about forty-five minutes. When we got to his room on rounds, he was on the floor and unconscious, his pulse was slow, his blood pressure was up, and his pupils were sluggish." She stopped to take a breath. "You must know that I have never even had a neurosurgery rotation as a student," said Elizabeth.

"Dr. Roberts, you must act quickly," Dr. Cabellero said. "This man has a closed head injury, and the bleeding inside his head is literally compressing his brain tissue. There is nowhere in his skull for his brain to go. You must do exactly as I say. Intubate him. Get his airway under control. Start oxygen immediately, and breathe very fast for him. Give him steroids, Mannitol, and intravenous fluids. Hyperventilate him immediately. I will call you back in a minute. Oh, and get a quick skull X-ray, if possible," said the neurosurgeon as he hung up to return to his patient in the OR.

Elizabeth knew that all the procedures recommended by the neurosurgeon were to take pressure off the patient's brain and allow him to retain some brain function. Her gut told her it was no use, but since she had never seen a person with this degree of head trauma, she followed Dr. Cabellero's instructions carefully. As she struggled to get a tube down his trachea, three nurses and students were starting IVs and getting the medications into Mr. Pierce. When Elizabeth looked into the patient's face, she realized both of his pupils were fixed and dilated. She knew that to be an ominous sign.

As she turned to tell Nurse Robichaud to call the chief surgery resident, Elizabeth heard the nurse yell into the phone on the wall, "Dr. McSwain, I know that you are in surgery at Tulane, but you have got to send someone down here *now!* We are in over our heads down here! The neurosurgery chief cannot come down, and the chief general surgery resident cannot be reached."

These communications could take place because Charity, Tulane, and the VA hospitals were connected by phone. Every emergency area in each hospital had wall phones with speaker mechanisms. Doctors and nurses could continue working while orders came over the speaker. Surgical staff doctors could know what their residents were doing in several locations at one time and could instruct them.

As Elizabeth secured the endotracheal tube to Mr. Pierce's face, she saw her hands shaking. For the first time in her life, she felt completely incompetent. She did not know what to do to help this man, and she knew he was going to die. With all of her being, she wanted to be somewhere else—anywhere else would do.

"Burr hole?" she heard Nurse Robichaud say. "Are you kidding me? You want an intern to drill a burr hole in this man's head in the emergency room?" She sounded incredulous. "Yes, Norman, I know he will die without neurosurgical emergency care. Yes, sir. I will get everything set up. But, sir, I don't like this idea," said the nurse. She hung up the phone, muttering, "This is crazy…intern… burr hole…crazy…"

Elizabeth looked into Nurse Robichaud's eyes. Her usual cockiness had vanished, and the nurse looked worried and afraid.

Elizabeth's panic rose. Her palms were sweaty, her heart hammered in her ears, and her bowels rumbled.

"Have you ever seen or read about using a Hudson-Brace handheld drill for drilling burr holes in the human skull?" asked the nurse.

"No, I have not," said Elizabeth as she repeated her physical examination of the patient. Nothing had changed. The initial attempts at resuscitation had been unsuccessful. The patient was still unresponsive. His pulse was still slow, and his pupils remained fixed and dilated. He was no better, but he was no worse. All the suggested drugs had been administered.

The phone rang in the trauma room, and Dr. Caballero's voice was placed on speaker. Elizabeth continued to breathe rapidly for the patient, using the handheld Ambu bag attached to his endotracheal tube. At that moment, the

X-ray technician threw Mr. Pierce's skull X-ray onto the view box on the wall, and Elizabeth gasped. From across the room, she could see the long temporal fracture that ran right over the middle meningeal artery on the left side of the patient's head.

"How is he doing, Dr. Roberts?" asked the neurosurgeon. "I am not going to be able to come and help you, and my two residents are tied up at the VA."

"He is worse, sir. His coma is deep. His skull X-ray shows a fracture along the right temporal bone. He is completely unresponsive. His pupils have gone from being sluggish to being fixed and dilated. When I shine light in his eyes, nothing happens," said Elizabeth.

"Well, then, you have *no* choice but to open his head. His brain will completely herniate, and he will die if you do not remove the pressure. You must drill the burr holes. Nurse Robichaud has seen it done a few times. She will help you."

Elizabeth thought, *Well, I am a doctor and a surgeon in training, and I am the only help that this man is going to get. I had better get on with it…*

Elizabeth's body held completely still and her mind gave her complete attention to Dr. Caballero's voice on the speaker phone: "Get the fourteen-millimeter clutch drill bit, and attach it to the handheld drill. Have someone hold the patient's head very still while you drill the first hole right behind his ear on the side of the fracture. If he does not improve, just keep breathing him down quickly, and move to the frontal, temporal, and parietal areas, and drill holes until he perks up. It is the *only* chance he has, Dr. Roberts. Do your best. Good luck," said Dr. Caballero as he hung up again.

Elizabeth felt lightheaded and nauseated as Nurse Robichaud handed her what looked like a drill for installing screws in a wall and hanging pictures.

The largest medical student moved to the top of the bed and held the patient's head slightly to the side. Another student, a tiny female, was tucked into the space under his arm, continuing positive pressure ventilation with the Ambu bag to breathe for the patient. They all stared at Elizabeth in anticipation.

"The head is bumpy, curved, and easy to slide off of," Nurse Robichaud said. "When you press on the skull, you want to push in a little bit with the drill or else you will just cut the scalp and never get through the bone."

"What if I push through the skull and get into the brain?" asked Elizabeth.

"The tip of the drill bit is short and designed to only go through the bone. But, Elizabeth, at this point, it hardly matters. This is his last hope, and the sooner you start, the better his chances are," said the nurse.

Elizabeth realized what she was seeing in Nurse Robichaud's eyes was raw pity. Elizabeth felt anger that her chief resident was nowhere to be found. She felt fear that she would not be able to do an adequate job at something she had never even seen before. She felt determination to do her absolute best for her patient.

She put on sterile gloves, wiped the area of the man's head where she was going to drill with antiseptic betadine to kill as many germs as possible, and began to hand crank the drill into the unconscious man's skull. As she pushed on his skull and turned the handle on the drill, she felt vomit rising in her throat. As she drilled and pushed, she felt the bone give way, and she felt the tip of the drill meet the soft matter of the patient's brain. She lifted the drill. A large blood clot shot out of the hole. She knew she had found the right spot and had entered the hematoma.

Elizabeth felt a moment of excitement and accomplishment. She knew that the burr hole had decreased the pressure on her patient's brain a bit. Her silent prayers were that it would be enough.

She hoped anxiously for any sign of improvement.

She performed her physical examination again, but nothing had changed. Mr. Pierce was still comatose and unresponsive. She drilled the next hole as Dr. Cabellero had instructed. Purposeful activity had always been an antidote to panic for Elizabeth. As she focused on her work, she prayed and drilled. Her panic subsided. Drilling into bone with a hand drill was strenuous physical work, and she began to sweat under the hot surgical lights of the trauma room. She felt her perspiration run between her breasts and down the backs of her legs.

Holes in the temporal bone and the frontal bones had been drilled. She was about to start the hole in the parietal bone as a nurse yelled, "Our patient has lost his pulse, and he has no blood pressure! Begin cardiopulmonary resuscitation now!"

As Elizabeth had moved from the top of Mr. Pierce's head, around the side, and to the back of his head with the drill, she had worked in a focused trance.

Now the trance was broken, and her patient was dying in earnest. She followed the well-established protocol for coding a patient. The team was very familiar with this part. They had just done this part of the routine an hour ago in the same room. The drugs were given, and the heart was shocked, but the patient died, despite everything.

For thirty minutes they continued working on Jeremiah Pierce. He was a young, healthy man with a wife and three children sitting in the waiting room of a major hospital. His wife and three kids were eating Burger King burgers and waiting for his discharge home. He couldn't just die. Elizabeth and Nurse Robichaud would not give up. They kept breathing for Mr. Pierce and pumping drugs into his veins and shocking his heart. None of the team members could make eye contact with each other.

None of them could bring themselves to call the code and stop the work, even though their patient was obviously dead.

Suddenly the doors swung open, and Dr. Caballero ran through them. He lifted the patient's eyelids, touched his wrist, and asked, "How long since his heart stopped?"

Elizabeth whispered, "Thirty-two minutes."

"It is time to stop. He is gone. There is nothing else to do," said the neurosurgeon.

As Elizabeth removed her hands from her patient, the room spun slightly. She felt as if her body and her brain were not fully connected.

She knew to focus on something nearby. Her eyes fell on Dr. Cabellero.

He was immaculately groomed, just as he was when they were having dinner at Commander's Palace. His confidence was apparent. With a thirty-second examination, he realized that the hopeful nurse and the horrified intern were on a fool's errand. His acceptance of the man's death was immediate. He did not look sad. He looked resigned and in control. Elizabeth knew this wasn't the first time he'd had to pronounce a patient dead. He had experience.

"Elizabeth, have you spoken to the family?" asked Dr. Caballero.

"No, none of us has met them yet," Nurse Robichaud answered.

"Well, that is about to change," said the neurosurgeon.

The doors swung open again, and Dr. Norman McSwain came through.

His face was tense and agitated. "What happened here?" he asked as he pulled back the white sheet to survey the dead patient. The professor was breathing hard; it was obvious he had run the whole block from Tulane Medical Center. His face was red, and his intense focus was on Elizabeth.

"He was hit in the side of the head with a baseball bat," began Dr. Caballero.

Dr. McSwain loudly interrupted, "*No*, Ernesto, I am asking her! She is the Tulane Surgery charge resident down here, and I want to know, from her, exactly why a patient died on her watch!"

Elizabeth was terrified at Dr. McSwain's stern tone, but mostly she felt sick with sadness. "We were busy working on the gynecologist conventioneer with the airway obstruction in Room Four, and by the time we got out and started making rounds, this man had gone from sitting up and talking with his family to on the floor and comatose."

"Really?" said McSwain. "And where exactly were you, doctor?"

"I was standing next to you in Room Four, Dr. McSwain," said Elizabeth.

"So, let me get this straight. Nobody was making rounds on the people in the exam rooms while you were helping in Room Four? Is that correct?" asked McSwain.

Elizabeth thought to herself, *The nurses and the students were.* But she had learned the Tulane Surgery way. She knew that no matter what, she was responsible for this patient.

"Yes, sir, that is what happened. I did not appreciate the fact that a person who had never lost consciousness and who walked into the emergency department could bleed into his brain and be dead in less than an hour. The error in judgment was completely mine," said Elizabeth.

"By the time you are through cleaning up this mess, Dr. Roberts, this man, his family, and his injury will be forever in your memory. This moment in time is branded into your psyche. If you are a good doctor, he will never leave you. This tragic mistake will be one that you will never make again," said Dr. McSwain sternly. He stared into her eyes without blinking. Elizabeth felt the weight of his proclamation. She knew he spoke the truth. She looked into the face of her dead patient, shuddered, and knew he was forevermore part of her life.

She started to shake all over, and she wondered if Dr. McSwain would fire her today or if he would wait until December and prolong her pain.

Dr. McSwain, ignoring her, studied the dead patient. "Poor bastard, this should never have happened. The burr holes are perfect. Who drilled those?"

"I did, sir," said Elizabeth.

"Caballero, did you help her?" asked McSwain.

"No, Dr. McSwain, I was upstairs doing a brain tumor and could not come down," said Dr. Caballero. "She was alone."

"Livvy, did you help her?" asked McSwain.

"No, Dr. McSwain. I got the drill and reminded her to have someone hold the head good and tight, but she figured it out on her own," said Nurse Robichaud.

As Dr. McSwain turned the dead man's head from side to side, he looked around at the nurses, nursing students, medical students, and orderlies standing frozen in the crowded room. All present were holding their breath, waiting to hear what would come next. As a professor, it was Dr. McSwain's job to make sure every encounter with any patient was a teaching moment. This one would be no exception.

Dr. McSwain took a deep breath and began, "Dr. Roberts made a huge mistake in not recognizing the mechanism of injury could be serious, in not getting him X-rayed quickly, and in not keeping a closer eye on him. But in all honesty, I really do not know if it would have made much difference. He is properly intubated, he has three functioning intravenous lines, and these burr holes are textbook perfect. Even if Dr. Caballero had been standing here, I do not see what he could have done better. With no operating room available, this poor guy was likely to die, no matter what." He sighed. "I am mad as hell about this, but I really think all that could have been done was done. Nurse Robichaud, get him cleaned up for the family. Dr. Roberts, come with me."

Elizabeth was filled with gratitude that he had not blamed her totally and that he had examined her work and found it acceptable. But she was filled with fear at the anticipation of what came next. Getting fired was not what she wanted.

She followed Dr. McSwain into Nurse Robichaud's small office. He held the door for her, followed her in, and shut the door. He did not sit down, and he did not invite her to sit. Elizabeth was tall at five feet, ten inches, but Dr. McSwain was taller. The top of his chest was in her face, and his breath was full of coffee and anger.

"You have killed your first patient, Dr. Roberts," he began. "It happens to all of us. At least yours was a sin of omission. Now you have to do the cleanup and learn to live with your error. First, you have to explain this to his family. Then you will go to his autopsy and look inside his brain to see exactly what those sixty minutes of your inattentiveness meant to this man's life. Lastly, you will stand before your peers and your professors on Friday afternoon at the Surgery Death and Complications Conference and explain exactly what occurred. You will be brutalized, and you will never forget it," said Dr. McSwain.

Elizabeth felt hot tears form in the corners of her eyes. She had never felt such shame.

When Dr. McSwain saw her tears welling up, his eyes flashed anger, and his jaw became hard. "There is no crying in Tulane Surgery! Dry it up. You are about to meet people who really have something to cry over. Pull yourself together, doctor!"

"Yes, sir," said Elizabeth.

"After someone has died, you have to go out into the waiting room and tell the family," he told her. "You always tell them the truth. No matter how badly things have gone from a medical standpoint, they have a right to know. You will stand before them, be as kind and as compassionate as you can be, and you will tell them the truth. Do you understand?"

"Yes, sir," said Elizabeth. Her father had taught her that she was better off taking a beating while telling the truth than trying to rebuild a relationship after a lie. She really had no experience in lying. It was not the way of her family or her Southern culture. Even in her terror and shame, she was relieved that it was her duty to tell the family the truth.

"Dr. Caballero and I will be with you. You will introduce us, but you are responsible for informing the family and handling this situation. Nurse Robichaud will get the patient ready for the family to see him, if they choose to see him. If they do, you will bring them back here and stay with them while they look at their dead family member for the last time. Let's go. You owe them this, Dr. Roberts," said the professor.

As they exited the nurse's office, Dr. Caballero stood waiting in the hall. He looked professional and somber. To Elizabeth, he resembled a famous Spanish opera star. As Elizabeth felt her panic rise, she heard music from *Madame Butterfly* playing in her head, which helped her fight the urge to run in the opposite direction as fast as her feet would take her. Cutting and running in the face of deep pain was an ingrained coping mechanism in many people. She felt the strong desire to run now. Focusing on the familiar sound of the famous aria in her head helped her to move forward toward the waiting area and overcome her natural instincts.

Elizabeth immediately identified Mr. Pierce's family. Three towheaded boys ranging in age from four to nine sat with a relaxed, overweight, and jolly-looking woman. They had gotten food from the Burger King across the street, and each boy had his hand in a Burger King bag. The mother looked up as the three doctors approached. Her face transformed from the smile that came with lighthearted laughter with her young children to anxious anticipation. Elizabeth was never one who could hide her feelings. The young mother could see what was coming on the young doctor's face.

Mrs. Pierce began to quiver and cry.

"Mrs. Pierce, I am Dr. Elizabeth Roberts, and this is Dr. Norman McSwain and Dr. Ernesto Caballero. We are the team who has been caring for your husband," said Elizabeth. Her urge to cut and run was growing. Her feet actually felt itchy, and it was hard to stand still.

"Hello," the woman responded. "I am Naomi Pierce, and these young men are Jeremiah Jr., Jonah, and Joshua. How's their father? When can we see him?"

The waiting room was crowded. Every green plastic chair had someone sitting in it, and some people were standing while they waited. Privacy was impossible. With mounting horror and regret, Elizabeth said, "I am terribly sorry to have to inform you, but your husband did not make it, ma'am."

"*Make what?* What did he not make, doctor?" asked Mrs. Pierce in disbelief.

The boys immediately sensed their mother's anxiety, dropped their bags of food to the floor, and came to complete attention, focusing on the adults before them.

"Where's my dad?" asked Jeremiah, the oldest. The three boys stood and moved closer to their mother.

Elizabeth could not bring herself to look at the child. She said, "Mrs. Pierce, I know it is hard to believe, but your husband has died. We did everything that we could for him, but he passed away a few minutes ago."

The woman let a small scream escape her tight lips and fell back into her chair. "We just saw him a little while ago," she said. "What do you mean that he died? He is young, and our children are small. What do you mean? We were at a Little League baseball game. Grown men do not die from baseball games!"

Elizabeth touched her arm to try to make a connection between them. The boys sat down and touched their mother's back and arms.

"When the bat hit him at the baseball game, it caused a small artery in the side of his head to bleed. It bled slowly, and it took a while to become apparent. Once it bled enough, his brain became swollen and he could not get oxygen. When that happened, he quit breathing, and he died. I am so sorry," said Elizabeth.

"But he was in a hospital. He drove himself here, and he was in the emergency room. Charity is famous for saving people. How can a man walk in here and die? How, doctor? How?" asked Mrs. Pierce.

Elizabeth realized neither Dr. McSwain nor Dr. Caballero was coming to her aid. She felt abandoned and lost. But her patient's family needed answers.

"We did everything that we could do to try to save him, and nothing worked," said Elizabeth simply. The young mother looked baffled and uncertain of what to do next.

The group sat quietly for a moment as the uncomfortable doctors waited. The silence was broken by young Jeremiah. He reached toward Elizabeth and pulled on the bottom of her white coat. "Miss Doctor Lady," he addressed her, "may I ask a few questions?"

Elizabeth instinctively squatted beside the boy and said, "Of course, sweetie."

Her heart was broken by the courage of the towheaded Little Leaguer with his tan freckles and fear-filled blue eyes. "Did my daddy say anything before he died? Did my daddy hurt? Did he know we were here waiting on him? I don't think he would go if he knew we were waiting on him," said Jeremiah.

Completely forgetting Dr. McSwain's admonition to never lie and never cry, Elizabeth looked into the child's eyes and said, "Your father loved you very much, and he did not suffer. He went quietly." Tears streamed down her face, and Jeremiah's tears streamed down his.

"Thank you, ma'am," said Jeremiah politely. "Is that my daddy's blood all over your nice pearls?" Elizabeth touched her own neck and felt the crusted blood on her skin and on her pearl necklace. His simple question wounded something deep in her soul. She knew this wound would never leave her, just as young Jeremiah's wounds would never leave him. She could not speak and merely nodded at the young boy to let him know that the blood on her pearls was indeed that of his dead father.

Dr. McSwain cleared his throat to indicate it was time to terminate the conversation. Elizabeth turned to the boys' mother and asked, "Mrs. Pierce, would you like to see your husband now, or would you prefer to see him at the funeral home?"

"I want to see him now, doctor. I think that Jeremiah should see him, too. They were very close, and he is very mature for his age," said the mother.

Dr. McSwain said, "Mrs. Pierce, your son is awfully young. I think it best if he stays out here to support his brothers, ma'am."

"I'll be the judge of what is best for my children, doctor," said Mrs. Pierce. She and young Jeremiah Jr. stood united.

Elizabeth was horror-stricken at the thought of this little boy going into Room Four to see his dead father. But she was doing this for the first time, and she had no idea what to say to try and dissuade Mrs. Pierce or how to say it, especially since Dr. McSwain's objection had not swayed her.

The triage nurse, Aoife, had been watching and listening to the entire scene from her desk. She walked over and said, "I can keep an eye on the little ones for a few minutes."

Dr. McSwain turned to leave. Dr. Caballero took the hand of nine-year-old Jeremiah, and Elizabeth supported the elbow of the mother. The group walked back down the long ugly hall to Room Four together.

To Elizabeth's surprise, Room Four had been transformed. The scariest equipment had been moved into the closet, and the floor had been mopped. Mr.

Pierce's head had been completely dressed with spotlessly clean white gauze, and he was lying peacefully on his back with a clean white sheet up to his chest. He looked like a hero taking a nap. His tan arms were folded over his chest, and his gold wedding ring was shining.

Jeremiah Jr. ran to the side of the table and immediately took the hand of his father. Big hot tears ran down his face. His mother threw herself across her husband's chest and said, "Oh, Jerry, I was going to surprise you tonight after the game and tell you that another little one is on the way. Oh, baby, why'd you have to leave me now?"

For all of Elizabeth's life, she had felt the presence of the newly dead near their bodies. She did not know if it was the spirit, a ghost, or some figment of her imagination, but she frequently felt something in the room near the time of a death. It did not occur every time, but sometimes she could sense something. Right now, she was certain she did feel a presence. It was very near the mother, and it expressed the idea that everything would be okay.

Elizabeth looked from the child to his mother and back to Dr. Caballero. Nobody else seemed to notice what she was feeling. Elizabeth shook her head from side to side and thought that maybe she was imagining it. Nonetheless, she felt a sense of ease and comfort in the room, and she hoped the wife and son felt it, too.

Young Jeremiah gave voice to what Elizabeth sensed. "My daddy looks peaceful," he said. "I think it is going to be okay, Mama." He patted his mother's trembling back.

"No, son, it is never going to be okay for me," said Mrs. Pierce.

Nurse Robichaud entered and handed the mother and child some tissues. The head nurse stood solemnly at the side of the grieving woman. Her face was filled with sadness. "Your other children are getting a little restless, Mrs. Pierce," she told her. "I think you might better head back to the waiting room. Someone will meet you there to work out the details. I sure am sorry that your husband passed."

Elizabeth saw the courage and determination on Jeremiah Jr.'s little face. His great courage matched her great shame. As Dr. Caballero steered what was left of the little family back to the waiting room, Elizabeth ran to the end of the hall, sobbing as she flung herself into the linen closet. The six-by-four-foot room was stocked floor to ceiling with freshly washed and bleached bed linens. She pressed her face into the piles of clean sheets and sobbed so hard she nearly threw up. The young doctor was grateful for the few moments of solitude.

Eventually, she washed her face with cold water from the utility sink, and she used the toothbrush from a patient admissions kit to clean the blood from her pearls. She sobbed again, counting the pearls like the beads of a rosary. She was not Catholic, but she needed solace. As she cleaned Mr. Pierce's blood from her grandmother's pearls, her body felt heavy, like it was made of brick. *Whatever made me think I could be a surgeon?* Earlier, she was hoping for greatness, and now she worried she might be fired. *How stupid am I?*

How could I possibly have failed these people so badly? She wanted to quit, run out the back door, and keep running. She never again wanted to see the look of disappointment and mourning that she had seen in the eyes of that child and his mother. She knew that Dr. McSwain was right. She would never, ever forget Jeremiah Pierce, a man who died because she was not diligent enough, or his grieving family. She could never remember having felt such guilt and remorse. In the middle of her breakdown, she heard the linen closet door open. "I hate to interrupt you in your nice office and all," she heard Nurse Robichaud say, "but there are twenty-one people sitting out here waiting for their doctor, Crème Puff. Wipe your face off. Put your pearls back on, and get out here." Elizabeth turned to look at her.

"Every surgeon loses a patient," the nurse told her. "Nobody saves them all. Your first death came early, in a very dramatic way. But this experience is part of the deal. Some live and some die, and your task is to do the absolute best that you can do. Who makes it and who doesn't make it is a mystery too deep for you and me. Now, stop thinking about yourself and get back out here," Lavinia Robichaud told her. "You are a Tulane surgeon, Elizabeth, and your patients need you."

CHAPTER 13
The French Quarter

T he long day and longer night were finally over. Elizabeth had seen twenty-three people with traumatic injuries during her twenty-four-hour shift. After the death of Jeremiah Pierce, she felt as if she were moving through a dream. The entire emergency room seemed draped in gray gauze, and she felt detached from reality. So much had happened. The shift had started dramatically, with the emergency tracheostomy of the drunken gynecologist conventioneer who aspirated his own vomit and coded.

Then came the struggle to save Mr. Pierce, his senseless death, and informing his family. The looks on the faces of the dead man's wife and their three sons would not leave her, even for a moment. There was no respite. The scene in the waiting room with the children kept replaying in her mind. Their entire world had been completely and forever shifted by a few words. Elizabeth wondered if her inner voice would ever stop reminding her of this terrible mistake.

She was grateful the remainder of her shift had been routine injuries from fights, car wrecks, domestic disputes, and superficial stab wounds; today her spirit was wounded more than most of the patients' bodies. She felt deeply ashamed for not having done her duty to the best of her ability. The importance of her job weighed heavily. She wondered how the family was doing. She wondered when Dr. McSwain would fire her. Mr. Pierce's death was a permanent scar on Elizabeth's otherwise clean conscience. She stood in the hall of the trauma suite feeling lost and alone.

Nurse Robichaud walked toward her. "Have you finished checking out all the patients to the LSU guy yet?"

"Yes, ma'am," Elizabeth told her. "He has seen everyone, and he knows what is going on."

"Okay, then," said Nurse Robichaud. "Get your things and let's go for a walk in the Quarter."

"But it is seven in the morning," Elizabeth protested, "and I have not slept in over a day. I was thinking that I'd just go upstairs and take a nap before I had to go to clinic." She did not feel like walking or having company. And she certainly did not want to continue the harangue about her failures as a doctor and her chances of not making it to December. She needed sleep, and she needed to get away from the other people in the accident room. She needed to grieve in private and grapple with her sense of shame. Shame was a new emotion for Elizabeth. She had always done her duty and never had much to be ashamed about. But now she was steeped in painful humiliation. She never wanted to feel this way again.

"You are not going to clinic for three hours," Nurse Robichaud said firmly. "Please come with me, Crème Puff. Once you are alone, the real demons will come. You won't be able to sleep, and you will feel awful. I know these things. Come and walk with me in the Quarter for an hour, and then you can get your nap. Come on, clinic does not start till ten," said Nurse Robichaud.

Elizabeth realized that the nurse had never before said "please" to her. The look in Lavinia Robichaud's eyes was pleading.

"I don't even know exactly how to get to the Quarter on foot from Charity," Elizabeth admitted. "I've only been on the side streets on the edge of the Quarter between my apartment and Café du Monde. Do I need my car?"

"No, Crème Puff. As in all things, just follow Nurse Robichaud. I will show you the jewel of our city," said the nurse.

Very reluctantly, Elizabeth followed her, dreading more admonishment. She could only think of sleep, and the French Quarter, the so-called Jewel of New Orleans, held no attraction compared to that of her bed. She thought it might kill her if she had to endure any more criticism. But knowing sleep would bring dreams, she decided to follow the nurse. *It will take less energy to do as Nurse Robichaud wants than it will take to argue with her,* Elizabeth decided.

Nurse Robichaud hung her white lab coat on a hook in the nurses' station. She put her small wallet into the front pocket of her scrubs. Nobody carried a purse around Charity. Muggers were ubiquitous, even within the hospital. Elizabeth had nothing to take with her. She kept five dollars pinned inside the pocket of her scrubs for emergency food at The Fistula. She was ready to go.

"To get to the French Quarter," Nurse Robichaud began as they started to walk, "you go out the front door of The Big Free, take a right on Tulane Avenue, and keep walking. At any time, you can hang a left. You will walk into the French Quarter eventually. The street signs all say Vieux Carre once you are in the Quarter."

Elizabeth said, "How do you decide which street to take?"

Nurse Robichaud said, "I like the scenic route myself, so I usually go down Bourbon Street if I am in the mood for a freak show. Drunks from the night before are still wandering Bourbon Street hoping a naked gal swings out of a window in a bar. I go down Royal Street if I want beauty and quiet. Royal Street is pure elegance. We had enough of the freak show last night. I say we go for the beauty."

Elizabeth felt like a zombie, her free will obliterated by physical and emotional exhaustion. She obediently followed the swinging hips of the jabbering nurse in front of her.

As they walked past the back door of the emergency department of Tulane Medical University Hospital, Elizabeth noticed an old wooden building on her left that looked completely out of place near a sprawling medical complex. The relatively new Tulane Hospital was only ten years old, and the rickety wooden structure looked one hundred years old. "What is that?" she asked.

"That old shack is Joe's," Nurse Robichaud replied. "I know that it looks like it could fall down any minute, but it has been there a long time. Every medical school has a favorite watering hole, and that one is Tulane's. It is an institution. Many think it might be the devil's den, as it has survived four hurricanes." She smiled, and then continued, "It is a place of comradery and debauchery. The walking wounded go there for drinks on Friday night after the Friday afternoon Death and Complications Conference. It is one of a few places where you see students, residents, fellows, nurses, EMTs, and some professors hanging out together. Whatever happens at Joe's is sacrosanct. It is packed every single Friday night. I'll take you one day," offered Nurse Robichaud.

Elizabeth shuddered at the thought of the Death and Complications Conference.

As they strolled by the old wooden building, Elizabeth said, "I'm not really much for bars."

She remembered her father's words of advice: "If you are going to be the only woman in your work environment, it is probably best to maintain decorum. You want to be completely above reproach, and you want to keep your personal life private. Be especially careful with the men. Be kind, courteous, and friendly to everyone. Be helpful at all times, but don't get romantically involved with your coworkers."

Elizabeth had steadfastly followed her father's advice. She had seen in college and medical school that the girls who crossed those lines with other students, teachers, and professors were not well respected. Elizabeth had little romance, but no trouble. So far, her father's advice had served her well. Hanging around in a dark bar with a bunch of drunken men was not anything she would willingly seek out.

As they walked, Nurse Robichaud watched Elizabeth and continued talking.

"You'll find that attendance at Joe's is mandatory. You can't be part of the team if you don't go over there and at least stand around for an hour on Friday night. Tulane Surgery is steeped in tradition. If you want to fit in, Elizabeth, you have to go there," insisted Nurse Robichaud.

"Okay, I am prepared to do whatever is necessary," said Elizabeth. If standing in a bar could numb this pain she felt from last night's debacle, she'd willingly stand there all night. She felt heavy and numb. She thought, *Too bad I'll likely get fired at the next Death and Complications Conference and miss the opportunity to stand around with drunk students and residents.*

The pair crossed Canal Street, navigated across the tracks of the double streetcar line that ran down Canal, and passed Burgundy Street, Dauphine Street, and Bourbon Street. Finally they turned left onto Royal Street.

When Elizabeth had interviewed at Tulane, she had taken a cursory cab drive through a few streets of the French Quarter, but she had spent most of the cab ride looking down at her notes and preparing for her Tulane interview. She had no remembrance of what there was to see in the Quarter, and had never explored the area on foot. Now, standing at the entrance to Royal Street in the early morning mist, Elizabeth felt transported to another world. As they walked down Royal Street toward the curve of the great Mississippi River, she was stunned by the beauty.

Elizabeth's eye was immediately pleased by the elegance. The facades of expensive antique shops, the elaborate iron-lace balconies with purple bougainvillea tumbling over the sides, and the rainbow of colors on the storefronts soothed her.

Nurse Robichaud said, "I love the activity on this street in the early morning. The owners of the expensive shops hire folks to come out and wash the sidewalks and water the plants. The owners of the smaller shops do it themselves."

The streets were steamy in the early morning. The smells of tea olive and jasmine mixed with walls of bougainvillea and mandevilla were intoxicating to Elizabeth. She had never been to Europe, but this was how she imagined an old town in Italy would be. Elizabeth wondered why she felt at home here. She had never seen anything like Royal Street in the mist, yet being there seemed like a homecoming.

"Elizabeth, this is one of the most expensive and respected antique districts in the world," Nurse Robichaud said. "Rich people come from the world over to shop here, and it is best appreciated in the early morning. Many of the antiques you see in movies are bought right here on Rue Royale."

Elizabeth could not help but compare the poverty and hideousness of the trauma room at Charity Hospital with the affluence and allure of this famous street, located just a few short blocks apart.

The shopkeepers were friendly and smiling. The aroma of chicory-laced coffee was everywhere, emanating from cups in the hands of the people hosing down the sidewalks or perched on window sills a few feet away. Every now and then, as they maneuvered past one of the cross streets, Elizabeth got a waft of alcohol or fried food or horse manure. But Rue Royale was pristine in the early morning.

Neither woman talked for several blocks. The peace of the early morning Quarter was wonderfully soothing. As they made their way to the riverside, Elizabeth noticed the opulence increased, and the floral plantings hanging from the wrought-iron balconies grew more elaborate.

Elizabeth loved the pastel colors of the Creole cottages. They reminded her of the thirteen Georgian homes on Rainbow Row in Charleston. Even with the absence of the Low Country palmetto trees, she felt homesick as she admired the beauty of the Quarter. The more she thought of home, the more she missed her father. She'd love to talk to him about last night in the Charity ER. She wanted to confess her failure. Her father could always soothe her.

Elizabeth realized she was standing still in the middle of the sidewalk, and that Nurse Robichaud was staring at her.

"Earth to Elizabeth! Look at the golden antiques in these windows! There's big money in that window, Crème Puff," said Nurse Robichaud.

Still feeling in a dream, Elizabeth followed instructions as they walked.

Every few yards, she glanced into a shop. The style of Louis XIV was everywhere. Flamboyant gilded chairs and tables flashed through the store windows. No green plastic for these shoppers! Elizabeth had only seen furnishings like these in movies and museums. She felt a flash of anger, contrasting the poverty she witnessed a few blocks away from such wealth.

"How can one city have such poverty and horror right next door to such beauty and wealth?" asked Elizabeth.

The nurse laughed and said, "Baby, this is New Orleans. It is a truly integrated society. Your crack addict and your mayor live close to each other. Your Loyola professor and your oil rig worker buy their groceries in the same place. Your streetwalker and your priest likely eat their po-boy sandwiches at the same counter. There is no place like this crazy place. It was safer before crack came to town, I'll give you that. But New Orleans has always had your rich right next to your poor."

Elizabeth ogled a beautiful flower-lined walkway leading to a garden behind a Creole cottage. "Look back there, Nurse Robichaud! That garden behind that cottage is just gorgeous!" said Elizabeth.

"Yes, it is. You can spend years wandering down these old streets and never see everything. The most beautiful spots are hidden behind the fronts of the houses and cottages. If you were to walk ten yards off the street, down an alley beside one of these homes, you'd be in a secret garden. It would be quieter and cooler than the street and just magical. I dream of living here one day. But it's a long way from Chalmette to the French Quarter, honey," said the nurse with a laugh.

Elizabeth wondered why Nurse Robichaud was laughing at her own dream.

"My father told me that you can do anything you really want to do," said Elizabeth.

"Well, that may be true for some people, but I sure don't find it to be true for *all* people," said Nurse Robichaud.

Elizabeth thought, *I disagree, but am too tired to debate.* She kept walking.

"Can you feel the river yet?" asked the nurse.

Elizabeth stopped quickly and tried to perceive a change in her environment. She did not know the location of the river, but looked in all directions, excluding the direction from which they had come. She noticed a sleeping man propped on the concrete walk under a door down Ursuline Street. As she looked in the opposite direction, she saw a massive Rhone horse in the middle of the street carrying a young policeman dressed in a navy blue uniform and black riding boots. The early morning sun caught the glint from his boots, his mirrored sunglasses, his brass uniform buttons, and his watch. He nodded solemnly in their direction and continued to sit on his horse, like a statue in the middle of the street. Elizabeth heard dripping from most balconies as plants were freshly watered. Drops of cool water blew off the balconies as they passed. But she could not fully sense the river.

"Why doesn't that policeman help that guy on the ground?" asked Elizabeth.

"He has probably already checked on him. The police down here are excellent. They have to let the good times roll and keep it all happy and vibrant. New Orleans tourists interpret the phrase *laissez le bon temps rouler,* which translates to *let the good times roll,* seriously. The police deal with amateur drunk tourists every day and night, the same people we see in the ER at Charity. There are always folks left over from the night before. The police try to round up the homeless, but there is the occasional passed-out tourist or straggler napping in the doorway of some store. Police in every city deal with tourists, but the New Orleans police have to deal with throngs of *drunken* tourists. A policeman's worst nightmare is an injured tourist. A hurt tourist is bad for business. So rest assured, he is on it, Crème Puff," Nurse Robichaud said. "Now answer my question about the river."

"I can't see it, if that is what you are asking. I don't even know in which direction to look. This is my first time on foot in the Quarter, and I am a little turned around. My sense of direction is not that great on land anyway," Elizabeth admitted. She did not feel like being quizzed on geography after that last ER shift.

"I can usually feel it by the time I get to Dumaine Street," Nurse Robichaud told her. "It is a mighty river, the Mississippi, and it takes a bend right at this part of the Quarter. To me, it roars like a grumpy old grandpa. I can hear it and feel a rumble when I get about here."

The nurse reached out and pulled Elizabeth to a stop. "Focus on the ground beneath your feet and see if you can detect a little tremble," she ordered.

"No, I really can't say that I feel anything," replied Elizabeth. "And the only rumble I am experiencing is my stomach. I am starving. If I don't get some coffee in me soon, I will be asleep in one of the doorways with that policeman jabbing me with his baton to see if I'm alive."

"You have been here no time at all, and already you are such a Tulane Surgery intern! Food, coffee, sleep, and sex are all you think about. Don't look at me so shocked! I saw you gawking at that hunky policeman on the horse. Your little mouth was watering, and your blue eyes were gleaming. You think he is *sexy*! Yep, you are a typical intern—sex, surgery, food, sleep." She laughed. "And, Crème Puff, I know you want that policeman to poke you with more than that billy stick," said the nurse.

Elizabeth was outraged and embarrassed at her transparency. "Nurse Robichaud, I was thinking nothing of the kind! I am, however, quite interested in some food!" Elizabeth wondered if her companion were a mind-reading voodoo queen. She'd have to be more guarded with her thoughts and facial expressions in the future.

"When you try to lie, which you really suck at, by the way," the laughing nurse said, "your drawl gets very pronounced, and you get very proper. I bet if you tried to tell a big lie, you could give Scarlett O'Hara herself a run for her money. You are very entertaining, Crème Puff."

"I thought we agreed that you would not bully and demean me as much," said Elizabeth.

"I am *not* bullying you or demeaning you. I am making observations," said the nurse.

Elizabeth stood tall, planted her feet, and put her hands on her hips, then turned to block the nurse from walking farther.

"Well, here's *my* observation. *You* like to keep the topic on other people so nobody knows anything about you. You want to know all my business, but won't even tell me your full name," said Elizabeth.

Both women held their breath and glared at each other. Elizabeth nervously wondered if she had stepped across a line that should have been respected.

After a very deep breath, Nurse Robichaud put her hands on her hips, cocked her head to one side, and said, "My name is Lavinia Adele Robichaud. My friends call me Livvy. If you ever call me Adele, I will kill you. I prefer that you call me Nurse Robichaud, for now. When you are no longer in my ER, if they don't fire your butt, you might be able to call me Livvy, but in private, not in front of other people. And definitely not until I say so. I insist all interns and residents give me proper respect."

"Okay, Nurse Robichaud, I am fine with that," said Elizabeth. *After all*, she thought, *Louisiana was part of the South, and proper manners did matter.* She just did not understand why deference and consideration did not go both ways. But Tulane Surgery was more like the military than a proper Southern institution. And as best she could tell, Elizabeth was considered a grunt.

The women walked another two blocks. Now Elizabeth, too, could feel the river. It was a slight rumble under her feet, and a low but audible roar in her ear. "I think I feel it. But I still can't see it."

"You won't be able to see it," Nurse Robichaud told her. "The banks are encased by a levy system so you have to climb up on the levy to see the Mississippi. You can't appreciate its full glory unless you are above the river, looking down. One night, you should go up on the rooftop of the Hotel Monteleone and look out over the river. That's the way to really appreciate its power and beauty."

"When I was in college, I was on the sailing team, and I sailed all over the Cooper and Ashley rivers around Charleston. I love the water. Can one sail the Mississippi?" asked Elizabeth.

"This is not a river like that," Nurse Robichaud said. "This river is at the bottom of our country, and it has accumulated the waste and power of all the areas that dump into it. You could not sail on this monster river. It does what it wants, and you just go along. When you sit near it, you can feel the power. It seems to say, 'Jump in here and I will mess you up.'"

Elizabeth believed her.

"If you doubt its power," Lavinia Robichaud continued, "just ask tugboat captains. I love to sit and watch them guide a big cargo ship through this river." She smiled. "This is no calm, meandering, clean little South Carolina river. This is the big, mean, muddy Mississippi. It drags all the toxic waste down from the middle of our great country and deposits it right here. That is what makes our shrimp and crawfish and oysters so fabulous! The nasty, muddy Mississippi flavors them up real good," laughed the nurse.

"That is disgusting!" said Elizabeth.

"Trust me, girl, after you have eaten them for a few years, nothing else will satisfy you. You will be hooked, and you will always want what you find so disgusting today. One day, you'll be living somewhere that is clean and neat and calm, and you'll be damn homesick for this nasty city and all its treats," said the nurse.

"I can't imagine. Are we getting close to food? I am starving," Elizabeth reminded her.

"We are nearly there. We are headed to the lower part of the Quarter on Decatur Street. It is the last street behind Jackson Square before you hit the levy. Is this your first time to Café du Monde?" asked Nurse Robichaud.

"No, I have buzzed up Esplanade in the dark to get coffee here. But I have not walked through the Quarter to get here, and I have never had the time to sit down inside. Usually I am half asleep when drinking my coffee and taking some to Aoife at the triage desk. I know the coffee is famous for having a chocolate flavor due to the chicory. I know the place is old and was started by the French. Right now, I could eat the awning," said Elizabeth.

"Typical intern!" said the nurse.

As they crossed Decatur Street and approached Jackson Square, Elizabeth saw old men feeding and brushing their horses for the day's work of pulling tourists around in their carriages. Each carriage was uniquely decorated with brightly colored flowers. Everyone was friendly and smiled at her, just like in Charleston. The smell of horse manure reminded her of working at her grandfather's farm in the summer and was strangely comforting. The famous statue of Andrew Jackson was behind a tall, black, wrought-iron fence. Elizabeth could see a few artists setting up easels in the square.

A short line was already forming at Café du Monde, which stayed open twenty-four hours a day. The sign out front proudly proclaimed, "The only time we close is Christmas Day and a few days when the occasional hurricane comes too close to New Orleans." Elizabeth chuckled as she read. Being familiar with coastal Carolina, she could relate to the idea of life being interrupted by the "occasional hurricane."

The women were seated outside under the green-and-white-striped awning with most of the other customers. It was getting hot, even though it was only seven-thirty in the morning. Elizabeth knew July and August to be brutally hot months throughout the South. In New Orleans, it could be hot even in November.

When the waitress arrived, Elizabeth noticed no menu was offered. But breakfast was breakfast the nation over, wasn't it? She excitedly ordered, "I'll have coffee without chicory, two scrambled eggs with ketchup, two sausage patties well done, and two biscuits with butter."

The waitress looked surprised and laughed as Lavinia Robichaud explained, "She's new. She don't know nothing yet, daw'lin. She'll have café au lait and three beignets, and I'll have iced coffee and three beignets, also."

"I have not eaten the food yet. What is a beg-net?" asked Elizabeth as she finally read the sign on the wall.

"There is no such thing as a 'beg net.' It is a French word, and it is pronounced *ben-yeh* and spelled b-e-i-g-n-e-t, silly. This place has been here since 1862, and they serve only a few things. You can get coffee with chicory, coffee with chicory and milk, iced coffee with chicory, orange juice, milk, and beignets. Beignets are fried hot, sugary doughnuts covered in powdered sugar. Those are all the choices. But as I see it, there is no good reason to eat anything else for breakfast," declared the nurse.

"It sounds delicious," said Elizabeth.

"I can't believe you have been coming here for takeout coffee and have not eaten here. I guess The Big Free has taken all of your focus," said Nurse Robichaud.

"Maybe I should have gotten the iced coffee, too. It is certainly warm out here for this early in the morning," said Elizabeth.

"No, you'll be fine with the coffee I ordered for you. One thing about New Orleans is that you can only get but so hot. Adding spices to the food and drinking hot drinks really can't make much difference. In July, it is hot as hell, and it does not matter much what you do or what you eat. Hot as hell is what you will be in July and August in New Orleans," said the nurse.

The food came quickly. Elizabeth gobbled the hot, fried, sweet dough and chased it with chicory coffee. This might have been the best breakfast of her adult life. As she finished her last beignet, Nurse Robichaud signaled for another order of three.

"You need to eat up," she admonished Elizabeth. "You are quickly getting too skinny. These little babies will perk you right up." She put all three beignets in front of Elizabeth.

"Thanks," said Elizabeth. She wondered what her father's mother, her granny, would say if she could see her shoving hot doughnuts in her mouth as fast as she possibly could. Elizabeth had been raised to be a proper Southern woman, and gobbling food was forbidden. But not eating for twelve hours at a time seemed to relieve her of the responsibility for adhering to all rules regarding the etiquette of eating. Since starting work in the trauma department, the new rules for eating were eat all you can, as fast as you can, because it may be a long time before you see food again, and don't waste time eating that could be used for sleeping.

Elizabeth looked up from the last beignet to see Nurse Robichaud laughing and looking at her again. "What now? What's so funny now?" asked Elizabeth.

"Crème Puff, you look like an addict covered in cocaine. You are skinny, have black bags under your eyes, and have white powder from one end of you to the other. There is powdered sugar in your eyelashes, honey! Next time," she advised, "lean over the table to eat the beignets, and don't blow the powdered sugar all over yourself. You could get arrested." She laughed again. "Oh, I forgot, that might be your goal. The cute cop on the horse could be the one arresting you. Did you spill that powdered sugar all over yourself on purpose?"

"Stop it with the policeman. I was just hungry," said Elizabeth grumpily. She looked around and noticed many other patrons were also covered in powdered sugar. Only the locals seemed to know how to avoid it.

For the first time in a day, Elizabeth felt relaxed. She sat back in her chair, sipped her delicious coffee, and felt almost human. She had never been out in public dressed in scrubs, but nobody seemed to notice. Casual was how many people were dressed. There were also people in elegant evening attire, coming in for coffee dressed from the night before. New Orleans welcomed everyone, whether you were in a business suit, a ball gown, a costume, shorts and flip-flops, or wrinkled scrubs. That accepting mentality was different from home. In South Carolina, you were expected to be properly attired at all times.

Nurse Robichaud interrupted Elizabeth's reverie. "So tell me how you ended up down here?"

"It's a long story, Nurse Robichaud. But I'll give you the CliffsNotes version. Even though it is 1982, there are only forty women in urology in the world. I want to be a urologist. I have to do two or three years of general surgery to be considered. With only around forty women in urology in the world, I figured that I'd better be well-trained to be fully accepted."

Nurse Robichaud listened silently and intently.

"I was an academically strong student," Elizabeth continued, "but when I interviewed at home, in South Carolina, nobody wanted a woman in their urology program. The chairman here at Tulane did not seem to care whether I was a man or a woman. He seemed to be looking for people who are dedicated. In fact, during my interview, he said, 'I don't care if you are a one-eyed purple cyclops; as long as you take excellent care of these patients, we'll get along well.' So I came partially for him and his attitude. The chairman of urology at my home medical school told me that 'even though you are a good student, we don't really want women in our program, yet.'" She noticed Nurse Robichaud was listening closely and leaning in toward Elizabeth. "That seemed to be a prevalent feeling at many places where I interviewed, other than Tulane. I signed up for three years of Tulane Surgery, even though only two years was the mandatory requirement before entering urology training. I figured if I was going to be one of the first women in a field, I'd better be above reproach. If Dr. McSwain doesn't fire me this year, I hope to transition into urology after my three years of general surgery," said Elizabeth.

The nurse gave Elizabeth her full attention. Elizabeth thought, *How odd! Nurse Robichaud seems genuinely interested in me.*

"You don't really seem like the trailblazer type to me," Nurse Robichaud told her. She cocked her head to study the young doctor. "I can't quite see you as the bra-burning-feminist type. That doesn't fit what I have seen in you so far. I would not have guessed you to be the kind of woman to be the first to do anything."

"You have me pegged correctly," Elizabeth assured her. "I am not a big feminist, but I do think men and women are equal in most ways. I saw my grandmother and grandfather work side by side doing most tasks on their farm. My thirty-two cousins and I worked all jobs on the farm all summer, and there really was not much difference between what the boys did and what the girls did. So I guess the whole idea that someone would not want me to do something because I am a girl caught me off-guard. It was not something I had considered an obstacle. But when that chairman of urology told me that I could not do it, I became more determined to do it. I think I might be more stubborn than I am a feminist," concluded Elizabeth.

Nurse Robichaud looked intently at the young doctor and asked, "Why choose Tulane General Surgery? It is one of the three most difficult programs in the country. You don't need all this trauma surgery to be a good urologist. Why would you do that to yourself?" She seemed genuinely puzzled. "You could have gone somewhere nice and cushy and done two years of general surgery and then come for urology here and not have been so exhausted. That easier path is what most urologists take. Did you consider that?"

"I considered it," Elizabeth replied. "But I figured that if I am going to be one of the first women in a particular field, and if the chairman at Tulane is going to give me a big break in accepting me, I owe it to them to be the absolute best I can be." She sat up straight and looked directly at Nurse Robichaud. "I am not afraid of hard work, Nurse Robichaud. Nothing is much harder than hoeing peanuts, pulling cotton, and picking tobacco in that hot Carolina sun. The only thing that scares me is not doing a good job with my assigned duty. I come from a long line of people who do their duty."

"I really can't imagine you as a tough farm girl," said the nurse.

"I was a town girl nine months out of the year, and a farm hand three months out of the year. I had the best, or worst, of both worlds, depending on how you view it. Now, enough about me; tell me about yourself," said Elizabeth.

"Not much to tell. I am a black woman from Chalmette, Louisiana. Chalmette is French for pastureland. We are on the Mississippi east of New Orleans. Ninety percent of the people in our parish are white. Chalmette is a haven for Louisiana rednecks. Locals from my area are called 'Chalmettians' and our parish, St. Bernard, is called 'Da Parish.' My family all had blue- collar jobs. I wanted better. I went to nursing school on scholarship at The Big Free. I have never been out of Louisiana except to go to the beach in Panama City a few times. Dr. McSwain gave me a chance, and I have worked my way up from the bottom in that trauma suite. I was a nurse's aide in the trauma area while I went to school. I love Charity and I respect Dr. McSwain. My whole life is in the walls of that hospital. I have never worked anywhere else and don't really care to. The Big Free is my chosen life," said Nurse Robichaud.

Elizabeth wondered why Nurse Robichaud had reported nothing particularly personal. She seemed to want to know all about Elizabeth, but offered little of herself. Elizabeth was fine with that, for now. In South Carolina, it was considered rude to ask personal questions. Religion, politics, and sex were not typical topics of discussion in her family. She could wait for more to be revealed. Elizabeth suspected most people got much less detail from Nurse Lavinia Robichaud.

"How are you feeling about that death last night?" asked Nurse Robichaud, abruptly changing the subject and interrupting Elizabeth's train of thought.

Elizabeth felt a spark of anger. The room seemed to tilt and her heart pounded. She felt a dark pall start to cover what had been a sweet and calming time.

"I feel terrible about it! How in the world would you expect me to feel, Nurse Robichaud?" said Elizabeth.

"I can see that you are taking it harder than most," Nurse Robichaud said. "Every single surgeon loses patients. It is part of the work." She paused. "It is one of the reasons why I am a nurse and not a doctor. At the end of the day, I am not the one in charge, and I am glad for that. Dr. McSwain makes all the hard decisions, and I follow his orders. That way, I sleep a little better at night," admitted the nurse.

"Well, it is a little late for a career change!" Elizabeth exclaimed. "Thanks for the great advice—that I should have been a nurse instead of a doctor. I really appreciate your words of wisdom," sneered Elizabeth. She blinked back tears as her pain and sadness and shame came roaring back.

"Don't get that way with me, Missy," said Nurse Robichaud. "All I am saying is that I fully understand the weight on your shoulders. I understand it so well that I knew it was not for me."

Elizabeth felt her anger subsiding.

"Being able to shoulder that kind of load and not drink or drug yourself into oblivion requires a modicum of greatness, Elizabeth," the nurse went on. "And I think you could have what it takes. I saw you were absolutely crushed by what happened. I heard your sobs in that linen closet, and I saw your pain. I watched you get right out of that laundry closet after you cleaned your pearls and wiped your face, and go out into that emergency room and keep working."

Elizabeth felt surprised that Nurse Robichaud thought she would do anything else. Doing her duty was instilled in her core by her family. How you felt while doing your duty had little to do with anything.

"Whether you realize or not," the nurse continued, "somebody raised you right. Part of your ability is God-given. Part of your ability is uniquely you. And part of your ability is the people who brought you up. All that combines to give you a little bit of the quality called greatness." She paused a moment to let that sink in. "All the great doctors care so much that it hurts them. I see it in Dr. McSwain, and Dr. White, and I see it in you, girl. That is all I am trying to tell you."

Elizabeth's lip trembled, and her tears stopped as she accepted the best compliment she had ever received in her life.

"Thank you, Nurse Robichaud," said Elizabeth, sincerely. "I find it hard to believe that I will ever be as capable as Dr. McSwain, Dr. White, and Dr. Caballero. They seem like they are in a whole different category. I do, however, think that I could be as good as Dr. Peterson. Quite frankly, he does not seem to try very hard."

"No, you will easily surpass Dr. Peterson," Nurse Robichaud assured her. "He thinks way too much with his little head. That man is a big old Romeo. His brain is stuck on sex, sex, sex, cigar, Jack Daniels, operate a little, take a nap, sex, sex. You can beat him just by breathing and showing up. He really wanted to be a rich banker, but his granddaddy said he would disinherit him unless he became the fourth generation of surgeons in the Peterson dynasty."

"You sure do like to gossip," said Elizabeth.

"No, I don't," Lavinia Robichaud asserted. "I observe. I just don't have much else going on in my life." She looked down at the table, then up to meet Elizabeth's eyes. "What I really wanted to tell you this morning is that your patients will be with you always. Whether you think you saved them or whether you think you killed them, they will always be with you. What I want you to remember is what I told you on your very first day. You are not in charge. Dr. White did not save that man with the gunshot wound, and you did not kill that man with the head wound. Something a whole lot bigger than you or any other doctor is running the show. You are just privileged enough to get a ringside view for the ride. Don't ever think it's all you—one way or the other. It's not. And never forget how rich your life is for being on the front lines, Elizabeth."

"Thanks, Livvy. I appreciate it," said Elizabeth. After a few moments passed, Elizabeth realized Nurse Robichaud had not corrected her use of the familiar.

The nurse drained the last of her chicory coffee.

"Come on, Crème Puff, I need to run next door to the open market and pick up some fresh tomatoes for my grand mere's gumbo today. Lucky for me, they are selling tomatoes there these days and not slaves! I'd hate to be on the block today. As tired as I am and as raggedy as I look, somebody might mistake me for a field slave instead of a house slave," laughed Livvy.

For a second, Elizabeth was shocked. *Ah, there goes that gallows humor again.*

"Don't worry," Elizabeth told her. "I doubt anyone would buy you. You are too mouthy, and you gossip too much. I hear that in the old days, a good slave was valued for her discretion," said Elizabeth, squealing and stepping out of reach as Livvy swatted at her.

"Oh, no! *I am gonna git you, girl!* I am gonna git you good. You'd better hope that hunk on the horse is nearby to save your scrawny white ass, 'cause I am gonna git you!" hollered Livvy as she chased Elizabeth down Decatur Street toward the vegetable market that used to be a slave market.

Powdered sugar flew from Elizabeth's scrubs as she easily outpaced the full-figured nurse. Both women squealed as they ran.

CHAPTER 14
The Autopsy

Elizabeth moved quickly through the French Quarter after she and Livvy parted at the old slave market building that now housed a popular produce market. Elizabeth was assigned to the private professor's clinic at Tulane Medical Center today, to help in Dr. McSwain's post-op clinic. It started at ten, which meant she had twenty minutes to rush to the call room, shower, and change into a skirt and blouse. After that, she had to grab a clean white coat and run back to Tulane Medical Center. The professors did not tolerate poor grooming from the interns assisting in their private clinics. The patients at the private clinic were clean, usually not bleeding, and they paid for their care. She had to look her best.

In the humid New Orleans summer, Elizabeth knew, the effect of her shower would only last thirty minutes. By the time she crossed Tulane Avenue, she'd look wilted again. But at least she'd be clean. The work in the post-op clinic was easy and mindless, and the patients usually were nice. She'd remove stitches, change dressings, and report any infections to Dr. McSwain. As a student in Charleston, she had spent many hours in the post-op clinic of the many local surgeons who allowed students to rotate through their offices. She felt confident in that environment. Her work in the post-op clinic would go quickly; Dr. McSwain liked to care for most of his patients personally, checking behind the intern on every case. Elizabeth thought, *Today should be an easy day.*

As Elizabeth walked toward Charity, she noticed the French Quarter had been getting busy while she and Livvy were eating and talking at Café du Monde. Delivery trucks carrying vegetables, fresh seafood, liquor, and beer lined streets that previously were empty. Restocking the stores and restaurants took an army, and the activity resembled a busy beehive. Men and women in shorts and T-shirts rapidly pulled overflowing boxes from trucks on every narrow street.

Elizabeth inspected the open containers of fresh produce as she walked by. She had loved going to the farmers' market with her grandfather to sell his produce in South Carolina. The colors, smells, and freshness of food that only recently had been harvested intoxicated the senses. During summers at her grandfather's farm, she ate fresh fruits and vegetables right off the vine, and today she longed to grab a tomato or green pepper off the stack and dig in. "Dust the dirt off on your shorts and dig in," her older cousins had instructed. *All fruits and vegetables taste better when warmed by the summer sun.*

The doors to the restaurants were open, and Elizabeth felt short blasts of cold air-conditioned air as she walked past them. The seconds of cold air were a respite from the otherwise exhausting heat. A constant parade of workers passed through the restaurant doors with rolling carts, each one piled high with boxes. A second line of workers exited swiftly with empty carts, headed back to the trucks for refills. The usual slow pace of New Orleans was forgotten during the early morning frenzy of restocking the French Quarter. Everything had to be ready to open by ten o'clock.

As Elizabeth moved toward the Canal Street side of the Quarter at a faster pace, she again saw the policeman on the big red horse. Her heart sped up and she instinctively took a street that went in the opposite direction. Her duty awaited her, and time was short. Handsome men were low on her current list of priorities.

Just as she crossed Canal Street and headed to Charity Hospital, her pager went off. The pager, which weighed about five pounds, pulled on the waistband of her scrub pants and underwear and screamed out like a speaker at the drive-in movies in her hometown. Some doctors higher up in the pecking order of students, interns, residents, and fellows had more modern pagers, ones that were a little smaller and lighter. But the interns carried around the equivalent of a small speaker. The Tulane operator's voice squawked loudly, "Dr. McSwain's post-operative clinic is canceled today. He wants you at the autopsy lab for ten o'clock. I repeat, no clinic for you today. Be at the Charity autopsy room for ten o'clock today."

Unfortunately, anyone within a twenty-yard radius could hear her loud pager. All activity paused for a second as everyone in her immediate vicinity stopped to see who was going to an autopsy today. Elizabeth was embarrassed. The beauty of the French Quarter dissolved around her. The shame and sadness of Mr. Pierce's death was once again all encompassing. Elizabeth felt conspicuous standing in her wrinkled scrubs in the middle of the antiquing district in front of Brennan's restaurant, being summoned loudly to an autopsy. She felt as if the entire street must know she was recently implicit in someone's death and that she would be called before the Tulane Medical School equivalent of a firing squad to answer for it. What they did not know was that Elizabeth's memory of Mr. Pierce's sad little sons was worse than anything that could occur at an autopsy.

She slowed her pace, realizing a shower was not necessary this morning. Being clean was not required in the autopsy room. Elizabeth was filled with angst. Her contented mood evaporated, her shoulders tensed, and her jaw tightened.

She had helped with many autopsies. One of her many student jobs was working as an assistant in the autopsy lab. She did not enjoy work in the morgue as death was always sad to her. The formaldehyde smell and the smell of death were unpleasant to Elizabeth. But she had learned a great deal of anatomy and had learned much about how disease could ravage the body. All her prior autopsies had been on people that she had not treated as a doctor. She functioned as a technician in her past experience and had never known the people in life. This morning's autopsy felt personal, and she dreaded it.

As she walked through the front door of Charity Hospital, she realized it was a quarter of ten. She saw Dr. Peterson standing in front of the elevators to the basement.

"Good morning, Dr. Peterson," said Elizabeth as she approached.

"Well, good morning to you!" he exclaimed. "I guess it is time for you to go and see exactly what happens to a person when their doctor does not pay attention to what they are supposed to do," he said with a cruel smile.

Elizabeth thought, *That statement could apply to you, too. You are my boss and you were nowhere to be found when we needed you.* She knew better than to reveal her thoughts. After all, Tulane Surgery and the military were similar in their complete respect for the chain of command. She turned her head away from him and to the elevator doors.

He talked to the back of her head while they waited on the elevator. "You know, Elizabeth, you are a beautiful woman. Surely you could marry some nice Charlestonian and avoid all this mess," said Dr. Peterson.

When Elizabeth didn't rise to the bait, he continued, "You know you don't really fit in here, don't you?" he taunted her. "Being somebody's nice, mannered wife should be your goal. You'd be a really nice wife. Want to be mine? You could quit now and avoid this whole autopsy thing. Surely the thought of getting grilled at the Death and Complications Conference is enough to make you jump into my arms? Come on, be mine!" Dr. Peterson mocked her as he bowed, got on one knee, and pretended to offer an engagement ring.

Elizabeth wondered, *Why does he feel the need to taunt me?* She recognized his privileged past and his lazy streak, but she had not realized how mean-spirited he was. She had been taught to accept others and to forgive little slights. Her father always told her, "Most people are doing the best they can at any given time." Elizabeth did not think Edward Peterson was doing his best, and she did not understand why people felt the need to be mean. She despised unnecessary meanness.

But rather than striking back, she played along. Using her most exaggerated Southern-belle voice she said, "One fateful day, I put the wrong fork in the wrong place on the white linen tablecloth at Christmas dinner, and I was ousted from the family forever and forced to go into exile and work for a living. What happened to *you* that caused you to have to seek employment?" Fear and shame, she realized, could make her mean, too.

Dr. Peterson jumped up, frowned, turned his back on her, and entered the elevator. They rode to the pathology department in stony silence.

As they exited the elevator and entered the pathology department, Dr. Peterson said, "Elizabeth, you choosing to get huffy with me will not help you, girl. McSwain is not happy about this death occurring in July, and I can assure you that the snobby Cuban opera expert, Dr. Caballero, is not going to get his hands dirty helping an intern who won't make it to December. I'm your only hope come Friday's Death and Complications Conference. You'd better show me some respect." His voice was threatening, and his eyes were cold.

Remembering again that Tulane Surgery was like the military, Elizabeth replied, "Yes, sir!" She doubted, seriously, that he would offer her any aid. She accepted that she would be alone at Death and Complications Conference on Friday.

The doors to the autopsy suite swung open as the autopsy technician, whose badge identified him as George, pushed his way out with an empty gurney. He was covered from head to toe with pale blue paper hat, mask, scrubs, shoe covers, and thick surgical gloves. Course gray hair escaped the edges of the surgical cap, and dark, shiny skin with ropelike veins peeked out in the area from his hat to his shoulder. He was tall and wiry, but moved slowly with age. "Morning, Doc Peterson. It was time for a pickup on the cancer ward. That ward keeps us hopping. LSU lost one this morning." He paused and then changed the subject. "I missed you at the Saints' game last week. You usually never miss a game. Where were you?" George asked.

"It is November," Peterson told him, "and I have to keep my eye on these interns. They'd be killing people every fifteen minutes if I left The Big Free to go to a football game. I have to hang close to the hospital until at least the middle of December. By then, I will know who is *Hodad*!" said the chief resident.

"Well, I will keep your seat warm for you," George assured him. "The Cajun Cannon is *hot* in the preseason!"

"Yep, that Bobby Hebert is turning into quite the quarterback. I have season tickets, and I hate to miss seeing him. But I have to keep this girl from killing anybody else," Peterson said. "You know Tulane—always the *equal opportunity employer*," said the chief resident, pointing his thumb over his shoulder at Elizabeth.

George ignored Dr. Peterson's derogatory comments. So did Elizabeth.

George pushed the empty gurney down the hall toward the elevator and picked up a full gurney left in the hall by the nurses from the cancer floor. As he unloaded the patient from the cancer ward onto one of the pristinely clean metal tables and covered the dead patient carefully with a clean white sheet, Elizabeth noticed his respectfulness to the dead. He was preserving the patient's privacy, even in death.

Elizabeth and Dr. Peterson waited patiently for George by their assigned metal table. Elizabeth asked Dr. Peterson, "What is *Hodad*?"

"It is an old Tulane term used mostly for professors who are very smart but cannot operate well. It stands for *Hands of Death and Destruction*. We have some teachers who are brilliant researchers but not great surgeons. At our awards banquet at the end of the year, we give out awards. Some are for excellence. Many are for fun. You could get the *Hodad* award for this man's death. But then, I doubt you'll be here after the big cut in December. Yeah, I'd say that about now, your head is the first for the chopping block."

Elizabeth was washed anew in a bath of shame. She refused to look at Dr. Peterson for fear her facial expression would betray the combination of anger, determination, fear, and humiliation she was feeling, so she looked at the table in front of her as Dr. Peterson pulled back the white sheet to expose Mr. Pierce's body.

Elizabeth was shocked to see that Mr. Pierce resembled himself in life only slightly. Whatever the animating force that made him the happy father and husband was long gone. He looked like a wax figure from a museum. All other emotions left her as again she was filled with pity for this man and his family and their loss. Those sad little boys were all she could see. Remembering the bravery of the oldest son broke her heart again.

She shuddered and fought back tears.

George had quickly returned with a full gurney, which he parked near the wall and covered with a sheet. One of the nurses from the cancer ward must have brought the patient to the elevator. The nurses did not like for anyone who had died to stay on the ward for long. The next body was waiting for the LSU team's turn in the autopsy room.

"Time to start, George," said Dr. Peterson as he lit a cigar. "I hate the smell of this place. But if McSwain shows up and we are not here, it will be ugly." He stood to the side and smoked his fat cigar, while George and Elizabeth went to work. Elizabeth had never seen anyone smoke in the hospital. But as usual, the rules did not seem to apply to Dr. Peterson.

Elizabeth stood mute, trying not to cry. She was very familiar with the routine of the autopsy. Part of her job as a student had been to record what the pathologist did and to weigh and catalog the organs. She knew the time-honored sequence of exploring a body for clues to death.

The autopsy technician moved with grace, respect, and obvious experience. At Charity, George and the surgeon did the autopsy and the pathologist was called only if anything unusual was found, or if the legal system was involved in the case. With thirty to forty deaths per day, the pathology department was swamped with work.

It seemed to Elizabeth that it took an eternity to saw open the patient's skull. She knew it had only been ten minutes, but the anticipation was miserable. As the brain was opened, she saw the giant clot of blood, now liquefied, that had pushed Mr. Pierce's brain down into his spinal canal, obliterated his breathing center, and killed him. She saw the fracture above his ear in the area of his temporal bone and peered into his skull at the torn artery responsible for the bleeding and brain herniation. She stifled a wave of nausea that she attributed to her shame and Dr. Peterson's smelly cigar.

The doors opened, and Dr. Norman McSwain marched through. "Anything unusual, George?" he asked.

"No, sir, this is pretty straightforward," George replied. "No other signs of any other trauma. It looks like something blunt caught him on the side of his head, ruptured the middle meningeal artery, filled his brain with blood, stopped his breathing, and here we are. Poor guy. Looks like these burr holes were drilled just right. One is right over the clot. I don't know why it did not drain the clot out. Come see, doc, the drill hole is right over the clot, sir," said George.

Elizabeth felt a second's respite from her shame as she realized that the hole she had drilled was where it was supposed to have been.

Dr. McSwain reeled around to face Elizabeth, standing a foot from her.

"Dr. Roberts, did you get a good look at your handiwork? You will be explaining this to your colleagues on Friday afternoon. George will provide you with a copy of the autopsy report tomorrow, after the pathologist confirms everything. I expect you to make copies of the autopsy report, one for each chief and the professors at the conference. I suggest you be very familiar with all aspects of this case. You will be standing in front of the group and explaining this man's demise. Any questions?" said Dr. McSwain.

Elizabeth felt a sense of dread unlike any she had ever known. "No sir, I have no questions. Dr. McSwain, I understand," said Elizabeth. She realized he was not requesting that she do these tasks. They were required of her, and she would comply. Already, she was bracing herself for what she feared would be the prelude to her getting fired. She had never experienced public humiliation in her genteel South Carolina upbringing. Her abdomen clenched at the thought.

Dr. McSwain reviewed the remainder of the technician's autopsy and paperwork and said, "Thanks, George, you're the best," as he exited.

Dr. Peterson grinned through his cigar smoke and said, "This Death and Complications Conference is going to be good. More than half the faculty and almost all the residents do not want women at Tulane Surgery. They are going to roast you like a Christmas goose, young lady." He smiled in anticipation. "Whatever you do, don't cry. They will fire you on the spot if you cry. I can't wait to have a ringside seat for this show."

In that moment, Elizabeth hated Edward Peterson. But more than hatred, she felt a keen lack of respect for her chief resident. He was supposed to teach her. He was supposed to toughen her up, but not tear her down. She thought his badgering her showed his lack of humility. She knew there would be men who would not welcome a woman into the male-dominated world of surgery. She knew that urology was 98 percent male doctors worldwide. She refused to even acknowledge sexism. She knew from the teachings of her father and the work on their farm that women could do anything. She would not waste her energy trying to change Dr. Peterson. She had more important ways to spend her time and energy. Simply learning the vast amount of knowledge required to be a surgeon was all-consuming.

"Are you about to cry, Dr. Roberts?" asked Dr. Peterson.

"Mr. Pierce's wife and children are doing enough crying for all of us," she said coldly. "You don't need to be cruel to me, Dr. Peterson. I see what can happen if a surgeon is not paying attention to every detail at every moment. I will not need to repeat this lesson."

Elizabeth knew that Dr. McSwain was right. The memory of this man and his family would never leave her. They were forever part of the fabric of her psyche.

Dr. Peterson snuffed out his cigar on the counter and left abruptly. Elizabeth wondered, *How can that pompous ass take no responsibility for this man's death?*

The technician, George, said, "Honey, try not to take this death too hard. If anybody has been down here more than Dr. Peterson, I don't know who it is. Don't let him get to you," he said kindly. "Dr. Peterson is just trying to pass his failures off on you. I don't want to speak out of turn. But just remember that every single one of them doctors who will be saying mean things to you on Friday has been in this same position, and many of them have been there multiple times. You just study this case from every angle and answer all their questions and you will be fine. I been doing this job for thirty-two years, and I done seen it all. Dr. Peterson is a good- enough doctor and pretty congenial outside the hospital. But everyone knows he likes to blame others. That is one of his weaknesses. We all got weaknesses. You just learn your patient's case from front to back and you will be okay on Friday."

Elizabeth felt somewhat reassured by his words. Intellectually, she knew all doctors lost patients. But Mr. Pierce was *her* patient. And doing her duty well was an all-consuming force in her psychological makeup. She could not accept failure easily.

"Livvy tells me that you are one of the good ones," George continued. "She always knows. It will be okay. Tulane wants to produce the best possible surgeons. Examining every aspect of every failure is part of the Tulane way." He paused. "I see from the look on your face that they have been beating on you real hard. But when you get done with your time in that trauma suite, you will never choke.

You will do surgery like Bobby Hebert plays football. Try to think of yourself as taking your hits early in the game to toughen you for the playoffs." He smiled. "It ain't nothing personal. Be proud that they are treating you just like everyone else. That means they think you have potential. Dr. McSwain is one of the fairest men I have ever known. If you are meant to be a Tulane surgeon, God will give you the strength. When they are getting on you, remember it is the Tulane Surgery way. And the ones that survived the experience and did not quit became great surgeons."

Elizabeth adored kindness at least as much as she hated meanness. This elderly black man with the grueling job was kind. His soft, melodic voice and lilting accent resembled Nurse Robichaud's. She felt comforted.

She looked down at Mr. Pierce for the last time and turned to walk out. "Thank you, sir," she said to George. "I appreciate your counsel. You have helped me greatly."

CHAPTER 15

The Soap Incident

I t was Friday, and Elizabeth was reliving yesterday's visit to the autopsy room in her head as she made her way to the on-call room, hoping to nap for a few hours and to study in preparation for the Death and Complications Conference that afternoon. Her work since the autopsy had been routine, and for that she was grateful. She had little appetite, but knew she needed to eat to keep her brain and body fueled. A fruit-stand vendor had appeared in front of The Fistula, and she had been grazing on fresh fruit and nuts for two days. Cracking open the pecans and eating the fresh fruit calmed her. The rhythm of the nut cracking reminded her of home. She and her cousins often sat with their grandfather on the big back porch at the farm and ate figs, grapes, and pecans. These little reminders of home soothed her. She hoped her appetite and time for a real meal would return soon.

She usually took the old, noisy, slow elevator for the pure pleasure of singing with Miss Albertha. But today, not even the jovial elevator operator and her beautiful gospel music could cheer Elizabeth. Instead, she punished herself by trudging up the twelve flights of dark, steep, stairs to the musty on-call room.

Elizabeth thought her first year as a surgical intern would be more academic, and not so exhausting. She expected higher education to elevate her life into the lofty realms of smart and forward-thinking people. After long days working in Charity's ER and the various clinics, she felt much as she had after a long day of hauling horse manure on her grandparents' farm—physically fatigued and mildly disgusted by her work. The exhaustion she felt today made her wonder what life would be like if she just stayed on the farm. At least she was good at farm duties, and farm work did not wear on her emotions. Her spirit never felt this heavy after farm chores. The worst chore at the farm was chasing down the farm animals in the middle of the night if they broke out of their fence. And even that chore usually involved laughter with her cousins and uncles. And best of all at the farm, she shared a room with other female cousins instead of two male strangers. As Elizabeth opened the on-call room door, she smelled the dank mildew odor of New Orleans. She recalled the rumors she heard at orientation about the horrible hazing that occurred at Death and Complications Conferences, especially toward new doctors who made errors in patient care. She shuddered at the thought of what might happen to her later that day.

Then she smiled as she looked at the first of the three old, sagging metal-frame beds. Surely they were prison surplus. Tony Parker was asleep in one, with his giant black head crushed into his pillow and loud snores roaring from the back of his throat. Elizabeth wondered how he got his bristle-brush hair to look symmetrical again—he usually woke up with one side mashed flat, while the other side stuck straight out from his head. She knew maintaining his short afro hairstyle was a constant source of hassle for him. She was thankful for her ponytail. She felt comforted knowing Tony was a sweet man, whether awake or asleep. She had grown to like and trust him. She considered Tony her friend.

Michael LeBlanc, their other roommate, sat at the only desk in the room, poring over a surgical text. The gray metal desk chair looked uncomfortable, and Michael looked frozen in place with his books.

He looked up when he heard the door open and whispered, "Good morning. Sorry about what happened to you. It must have been rough."

Elizabeth was surprised by his kindness, and she wondered what had changed his previously cocky and arrogant demeanor. Today Michael looked broken. He, like Elizabeth, was getting thinner, and he had deep, dark bags under his eyes. Elizabeth felt a wave of compassion for him, despite his prior poor treatment of her. Apparently, he'd had a rough week, too. Perhaps, Elizabeth thought, even though Michael had been a student at LSU and had worked at Charity Hospital a few years, being an intern and being completely responsible for patients' lives was a heavier weight than either of them could have envisioned.

She said quietly, "Thanks, it was a horrible experience. I worry about the family of the patient." She walked into the small bathroom they shared, quietly closed the old wooden door, and peeled off the scrubs that felt grown into her skin. Stains from at least two different body fluids from other people were recognizable on her pants. She noticed Michael's shaving kit, sitting open on the toilet tank. Condoms in foil packages protruded from the top, alongside his razor and toothpaste. Elizabeth wondered why he would bring condoms to the hospital.

She reached excitedly for her own toothbrush, anticipating the pleasure of clean teeth, and noticed the container holding her bar of Clinique face soap was open on the shelf by the shower. *Not a good sign.* Elizabeth always closed the container after using the soap. One long, thick, blond pubic hair stuck straight up on top of the soap bar. It was a deliberate provocation. It was just too much.

All the pain, emotion, and disappointment of the last week came flooding back as she ran out of the bathroom and into the common sleeping area. She abruptly halted in front of Michael, whom she supposed was the culprit. She was clearly furious. She did not realize that she was standing in the middle of the room in her bra and panties.

"*How dare you!*" she yelled at Michael, forgetting for a moment that Tony was sleeping nearby. "The *one* thing I asked of this crazy co-ed housing arrangement is that you *not* use my face soap on your behind. *How dare you* use my expensive personal face soap *on your private areas!*" Elizabeth screamed as she stood over Michael.

Her raised voice was enough to awaken Tony. He came to life in a fog of confusion and looked around as if he was not quite sure of his current location.

His blurry eyes focused on Elizabeth, and he asked, "What happened? Are you okay?" He averted his eyes as he realized what might have been a white two-piece bathing suit was actually her white cotton bra and panties.

Elizabeth turned to Tony, wildly waving her arms, and said emphatically, "No, I am not okay! That inconsiderate moron used my face soap on his butt and left his pubic hair on it!" She felt deeply betrayed. *What kind of a man uses a woman's personal toiletries? How could he be so rude?* Even her boy cousins at the farm knew better than to use their girl cousins' personal supplies. *Who raised this idiot, Michael LeBlanc?* Elizabeth felt she had lost all control over her life. The thin veneer of civility was gone, destroyed by this transgression. Michael's cocky attitude came flooding back. He stood up, defiantly, moving toward Elizabeth, encroaching on her personal space. "What makes you think it was me?" he inquired. "Three of us are living here, if you want to call this living, and I am only one of the three. Hell, you are so tired that you might have forgotten you used it yourself!"

Both men realized Elizabeth, in her fury, did not notice she wasn't dressed. Her white cotton bra and panties were certainly modest. But still, they were underwear.

Elizabeth looked from Tony to Michael. Tony looked horrified. Michael looked defiant.

There was nothing Elizabeth despised more than lying. Nobody in her family lied. It was not tolerated. Her boiling fury grew.

She screamed at Michael while pointing at Tony, "Well, for one, you lying bastard, he is black and you are white, and the pubic hair on my soap was *blond*. I doubt a black man has blond pubic hair, you moron!"

Michael grinned and said, "I knew they should have never let girls in Tulane Surgery." He could see Elizabeth wasn't finished, but he didn't want to pass up an opportunity to taunt her. "Control your emotions," he continued condescendingly. "For God's sake, Elizabeth, you have run out of the bathroom in your under—"

He never finished that sentence. Elizabeth swung around and decked him, her hand making contact with the left side of Michael's jaw. His head flew backwards from the impact. He stumbled, lost his footing, and squealed, "You are nuts!"

Elizabeth felt horrified and satisfied in the same second. She could not believe she had committed physical violence. Having proper manners was the cornerstone of her South Carolina upbringing, and she had been taught to maintain decorum at all times. The boys on the farm might fight regularly, but the girls were not usually physical. In the world she currently inhabited, however, physical violence seemed a reasonable response. "I'll get you fired for this!" screamed Michael, turning over the metal chair in his haste to put distance between himself and Elizabeth. As the chair clanged on the concrete floor, Tony got out of bed. He stood tall beside his cot and glared at Michael.

"I was right here, and I did not see a thing, Michael," Tony told him calmly. "I can't imagine why you'd pretend a skinny little thing like Elizabeth could hit you. And even if she had, what kind of man would admit it hurt?" asked Tony. "I can just see Dr. McSwain laughing when you whine that your sweet little blonde Carolina coworker beat on you! I hope you do tell someone, and I hope I am there when you do!"

"This is not the last of this matter, Elizabeth," snarled Michael.

Elizabeth noticed with a little pride that a red welt was forming on his chin. In the same moment, she realized her scrubs were on the floor in another room. She looked down, squealed, and streaked for the bathroom.

She went immediately into the shower, before the tears and shame could come. She felt defeated. Finding the pubic hair on her face soap was a symbol of her lack of control over anything. Her world had always been manageable. If she did everything right and worked hard, she had found she could perform better than everyone else, and her life ran well. She was embarrassed to have run into the common area in her underwear, but she was really embarrassed about losing her temper. Her father would have been extremely unhappy to know she lost control of her emotions, especially in the work environment.

As she cried in the shower, Elizabeth thought about her father and mother. Her parents adopted her when she was a baby. Everyone on both sides of the family always treated her just like everyone else. But she was acutely aware that she was the only person in her family who was not blood kin—the one who didn't belong. She always felt she had to be perfect to be worthy, accepted, and loved. Doing more and being more worked for her.

At Charity Hospital in New Orleans, no matter what she did or how hard she worked, life was unmanageable. The poverty, the racial tension, the overwhelming violence, the lack of funds for needed supplies, the paucity of staffing, the laziness of some employees, the anger, and the heat were more than anyone could bear.

She washed with ice-cold water, not wanting to use her defiled soap, and dried herself. Feeling calmer and more in control, she put on her clothes, even though she did not feel totally clean with no soap, redid her ponytail, and returned to the common area of the on-call room.

Michael sat mutely, his back turned to her.

Tony, in an effort to ease the tension, lapsed into an exaggerated island brogue. "Why don't ya sit down now, gull," he said to Elizabeth. She knew it was his attempt to lighten the atmosphere. "We will get ya another bar of that soap. I will go over to Maison Blanche mee-self, on Saturday. Ya just tired as can be. There is a fresh bar of Dial soap in there that has never been opened. Next time ya shower and get ya-self cleaned up, use that new bar of Dial until I can get ya a new fancy soap." He smiled at Elizabeth, and she smiled in return. His afro was still lopsided, and she adored him for his attempt to soothe her.

"Ya okay, gull. And if he touches ya new bar of soap, I will beat the hell out of him mee-self," Tony warned Michael, glaring at him. "He will get more than a little tap on the face, the arrogant little squirt."

Elizabeth started to laugh as tears ran down her face. Tony's island brogue reminded her of the familiar speech patterns of black people from John's Island in South Carolina. She found it comforting when he switched from educated Ivy Leaguer to Island Man. "Why can't you beat him now?" she asked. "I think the jerk deserves a good beating right now. My cousins and I always thought retribution was best delivered near the time of the offense," said Elizabeth, as she slumped on her own cot.

"That is one way to do it," Tony agreed. "But he has a big case due at the Death and Complications Conference, and I think you might just let the Tulane faculty whip up on him for ya," said Tony as he stood, leaned toward the cracked mirror mounted on the wall, and attempted to pick out his lopsided afro.

Elizabeth glared at the back of Michael's head. His nose was planted firmly in the book he was reading, and his concern for her was over. In that moment, she realized they would likely never be friends. A friend could make a mistake and be remorseful, and all could be forgotten. But someone who cared so little for the feelings of others was somebody who should not be trusted. Her father always admonished her to be nice to everyone, but to trust only a few. Tony was trustworthy; Michael was not.

Elizabeth decided to go back to the shower. She had stood in the cold water to cool her rage, but there was still time until the conference, and she was not truly clean. She took Tony's new bar of Dial soap and headed back to the bathroom. She undressed again and stepped into the dark, rusty, old shower stall. The plastic shower curtain was old and moldy near the bottom. The entire bathroom had not been remodeled in fifty years.

Hot water soothed her soul. She relaxed quietly in the hot steam and washed and washed with the fresh bar of soap. Eventually she started to feel her pain running down her clean body, into the drain, and out into the Mississippi River. She felt better. Surely that big mighty river could absorb the pain of one girl doctor.

She redressed in a khaki skirt, a pink polo shirt, and her grandmother's pearls. She noticed that the silk string of the pearls was still stained with blood. That blood would not come out, despite several washings. She carefully positioned the stained part of the string behind her long ponytail and placed the clean pearls in front at her collarbone. The pearls were a comfort.

She sat on her bed with her textbooks, making extensive notes regarding her dead patient, his medical condition, and what could have been done to save him. As she read, she realized she knew a great deal about Mr. Pierce's pathologic condition. But knowledge alone had not saved him. She was ready.

Elizabeth found her cleanest white coat, tucked her notes into the front pocket, and took a last glance in the mirror. Then she headed out the door for her first Death and Complications Conference as a fully-fledged doctor with a patient's death of her own to discuss. Tony and Michael followed closely behind her. As they got in the elevator, Tony smiled and winked. Michael ignored Elizabeth. His hands shook as he rearranged his notes.

CHAPTER 16

The Death and Complications Conference

Elizabeth walked briskly through the underground tunnel from Charity Hospital to the basement of Tulane Medical School with Michael and Tony following behind her. The tunnel was dark and dingy, and it smelled of mold. The last time she was here, she remembered, was the first day she worked with Sister Marion. She chuckled, thinking of Sister and her case of Bud Light. *It is hard to believe nearly six months has passed since my first prison clinic.* So much had happened this year. Time seemed compressed.

As they made their way through the tunnel to the conference, Elizabeth's confidence grew. She had determined the best course of action was to present her case truthfully and to the best of her ability. Having chosen a course made her less fearful of the presentation and its consequences. If they fired her, she would be mortified. *But today,* she thought, *I'm too tired to be frightened.* Working at Charity had depleted her of emotions. She could only get so frightened, so overwhelmed, or so exhausted before she simply could not respond.

Hitting Michael, she realized, dissipated most of her fear. The adrenaline jolt and release that came when her fist hit his chin rewired her thoughts, and she felt empowered and less anxious. On some level, she knew hitting another person was wrong. But with Michael, it felt so right. It was, she had to admit, a childish way to solve a problem. She and her cousins had sometimes solved problems in the woods away from their parents with a good fight. But that was a long time ago, when they were in middle school.

Elizabeth understood that the Death and Complications Conference was a time-honored way to share information, educate surgeons, and improve the quality of care for surgical patients. The specter of having to stand before your peers and explain your mistakes kept everyone on their toes and doing their best. In the time since Mr. Pierce's death, Elizabeth had had time to plan and to think. She remembered conversations with Dr. McSwain, Nurse Robichaud, and George, the technician from the morgue. Each one had explained that losing a patient was part of being a doctor. She refused to be upset that it was her turn to explain a failure. She would not allow herself to feel as if she were going to the gallows. She would not turn into a bowl of Jell-O and cry. In the Bible, in the Gospel of St. Luke, the physician, she remembered it says, "To whom much is given, much will be required." She felt she had been given many talents, and she was prepared for the imminent ordeal. She was certainly not the first surgical intern to run this gauntlet.

She was committed to telling the truth about what had happened to Mr. Pierce. She knew by being completely honest, she could help others learn from her mistakes and possibly save another patient's life. Death was one part of the cycle of life, and a true healer participated in all aspects of the cycle of birth, life, and death.

Today's gathering was her first Death and Complications Conference because she was working the emergency room most Friday afternoons and so could not usually attend the conference. She was here today because it was required.

As she walked down the underground tunnel, she wondered, *Will today be my last day as a Tulane surgeon? Will they fire me on the spot if I'm found unworthy?*

Or will I have to wait until they post the names of the people they intend to keep? Will I walk up to the list posted outside the conference room and not see my name? Someone at orientation said they post the last four digits of your Social Security number if you make it, which means, I guess, no names are posted. Or will Dr. McSwain tell me today? If he does, I hope Dr. White is not nearby...I really do not want Dr. White to see me get fired.

The three had reached the end of the tunnel. Elizabeth stood in front of the elevator doors and waited without speaking. Michael and Tony chatted nervously behind her. She blocked them out, trying not to focus on their anxiety.

While they waited, Elizabeth studied the Tulane emblem engraved on the elaborate brass elevator door, a beautiful oval with a green background, somewhere between hunter green and kelly green. Tulane folks called the color Tulane green.

At the top of the oval emblem was a creature that looked like a dragon. The founding year, 1834, was displayed, along with the Latin motto *Non sibi sed suis.* Elizabeth remembered its meaning; "Not for one's self, but for one's own." Most nurses and doctors she knew well were altruistic or simply loved the pursuit of knowledge. Others loved science. Many loved the patients. The best doctors and nurses loved the science and the care of the patients. She knew some chose medicine for the financial remuneration, but she really did not know those people. *Well, maybe Dr. Peterson. He might be in it for the money.* She thought, *You'd have to be a fool to go into medicine for yourself. It is just too hard.*

The door opened, and she stepped into the elevator. Michael and Tony followed her. "Here's one place you can really tell the difference between LSU and Tulane," remarked Michael.

"How so?" asked Tony. Elizabeth noticed that his afro was picked out perfectly and there was not one wrinkle on him. Tony was a second-year surgery resident and had nothing to present to the faculty today, but he respected the process. He was also trying to keep the peace between the two nervous interns.

"Just look at that elevator door. You won't see anything like that at LSU. Politicians keep the money for themselves," he maintained, "but rich old white people die and leave their money to Tulane. And, since the state is not subsidizing it, the tuition at Tulane is at least twice the tuition at LSU," said Michael.

Tony said, "I've never been in LSU. How are the two schools so different?"

"Just look at the differences in their physical plants. If you walk out the front door of Charity Hospital and turn right, you'll run into Tulane Medical Center, and you can see what money and power can buy. If you walk out the front door of Charity and go left, you'll see what former Governor Huey P. Long's resentments and control freak nature can get you," Michael said, laughing nervously.

Elizabeth realized Michael's nonsensical chatter was an outgrowth of his fear about the Death and Complications Conference. As an LSU graduate, he might be judged inferior by his Tulane colleagues.

"Is the quality of instruction different?" asked Elizabeth.

Michael said, "Not really. No matter what a medical student pays in tuition, whether at LSU or Tulane, everyone ends up at The Big Free, so we all have the same experience. There are more sick people at The Big Free per square inch than anyone could treat in a lifetime."

"So no matter where we start out, all interns and residents end up at Charity, where we see thousands and thousands of the sickest people anywhere," said Tony. They chatted as they exited the elevator.

"Yes, whether you come from LSU or Tulane, The Big Free will either mold you into a great doctor or tear you down and spit you out," said Michael. "If you are smart and you study, you can become an excellent doctor by taking advantage of the wealth of knowledge you gain from the throngs of sick and injured Charity patients."

"Supposedly the best surgeons come from schools where they get a lot of operating experience. I have been keeping in touch with some of my medical school classmates who went to smaller programs. They have not even touched a surgery patient yet," said Tony.

"And here we are, two out of three of us have already *killed* one," chuckled Michael.

"I don't think that is funny, Michael," said Elizabeth. She felt her anger rising again.

"I don't think it's funny either, you violent little stuffed shirt," Michael replied. "I am just nervous about what is getting ready to happen, and I was trying to relax by making a lame joke. It wouldn't kill you to loosen up a little bit, Elizabeth."

As the trio made their way down the long hall, Elizabeth felt a wave of panic. She opened the door to the Rudolph Matas Library at twenty minutes before the five o'clock start time to find the room three-fourths full. Surgeons were punctual people. Operating room schedules waited for no one.

As she stepped into the room, her heart hammered in her chest. *So much for not feeling scared,* thought Elizabeth.

The long narrow library was musty and lined with shelves containing hundred-year-old leather-bound books. The preserved brain of Dr. Rudolph Matas, the Department of Surgery's founder, was prominently displayed on a dark-green marble pedestal. A world-renowned vascular surgeon, Dr. Matas taught at Tulane for forty-two years. Tulane Surgery had some odd traditions, but displaying the brain of its founder in the library named for him had to be one of the oddest.

At one end of the room was displayed a large white projector screen, beside which stood a lectern and an X-ray viewing box. The table ran nearly the length of the room. It was old, scratched mahogany, and could easily seat twenty people. Every inch of the remaining space was packed with chairs. Small worn leather club chairs sat crammed together around the table. Smaller wooden folding chairs formed two rows behind the leather chairs.

The wall opposite the projector screen was a large green chalkboard. The only door to the room was the one through which they had just stepped. The bare wooden floors amplified every sound. The room was tight, with less than three inches between the chairs. The chairs made scratching noises on the wooden floor as students fidgeted.

The ceiling seemed low, and Elizabeth felt claustrophobic. In the center of the huge table sat a projector. A young doctor was nervously previewing slides.

Most people were quiet or speaking in hushed tones, but not Michael. "That poor bastard is the audio-visual resident of the month," Elizabeth heard him say. "It is a miserable job, automatically assigned to someone doing the pediatric surgery rotation. The equipment breaks all the time, and the faculty acts as if the AV resident is personally responsible. It is hair-raising, to say the least. I'd rather be explaining a death any day than working that godawful projector," Michael concluded.

Several older residents glowered at them.

"Where should we sit?" asked Elizabeth of a student with a Tulane badge on his clean white coat.

He explained, "The faculty sits around the table. The chairman sits at the head of the table. Students sit in the back row and residents, interns, and fellows sit in the middle row. The longer you have been in the program, the closer you get to the table. The only exception to these seating rules is if you have a case to present. Then you want to sit near the front so you don't have to crawl over everyone else to present your case. The faculty gets very agitated if you waste time."

Elizabeth thought, *Of course there's a pecking order to the seating. The gods of Tulane Surgery sit at the front and the peons go to the back. Unless, of course, one of the peons is going to be roasted by the gods.*

She sighed and headed for the front of the room. She was scheduled for roasting today.

As Elizabeth was moving to the front, Michael's pager screamed out, "Please call the ER *stat* at 903-3000." Elizabeth recognized the voice of a nurse Michael regularly dated.

Michael pulled the giant speaker that passed for a pager out of his jacket pocket and walked out the door to answer the page. Elizabeth knew the only acceptable reason to miss the Death and Complications Conference was working on an emergency patient. *Could Michael have arranged for the nurse to call him just to get out of the conference? What a rat!*

Elizabeth felt the weight of her own pager dragging down the front of her white coat. There was no volume adjustment on the contraption, and she hoped she did not get paged during the conference. Dr. McSwain had admonished her to never turn off her pager, but she didn't want any more attention drawn to her.

Elizabeth looked up to see Dr. Harrison Lloyd White III come into the room, head for the front, and sit at the table. He was not on the faculty, but he sat at the table anyway. He had been at Tulane for fifteen years, as an undergraduate, a medical school student, a surgery intern graduate, a general surgery residency graduate, and now the second-year fellow in cardiothoracic surgery. Rumor had it he would do further training as the Tulane pediatric cardiothoracic fellow. He did not greet anyone. He flipped open the *Journal of Cardio-Thoracic Surgery* and started to read intently, ignoring everyone else in the room.

His intense quiet scared Elizabeth.

Elizabeth studied his patrician profile, his pale skin, and his incredible blue eyes. His long fingers turned the pages of the journal with natural grace. She had never been attracted to delicacy in a man, but she acknowledged her interest in Dr. White was more than simply professional. His pulling the bullet out of the heart of the patient, Mr. Mac Jenkins, in the trauma suite was emblazoned in detail in her mind. She remembered every hair and every vein on the backs of Dr. White's hands as he worked, and she could envision the exact spots on his thin wrists where his white sleeves covered the tops of his surgical gloves. Surprised by her own thoughts, she drew her attention to the stack of papers she held in her trembling hands.

She sat three seats from the end of the room, in the middle row, waiting. She was relieved to see the neurosurgeon, Dr. Cabellero, file into the room, holding Michael LeBlanc by his coat sleeve. Dr. Cabellero apparently had thwarted Michael's attempt to flee, and he appeared to be dragging the intern back into the room. Michael's case was a neurosurgery death; Dr. Cabellero was not planning to shoulder the explanation alone. Dr. Cabellero took a seat in front of Elizabeth. He gave her a slight smile as he sat down.

Remembering their dinner at Commander's Palace, Elizabeth felt embarrassed all over again, recalling it had taken two days to get the garlic smell of the remoulade dressing from her hair. Dr. Cabellero was a darker, more solid version of Dr. White. He was more muscular, and his bone structure was less delicate. His deep, quiet confidence was similar, however.

Clearly, Dr. Cabellero had financial resources beyond the usual intern and resident stipend, thought Elizabeth. She could smell his exotic cologne, which had a lime base with a musky overtone. *Delicious,* she thought. She noticed that his dark wavy hair was perfectly coiffed, like someone had shaved his neck and trimmed his hair five minutes before. His stiffly starched, pale-blue shirt contrasted with his white doctor's coat and his light-brown skin. From her seat behind him, she could see his broad shoulders. Lavinia Robichaud told Elizabeth that Dr. Cabellero had been a fencing champion as a Tulane undergraduate. *Why am I thinking about this? This is a Death and Complications Conference. Maybe my mind is filling with trivia to try to calm itself.*

Dr. Cabellero reached out to grasp a book from the mahogany table, and Elizabeth saw his hands. Elizabeth especially liked hands. His were tanned deeper than natural olive-toned skin, and his nails were perfectly square and white. On his wrist he wore a gold watch. The face said Rolex. Elizabeth had never heard of that brand of watch. *Was it the Cuban version of Timex?* Her family was not much for jewelry, and her very proper father's mother maintained "only people with new money wore lots of jewelry." The gold watch looked stylish and appropriate on Dr. Cabellero.

By 4:50 p.m., all the students and residents had found chairs, and the room was getting packed. A room designed to hold twenty people now contained sixty. Young doctors and students nervously shuffled papers and opened and closed their textbooks. Eyes darted around as the newer doctors and students surreptitiously appraised one another. Dr. White continued fervently reading, acknowledging no one.

At 4:58 p.m., the chairman of surgery, Dr. Robert Waites, walked to the front of the room. Everyone stood as he entered and did not sit until he took his seat at the head of the table. Elizabeth had met him twice, but had heard gossip about him from people in the medical system. People said that he was a quiet man drawn more to research than to surgery, that his research grants brought large amounts of money to the department, and that his Ivy League education and connections brought prestige. Many of his predecessors were brilliant, irascible, and passionate. In the long colorful history of Tulane Surgery, some surgeons had reportedly dueled in front of Charity Hospital concerning disputes over patient care. Elizabeth was happy to be a student in Dr. Waites' time. Of all the Tulane Surgery chairmen, he was known as mild-mannered and less flamboyant.

For the first time, Elizabeth realized she was one of only two women in the room. The other, a beautiful female student, sat behind Dr. Edward Peterson. The female student leaned forward, laughed, and whispered something to the back of his head. He smiled and nodded. Even though he was chief resident and technically responsible for both deaths that occurred this past week, he did not sit near the front. Elizabeth and Michael, the interns, sat at the front, and their chief sat in the back. Good leaders supported their troops, but Dr. Peterson positioned himself near the door, detached from his interns. *This is not a good sign. It doesn't look like he is planning to help us if we falter...* Elizabeth began to perspire as the room heated up, literally and figuratively.

She could smell fear seeping from her pores.

Dr. McSwain was the last of the faculty to arrive. He swept into the room, closed the door loudly behind him, and came to the front to stand by the podium.

Dr. McSwain dressed differently. All the other men wore either a coat and tie or a starched white doctor's coat with the Tulane emblem. But Dr. McSwain wore a cotton turtleneck. A large turquoise bear claw hung around his neck on a thick silver chain. In Native American mythology, Elizabeth recalled, bears were thought to possess magical healing powers, and the bear claw was a talisman for strength, resilience, and leadership.

With his turtleneck, Dr. McSwain wore tight jeans, a belt with a large turquoise buckle, and cowboy boots. His white coat, held back over his hip, exposed three large beepers and a walkie-talkie attached to the thick belt. *He looks more like a rodeo star than a medical school professor.*

As always, Dr. McSwain exuded masculinity, virility, and personal power. As he strolled past the department chairman, the contrast between the two men was drastic. Dr. McSwain was tanned, athletic, and powerful. His skin was olive and his hair was black. Elizabeth wondered if he were part Cherokee. Dr. Waites, obviously never an athlete, was pasty white, doughy, smaller, and studious. The two men exchanged a smile. *Tulane seems to have room for all kinds of people.*

Dr. McSwain stood at the podium, and his smile vanished.

"I now call the Tulane Death and Complications Conference to order," he said. "We have much to discuss today, unfortunately. It is July, and each case is a teaching opportunity. There are copies of the agenda on the table. Please take one, pass them around, and follow along."

The first case on the agenda was Michael's. Elizabeth felt anxious for him. She saw the look on his face when he realized he was first. His eyes grew wide, and he bolted up straight in his chair. He looked around the room for Dr. Peterson, who was avoiding eye contact with anyone, looking down at the agenda. Michael had a feral look as his eyes darted from one senior resident to another, looking for assistance. His gaze settled on Dr. Cabellero, who nodded in support. His eyes seemed to say, "*I am here.*"

Michael sat back, waiting for his name to be called.

Dr. McSwain said, "It looks like the neurosurgery team had a bad week this week. Both deaths occurred on the neurosurgery service." Elizabeth knew that was not strictly correct. Dr. Caballero did not see one patient until after the patient was dead, and the other died while he was operating at a different hospital. But Tulane Surgery, like the military, beat up on the most junior person and blamed the senior resident or fellow. Dr. Cabellero seemed calm, but focused. "Yes, sir," he said.

McSwain continued, "Dr. Michael LeBlanc, intern, please come to the podium and explain your death, sir."

Elizabeth crossed her fingers in her lap and hoped Michael would do well. Though she detested his selfish behavior, he was part of her group, and she was pulling for his success; she realized he might not feel the same way about her. Elizabeth viewed loyalty to one's peers as a part of overall good character. She might privately argue with Michael or slug him, if she felt he needed it, but she did not wish public humiliation for any of her colleagues. On the farm, the cousins always fought it out, made up, and kept the adults out of the fray.

Michael fought through the crowd to get to the front, stepping on toes in the process and nearly landing in the lap of one professor. He looked terrified. His usual bravado was eclipsed by fear, and he stammered when he started to talk.

Elizabeth knew Michael would be discussing the hideous attempted suicide of the beautiful young Hispanic woman who was seen during her trauma shift. Elizabeth's anxiety rose with Michael's.

"My patient was a twenty-three-year-old Hispanic female. She attempted suicide by self-inflicted gunshot wound to the head. She was resuscitated successfully in the trauma room and brought to the operating room for debridement of the left side of her face. Her left jaw, left eye, left upper teeth, and entire cheek were blown off from the gunshot blast. The team in the operating room consisted of neurosurgery, ophthalmology, ENT, plastic surgery, maxillofacial and oral surgery, vascular surgery, and general surgery. She had extensive loss of tissue and her airway was compromised by extensive swelling from the blast. At the time of the debridement of her face, it was decided to place a tracheostomy tube, as she was expected to require multiple procedures. She was admitted to neurosurgery, as she had quite a bit of brain swelling, and we were managing that aspect of her care."

"Who was her main doctor?" asked Dr. Waites.

"Dr. Cabellero and myself, sir," said Michael.

"Was her family involved?" said Dr. Waites.

"No, sir. We met a sister the day the patient came in. But nobody came back after the first day," said Michael.

"So, she did not have a Do Not Resuscitate Order, did she?" said Dr. Waites.

"No, sir. We were doing everything possible to save her," said Michael.

Elizabeth watched as Dr. McSwain focused, laser-like, on Michael. Dr. Cabellero sat tall and serene. Dr. White quit reading.

Suddenly, Dr. White spoke. "So, intern, *seven* different surgical teams spent eight hours of operating room time trying to put this poor woman back together, and what was *your* job in all of this?"

"My job, sir, was her post-operative care," said Michael, in a whisper.

Dr. White spoke loudly, "I didn't hear you, intern."

Michael looked into Dr. White's intense blue eyes and said in a louder voice, "Dr. White, it was my job as the intern to care for her after surgery."

"And what was the most important part of that care?" said Dr. White.

"Keeping her airway open and functioning, sir," said Michael. He was visibly trembling and clinging to the lectern for support.

"What *exactly* caused your patient's demise, intern?" said Dr. White. Elizabeth had never seen such disdain and venom from one person toward another. *Did Dr. White really need to be that aggressive?* She felt protective of her colleague, but sensed this was no time to speak in his defense.

"Every time the patient came to the end of her sedative dosing interval," Michael began, "she would wake up and try to pull out her tracheostomy tube. If we sedated her more, she could not take a deep breath. When we kept the sedation light enough to allow her to breathe, she would wake up every four to five hours and fight to pull out the tube. The last time, she succeeded," said Michael as he looked down at the podium.

"So, intern, you killed your patient by not providing adequate care. You knew she was a suicide risk, and you knew that tracheostomy tube was her lifeline. And yet here we are. What do you have to say for yourself?" asked Dr. White.

Michael's hands shook, and his shoulders slumped. Every eye in the room was riveted on him. "Dr. White, I could not be at her bedside every moment. I blame the nurses for not keeping an eye on her while I was in the operating room assisting Dr. Cabellero…"

A great roar came from Dr. McSwain. "*You* are the doctor, sir. Nurses are *never* to be blamed for your poor planning. Nurses follow doctors' orders. Since you have no idea what you did to cause your patient's death, Dr. LeBlanc, you may be seated. Dr. Cabellero, take the podium and explain the errors of the neurosurgery team," said Dr. McSwain.

Michael skulked away, looking genuinely ashamed. Dr. Cabellero took the podium. He made eye contact with Dr. McSwain, Dr. White, and Dr. Waites.

"Good afternoon, sirs. The chairman of neurosurgery sends his regrets that he cannot be here this afternoon. He is giving a talk in Germany. But he has been fully apprised of the failures of our department this week," said Dr. Cabellero.

Everyone relaxed a bit upon hearing the apology.

"Our patient's death is my fault," continued Dr. Cabellero. "I had to decide between keeping her sedation light, to avoid aspiration and pneumonia, and keeping her in coma with full ventilation. Each time I came by to see her, she was resting quietly. Dr. LeBlanc had told me of her intermittent agitation, and he also had expressed concern that she seemed to still be suicidal despite our intervention. I decided to ignore his concerns, and the error cost this woman her life…or what was left of it," said Dr. Cabellero.

Dr. McSwain said, "Okay, son, you made an error that led to death. Explain in detail to the young interns and medical students exactly what your choices were and how you came to the wrong choice."

Elizabeth immediately noticed Dr. Cabellero got respect from Dr. McSwain; Michael did not. *How does one gain Dr. McSwain's respect?*

"Yes, sir, I will attempt to explain," said Dr. Cabellero. "When a patient has a head injury, we have to breathe for them with a tube. If it is going to be a few days, we put them on a ventilator and put the tube through the mouth and into the trachea. We keep the patient in a drug-induced coma so that the patient is comfortable and not able to fight the ventilator. When the brain swelling has gone down, we take out the tube and allow the patient to breathe on their own," said Cabellero.

With nobody to grill, Dr. White had gone back to reading his journal. Michael slumped in his chair and fidgeted with the agenda. Dr. Peterson looked bored. Elizabeth thought, *It is so unfair that Dr. Peterson, the chief of the general surgery service, is getting off unscathed.*

"So why did you not do that with this woman, doctor?" said Dr. Waites.

"She was young and otherwise healthy, and I did not want to restrain her. The ENT service had put in a tracheostomy tube, which has less opportunity for aspiration," said Dr. Cabellero.

"Explain aspiration to the students, son," said Dr. McSwain.

"After any kind of surgery, we are always concerned that patients cannot control their saliva production. When they are in an altered state after surgery, their oral secretions can go down the trachea and into the lungs. Pneumonia and respiratory failure can ensue," said Dr. Cabellero.

"So, students and interns always remember this lesson," said Dr. McSwain. "You are responsible for making the best decisions for your patients when they cannot make them for themselves. The airway is your number one concern in every situation. If patients cannot breathe, their heartbeat will do them little good as they are circulating blood that cannot fuel their cells with oxygen. So make the death of this unfortunate young woman count. Every one of you should forever remember that poor airway management is the fault of the doctor, and death is the result. Dr. LeBlanc and Dr. Cabellero should have kept their patient more heavily sedated and better restrained until she did not require the tube to breathe. Please sit down, Dr. Cabellero," said Dr. McSwain.

"Thank you, sir," said Dr. Cabellero. As he pulled back his chair and wedged himself into it, the chair legs on the floor made an alarming squeal. The room was filled with the sounds of shuffling papers, but nobody spoke. The tension was palpable.

Elizabeth's eyes were glued to her lap, where she had placed the agenda. Next up for discussion at the conference was Dr. Elizabeth Roberts with the Death of Patient Mr. Jerry Pierce, Neurosurgery Service and Accident Room.

Elizabeth felt dizzy, and the room went in and out of focus. Everyone and everything in the room had a hazy edge. *Please, God, do not let me faint.*

Her pulse raced, and her palms sweated. She could not look up.

Somewhere deep in her consciousness, she heard Dr. McSwain's voice say, "Dr. Roberts, Dr. Roberts, you are up!"

She pushed back her chair, pulled down her skirt, and walked slowly to the podium. All eyes were on her. Her hands shook visibly, and her knees trembled, but she made it. She grasped both sides of the lectern for support and took a long deep breath. Something her father told her flashed into her mind, something he would say to Elizabeth when jealous classmates belittled her good grades or ridiculed her poor athletic performance: "Elizabeth, you are neither as good nor are you as bad as *they* say. You are you, and some days you are great, and some days you are just another bozo on the bus." She remembered Wavy the Clown and his quote used frequently by her father. *Just another bozo on the bus* was her father's way of saying we are all important, none more than others. She fought back an inappropriate giggle.

Her bowels felt loose, her eyes felt watery, and her knees felt jelly-like. But she was upright and ready to take a beating for her failure.

Dr. McSwain said, "Okay, intern, I can't wait to hear what you have to say for yourself about this death. In my mind, it was absolutely inexcusable. I strongly suggest that you not try to blame anyone else. We heard enough lame excuses from Dr. LeBlanc."

"Yes, sir," said Elizabeth. *Blaming others is not my way.* Elizabeth glanced out into the audience and saw Drs. White, Cabellero, and LeBlanc staring at her, anticipating a show. Only Tony Parker's face looked compassionate. He actually winked at her in support. Elizabeth found comfort in his friendly gesture. *It's always nice to see a friendly face on your way to the gallows.*

"Mr. Jerry Pierce was a quite healthy thirty-two-year-old Caucasian man, father of three little boys, who walked into the Charity Hospital of New Orleans after having sustained a hit to the left side of his head from a bat that flew out of the hand of a Little Leaguer while Mr. Pierce was acting as a first-base line coach."

Dr. White interjected coldly, "We aren't interested in all of the social issues, intern. This is *not* a social worker conference. In case you were unaware, this is the General Surgery Death and Complications Conference. We'd like to know exactly how you killed this man, from a surgical standpoint."

The room filled with snickers, and Elizabeth felt angry. Her anger calmed her rattled nerves as she gazed into Dr. White's penetrating blue eyes. He looked smug. *Does he kick kittens, too?*

"Yes, sir," said Elizabeth.

Dr. McSwain interjected, "Students, it is important to note that the patient was stable at the scene. He never lost consciousness from the head blow, and he did walk into the emergency department. Remember those factors, as they will be important later. And his mechanism of injury is important to the story. Continue, Dr. Roberts."

"I was the surgical charge resident in the accident room when he arrived. His vital signs were normal, and he was talking normally with his family. He had a slight headache where the bat had hit him. He was not examined immediately, and that was my first mistake," said Elizabeth.

"I had gone from examination room to examination room, attempting to triage my workload and decided he was one patient who could wait for evaluation," said Elizabeth.

Dr. Cabellero looked down at the table. Dr. White's glare intensified; Elizabeth thought he resembled a hungry wolf. Elizabeth shuddered slightly and went on, "Five minutes after I last saw Mr. Jerry Pierce, a drunken patient aspirated in the hall in front of me and was taken into Room Four for resuscitation. Getting an airway on the patient was very difficult, and Dr. McSwain did an emergency tracheostomy. By the time that code was over, the airway was secure, and ENT was taking the patient to surgery, I had forgotten all about the other patients in the ER."

Dr. McSwain said, "So let me be sure that I understand you, Dr. Roberts. You were having such an interesting time in Room Four that you *forgot* about the other patients for whom you were responsible? Is that correct, intern?"

Elizabeth knew then that this could be the prelude to being fired from the Surgery Department at the end of the semester. Her heart sank, but she was determined that the people who remained would learn something from her debacle that might save some other person's life.

"Yes, Dr. McSwain, in my excitement over the code and the emergency tracheostomy, I completely forgot about poor Mr. Pierce," said Elizabeth. Her shaming was complete. This time when she gazed out into the audience, she saw some doctors looked triumphant. Drs. White and Peterson looked particularly happy. Drs. Cabellero and Tony Parker had pity in their eyes.

Elizabeth stood tall and continued. "When the tracheostomy patient was transported to the operating room, I immediately resumed my rounds in the accident room. When I got to Mr. Pierce's exam room, he was unresponsive."

Dr. Waites asked, "What happened then, Dr. Roberts?"

Elizabeth never had wanted to run away from anything so badly in her entire life. Reliving the last hour of Jerry Pierce's life was the absolute last thing she ever wanted to do. But before they fired her for incompetence, she had to tell the story, take the blame, and be the messenger to other doctors about what happens when a doctor doesn't manage resources properly in a busy emergency room.

"I called a code, and the nurses and students came in. We started the protocol per Dr. McSwain's Advanced Trauma Life Support algorithm. As soon as I saw that Mr. Pierce's pupils were fixed and dilated, I called for neurosurgery backup."

Dr. White interjected, "Why didn't you just call the morgue? He was a dead man at that point, intern."

Elizabeth ignored his question and continued.

"The neurosurgeon on call was doing a particularly delicate aneurysm repair and could not come to assist. So he and the nurse on duty talked me through drilling multiple burr holes in the patient's skull in an attempt to reduce the pressure on his brain," said Elizabeth. She caught the eye of Dr. Cabellero. He seemed to be imploring her to ask for his help. She decided she would take all the criticism. *At this point, why drag any other doctors and nurses into the fiasco?*

"Our team in the emergency room worked for an hour. Mr. Pierce never regained any level of consciousness. The neurosurgeon arrived and pronounced his death after everything that could have been done was done," said Elizabeth.

Dr. White stood up, adjusted his starched white coat, pulled down his starched blue shirt cuffs, and said, "This mess is exactly why we have this conference. We are here to root out stupidity. We gather in this dusty, musty old room to determine who should be a Tulane surgeon and who should not. This room is the weeding-out arena. Anyone who cannot do more than one thing at a time is not fit for Tulane Surgery." He sat down.

Elizabeth felt the nails being driven into her coffin. In an odd way, she felt relieved. *Public humiliation doesn't get worse than this. Dr. White is mean as a snake. He gave me the full force of his venom, and I am still standing, barely.*

Dr. Cabellero stood and said, "Dr. McSwain and Dr. White, I would just like to point out that although the patient died, Dr. Roberts drilled perfect burr holes in the absolute perfect locations and followed the trauma protocols immaculately. Yes, the patient died, but the intern did everything exactly the way I would have done it, had I been there. Once she assessed the patient, she immediately realized the gravity of his condition, and from that moment forward, her work was impeccable." He sat down.

Dr. White said, "Great, now we are applauding people for working well on a corpse. This is ridiculous." Dr. McSwain stared at Dr. White, as if willing him to be quiet. But he did not say anything.

"Enough," said Dr. Waites.

"Summarize, intern," ordered Dr. McSwain.

"Yes, sir," she began. "What I failed to do in this scenario was this: I failed to dispatch one of the medical students to continually make rounds and check on the other patients while we were doing the emergency tracheostomy. Had I thought to do that, Mr. Pierce's condition might have been discovered earlier. I failed initially by not examining his head for a fracture. If I had simply rubbed my hand on the area where he had reported being hit, I might have felt the fracture, gotten an X-ray earlier, and seen that the fracture was right over a large artery."

Dr. McSwain interrupted, "Students, this case represents Dr. Robert's failure to do the two simplest things in any doctor's armamentarium. She failed to watch her patient, and she failed to examine her patient. These things are simple, but never, ever ignore them. Watching and examining are two of the most important things we do in the medical care of anyone. Once you have been doing this a while, it will become apparent to you that 90 percent of diagnoses are made by listening to the patient's story, watching the patient, and examining the patient. We've got lots of fancy tests, but nothing can replace the basics of taking a detailed history and doing a thorough physical examination."

Elizabeth had dreamed of being a shining example. Instead, she was a dire warning.

"What did the autopsy show, Dr. Roberts?" said Dr. Waites.

"The autopsy showed that the middle meningeal artery lying right under Mr. Pierce's temporal bone was sheared by the skull fracture. It had bled and filled his skull with a very large clot. He herniated his brain into the base of his skull and obliterated his respiratory center," said Elizabeth.

"And why did your *perfect* burr holes not work?" asked Dr. White caustically.

Elizabeth could not meet his intense glare; she looked down at the lectern and hung her head. "It was too late," she said quietly. "By the time I drilled the holes and released the pressure on his brain, it was too late."

"I could not hear you," said Dr. White.

She looked up, met his steely glare, and said, "Dr. White, it was too late. I failed Mr. Pierce by getting there too late." Her lip trembled and she forced back the tears. "My patient died because I did not watch over him carefully enough."

Elizabeth knew that this might be her last time to speak at this conference, just like she knew Jerry Pierce and his wife and three boys were forever part of her life. She would never forget one moment of this experience, but the conference and her humiliation were minor compared to her memories of the Pierce family.

The room was completely silent. No papers were shuffled. Nobody whispered. Time seemed to stop. The great truths—that surgeons are not infallible, mistakes can happen—hung in the air like black crepe.

Dr. McSwain broke the silence. "That's it for today's conference," he said. "Thank you to everyone who presented cases today. We learned a great deal, and that is the point of this conference. Good surgeons don't make the same mistake twice. Remember the Tulane Surgery motto," he reminded them. "Assume nothing, trust no one, and triple check everything." He closed the conference with a smile.

Elizabeth looked down and waited to be fired by Dr. McSwain.

CHAPTER 17

Joe's Bar

Elizabeth sat in her hard, uncomfortable, wooden folding chair at the Death and Complications Conference, waiting for the doctors at the end of the room to exit through the only door. She felt like she had been through a war and lost. She stared at the jar containing Dr. Matas' brain and wondered what made him a great surgeon and what she lacked.

It was stiflingly hot in the room, and nobody talked to Elizabeth. The professors discussed departmental matters. She heard the words *budget, clinic expansion, fiscal plant, operating room microscope, research grant...*

She realized their concerns had little to do with her. She was just a stupid intern who had made a stupid mistake and caused a death. The professors had a department to run and other considerations besides her humiliation. She saw Dr. Waites, the chairman, surrounded by professors jockeying for a moment with him. They looked like hungry children begging for a cookie.

She wanted to laugh, realizing her anxieties were petty to them. They had concerns she could not even imagine. *How does the complex system that supports Tulane Surgery hold together? How do they balance their full-time jobs as surgeons, teachers at the medical school, their responsibilities for students, nurses, interns, residents, fellows, clinics? Operating rooms at four locations, clinic staff, research laboratories, research staff? The grants, the budget, the personnel, hiring and firing everyone involved?* For a moment, Elizabeth imagined the burden of what the faculty had to do, besides caring for thousands of surgical patients.

The process of providing outstanding medical education while trying to take good care of sick patients was without a doubt a daunting task.

Elizabeth suddenly realized the reasons for their abruptness and lack of sympathy for the weak students and interns. *They do not have time for stupidity. There is too much to do. They must pick the strong people who can keep up with the pack and let the rest go.* The famous "Tulane Surgery cut" was about keeping the organization functioning with the best people. Elizabeth realized the cut was not personal. *Either you have what it takes to be a Tulane surgeon, or you do not...*

Everyone but a few professors and the chairman had left, and nobody had spoken to Elizabeth. Her presentation was over, and they had moved on to current events in the department.

She gathered her papers and looked up to see the head and arm of Nurse Lavinia Robichaud through the partly open door. She waved enthusiastically for Elizabeth to come out into the hall. Elizabeth groaned at the thought of being assigned some other doctor's emergency room shift this evening. She could think of no other reason Nurse Robichaud would be looking for her.

Resigned, she walked to the door and out into the hall. "Come on, Crème Puff, shake it off! You aren't the first intern to get scorched at D&C, and you won't be the last. We are going to Joe's to drown your sorrows," said Nurse Robichaud. Standing with her were Triage Nurse Aoife Patrick, Dr. Tony Parker, and Dr. Ernesto Cabellero. Chief Resident Edward Peterson and Dr. Michael LeBlanc were conspicuously absent.

Elizabeth was confused. "Joe's?" she asked.

"Remember the bar I pointed out the morning we walked to the Quarter?" said Nurse Robichaud.

"No, not really," said Elizabeth.

"Joe's is Tulane Medical School's main watering hole," Tony said. "Every college and medical school—and probably every law school, too—have a watering hole where students drown their sorrows."

"Thanks for the gesture of inviting me, but I don't really drink, and I don't particularly like bars," said Elizabeth.

"Well, that is too bad, Crème Puff," Nurse Robichaud admonished her, "because after D&C, an appearance at Joe's is mandatory. It's expected. You don't have a choice. You are going." She grabbed Elizabeth's elbow.

Elizabeth was in no mood to be bullied. She leaned over and whispered in Lavinia Robichaud's ear. "I thought we agreed that day in the French Quarter that you would not bully me. We also agreed you would not call me 'Crème Puff' in front of others." She raised her voice from the whisper. "I do not want to go to a bar," Elizabeth told her emphatically. "I want to go home and sleep."

"Too bad!" said Nurse Robichaud. "This is not about what you want. You are going. Gentlemen, kindly assist her."

Tony grabbed one of Elizabeth's arms, Dr. Cabellero the other, and Aoife pushed Elizabeth from behind. Elizabeth partially walked and was partially dragged to the elevator. It felt like being back on the farm with her cousins. Whether it was the first time she had driven a combine, or ridden a horse, or milked a cow, someone dragged her to do it. She could not evade her cousins, and she could not get away from this group.

The doors to the elevator opened, and the group packed in.

"So, who is Joe?" asked Elizabeth.

There was silence in the elevator. Eventually, Tony said, "We don't actually know who Joe is or was. The place has been there a very long time, and it has always been called Joe's, but nobody's ever seen him."

"So, Nurse Robichaud, what goes on at Joe's?" asked Elizabeth. She was afraid to call her Livvy in front of the others.

Everyone laughed. Tony said, "Nothing good."

Aoife offered, "Gossip and drunkenness."

Dr. Cabellero said, "People let their hair down and loosen up."

Nurse Robichaud chimed in, "Nothing at all goes on there that your stuck-up little lily- white butt will be interested in. And that is exactly why you have to go. We are going to try to help you fit in a little better with Tulane Surgery."

Elizabeth wondered why Livvy could not just be nice to her. *Why did everything have to sound like a threat?*

Elizabeth said, "It may come as a big surprise to you, Nurse Robichaud, but I tended bar for four years in college. I worked at Captain Harry's Blue Marlin Bar in Charleston, South Carolina, and I actually served Jimmy Buffet many times."

"Who is Jimmy Buffet?" asked Nurse Robichaud.

Elizabeth's jaw dropped. *How could she not know Jimmy Buffett?*

"He's a musician," Elizabeth explained. "Ever heard the song 'Margaritaville'?"

"Can't say I have, Crème Puff," said Nurse Robichaud. "Is that some silly white people music your folks play in South Carolina? 'Cause down here, we listen to real music, like Erma Thomas, The Neville Brothers, the Meters, and Mr. Allen Toussaint. New Orleans music is music worth listening to," said the nurse.

Of course, anything of Livvy's is better than anything of mine! How could I forget that?

Across the street from the back door of the Tulane Medical Center Emergency Room, Elizabeth saw a ramshackle wooden building. She remembered passing it before, but it didn't look like the kind of place she would ever enter of her own accord. But Elizabeth was too tired to fight. She'd endure an hour at the bar, she decided, and then head home to sleep.

A sign painted on a crooked weathered board that hung above the door proclaimed: *Rx. For What Ale's You!*

Dr. Cabellero held the door for the group. Elizabeth entered last. As she stepped into the dark, stinky, crowded, and smoky shack, he leaned over and said into her ear, "All hope abandon, ye who enter here."

Elizabeth laughed, recognizing the quote, the inscription at the entrance to hell from Dante's *Divine Comedy*. Her father's mother, her Granny, loved all kinds of literature, and together they had read the entire works of Dante before Elizabeth entered high school. Elizabeth surmised Dr. Cabellero could tell by the look on her face that a dark, smoke-filled bar was her idea of hell.

"Hurts So Good" by John Cougar blasted in the background. The small bar was standing-room only and packed shoulder to shoulder. It took Elizabeth's eyes a few minutes to adjust to the dark and the smoke. Everyone cleared a path for Nurse Robichaud's ample figure as she herded them to a corner of the bar where a shelf attached to a wall served as a table.

Elizabeth was surprised to see many of the people she had met over the last few months in New Orleans. Tulane Medical students huddled together near the door. Most were not drinking. She recognized Jalpa Patel holding a cup of coffee, and Sally Smith with a can of root beer. Larry Silverstein, the student who had been trapped in the elevator with her, was scanning the crowd nervously. A few months of third-year medical school rotations apparently had not calmed his jitters.

Elizabeth smiled at the group of students and gave a friendly wave. Jalpa and Sally waved back. Larry stood and stared. He had dark circles under his wide, darting eyes.

"Okay, Crème Puff, whatever you do, don't get drunk and embarrass me," Nurse Robichaud said loudly. "I am not in the mood for pulling you off the table while you try to pretend to pole dance." Shocked, Elizabeth glared at her. Tony and Aoife laughed.

"I don't intend to drink, and I have never been on any table in any bar, thank you, Nurse Robichaud," said Elizabeth primly. *In point of fact, I am usually the one pulling somebody else off the table.*

"Just kidding, Crème Puff," the nurse replied. "I know you are too uptight and stiff to get drunk in public and dance around. I didn't really think you'd do that, but the thought does entertain me. Please don't spoil my fantasy."

Elizabeth leaned into the nurse's shoulder and hissed, "In *my* fantasy, you stop calling me that stupid name and start acting like a friend should act."

"Well, all right then, *Elizabeth*. I will try to comply," said Livvy. She smiled and scanned the room.

Dr. Cabellero took their drink orders and headed to the bar. Elizabeth noted one skinny, harried, jovial server tended to the professors. The students, interns, and residents were crowded around the bar awaiting their turns to order. *Even at Joe's, there is a pecking order.*

Elizabeth saw Dr. Harrison White leaning against the far wall under a flashing neon sign advertising beer. Next to him stood a Nordic goddess—a tall, leggy blonde. Livvy followed Elizabeth's eyes to the doctor and his admirer. "That woman, Rose Anders, is the best cardiac nurse in New Orleans. She assists on all the difficult cases. Every heart surgeon in town wants her to work for him. She has her choice of jobs in the heart room. She has the biggest set of knockers in Louisiana, and she has her heart set on marrying Dr. White."

Elizabeth watched the couple. Dr. White did not look at Rose Anders. He stared into the room and sipped his beer, nodding every few minutes to acknowledge Nurse Anders, who leaned her large right breast into his left lower arm, dipped her platinum-blonde head into his field of vision, and talked constantly. For Rose, there was no one in the room but Dr. White.

Elizabeth felt disappointed as she watched them. She laughed to herself and wondered why that was.

Dr. Cabellero returned with their drinks and said, "Elizabeth, they are brewing a fresh pot of coffee. It might be a few minutes before it is ready, but it will be worth the wait. The old pot looked as thick as motor oil."

"Thank you, Dr. Cabellero," said Elizabeth. Even though they had been on what might be called a date, she decided being professional was best and avoided using his first name, even though they weren't at the hospital.

Billy Idol's "Hot in the City" blasted from the ceiling speakers as Elizabeth continued to look around. Nurse Robichaud said, "I can tell that you don't like this, *Elizabeth,* but could you try to get that I-just-sucked-a-lemon look off your face? Try to loosen up and fit in. This is the Tulane Surgery bonding ground. Most folks here probably need psychotherapy after everything they see in The Big Free emergency room. Instead, they come here to drown their sorrows, be with similarly warped beings, and try to have some fun. You should, too."

Elizabeth thought, *Why should I bother? After today's D&C Conference, I am the most likely to be fired! It won't be long now.* She tried to smile and relax as instructed.

Dr. McSwain walked by, a beer in his hand, and smiled and spoke to each of them. He seemed relaxed and at home. He surprised Elizabeth by joining a group of students, and she observed the students laughing with him. Above the roar of the music, she heard him ask, "So what have you students done for humanity today?"

Again, Livvy followed Elizabeth's gaze. "Dr. McSwain is a great teacher. The kids just love him, once they get over their fear. Every Tulane student is afraid of him, respects him, and grows to love him as a teacher. He has all the characteristics of a good father. He's stern, but fair."

Elizabeth turned her full attention to Nurse Lavinia Robichaud. *This woman is one mystifying being. She's gorgeous, buxom, cagey, Creole, and intelligent, not to mention flirty, mean, and apparently loyal, at least to Dr. McSwain.*

Livvy waved her hand in front of Elizabeth's face. "Earth to Elizabeth! Wake up! What are you thinking about? Those baby-blue eyes are intense, wide open, and staring at me," observed Livvy. "What gives?"

Fatigue was taking over, and Elizabeth was lapsing into daydreaming. "I was thinking about you," she replied. "I was wondering exactly what kind of woman you are."

"Oh, that's easy," said Livvy. "I am all tough on the surface, but my heart is as big and soft as my big chocolate behind, baby."

Elizabeth laughed as Livvy walked off to talk to George, the technician from the morgue who had been so kind to Elizabeth.

Elizabeth looked across the bar and was surprised to see Nurse Mikey Sherman deep in conversation with Dr. Edward Peterson. They both drank from tall glasses that were filled with clear liquid and no ice, and both seemed to sway a bit. Remembering Nurse Sherman's smell from clinic, Elizabeth thought it likely their glasses held straight-up vodka. Dr. Peterson wore a coat and tie and looked dressed for an evening out. Nurse Sherman wore his green VA scrubs. Never would Elizabeth have thought they had anything in common, but they seemed to know each other well and have much to discuss. She remembered from her days as a bartender that drunken people always found one another fascinating right up to the point when they started to fight. The thought of Nurse Sherman and Dr. Peterson in a fistfight made her laugh out loud.

Dr. Cabellero returned with her coffee, and Elizabeth felt Tony touch her elbow. She turned to him, and he smiled and tried to talk to her. But someone had turned up the volume, and Rod Stewart's "Young Turks" made talking impossible. It was so crowded that nobody could actually dance, but nearly everyone was bobbing up and down to the music, dancing in place while knocking into others. "Young Turks" seemed to be a crowd favorite. Even Dr. White smiled when the song started.

Michael LeBlanc had cornered a cute redheaded nurse near the door to the only bathroom. In the dark bar, faces blurred in the cigarette smoke. Intermittently the bathroom door opened, light flooded the area in front of the door, and Elizabeth saw Michael's face for a flash of a second. He leaned over and kissed the nurse repeatedly. He seemed unstable on his feet, too.

The volume decreased as "Young Turks" ended and Earth, Wind, and Fire's "Let's Groove" began.

Tony leaned down to Elizabeth's ear and said, "You are smart to drink coffee. This place turns into a shark tank, and people pair off with whoever has the same level of drunkenness they do. Folks come in here looking like Cybill Shepherd and Richard Gere and go out looking like Phyllis Diller and Keith Richards. You want to be friendly, smile, speak when spoken to, and get out before folks start turning into pumpkins," he advised.

Elizabeth thought, *Tony has been talking to my father. His advice is sage and familiar.*

"Thanks, Tony," she told him. "I think you are right."

Elizabeth sipped her coffee and wondered how much longer she had to stay to satisfy Livvy. She felt someone staring and looked up to see Dr. White's full focus on her. She felt an electric jolt.

The cardiac nurse was clinging to his arm, pressing her body into his, as if to block him from the crowd. He stared at Elizabeth. He did not smile or nod. He made no attempt to make any kind of greeting across the room. He did not avert his gaze. He just stared openly at her.

Elizabeth could not hold his steely gaze and looked down into her coffee cup and took a long sip. Livvy was immediately at her side, turning her in place so her back was to Dr. White. "Honey, do not look over there," she told Elizabeth. "That man is uptown New Orleans Audubon Street old money. He is the smartest, most difficult man God ever made. I am serious, Elizabeth. He might be the best doctor that Tulane has ever produced, and so his eccentricity is tolerated. But stay the hell away from that one. His goal during this part of the academic year is to cull the herd. He is looking for weak interns, and he plans to get them fired. If he is staring at an intern, it is for one reason. I know you are used to men staring at you in bars, as pretty as you are, but that is one man you do not want staring at you."

"Is that nurse his girlfriend?" asked Elizabeth, trying to change the subject.

"She thinks she is. He uses her to get the best work for his patients. She makes everything absolutely perfect in the operating room for every one of his cases because she is stupid enough to think he will reward her for that by asking her to be his wife. She is not from New Orleans," Livvy explained, "and she does not understand the rules. *No* man from uptown marries a woman for her looks."

"Wow, that sounds a lot like Charleston. The old families marry the old families, no matter who they might love," said Elizabeth.

"Sure, Dr. White likes her rubbing those big boobs on him in front of other doctors," Livvy went on. "But what he really likes is having the right instrument handed to him while he's operating on a human heart. I have never seen it myself, but everyone who works in their operating room says those two are like four hands on the same body when they do a heart operation."

Elizabeth was again surprised by a feeling of disappointment.

Blondie's "Rapture" blasted out the speakers as Elizabeth drained the last of her coffee.

She smiled at Tony and mouthed goodnight. Aoife pointed toward the door. Elizabeth waved at Nurse Mikey and George the morgue technician and bolted out the door before Livvy could stop her. Once again, she had done her duty. Now she wanted to go home and cry. She realized that she could not hold her pain much longer. The conference had drained her energy, and the Pierce family haunted her. Her chest felt constricted, and the bitter coffee roiled in her stomach.

Elizabeth walked as fast as she could to the Tulane parking garage behind the medical school building. Aoife fought to keep pace with her.

Aoife asked, "Did you see all those *hot* doctors staring at you, Elizabeth? Man, they looked like hungry dogs looking at a steak."

Aoife doesn't know right now I could not care less about that. Elizabeth tried to respond kindly. "No, I did not notice," she said, "and I am not interested anyway. I just want to get away from here for a few hours. I felt humiliated at the D&C Conference, and I want to get as far from Tulane Medical Center and Charity as I can."

Aoife grabbed Elizabeth by the arm and tugged her to a stop. The women stood on the sidewalk with Charity Hospital on one side and Tulane Medical School on the other.

"Elizabeth, the D&C Conference is not about you or your feelings of humiliation," Aoife said firmly. "Medical education, especially surgical education, is about molding and educating the best people to do the work of cutting open a patient's body to try to heal it. Your patient will lie on that operating table, undergo anesthesia, give up every human right, and trust that you know what you are doing. What you are doing is an enormous responsibility. Tulane is not going to allow that responsibility to just anyone."

"I know that! Why do you think I've come to one of the most difficult programs in America? I want to be the best," said Elizabeth. She did not want to cry on the sidewalk in the open.

"It is the job of the Tulane Medical staff to make sure that you won't choke when nobody else is there to help you. They will not turn you loose on the public with a shiny Tulane diploma unless they are absolutely certain you know what you are doing. Yes, they are trying to weed out weak doctors. It's their job and their responsibility," said Aoife.

The two stood on the street, glaring at each other.

"It just seems a lot meaner than it needs to be," said Elizabeth finally. She wanted to run to her car, speed to her apartment, lock the door, and sleep. But she stood firm and listened. She knew Aoife was one of her few friends at The Big Free. And she understood the wisdom and kindness in Aoife's words.

"Look, Elizabeth, I am not smart enough to do what you are trying to do," Aoife said. "I could never pass the tests to even be considered. I see how hard they work you. I see the doctors they fire, and I see the ones who make it through." She stopped to take a breath. "If you don't make it here, there are many opportunities to be had elsewhere afterwards."

"But…" Elizabeth began.

"But if you make it," Aoife interrupted, "you will be great." She smiled and then looked serious. "With your good heart and your commitment to the patients and your kindness and compassion, you will be one of the great ones," she told Elizabeth. "I know it. That is, if they don't fire you first." She smiled again.

The thought of being fired felt like a death threat. Elizabeth could not accept being fired. She had always done everything that had been required of her, every day of her whole life. Elizabeth shuddered at the thought of failure. She said, "I have never failed at anything, so far."

Aoife laughed. "Don't worry—I have failed enough for two. Soon you will know if you are in or out. That decision is in God's hands. Go home and rest. I will see you in the morning. Try not to worry. Whatever is going to happen is going to happen."

Elizabeth searched the nurse's face for duplicity.

"Aoife, do you think the professors are purposefully trying to get rid of me, just because they don't want female surgeons in their club?" asked Elizabeth.

Aoife wrinkled her face, stood extremely still, and looked up at the Tulane crest over the door to the medical school. Elizabeth held her breath.

"You know," she said thoughtfully, "I really do not think so. I have seen Asians, blacks, and Indians, lots of plain old white Metairie boys, a couple of girls, and a few Hispanics graduate from the surgery department. I know Dr. McSwain does not care about anyone's outside package. Of course, some of the guys don't want women. They really like the Old Boys' Club aspect of surgery. But from what I have seen, Tulane breeds excellence. Excellence is the only criteria," said Aoife.

"Thank you," said Elizabeth. "That helps. If my name is not on the list of doctors who made the cut, at least I will know it was fair."

"Livvy and I will be sad if you don't make it. You brighten our day with your silly formal South Carolina manners and your determination. I have to get back to work. Drive carefully— you look awfully tired," said Aoife.

The two parted, Aoife walking toward the back door of Charity Hospital and Elizabeth to the parking garage, and eventually, at last, to her bed.

CHAPTER 18

The Cut

Wednesday, December 15, 1982

Three weeks had passed since the Death & Complications Conference and her post-conference visit to Joe's, and Elizabeth realized the rhythm of working the trauma room had become her life. She was adapting to the unpredictable sleep cycles, eating infrequently, confronting death and dying on a daily basis, and interacting with the varied personalities of the staff members at the hospitals Tulane Medical School covered.

She had learned so very much in five-and-a-half months—her short time at The Big Free had taught her more than she had learned in two years of clinical time as a medical student in South Carolina. Today she would learn whether she would need a new job in seven months. If she did not make the cut, her time at Tulane was up in June.

Elizabeth twisted her grandmother's pearls all day, a sure sign that she was more anxious than usual. She had learned to focus on what was right in front of her, and her daydreaming had diminished. But as she worked through her shift in the ER that day, she wondered all day what it would feel like to be fired. She really did not see a path to redemption. If she were Dr. McSwain, she would fire her. The death of Mr. Pierce was, in Elizabeth's estimation, a truly unforgiveable mistake.

As she waited for her shift to end, Elizabeth realized Nurse Robichaud had avoided interacting with her most of the day. *Either she knows and is not telling me, or she has no idea and does not want to be part of my angst.* Neither thought was particularly comforting.

In times of greatest stress, I miss my father the most... Elizabeth realized how much her family meant to her and how very much she missed them. If they were here today, her cousins would joke and her father would reassure. Elizabeth felt lonely again.

Dr. White had come through the emergency department earlier to check on a patient with a chest tube. Since Joe's there had been no more long stares from Dr. White. He ignored her and talked only about patient care. Elizabeth studied his face for a sign of whether she was in or out, but he gave nothing away.

"The chest tube looks very secure, intern," he told her. "Looks like you've learned at least one thing in half a year. I don't see how it could fall out with him taped up like a mummy. Charity will have to put in for an increase in its tape budget, though, since it looks like you are putting an entire roll of tape on every patient."

Elizabeth thought, *He's being his usual self. Slightly critical. Always condescending. Nothing new or different here.* "Thanks, sir," she had replied, ignoring the remark about the tape budget. "May I send him to the ward?"

"Of course he can go to the ward. Where else would he go? Home with you?" Dr. White laughed as he walked away.

Home with me? Does he mean that I am going home and not coming back? Stop it, Elizabeth! she told herself. She would know today. At six-fifteen, when her shift was over, she would go to the surgery department and look for her name on the roster. *My name will either be there or not. Fretting will not change the course of events.*

At four o'clock, Dr. Michael LeBlanc walked through and whispered in her ear, "I made the cut." Elizabeth spun around, looked into his joyous face, and asked, "Did I?"

"Don't know," he replied. "Instead of our names, we are posted by the last four digits of our Social Security numbers on a white sheet of paper hanging outside of the Matas Library. We started out with thirty interns, and there are only sixteen numbers on the sheet. If you give me your number, I will go and look for you," said Dr. LeBlanc.

Even though Elizabeth was apprehensive and dying to know, she felt knowing her fate was best experienced as a private moment. "Thanks, Michael, but I will wait and go over there after my shift. I want to stay focused on work until the shift is over. Thanks for your offer, and congratulations to you."

"Elizabeth, I know we have had our differences, but I do hope that you make the cut," said Michael. "I really did not want women in the surgery department. But you are a very hard worker, and I admire that about you. Good luck!"

"Thank you, Michael. That means a lot coming from you," said Elizabeth. She thought she saw pity in his eyes as he turned to walk away. *Well, that is a surprise. I thought he despised me…but from the look in his eyes, he thinks that I did not make the cut.*

Behind her she heard the distinctive loud clatter of Dr. Norman McSwain's cowboy boots.

"Hey, Dr. Roberts! What have you done for the good of mankind today?" asked the professor. He always started trauma room rounds with this same question, unless he arrived in the middle of a life-and-death emergency.

Elizabeth turned in the hall to see the man she had so thoroughly grown to respect. He still looked and dressed like a cowboy, but he really was the best teacher she'd ever had. She did not detect any change in him or the way he treated her today. She looked closely into his warm brown eyes and saw no hint of whether she had made it or not. He was himself, and always the same. He wanted everyone in his environment—every student, intern, resident, and nurse—to ask themselves, "What have you done for the good of mankind today?" To Elizabeth, his simple question spoke volumes about the surgeon. She had grown to know that Dr. Norman McSwain really cared about each and every patient under his care.

He and Nurse Robichaud and Elizabeth made checkout rounds and prepared the emergency area for the next shift of doctors and nurses. The ER was quiet, unusually quiet for Charity. As Dr. McSwain walked away he said, "Good luck, Dr. Roberts."

So he knows! Of course, he knows. He helped choose who goes and who stays, but he is giving away nothing!

Thirty more minutes and she could go to the surgery department and know for certain.

Elizabeth stitched the last laceration of the shift with great care. The patient was a twelve- year-old kid who had fallen from his bike and gotten a big laceration on his calf. He was stoical and quite curious about the trip to The Big Free. He, like many of the kids in the St. Thomas project, was being raised by his grandmother. His mom and dad were not around today, or any other day.

"Doc, does he need one of them tetanus shots?" asked his grandmother.

"No, ma'am, Mrs. Bailey, James got his tetanus at the Charity Pediatrics clinic right on time last year. You are doing a great job of keeping up with his shots," said Elizabeth.

As Elizabeth stitched, the young adolescent was still and calm. His grandmother held his hand, and they smiled at each other.

"What's it like to be a doctor?" asked James. "I think I might like to be a doctor. I'd like to be one of those bone doctors. It would be fun to put casts on folk's broken arms and legs that they can decorate."

"Well, James, I think you'd make a fine doctor. Those bone doctors are called orthopedic surgeons, and I think you should definitely do that. In fact, remember the word Harvard. I want to see you go to Harvard. Write that word on a piece of paper and put it above your bed, and every night think about the wonderful place that you can go after you graduate from Tulane Medical School."

James laughed and said, "Yes, doctor, I will do that. But, for now, I just hope to get out of St. Thomas. When I do, I am buying me and Grandmamma a nice house away from those drug dealers. Those people give me the creeps."

A shadow of worry passed over the face of the grandmother. She frowned and looked down at her large purse in her lap.

Elizabeth said, "James, being a doctor is the best job in the whole world. There is no other job where you get in your car to go home every day and realize that you have definitely helped some people. Teachers help people. Police help people. But doctors save lives and really help people. You must do it. I am pulling for you."

He and his grandmother broke into broad smiles, and Elizabeth realized that no matter what happened with the Tulane Surgery cut, she was still a doctor and she still had the best job in the world.

Every stitch was filled with memories. The horror and the humor of practicing medicine in the trauma ER came to her in vivid vignettes: the prostitute with the broken tooth who was her first patient, teaching the male genital exam to the female medical students, the sweetness of Nurse Mikey Sherman and his unflagging devotion to the veterans. She thought about the failed suicide patients she had attended, of Sister Marion and the Angola prisoners, and of her embarrassing dinner date at Commander's Palace with Dr. Cabellero. She sadly recalled the death of Mr. Pierce, the forlorn faces of his sons and wife, the beauty of the French Quarter in the early morning, and the humiliation and stress of appearing at the Death and Complications Conference. She remembered moments of mutual merriment and laughter with all the wonderful nurses, and sharing an on-call room with Michael and Tony. Many days and nights of exhaustion flashed before her as she stitched. *No matter what happens today,* she told herself, *I am forever grateful for this opportunity.*

She changed from her bloodstained scrubs in the emergency room bathroom and headed to Tulane to meet her fate. As Elizabeth was leaving the ER, Nurse Robichaud appeared and stood in the middle of the hall, staring intently. She said nothing, but gave Elizabeth a little smile and a wave. Livvy looked like she cared. Her smile had displayed none of its usual haughtiness. *There is really nothing to say.*

Elizabeth walked through the long underground tunnel between Charity Hospital of New Orleans and Tulane Medical School. She knew every step by heart. The closer she got to the library, the taller she stood. Whatever her fate, she had decided, she would accept it and be grateful. The Big Free was a miraculous training facility. She was grateful to the patients, the nurses, and her teachers. The Big Free was a tough taskmaster, full of horror and humor. Elizabeth had learned sometimes the horror *is* the humor, and she realized she both loved and hated Charity. It had broken her and healed her. Instead of destroying her, it had chewed her up and spit out a better version of her. Overwhelming gratitude was Elizabeth's primary emotion as she walked up to the white piece of paper taped to the door of the library.

She took a deep breath, leaned toward the page, and searched for 7186, the last four digits of her Social Security number.

And there it was! Four numbers from the bottom was her number. She reread the digits three times to be sure that she had not imagined what she saw. There she was! *I have been chosen. I am good enough. I have the opportunity to do my duty. I will be a Tulane surgeon.*

Elizabeth leaned back from the white page on the wall. She had expected to feel elated at being chosen. Instead, she was ambivalent, and her mixed feelings shocked her. Yes, she was ecstatic to be chosen. Being chosen meant she would have the opportunity to be as good at fulfilling her duty as she could hope to be. But being chosen also meant seeing her family only occasionally, rarely getting enough sleep, and having no time to date. It meant maybe no marriage and maybe no children. For certain, being chosen meant she'd have constant stress and pressure and more opportunity to make mistakes and fail, as she had failed the Pierce family.

As she walked slowly back to the elevator, she could not believe that she could simultaneously so deeply desire two opposite things. One part of her still wanted to do anything necessary to be as competent a surgeon as Dr. White. A different part of her wanted to be relieved of the demands that being a good doctor would put on her life. She wanted to dance for joy and celebrate, and she wanted to run for her car and drive away, never to return. She wanted to laugh, and she wanted to cry. She got everything she had been working so hard to get, and she was devastated.

When she had chosen Tulane Surgery as a medical student, she did not know what she was really choosing. Now, she knew exactly. *Would the price be too high?*

As the elevator doors closed, Elizabeth pressed the button that would take her to the street level. She needed fresh air. She walked out the front door of the Tulane Medical School building and turned left on Tulane Avenue. Even though it was December, it was still muggy and warm in New Orleans. As she approached the corner, she looked to the left at 1532 Tulane Avenue. She gazed up at the façade of the twenty-story Art Deco building known as Charity Hospital New Orleans, or The Big Free.

Elizabeth had been transformed in that building from a shy Low Country girl to a hardworking, mostly competent surgeon. But did she want more? *What would be the price?*

She entered the Charity Hospital lobby and was grateful not to see anyone she knew right away. She hoped Tony and Michael would not be in the on-call room so she could have some privacy. She needed time alone to think, and she needed to call home. She needed to hear her father's voice.

As the elevator doors opened, the smiling face of Mrs. Albertha Simmons was before her. Mrs. Albertha was chatting in the warm, musty elevator with Mrs. Yolanda Wilson, the lady who cleaned the trauma suite in the emergency department. Mrs. Yolanda leaned on her big mop and wash bucket with wheels on the bottom. The bucket was jammed into the corner of the elevator, and Mrs. Yolanda seemed to need the mop's support. Her fatigue was deeply etched on her shiny black skin.

Elizabeth was glad to see them. She liked both women, and gave an easy smile.

Mrs. Albertha asked, "How you doing today, baby? I heard they are announcing the cut list for Tulane Surgery today. You got any good news for me?"

Both women froze in anticipation, waiting for Elizabeth's answer.

Elizabeth said, "Yes, ma'am, I have news. They picked me!"

Mrs. Yolanda and Mrs. Albertha hooted in unison. "Yee hee! We been praying, baby. We been praying!" said Mrs. Yolanda.

The doors closed, and they were alone. The elevator moved slowly upward.

Mrs. Albertha studied the expression on Elizabeth's face. "You don't look too happy, baby. What's wrong?" she asked.

Elizabeth wanted to cry. "Oh, Mrs. Albertha, I don't know if this is for me or not," she told her. "Of course I am very grateful they picked me. But I wonder if I really have what it takes to be a surgeon. I wonder if they made the right choice," said Elizabeth.

Mrs. Albertha brought the elevator to a stop between the sixth and seventh floors.

Mrs. Yolanda stepped away from her mop, propped it against the elevator wall, and moved toward Elizabeth, her hands on her thin hips.

"Of course you got what it takes, young lady," Mrs. Yolanda told her. "Albertha and I been watching you for half a year. We know you got what it takes."

Elizabeth said, "I hope that you are right."

Mrs. Yolanda became adamant. "Honey, when you clean up behind people day in and day out like I do, you learn what's in their souls. There are some doctors who never speak to me. They treat me like I am part of the wall. They walk right past me and never even say good morning. Those doctors may have all the skills in the world, but they got no love of people." She paused, exchanged a look with Mrs. Albertha, took a deep breath, and then continued. "You are not like that. You see everyone, and you treat everyone the same. You don't smile at Dr. McSwain and ignore me and Albertha. To you, we all have the same value. When you do an operation, you clean up behind yourself because you care that I don't have to clean up your mess. You treat them prostitutes and them drunks and them drug addicts with kindness. You don't have a mean bone in your body. God made you a healer, girl. Course you gonna stay at Charity!"

"She's right," Mrs. Albertha concurred. "We might be the lowest on the Charity Hospital totem pole, but we can spot greatness, and you got it, Dr. Roberts. Your people raised you right. You came to Tulane with everything you needed to be the best. We watched you be scared and tired and still be polite and kind to everyone. We saw how hard you worked. You *care* what happens to these people. That is how a doctor should be, honey." Mrs. Albertha smiled at Elizabeth.

"The Big Free can cut you down, or it can saw off the rough edges and make you great," Mrs. Albertha continued. "But it can only work with what you bring to the table. And what you bring to the table came from God and your people. God gave you brains and drive, and your people raised you to be decent. Of course you are staying."

Elizabeth's decision was made in that elevator trapped between floors six and seven by a housekeeper and an elevator operator. Mrs. Yolanda and Mrs. Albertha had spoken. Clearly, she had a new family.

Mrs. Albertha started the elevator and deposited Elizabeth on the floor where the intern on-call rooms were located. All three women were silent as Elizabeth exited.

As Elizabeth stood in front of the old wooden door with her key in hand, she realized the truth of what the ladies told her. She had left home with everything she needed to succeed. Though she didn't realize it at first, all her fear and worry had been for naught. Her family and her faith had brought her to the place where she now stood, wiser and more confident, ready to take on new challenges and claim her new identity. She was a Tulane surgeon.

The End

ACKNOWLEDGEMENTS

My greatest debt goes to Charity Hospital of New Orleans. It opened its doors in 1736 and they were permanently closed by Hurricane Katrina in 2005. Like many urban charity hospitals, it provided the best training ground for young doctors and nurses. I lived in that hospital for six years and am forever indebted to every patient, nurse, doctor, EMT, policeman, orderly, housekeeper, and administrator of Charity. My Tulane education at Charity Hospital was the best!

I'd also like to thank Morgan James publishing and David Hancock for giving me a chance as a first-time fiction author. The entire process has been a pleasure. I appreciate the assistance of Megan Malone at Morgan James. Publishing can be fun!

Phyllis Mueller and Laura Jensen were great editors. I deeply appreciate their work.

I appreciate my friends and readers, Rosemarie King, Glory Sanders, Janet Brumfield, Mary Anne Walser, and Jesse Boone.

Thanks to my lawyer, Mark A. Baker.

Thanks to my photographer, Karen Burns.

I'd like to thank Dr. Norman McSwain posthumously. I have written stories since I was a young girl. Dr. McSwain started reading my stories and encouraged me to write them in novel format. Dr. McSwain was a very busy and world-renowned trauma surgeon. Despite his very hectic work life, he found time to read my stories on airplanes and on Sunday mornings at his French Quarter home. He frequently hounded me with *where's the next story?*

Even though Dr. McSwain was my professor more than twenty-five years ago, he remained my teacher. My husband and I had gone to New Orleans for a urology meeting and planned to have dinner with Dr. McSwain. We stood in the rain outside the Windsor Court Hotel waiting for him to pick us up in the summer of 2015. We were planning to have dinner at Commander's and talk about my book. Dr. McSwain never made it. He was in the ICU at Tulane and could not call. My husband tried to reassure me by saying *I am sure that he is stuck in some operating room somewhere and he will resurface...* But I knew something awful had happened. Dr. McSwain was not a person who did not make his commitments. He called me three days later from the ICU to apologize for leaving me waiting in the rain. The next time I was in New Orleans was for his funeral.

Dr. McSwain wore many hats. He was a loving father to Merry. He was a researcher. He loved Tulane and Charity. He loved the New Orleans police and was their doctor. He adored the emergency medical technicians and was their champion. He worked tirelessly for the military to improve their outcomes in the battlefield. And he found time to read my stories and reminisce about Charity. We had lots of laughs. His greatest gift was that he cared about people.

My deepest heartfelt thanks go to my family. Jesse, Sarah, and Jenna are the joy, fun, laughter, and love that keep my life on track. I adore you guys! There are lots of laughs at our house. We travel and sail and cook. Jesse is the last of the true "Renaissance" men. Whether you want your boat sailed, a fish caught, your novel formatted, or macaroons for dessert, he's the man.

I speak in my stories of the farm, my cousins, and South Carolina. I am deeply indebted to my family, the Bessinger and Boatwright clans, and the hard work and values they taught.

In thirty-three years, I have seen over 175,000 patients. None of my stories are about any specific patient. The stories are an amalgamation of the struggles, bravery, and deep respect that I have shared with each and every one. The intimacy and the honor of sharing people's lives as their doctor have given me rich and vivid life experiences from which to draw. I am forever grateful to my patients.

ABOUT THE AUTHOR

Martha B. Boone is a private practice urologist. *The Big Free* is her first novel. She did her surgical and urology training in New Orleans at Tulane and worked for six years at Charity Hospital.

She is one of the first one hundred women in the world trained in urology. She writes the humor and horror of the world of medicine as only a true insider can write.

She lives in an Atlanta suburb with her husband and two stepdaughters. Their family likes to sail, travel, and cook.

Morgan James
Speakers Group

We connect Morgan James published authors with live and online events and audiences whom will benefit from their expertise.